Dear Roomie
Valerie Kain

Copyright © 2024 by Valerie Kain

All rights reserved.

No part of this publication may be reproduced, distributed, or transmitted in any form or by any means, including photocopying, recording, or other electronic or mechanical methods, without the prior written permission of the publisher, except as permitted by U.S. copyright law. For permission requests, contact valeriekain.writing@gmail.com.

The story, all names, characters, and incidents portrayed in this production are fictitious. No identification with actual persons (living or deceased), places, buildings, and products is intended or should be inferred.

Book Cover by Andy Payne

Edited by Brooklyn Marie at Brazen Hearts Author Services

1st edition 2024

This is for all the *difficult* women.

Never minimize yourself for the approval of others.

Content Warnings

Dear Roomie is not a dark romance, but at times does contain darker themes. These include:

- Drug use

- Grief/loss/mourning

- Abusive relationships (not between the main couple)

- Cheating/Emotional affair between the MCs

Contents

Chapter 1
Morgan

Aluminum teeth bite into my thumb and forefinger every time I twist the key through my nervous fingers. No matter how many times I've done it, starting over somewhere new never gets any easier, but the dull lick of pain helps distract me from the growing pool of dread in my gut.

Athens, Georgia: population 128,711, more bars per capita than any other city in America, home of the Georgia Bulldogs, and the place I'll be spending the next three years of my life. I've done my research and spent hours familiarizing myself with the school's campus and the surrounding city, but no amount of online images or Google searches can prepare you for what a new place is actually like.

My new apartment sits on a triangular lot in the middle of a five-way intersection that marks the border between the city and the university. It's a bright building, painted with thick blocks of matte colors, contrasting with the monotony of aged red brick. That, coupled with its awkward shape, creates the illusion that it was painted directly onto the horizon. It's got a strange charm about it that helps make approaching it feel a little less daunting, and I'll take whatever I can get right now to not feel like I'm marching toward my doom.

Everything about this move has been a masterclass in jumping headfirst into the unknown. Who moves across the country to live with someone they've only interacted with through scattered text messages? Me, apparently. It isn't like I had any other options. My flight back from Peru was less than a week ago. I only had enough time to get my things out of storage and make the cross-country trip from Arizona.

I'd be lying if I said I only responded to the ad for this apartment, or that James would have been my first pick of roommate. His post was beyond vague. All it told me was where the apartment was, that they liked to keep things neat, and that they have a dog that doesn't do well with cats. What is a man supposed to do with that? I wouldn't have reached out if the first three ads I responded to hadn't shut me down once they realized we couldn't meet in person. Luck was on my side with the fourth. James was quick to reply and wasn't immediately put off by the fact my first day in Athens would be the day I moved in. We chatted some when I had access to Wi-Fi, and within a few days, my sublease was signed. Brief messages were exchanged throughout the summer, and while my roommate is still mostly a stranger, I'm glad I had the chance to get to know him some before I moved in.

However, I wish he'd be more responsive right now.

The last message I sent—letting him know I was ten minutes out—has been left on read since it was delivered. It would be nice to know what I'm about to walk into.

The sun catches on the rhinestone on my key as I twist it through my fingers again. I'm sure James thought it was hilarious to mail me the most feminine key he could find, thinking it would embarrass me or something. Truthfully, I'm too grateful to actually have a key to be ashamed of what it looks like. Most of the guys I've lived with over the years wouldn't have thought to have a new key made, let alone send me one so I would have an easier time moving in. My last roommate left me standing outside in the Arizona heat with my boxes for hours while I waited for them to let me in. I'll take a baby-blue key with tiny jewels and decorative script reading "HOME" over that any day.

He has been an absolute godsend with this whole move. He's been living here for a few years already and was more than willing to help me get everything settled remotely. I appreciate everything he has done to help, but that doesn't make the prospect of meeting him any less intimidating.

There's no use in delaying it, though.

I pocket my keys and load my arms up with boxes. The trunk of my hatchback slams shut before I make my way across the street and into the building. It's not hard to find the door labeled 208, but the brightly colored welcome mat out front makes it even easier. I knock on the door with my foot and wait for several moments. It becomes clear rather quickly that James either isn't home or isn't going to answer. I finagle the boxes into a precarious stack in one arm and fish my keys out of my pocket to open the door.

"Hello," I call out as I step over the threshold, but the only thing that greets me is silence.

Gravity starts to win out, pulling the tower of boxes out of my arms. I let them fall into a pile by the door and pause to take in the apartment. There's no sign of James or his dog, which takes some of the pressure off my shoulders. It gives me time to get my bearings first.

Two things immediately stand out to me: James was one hundred percent serious when he said he likes to keep things neat, and his idea of fully furnished is more than a simple sofa and a place to eat.

The common areas are decorated like something off Pinterest or out of a home-decor magazine. It's a decent veneer for the otherwise standard white walls and wood-grain vinyl floors. The space is divided by an island counter, which marks the transition from the living room to the kitchen.

Things seem to cover every surface, but in a way that makes it feel curated, not cluttered. I'm not quite sure how James pulls it off; I could have walked into HomeGoods blindfolded and gotten a near-identical assortment of art and decor, but it wouldn't have come together to feel this homey—because it's clear that's what this is: someone's home.

Framed photos are mixed in among the mass-produced prints. My curiosity gets the better of me, and I take a closer look at one of the pictures on the wall.

James and his dog are standing on a mountain overlook with the sun beginning to set behind them, but what catches my attention is the woman with them. She is one of the most beautiful women I have ever seen. It's clear she's his girlfriend from the way she's glued to his side and gazing at him like he hung all the stars in the sky just for her. But if James hung the stars, then his girlfriend is the sun.

Everything about that woman is wrapped in a golden aura, from her blond locks—which hang down her back in waves—to the glow of her sun-kissed skin. More than anything, I'm captivated by the radiance of her smile, which seems to light her up from the inside. The love between them shines through the image, and that alone is enough to make me stop my snooping and vow to forget these thoughts ever crossed my mind.

He sure is a lucky man.

He never mentioned having a girlfriend in any of the messages we exchanged over the summer, but it shines a new light on the whole situation. The key. The decor. All of it must be her doing.

I don't think James is going to be my only roommate this year.

The realization sinks in my gut like a lead weight. If I had known my roommate's girlfriend was going to be living here rent-free, I would have looked for other accommodations. I've dealt with it in the past and have no desire to do it again. Unfortunately, there's nothing I can do about it now without asking James to change his whole life. It isn't a fair ask. This is his home that he's been living in for years, and I'm practically a stranger.

I take a deep breath and mentally prepare myself for what's coming: a year full of witnessing PDA, moderating their fights, and hearing them make up through paper-thin walls.

Maybe they won't be as bad as the last couple I lived with.

I cling to that hope as I pick up my things and carry them toward my bedroom. It's easy enough to find; there's only one hallway that extends off the back wall of the living room, with only two rooms down it. The first room is clearly meant to be mine. The door is wide open, showcasing the vast emptiness contained between the sterile white walls. It's basic—no frills beyond a small closet and a door that leads to the shared bathroom—but it's mine for the next twelve months.

Chapter 2
James

My heart rate skyrockets as I read Morgan's text. She wasn't supposed to get here so soon. There's still so much I have to finish before she arrives. I need to mop the floors again and vacuum her room, and I wanted to bake cookies so she'd feel welcome and at home as she stepped foot in our apartment for the first time. At this rate, I'll be lucky if I'm even there to greet her.

This is all Chelsea's fault.

The small mesh-top table in front of me is covered with the empty appetizer platters Evelyn and I have picked over while we wait. Our friend was supposed to meet us for lunch half an hour ago, but apparently, there were delays at the airport. Something to do with customs. I didn't quite understand it all, but I've also never traveled abroad. I just wish she would have told us *before* we got to the restaurant. I'm not even hungry anymore. Between the apps and the anxiety, my stomach is a churning pot of lead.

"I'm back, bitches!"

All eyes in the restaurant's tiny alleyway patio snap toward the woman making a scene at the entrance. Chelsea doesn't falter under the gazes of strangers; she's used to being gawked at, and I think she relishes the attention. The girl is gorgeous. Her tall, willowy frame and untamable fiery curls draw attention wherever we go, and she learned long ago to embrace it.

"How were your summers?" she asks as she joins Evelyn and me at our table.

My dog, Grover, lets out a half-assed growl at her approach without bothering to lift his head from where it's perched on his paws. He isn't the most sociable of animals, but both of my friends have known him long enough to know he is all bark and no bite.

Evelyn jumps up to greet our friend with a hug while she gushes over her. I should do the same, but my mind is only half present at the table. Intrusive thoughts rattle around my head like a game of pinball, drawing my focus back to the growing pit in my gut, which is steeped in an aura of dread.

"I hope you two didn't get up to too much trouble without me," Chelsea adds as both girls sit.

"Who cares about our summers? I want to hear about Paris," Evelyn says, nearly bouncing in her wire-framed seat.

I can't find it in me to match her enthusiasm. What if Morgan is already at the apartment? What if she hates the place? What if the key I sent her doesn't work and she's stuck outside, waiting for me to get home? What if she thinks I'm rude for not being there and hates me?

No. I can't think about those things or I'll spiral, and I refuse to let that happen in public. Through sheer force of will, I make myself tune in to the conversation. It's not like I don't want to hear about my friend's summer abroad, but it's hard to focus when my heart is beating so hard I think it might explode.

"What do you want to know?" Chelsea asks, and Evelyn is quick to respond.

"How was the food? The fashion?"

"The men," I add with enthusiasm I don't feel.

"The food was to die for, the fashion was to kill for, and the men...well, a lady doesn't kiss and tell." Chelsea smiles like a cat that got the canary.

"Well, it's a good thing you aren't a lady," I tease, ignoring the way my stomach twists, and Evelyn chokes on a snort of laughter.

"Well, excuse me, Ms. Future First Lady. I'm sorry we don't all meet the level of class you've grown accustomed to."

"Oh, shut up." I throw my paper napkin at her face with a laugh. "It's Tanner's dad who's running for governor, anyway, not Tanner. That makes me Ms. Future Nothing."

"How is Tanner?"

That is certainly a question. One that only adds to the churning stew of anxiety.

My boyfriend has been…busy. I didn't actually get to see him much over the summer. His new job demanded too much of his time for him to make the trip to Athens, and my class schedule only let me go back home to Savannah every so often. It wasn't great. I think we fought more over the past three months than we have in the years we've been together.

I hate this distance, and I know he does too. Thank God we only have a few more months until we close the gap for good.

I'm not about to tell them that, though. I haven't seen Chelsea in months, and I don't want to kill the mood by moping about missing my boyfriend.

"Nope, we aren't talking about him. I want to know about the French men whose hearts you broke," I say, putting on the happy mask I know they expect from me.

"It was just one heart"—her porcelain cheeks grow pink—"but he wasn't French."

"Spill," Evelyn demands.

"His name was Ezio. He was from Italy but was spending the summer in Paris to find himself."

I look at Evelyn and mime gagging.

"Hey, I didn't claim he was very bright, but he was pretty. And the things he could do with his fingers…" She pauses and shivers in her seat. "Let's just say he kept me very satisfied."

"What happened?"

"What do you mean what happened? We went on a few dates, had a couple of fun nights together, and then the next thing I knew, he was confessing his love and trying to convince me to go back to Italy with him."

"I take it you dipped," I ask, swallowing back the judgment threatening to coat the words.

That's her typical MO once feelings get involved. I've known Chelsea for years, and in that time, she has left a trail of broken-hearted men in her wake. She isn't cruel—she gives them closure—but she also doesn't stick around once she knows it won't work.

I don't get it; I could never be so callous with my heart, but I also met my soulmate when I was seven. Most people don't get that. It's been me and Tanner since we were kids. Our relationship is the storybook romance people write about. We are endgame.

"I had a new hotel booked on the other side of the city that night," she confirms.

"Chels, that's awful," Evelyn chastises.

"That's life, babe. He was fun for the moment, but he had no long-term potential. He was an artist, for fuck's sake. He might as well have had a sign around his neck that said 'I'm unemployed.'"

I grit my teeth and keep smiling despite her words. It's not like I haven't heard similar sentiments my whole life, but it still hurts, even if it wasn't directed at me.

"You really didn't see him again?"

"Oh, I saw him plenty, he just didn't see me. I had to find a new café because he kept showing up at my favorite one like a sad, lost puppy. It was kind of pathetic. Enough about me, though. I want to hear about you two. How were your summers?"

"I spent most of mine volunteering with the Labre Mission like I always do." She tucks a lock of thick, dark hair behind her ear.

"Were you able to convince Jamie to join you this time?" Chelsea gives me a pointed look, and my eyes fall to the table.

It's not that I don't want to go with her to volunteer; the timing has never worked out. Between classes, finding a new roommate, and trying to arrange visits with my boyfriend, my summer was booked, and things only get crazier during the full-term semesters.

"No," Evelyn admits, but the cheery smile never leaves her face. "But maybe you both can come with me before the semester starts."

"Sure," Chelsea lies. She's never gone with Evelyn either. "What about you, Jamie? Did you get up to any wild adventures with that man of yours?"

This time, I'm unable to keep the pain off my face. I get that he's busy with his new job with his dad's campaign office, I really do, but each canceled plan was a blow to my heart. Is it really that hard to prioritize your girlfriend every once in a while?

"Nothing too crazy," I tell her with a forced laugh. "He is coming to visit next weekend, though."

"Did you ever get the new roommate figured out?"

"Yeah, I did. Her name is Morgan Hall." The frayed ends of my nerves spark to life again. I found her online, but her social media presence is abysmal, and we never got to meet in person due to her being out of the country. It's a recipe for disaster, but from the few messages we exchanged, she seemed to be the best option out of the candidates. She's older and about to start grad school, so I'm hoping she'll bring less drama with her than past roommates have.

"Do we like Morgan?" Chelsea asks.

"Undecided, but we should give her a chance. She doesn't know anyone else here."

"We can invite her to go downtown with us." Evelyn sits up a bit straighter, and from the look in her eyes, I know she's already planning all the ways we will include my new roommate this year—like roping her into watching those trashy reality shows with her. Lord knows, Chelsea and I don't have the patience for it. Maybe she'll be the one to actually enjoy them.

"Let's hold off on that until I've at least met her. She could be a psychopath or something."

"Fine," Evelyn huffs. "When is she moving in?"

I glance at the time and curse. "Right about now, actually. Shit, I should go. I wanted to be home when she got here. It will take her forever to move all her stuff in on her own."

I also wanted to do another pass over the apartment to make sure it was in perfect condition. First impressions are the most important, and I'll be damned if she thinks I wasn't serious about keeping the apartment spotless.

"But I just got here. I missed you guys," Chelsea says with a small pout.

"I know, I missed you too. Catch up with Evelyn today, and we can all go out for drinks tomorrow night. Want to meet at Magnolia's at ten?"

"Fine, go meet your new roommate," she relents with a playful smirk while rolling her eyes. "Call me if she's awful."

"She won't be awful," I tell her, but I have no way of knowing if my words are true.

I grab Grover's leash and hug them both before starting the walk back to my apartment. Each step closer fans the smoldering bundle of nerves in my gut, stoking my anxiety into a raging inferno. Morgan could be terrible. She could hate me and try to make my life a living hell for the next year. She could also end up becoming one of my best friends. I won't know until I meet her, but that doesn't stop the worst-case scenarios from playing out in my head like flashes of a nightmare the entire way.

Chapter 3
Morgan

The front door slams, the jarring sound snapping my spine straight. *James must be back.*

All too easily, I got lost in the mindless repetition of unloading and unpacking, but the idea of finally meeting my new roommate brings my reality back into sharp focus. My shoulders heave with heavy breaths as I take in the piles of boxes scattered around my room. It was too much to hope that he came back after I got everything cleaned up.

Beads of sweat roll down my back, gluing damp cotton to my skin. It's the slick, sticky type that comes from an afternoon of manual labor in the humidity. My whole body is drenched in it. Even my hair clings to my forehead in wet clumps. This isn't the state I'd prefer to be in to make a first impression. You never get a second chance there, and I dress with that in mind. At some point during the seemingly endless trips, the heat won out, and I rolled up the sleeves of my shirt and undid a few of the top buttons, leaving me in a disheveled state of half dress.

There might be time for me to freshen up.

Both options battle in my head while my eyes dart between the door to the bathroom and the hallway. The choice shouldn't be this hard. With a resigned sigh, I move toward the hall. We might as well get introductions out of the way now, and it's not like he won't see me in a variety of states over the next year—some probably worse than this.

The wind is yanked from my sails as I step into the living room, and I stumble to a stop. It isn't James who's entered; it's *her*.

She's even more beautiful in person.

I don't think she's noticed me yet. A huge German shepherd has all of her attention. Her face glows with a radiant smile as she unhooks him from the leash and scratches behind his ears. My stomach flutters like I'm a schoolgirl with a crush. That thought pushes the feeling away in an instant. Catching feelings for my roommate's girlfriend is the absolute last thing I need. Still, I mentally curse myself for not choosing the shower.

The dog, on the other hand, definitely notices me. Its hackles raise as it positions itself between me and the woman. I swear it looked smaller in the photos. It snarls at me, and confusion replaces the beautiful smile on the woman's face.

"Grover, wh—" James's girlfriend freezes when she sees me standing in the hallway, her eyes widening in fear. She takes a slow step toward the door and pulls her phone out of her pocket.

Well, crap. He must not have told her I was moving in today.

Before I can get a word out to introduce myself, all of the emotion drains from her face. She stands taller, and an icy mask freezes over the warmth she came in with.

"Who the fuck are you, and what are you doing in my apartment?" she all but spits at me. Her words are laced with venom, but the hint of a southern accent peeking through softens their impact.

"I'm Morgan Hall," I tell her and raise my hands where she can see them. The rapid pounding in my chest nearly drowns out my steady words. "James's new roommate."

"No you aren't. Try again." Her glare is murderous.

My jaw falls slack at the absurdity of her demand.

"Try what again, saying my name?" An edge of sarcasm laces my words, not helping the situation. I take a breath and try again, deliberately keeping my voice even. "I can prove it if you need me to. I've got my ID in my pocket, or I could call James and clear this whole thing up." I pull my phone out of my pocket and click on James's contact without giving her a chance to protest.

The dial tone plays in my ear, and the woman's face drops in absolute horror as her phone begins to ring. The cheerful, melodic tone hangs in the air, mocking us. She doesn't make any move to answer the phone, and I am too stunned to hang up. The ringing stops, and an awkward tension remains in its place. After another beat, she confirms what I already suspected.

"I'm James."

Her dog, Grover, growls again and stalks toward me. My gaze jumps between the dog and its owner, but she doesn't make any move to stop him. Despite being several inches shorter than me, she looks at me from down her nose, her face twisted with loathing.

"Can you get your dog?" I resort to pleading as my unease grows. "Please."

She rolls her eyes and lets out a sharp, two-toned whistle. Grover relaxes and slinks off to lie on a cushion near the couch.

"Thank you," I tell her, but she only glares.

"Okay, you are Morgan Hall," the woman—my new roommate—says after several minutes of tense silence. "How are we going to fix this?"

"Fix it?" My face scrunches in confusion. "I'm sorry, I don't quite understand what you mean."

"This is obviously a mistake. So what's it going to take to get you out of my apartment?"

For the second time in only a few short minutes, I'm struck by this woman's audacity. I don't think I've ever met someone with such an unashamed sense of entitlement.

"Our apartment," I clarify with a clenched jaw. It's all I can do to keep my tone pleasant.

"No, not ours. Mine," she says without making the same effort.

"I signed the lease too."

"I don't care what the fuck you signed, you aren't staying here." She crosses her arms over her chest and stares at me with a look that says she's serious.

"Where do you expect me to go?" I don't anticipate an actual answer; I'm hoping she will realize how ridiculous she's acting.

"I don't give a fuck where you end up, you just can't stay here."

"No, James, I'm not going anywhere," I tell her. I always try to be a good roommate, but I'm not going to let her steamroll me into sleeping on the streets. "What's so bad about this, anyway? Sure, it might not be exactly what either one of us expected, but this isn't really the worst thing in the world."

"Oh." She lets out a bitter laugh that sounds far too ugly for someone so beautiful. "I see how it is. You're enjoying this, aren't you?"

"What? No, of course no—"

"Don't even try to deny it," she interrupts. "I bet you planned this from the beginning in some twisted attempt to force some poor woman to act out your sick fantasies."

"Jesus Christ, why would you even think that? No, just no." I run my hand through my hair as I try to figure out how to salvage this situation. "We clearly got off on the wrong foot here. Hi, James. I'm Morgan. It's nice to finally meet you in person." I stick out my hand for a handshake, and she eyes it like I offered her a handful of trash.

"Go fuck yourself, Morgan," she hisses as she storms past me toward her room. "Don't get too comfortable. My dad will make this right," she shouts over her shoulder and then slams her bedroom door.

My shoulders slump once she's gone. I think I would have preferred a couple. There's nothing I can do about it now, though. I try to shake off the encounter as I resume unloading things. One thing is for sure, though. I won't have any issues forgetting I ever thought James was attractive. She may look like an angel, but that woman is a devil in disguise, and she's going to make my year a living hell.

Chapter 4
James

The door slams behind me, and all of the fight leaves my body. The armor of self-righteous indignation crumbles away, letting loose the raw panic that had been locked away underneath.

What the actual fuck did I just do? In what world is provoking a strange man behind closed doors a good idea? I'm lucky Morgan responded the way he did instead of with anger or violence. Things could have gone so much worse, and for what? My own ego?

I'm such a fucking idiot.

My heart grows erratic, and my breath comes in shallow gasps as panic claws its way through me, tearing through my carefully constructed walls with ease.

I stumble toward the bathroom and run through one of my coping strategies.

Ten...

Nine...

Eight...

Seven...

Six...

Five...

Four...

Three...

Two...

One...

Breathe.

I repeat the process, but it does nothing to calm the raging beast inside me. My body functions on autopilot as I cross the threshold into the Jack and Jill bathroom and ensure both doors are locked. White-knuckling the countertop's edge, I stare into the mirror. The girl who stares back with wild green eyes looks like a feral animal caught in a hunter's snare. I don't recognize her; the woman struggling for air while she clings to the counter is an impostor wearing my skin.

I start my count again, but it's apparent that it isn't enough to leash the panic. With shaking hands, I reach for one of the drawers and dig out my emergency medication.

"Goddamnit, James, pull yourself together," I hiss at my reflection and swallow back the tiny white pills. "You are going to shower, call your dad, make dinner, and act like a civil human being. It's only temporary. Dad will fix everything, and you won't ever have to think about Morgan Hall again."

I push away from the counter and turn the shower on to the hottest setting. After waiting a few moments, I step under the scalding spray. The water singes my skin, and the pain centers me, giving me something to focus on while I wait for my meds to kick in.

Feeling more composed, I turn the water off and head back to my room. I start to throw on my normal house clothes—an oversized T-shirt and athletic shorts—but think about Morgan and his stupid outfit and pause. Who wears business casual to move, anyway?

Fuck him.

I won't let him or his pretentious judgment dictate how I live in my own home. That's the lie I tell myself, at least, but I tuck the clothes back into my drawers and opt for a pair of jeans and a nicer tank top instead.

I check the time and grab my phone to call my dad. It's six hours later where he is stationed, and it's already pushing the "too late to call" point for the night.

"Hello." The familiar drawl of his voice comes through the line after a few rings. Hearing it is a balm, soothing all my worries. He sounds groggy; normally,

I would feel guilty about calling him this late and waking him up, but any guilt is overshadowed by relief.

"Hi, Dad." My voice cracks as my emotions threaten to spill out.

"Ophelia, what's wrong? Are you all right," he asks, sounding more awake.

"I'm fine," I lie, which earns me a disapproving hum. I've never been able to hide anything from him.

"Okay, I'm not fine," I amend with a sigh. "I met my new roommate today, and there is a pretty big problem."

"What kind of problem?" His voice takes on a protective edge.

"Morgan is actually a man." I drop the bomb and brace for my father's reaction.

"Okay, and?" he questions without a trace of the validating anger I hoped to hear.

"I am a woman who will be living alone with a guy she doesn't even know. It isn't safe."

"All right, if this is an issue for you, I can call the leasing office tomorrow and break your lease. It will probably be difficult to find somewhere else for you on this short notice, but I'm sure we can find something."

"No, I'm not moving. I want him out of my apartment." The idea that I would be the one to move is outlandish. I was here first. I've lived here for three years, and I'm not about to move because some asshole didn't tell me he had a penis.

"Is his name on the lease?" His voice carries the same tone that has always meant I'm not getting what I want.

"Yes," I admit with a pout he can't see.

"Has he done anything to violate the terms of the lease?"

"No, but—"

"There are no buts," he interrupts me, using his drill-sergeant tone. "You are out of luck, kid. This boy signed a lease and is legally in his rights to live in that apartment. The way I see it, you've got two options here: move out or suck it up and try to make the best of the situation. If you genuinely feel unsafe, I will get you out of there tonight. We can get you a hotel room, and you won't have to see him again. It's your call here, kid. I'll support you in whatever you choose, but forcibly removing a paying tenant isn't on the table. Do you understand me?"

"Yes, sir," I grumble.

"Good. Do you feel like you are in any danger?"

I think about it for a moment before begrudgingly admitting, "No."

"Okay then, think over your options, and let me know what you want to do in the morning. It's past one in the morning here—"

A loud crash from the room next door distracts me from whatever my dad is saying.

"Hey, I've gotta go," I cut in. "I love you, Dad."

"Love you too, kid," he says, and the line goes dead.

I dash back into the bathroom and push the door to the other bedroom open without knocking. My roommate is sprawled on the floor, surrounded by boxes that have been strewn about in haphazard heaps. There aren't many of them, and there's no furniture, but those things are probably still in his moving van.

He lets out a groan of pain, summoning me to his side in an instant. Alarms blare through my head as he stares up at the ceiling with dazed eyes.

"What the fuck? Are you okay?" I crouch beside him to get a better look. He looks fine, from what I can tell, except that his glasses are skewed. I hadn't noticed before, but the eyes behind them are hazel, shining almost amber in the light.

"Yeah, I'm fine," he says as he sits up, but the strain in his voice tells another story.

It only takes a second for me to figure out why.

A small television broke his fall, its sharp plastic corners lining up perfectly with his spine. He notices it too, and his face falls. He scrambles around on his hands and knees to stand the TV up and plugs it into the wall. Muttering something under his breath, he clicks the power button. The screen flashes to life, but the display is nothing more than a black-and-white web of destroyed pixels.

That isn't what catches my attention, though.

A small patch of blood, which is growing as the seconds pass, stains his white dress shirt.

"Fuck."

"Yeah," he sighs as his shoulders sag. "It's definitely broken."

"No, Morgan, 'fuck' as in you're bleeding," I snap.

He cranes his head to see the spreading stain, and his expression falls even further. The dejected look on his face pulls at something in my heart. There is no way I can leave him here when he looks this sad. It would be cruel, like kicking a puppy.

"Come here." I grab his arm to pull him to his feet and then guide him to the bathroom. He follows without protest, but his brows are pinched in obvious confusion.

"Sit," I command, directing him to the lid of the toilet. "Take your shirt off."

He does what I ask while I grab the first aid kit from under the sink. I turn back around and find him straddling the toilet seat with his back to me. For a brief moment, I'm caught off guard by how sculpted the muscles there are—it's the last thing I expected to see underneath the geeky, try-hard attire—but the oozing cut near his spine quickly draws my full attention.

"Let me look." I kneel behind him and run my hand over the bruising skin. My fingertips tingle from the warmth radiating off him; it's almost electric. He lets out a soft hiss at the contact, and I jerk my hand away. "I'm sorry, did I hurt you?"

"No, I'm fine," he says through clenched teeth. "What's the verdict, doc?"

I choke back a snort of laughter. "I'm no doctor, but I don't think you'll need stitches. I do want to clean and bandage it, though. If that's all right."

All at once, I'm aware of how inappropriate I'm being. I barged in and forced him to get half naked while I ran my hands all over his body.

What the fuck, James?

My cheeks grow hot as my embarrassment floods through me. I clean and dress his wound as quickly as I can while still making sure things are done right.

"There, good as new," I tell him, pulling away.

He turns to face me and gives me a heart-stopping smile. It's not perfectly symmetrical—one side pulls higher, and only his left cheek dips with a pronounced dimple—but those imperfections only make him more attractive. Because, holy fuck, Morgan Hall is attractive.

"Thank you, James," he tells me, his voice dripping with sincerity.

"I—uh—I'm gonna go make dinner," I stammer, growing more flustered. "You can join me if you want...I'm making tacos."

I don't wait for him to respond as I flee the confined space into the refuge of the kitchen. There isn't much room, but I've meticulously organized all of the cabinets to optimize what I do have. I'll need to teach him where things go.

Fuck, I guess he will be sticking around.

I put in my earphones, turn the volume up as loud as it will go, and dance around to the bassy rifts while I brown the beef. A tap on my shoulder causes me to jump and my heart rate to skyrocket. I turn around, brandishing my spatula as a weapon in one hand while I pull an earbud out with the other. Morgan is behind me, holding his hands up in surrender with a sheepish look on his face.

"You scared the shit out of me," I admonish.

"I'm sorry. I just wanted to see if you needed any help."

He's changed into a clean button-down but left it untucked from his khaki pants. His bare feet poke out from the bottom of his slacks, ruining the whole junior-accountant vibe he's got going on.

"Don't you have more to unload?"

"No, that was it." His shoulders tense as his gaze drops to the floor.

"Oh." *Oh.* How could those few boxes be all he brought with him? He didn't even have a bed; what is he going to do, sleep on the floor? It's clear from the way he refuses to meet my eyes that he's uncomfortable talking about this. "You can set the table, then," I suggest, changing the subject. "The plates are in the cabinet next to the microwave, silverware is next to the fridge."

His shoulders relax, and he moves to follow my instructions, setting us both a place at the small table tucked away behind the couch.

"Cups?" he asks, and I direct him to the right cabinet.

I bring all of the food over to the table, and we both fill our plates. Several minutes pass, blanketed in an awkward silence while we eat. My skin crawls from the uncomfortable pressure.

"You can use the TV," I blurt out. "The one in the living room, I mean. If you want to. Since yours broke."

"I don't want to impose," he starts to protest.

"You wouldn't be," I cut in, and I'm surprised to find I mean it. "You live here now too."

"Do I?" he asks with a small smile playing on the corner of his lips. "I take it your conversation with your dad didn't go the way you hoped, unless that was a bluff."

"Not a bluff." My eyes fall to my plate as I tear a tortilla into tiny pieces. I suck in a deep breath and swallow my pride. "I'm sorry about earlier. I freaked out and lashed out instead of thinking things through. If you are still willing to try, I'd like to start over." I look up at Morgan, and he's giving me another one of those breathtaking smiles.

"I'd like that." He reaches a hand across the table. "Morgan Hall."

I shake his hand, and my lips curl with a smile. "Ophelia James Clarke, but I go by James."

"It's nice to meet you, James." He pulls his hand away and resumes eating. "Tell me about yourself."

"I have a boyfriend." The words come tumbling out without thought.

Why did I just say that?

I cringe and brace for Morgan to tell me off, but he just laughs.

"I know, I saw the pictures of you together. I just thought you were going to be him."

"Oh."

"How long have you two been together?"

"A little over ten years," I tell him, and he lets out a long whistle.

"That's impressive. I can't imagine being with someone that long. You're, what, twenty-one?"

"Twenty-two," I correct. "I'm a fifth year."

"So you were twelve when you got together?" He shakes his head as he absorbs that information. "Where is he now?"

"Tanner graduated from Georgia Southern last December and has been working at his dad's campaign office back home ever since."

"The long-distance thing must be tough."

That's an understatement. We went from seeing each other every day for years to only seeing each other a few times a month, and it sucks. It's been over four years, and it's never gotten easier. I miss him. Even more now that his job keeps him too busy to visit as often. Ever since he graduated, it barely feels like we are in a relationship. When we are together, things are good, but finding time for that seems to be growing rarer and rarer as the election approaches. Things will be like they were before once I graduate and we close the gap. I just have to get through this year.

"It is, but we make it work." Melancholy swells for a moment before I shake it away. "What about you? Anyone special in your life?"

"No, I haven't dated since undergrad. After I graduated, I joined the Peace Corps and haven't had time for relationships since then."

"What brings you all the way from Peru to Athens, Georgia?"

"Law school. It was time for me to go back to school, and the University of Georgia offered the best financial-aid packet. It was a no-brainer, really."

We fall into a comfortable conversation throughout the rest of dinner and continue even after our plates are clear. I tell him all about my dad being in the

Air Force and how I spent his deployments with my Grandma Anne in Savannah. That's where I met Tanner for the first time when we were seven. Morgan tells me about his time in Peru, and I learn he is originally from Michigan but got his bachelor's degree at Arizona State University on a wrestling scholarship. Neither one of us pushes for anything more than surface-level information, but it's nice, and the contrast to our first interaction is a welcome surprise.

The conversation hits a natural lull, and we fall back into silence, but this time, it lacks the oppressive edge. I start to clear the table, but he stops me before I can lift a plate.

"What do you think you're doing?" Morgan asks. His voice is stern, but there is a playfulness behind the tone.

"The dishes," I tell him, but it sounds more like a question than a statement. Oh God, he's a slob, isn't he? I knew it was too good to be true. He got points in the green-flag column for offering to help and not being weird about Tanner, but this might ruin it all.

"No you aren't. You cooked, I'll clean."

Oh. *Make that three points in the green-flag column.*

"Thank you for dinner, James, and for the company, but I've got it from here. Go relax and enjoy your night."

I'm too dumbfounded to do anything but listen. I can't remember the last time Tanner cleaned up after a meal, and I don't think he ever has without me nagging him first. I'm going to have to check his work in the morning, but for tonight, I'm content to let him handle it. If things stay like this, living with him might not be so bad.

Chapter 5
James

By the time the first rays of the morning sun start to peek over the horizon, I'm already drenched in sweat. Grover trots alongside me as my feet pound into the sidewalk that zigzags across the idyllic fields of North Campus. We keep pace with the music blaring in my ears; the brain-rattling bass and hardcore riffs clash in comparison to the tranquil scenery around me. Early mornings are my favorite time to run. The sweltering summer heat isn't nearly as unbearable, and, more importantly, it's one of the few times the campus isn't swarming with other people. It's peaceful, and you don't find that often in Athens.

Normally, these runs would put me into a meditative state, but I can't get Morgan out of my head. Everything would be so much easier if he was an asshole, but instead, he has the gall to be decent. He's fun to talk to, he cleans up after himself, and overall, he seems to be respectful and well-mannered. It's awful.

I think I actually like him.

I expected to have to do a second pass on the kitchen this morning, but I found it spotless and damn near swooned. He would be the perfect roommate if his stupid smile didn't make my stomach flutter.

Shaking my head, I try to force those traitorous thoughts from my head.

A robotic voice cuts through my music, announcing an incoming call from Tanner Nicholson, causing me to stumble over my feet. His call is a welcome surprise, especially since he wasn't able to talk last night. He had a late night with his team from work; it sucked not hearing from him, but I understand why.

My heart swells as two overexcited voices greet me as soon as the line connects.

"Ophie," Tanner's sisters shout into the phone. The twins, Kinsley and Raelyn, are only nine and are the closest things to siblings I have. Tanner's parents didn't plan them—they were happy with their picture-perfect family of three—but, as they like to tell everyone, "God had other plans."

"What are y'all doing up so early?" I ask.

"Tanner took us to breakfast—"

"And now we are going to the mall—"

"He said we can get our nails done—"

"And have ice cream—"

"But we aren't supposed to tell Mom 'cause we had waffles too."

The twins talk over each other, butting in to finish each other's sentences when their excitement overwhelms them. I don't bother trying to keep track of who's talking.

"That sounds fun. I bet you could convince him to get his nails done too," I add with a sly grin.

"But he's a boy," one of them says, and they burst into a fit of bright laughter.

"I guess you're right." But knowing my boyfriend, he would do it in a heartbeat if they asked. "Do you think I could maybe talk to him too?"

They both grumble but hand the phone over to my boyfriend.

"Hey, Ophie," Tanner says with a playful drawl.

My lips tighten into a small frown. I hate that stupid fucking nickname. Tanner has called me that for as long as I've known him—he wasn't able to pronounce Ophelia when we met—and he knows how much I dislike it, but the nickname has persisted despite my protests. I don't even bother to correct him anymore. It's not like he stopped when I was in tears because kids kept calling me Ophie the Oaf, so why would he now?

I started going by James in middle school to distance myself from that.

"Hi, love." I push the budding annoyance down and bury it deep. "Special day with the girls?"

"Yeah, I wanted to spend some time with them before they go back to school. Dad said things at the campaign office are about to ramp up, so I know I'm not going to be able to spend as much time with them as I want."

"That sucks." And it means he will have less time for me too. "You are still planning on coming up to visit next weekend, though, right?"

"About that, O," Tanner hedges, and my heart plummets. This happened all summer too. Any plans that didn't involve me going to visit him fell through without warning, and the only excuse he offered was that he was too busy with the campaign. I brace myself for the words I've already heard a dozen times. "I've got an important meeting that weekend that was just put on the schedule. You are still coming down next month for the fundraiser, though, so I'll see you soon."

"Right." My voice drips with bitter sarcasm.

"Babe, don't be like that," he groans. "It's only a few extra weeks. Tell me about the new roommate. Is she a total bitch?" It's a sorry attempt at changing the subject, but I let him have it. I don't have the energy to fight with him this early.

"They seem fine, but there was a bit of a mix-up," I tell him with a light chuckle. "Morgan is actually a guy."

He doesn't say anything; silence so pristine that I could hear a pin drop is the only thing that rings through the line.

"Are you still there?" I let out another chuckle, but this one is twisted by nerves.

"I'm sorry, can you repeat that?" His voice is eerily calm. "Because it sounded like you said your new roommate is a man."

"He is," I confirm and then suck my bottom lip between my teeth.

"What the fuck, James," he growls. I recoil, not only from the tone but also from the use of my preferred name. He only ever calls me James when he's mad. "And you just expected me to be okay with this?"

"Okay with what?"

"The fact you are living with another man," he shouts, and I can hear something crash in the background. "Did you plan this?"

"Of course I didn't fucking plan this. Morgan was just as confused about the whole situation as I was, but there's nothing I can do about it now."

"So that's it, then, you are just going to roll over and accept things?"

"What else do you expect me to do," I shout, my voice rising to match his.

"Anything but playing fucking house with someone else while I'm stuck at home working to build our future." His words are a sharpened lance, piercing straight through my heart.

"Tanner, please don't do this," I plea as hot tears fill my eyes.

"Do what? Point out just how much you're cucking me right now? Because you are, James. This *Morgan*," he sneers, "is going to try to fuck you. The only question is when."

"Tanner—"

"Think about how this looks on me—on my family. With the right spin, this story could ruin Dad's campaign. I can't—"

I hang up the phone.

I'm paralyzed for several seconds, with silence ringing in my ears. That wasn't the Tanner I know. He's never spoken to me like that before, and I'm sure as hell not about to let him start. If he wants to finish this conversation, then he can apologize and talk to me about it like an adult. Not whatever the fuck that was.

The music resumes, kicking my ass back into gear. I don't have it in me to finish my run, so I turn toward home. Angry tears sting my eyes, and I fight to keep them from spilling over. Attempting to distract myself, I focus on the lyrics blasting in my ears, but even that fails once I make it back to the apartment. I let Grover off his leash and beeline toward the bathroom. The floodgates open as soon as I cross the threshold. I splash a handful of cold water on my face, and when I look up, I realize I'm not alone.

My gaze locks with my roommate's wide-eyed reflection. He's standing in the shower with the faucet running, frozen like a deer caught in headlights.

A very *naked* deer.

I could tell he worked out from his honed back muscles, but that didn't prepare me for how cut he actually is. Morgan isn't an exceptionally large man—his muscles are lean instead of bulky—but every inch of him seems to have been chiseled out of stone. I didn't think *this* was what he was hiding under those stupid Oxford shirts.

My eyes move of their own volition, trailing over every perfectly sculpted line on his tanned torso. They drink in his defined abs, dropping lower to follow the carved V all the way to his pelvis and stop on what lies below.

Maybe he *is* a large man.

What the fuck, James?

My eyes snap back up to his, and a hot blush spreads over my neck and face. I just checked him out. I just checked him out and *liked it*. Maybe Tanner was right; we aren't even two days into this arrangement, and things are spinning out of control.

My boyfriend is the only other person I've seen naked, and he stays in shape, but it's nothing compared to Morgan's physique. A wave of guilt crashes through me, turning my stomach to lead. But an undercurrent of curiosity comes with it. Part of me wants to look closer, to compare the two even further, but I keep my eyes glued to the reflection of Morgan's.

He stumbles out of the tub, his lips moving with silent words. I yank the earbud from one ear and catch the last few words of his question.

"—you all right?" He places a gentle hand on my shoulder and looks at me with concern etched on his face. He doesn't share that same concern for his state of undress.

"Morgan...naked..." I stammer and slam my eyes shut. That's what I should have done the moment I saw him in here.

He jerks his hand away like it was burned by my touch. "Ope, yeah, no, sorry."

The damp plodding of footsteps, followed by light rustling from his room, signals his exit, but I don't hear the door close, so I keep my eyes sealed shut.

"Seriously, James," Morgan says, sounding closer than before, "are you okay."

The genuine care in his voice catches me off guard. I risk it and crack my lids open. Morgan is standing in the doorway, thankfully fully clothed in plaid pajama bottoms and a T-shirt. He's looking at me with a furrowed brow, the worry clear on his face.

"Of course. Why wouldn't I be?" My voice carries the lie an octave higher than normal. "You weren't what I was expecting to walk into, and I'm still reeling from that shock."

"You were crying when you ran in here," he challenges and folds his arms over his chest. "That doesn't seem all right to me."

Shit. I was hoping he hadn't noticed that. I don't want him to see me weak.

"I don't think that's any of your business." I throw up my defensive walls, snapping at him with a bitter-cold edge. Anger is safe. It's an uncomplicated emotion. One I cling to despite knowing it will do more harm in the long term.

Morgan takes a step back and raises his hands in mock surrender. "There's no need for that, now. I was just checking on you, not trying to pry. Won't happen again."

"What the fuck were you doing in here, anyway?"

Morgan flinches at my hostile accusations, and I have to shove down my creeping guilt.

I thought we could be friends, but I was wrong. He doesn't seem like a bad guy; he seems like someone I could grow to actually like, and that's the problem. Tanner's words run on repeat in my head, urging me to burn this bridge once and for all.

It's better for everyone this way.

"I was about to shower." It sounds more like a question than a statement.

"And you just happened to leave the door unlocked? Yeah, right," I scoff. "You set this up, didn't you? You wanted me to walk in on you." I ignore the pain that flashes in his eyes as my baseless accusations hit their target.

"Jesus, James." He runs a hand through his hair and lets out an exasperated sigh. "Why would you even think that?"

"Why else would you leave it unlocked?"

"Because I forgot," he says, pushing back against my loaded words. "You barged in on me. You didn't even knock."

"Oh, save it for someone who cares. I'm not buying your Mr. Perfect act, and I want nothing to do with it. We aren't friends, and I don't want us to be. Stay out of my way, and we won't have any problems. Got it?"

He lets out a long breath, and the life seems to drain out of him.

"Okay, sounds good to me." His voice takes on a strange, hollow tone that makes something in my chest ache. It's almost enough to make me give up this facade and beg for his forgiveness. "You can have the bathroom. I'm done here. I'm sorry for not locking the door. It won't happen again."

He steps back into his room, pulling the door closed behind him. It latches with an almost inaudible *click*, but that tiny sound stabs into my chest with the force of a dagger. That felt final; it felt like I shut the door on any chance I had of getting to know the man I'll be living with. It was the right thing to do—Morgan Hall is already getting too deep under my skin—but knowing that doesn't make it hurt any less.

Chapter 6
Morgan

It might be cowardly, but I don't stick around for my turn in the bathroom again. The risk of running into *her* is too high. She's made her opinion perfectly clear—I'm the bad guy here. I'm not welcome, and I've never been the type who needed to be told things twice.

I guess this is as good a time as any to explore the campus. It's not exactly what I had planned for today, but anything is better than spending another moment stuck in that apartment with the she-devil.

The apartment butts up against the northernmost edge of the university's campus. It's the main reason I chose it. All of my classes will be held in the law building, which should only be a few minutes' walk down the road, and if the research I did over the summer is to be believed, I'll pass a handful of the school's landmarks along the way.

I wander aimlessly through the manicured lawns and picturesque gardens, taking the time to appreciate the campus's beauty. Because, despite the less-than-warm welcome, Athens is beautiful in its own weird way. James might be making my living situation hell, but I refuse to let that taint the rest of my experience here. I won't let one woman make me miserable.

My gaze catches on a fountain in the middle of a small field. The sunlight reflects off something in the water, creating a ripple of silver in the otherwise blue pool. I move closer for a better look and find...tinsel?

"You jumping in?" a masculine voice calls from behind me.

I turn around and find a man watching me with an amused expression. He looks to be around my age and is rocking the surfer-bro look despite there not being a beach for hours in any direction.

"Why would I do that?"

"I don't know, man, it's one of those freshman traditions. People jump in and take pictures. It's a whole thing."

"I guess that explains the tinsel," I say, mostly to myself.

"That it would." The stranger chuckles.

"I'm not a freshman, though." I extend my hand. "I'm Morgan. I'm about to start law school."

"Nathan," he says with a firm handshake. "I'm also in grad school, but I did my undergrad here too."

"Must be nice already knowing your way around." I let out a small huff and drag my fingers through my curls. "I'll be lucky if I can find my classes without a map come Monday."

"I can show you around if you want," the stranger offers, and his lips fall into an easy grin.

"Really?" The knot of nerves in my chest loosens. "That would be great. You're only the second person I've met in Athens, and the first wasn't exactly welcoming." I recoil as the words bring James back to the forefront of my mind.

It's been less than a day, but her split personality already has me on edge. The venom-spitting she-devil is a terror, but I saw a glimpse of a different James last night—one who was calm and pleasant to be around. I almost liked her. I don't even know where to place the woman crying in the bathroom, but everything in me wanted to take away her pain.

"Now, *that* sounds like a story," he says as he starts to guide me.

"You could say that," I scoff. "My new roommate is..." I struggle to think of a word that accurately describes James. "Difficult."

"Difficult how? Is this a zero-hygiene situation, or is he an asshole?"

"He is a she, who thought I was also a she, and I thought she was a he." My explanation comes out all sorts of convoluted.

Nathan freezes and cocks his head to the side as he tries to make sense of my ramblings. After a moment, he gives up and laughs. "Yeah, man, I'm lost."

"My roommate's name is James. I thought James would be a guy, but she is most definitely not. When she saw my name was Morgan, she assumed I was a girl. Which, again, I very clearly am not. She doesn't seem to be handling the fact that I have a penis well." A penis that she has now been briefly acquainted with. My cheeks flush at the thought.

"No shit," he says with a chuckle. "How bad is it?"

"Well, so far, she has sicced her hellhound on me, threatened to have her dad kick me out, and this morning, she accused me of setting her up to see my dick."

"What a bitch." He shakes his head in disbelief.

"No she's not." I jump to her defense. "That's what makes it worse. Between all the madness, I've seen glimpses of a different side of her, and I actually liked that version. It just didn't stick around very long."

"Man, that is rough," he agrees. "You should come out with me and my friends tonight. We like to hang out at a bar downtown, Cutter's Pub. My buddy Gage works there and hooks us up with free drinks all night. We typically meet up around nine. Let me show you the type of people Athens truly has to offer. I can't let James poison the city to you. We aren't all crazy."

"Sounds like a plan," I tell him, and for the first time since James walked into the apartment, I have a good feeling about this year.

***

I thought I had escaped the humidity when I left Peru, but I was mistaken. The Athens air is thick with moisture that clings to my skin, coating me in a layer of sweat that sticks to my clothes. My need to wash away the day's grime overrules my desire to stay away, and I find myself back at the apartment as the last of the sunlight fades.

James's hellhound is asleep on the couch when I return. I creep through the dark apartment in a poor attempt at stealth, hoping the dog doesn't notice me without James here to leash it. I could call for her if I need to be rescued, but knowing her, she'd let him eat me and laugh while I scream. My shin bangs against something hard, and the noise resounds through the room with a deafening echo.

The hellhound raises its head and lets out a low growl, paralyzing me with fear. My heart pounds in my chest as we stay locked in a silent standoff. Thankfully, after several tense seconds, he drops his head back to his paws, and I let out a breath of relief.

I don't wait around to see what else he does.

After slipping into the sanctuary of my bedroom, I head toward the bathroom, pausing to make a point to knock on the door. A moment passes with no response, so I enter and lock both doors.

I won't be making that mistake again.

My shower is quick, but it gets the job done. The mirror hasn't even had time to steam over by the time I shut the water off. An orange piece of paper sticks to the reflective surface, catching my attention as I step out and reach for a towel. Curiosity gets the better of me, and I grab the bright Post-it.

> Dear Roomie,
>
> Remember to lock the door
> next time. And don't store
> your toothbrush on the
> counter. It's unsanitary.
>
> Thanks,
> —J

Of course she left a note.

I crumble it in my fist and toss it into the bin in my room. The she-devil isn't worth my time or energy. It's clear she's playing a game with me, but I'm two steps behind and missing the rule book. Drinks and good company are exactly what I need.

This early in the night, the city is only just beginning to stir. The streets are illuminated by the neon signs that clutter bar windows—bars that will only grow more packed as time progresses. The University of Georgia isn't all that different from any other party school; over the next hour or so, the stench of stale beer will overpower any floral notes drifting in from the campus gardens, and the sidewalks will be flooded with drunken students who, for the most part, are probably underage. I've lived it before—heck, I've been that kid. The familiarity of it all settles the unease toiling in my chest.

Walking over to Cutter's Pub only takes me a few short minutes. A bored bouncer checks my ID at the door and doesn't give me a second glance as I enter the vaguely Irish-themed pub. My attention is immediately drawn to the large square bar in the center of the room. It's stocked with an impressive selection of beers and liquors and has an array of TVs overhead displaying various sporting events. Dark walls and exposed brick make the space feel smaller, creating a more intimate atmosphere, and the sounds of pool balls and dad rock fill the air. It's got the vibe of a dive bar but with a different clientele. I'm not sure if that's a good thing yet.

I spot Nathan leaning against the far edge of the bar, drinking alone. It's not exactly what I'm expecting, but I head in his direction regardless. He notices me and tips his glass in my direction with a relaxed smile.

"Hey, man, glad you could make it." He pulls me into an unexpected bro-hug. The causal touch catches me off guard; I can't tell if it's his personality or if he's already drunk.

"Thanks for inviting me. Are we the first ones here, or did your friends bail?"

"Well, that ugly bastard is Gage." He points to the giant of a man serving drinks to a group of giggling women on the other side of the bar. "He'll join us when he can. And Karis is running late, as usual."

"You said meet around nine, not at nine. Very different things, and therefore, I'm not late," a snarky voice cuts in.

A woman joins our group. She's dressed head to toe in black, from her dyed asymmetrical bob to the tattoos that cover her arms and chest. It's almost enough to distract from her size. Karis has to be one of the shortest women I've ever met. There's no way she even approaches five feet; despite that, she has a presence about her that makes her seem bigger than she is.

"Speak of the devil," he says with a playful smirk.

"Oh, please, the devil's got nothing on me." She winks at my new friend and turns her attention to me. "So you're the newest stray?" The playfulness she had with him disappears as she cocks her head and appraises me with predatory eyes.

There must be something in the water that makes Athens women this aggressive.

Nathan winces and gives me an apologetic look. "Come on, Kare Bear, play nice."

"Fuck off, Butler, I am playing nice," she snaps in his direction. "We've all been there." She turns back to me with the same assessing attitude. "He found me half overdosed on caffeine in the library last fall, and I've been stuck with him since. Gage and I train at the same MMA gym, and Nathan adopted him after, like, the second class I drug him to. The point is, we were all strays at one point."

"Morgan, this lovely creature is Karis." Nathan's voice drips with sarcasm.

"Nice to meet you," I mumble, but the truth of that statement is still to be determined. "So you guys do MMA?"

"Recreationally," Nathan says.

"Except for Gage. He went pro there for a while," Karis adds. Her words make sense; Gage has the look of a professional fighter. He has the flattened nose of a man who's had it broken one too many times, and his ears are swollen with the same pockets of blood I always got during wrestling season.

"That's cool. I actually trained some when I was younger." I twist my fingers in my hair and fidget with the strands. "I prefer grappling to sparring, though."

"No shit? You need to come to Double Teep with us, then," he says, clapping me on the back.

"Maybe once I get settled into classes." And even then, I probably can't afford it, but I'm not going to get into that with strangers.

"What other secrets are you hiding?" the woman asks, giving me a toothy smile. I think it's supposed to be friendly, but her too-wide grin comes across as feral.

"Morgan Hall, twenty-four, Scorpio, about to start law school, scared of frogs, and I'm pretty sure my roommate is the devil's daughter," I rattle off.

"I wanna hear more about this roommate," Karis says at the same time Nathan asks, "Frogs?"

They turn and face each other and have a silent argument with their eyes. "Fine," he says with an exasperated sigh. "I've already heard the story about the bit—witch, though." He pouts a little, putting on a show of it.

"What witch?" Gage asks as he joins us, and he hands both Karis and me a beer.

"Morgan's new roommate. From what he's told me, she's absolutely crazy."

Nathan's friends look at me with expectant expressions. I take a sip of the beer and tell them about the roller coaster the past day and a half has been.

"Yup, she sounds like a certified psycho," Karis concludes when I finish the story.

"Are you sure you've never met her before yesterday?" Gage asks. "This feels like grudge shit. Maybe you killed her cat in a past life or something."

"No, I'm sure I've never met her. But get this: when I stopped by the apartment on the way here, I found a note that she left for me."

"What type of note?" Nathan asks, instantly refocusing on the drama and the part of the story he hasn't heard yet.

"A passive-aggressive Post-it Note reminding me to lock the door and criticizing where I keep my toothbrush."

The three of them stay silent for a moment before Karis and Nathan burst out in laughter.

Gage places a hand on my shoulder. "You are a stronger man than me. I would have lost my shit within the first few hours."

"I would have been throwing punches in the first five minutes," Karis agrees. "Bring him something stronger, he deserves it after what he's been through."

The mountainous man grumbles at her order, but only affection shines through in his eyes as he pours four shots out on the bar. "To Morgan's endless patience," he says, holding up a shot glass for a toast. I throw mine back with the rest of the group, wincing as the alcohol burns its way down my throat.

"Do you know how to play pool?" Nathan asks, guiding us to an empty table and leaving Gage behind the bar.

As it turns out, I don't.

After two hours and a few too many drinks, I'm still barely able to hit the cue ball. That doesn't mean I'm not having fun. I realized pretty quickly that I had misjudged the prickly woman. She's good people—they all are. Never in my life have I meshed so easily with a group.

"Holy shit, man, do you see her?" Nathan says as he slings an arm over my shoulder and turns me toward the tiny dance floor.

The world spins for a moment as I regain my bearings. Three women writhe together on a dance floor of their own making, drawing the eyes of every man in the room: a willowy redhead with wildfire hair, a curvy brunette who moves her body with practiced grace, and a blond angel who is blessing the bar with her carefree jubilation. I can't get a good look at her face, but she glows against the grungy atmosphere.

"We gotta go talk to them," he insists and drags me, stumbling, toward them.

I don't put up a fight, because he might have the right idea. As we approach, the angel twirls, laughing as she dances with her hands in the air, and my stomach turns to ice.

It's James.

I freeze, pulling him to a halt with me.

"What the hell, man?"

"That's *her*," I hiss.

"The redhead is your roommate?"

"What? No, the blond is."

"Oh." He thinks for a moment, and a broad grin splits across his face. "Good. Let's go see if she's as bad as you say."

"I don't think that's a good idea," I try to protest, but I'm already being dragged forward again.

He puts on a charming smile and slides up to their group with relaxed ease. "Ladies," he greets the group, but his attention is on the tall ginger woman. "Mind if we join you?"

James's bright smile falls when she recognizes me, and a look of disdain takes its place. Her two friends don't seem to notice her discomfort, though. They are both too focused on our arrival. The redhead drags her eyes over Nathan's body and moistens her lips.

"Not at all." She twirls a strand of her fiery hair around her finger and moves a step closer. "I'm Chelsea."

"Nathan," he responds, "and this is my buddy Morgan, although I think he's already acquainted with your friend." He tilts his head toward James.

Both girls turn to look at James, their eyes blazing with questions.

The brunette thinks for a moment before understanding dawns on her face. "Morgan...like, new roommate Morgan?"

Her shoulders slump as she lets out a sigh.

"Evelyn, Chels, this is my new roommate, Morgan Hall." James's tone is pleasant, but she glares daggers in my direction. The brunette's—Evelyn's—dark eyes widen, and Chelsea's mouth falls agape.

"What the hell, Jamie? Why didn't you tell us about this?" Chelsea asks.

"It's only been a day. I haven't had the chance to bring it up," she says with a shrug.

They both stare at her like she's grown a second head, and the man beside me can't keep the sly grin off his face.

"Let us buy you a round, and you can get to know the guy." He slips his arm around the redhead's waist, and she melts into his touch as he leads her back toward Karis.

James follows them with a huff, leaving me alone with the softer woman. She drops her eyes to the ground and gives me a tentative smile from under thick lashes.

"We should probably go too," she says to her feet. "I'm Evelyn, by the way."

"It's nice to meet you, Evelyn. I'm Morgan, but I think you've already been told that at least twice." I cringe and rake my fingers through my hair. "Yeah, let's just go."

She laughs at my awkward rambling and urges me forward. Her arm brushes up against mine with every step we take, and she continues to give me shy glances out of the corner of her eyes.

Nathan already has Chelsea enthralled by his charismatic aura; he's got his arms wrapped around her, whispering words I never want to hear against her porcelainlike neck while she lines up her shot at the pool table. Karis looks unfazed by his blatant public display of affection, so I guess this is the behavior I should learn to expect from him.

My roommate stands apart from the group, curled in on herself, with her arms folded across her chest. Part of me wants to go check on her, but her words from earlier ring in my head, so I do exactly what she asked and stay out of her way.

"I'm going to get us drinks. I'll be right back." I leave Evelyn with Karis and flag Gage down at the bar.

"Who are the chicks?" he asks as he approaches.

"That would be the roommate and her friends." I don't bother to hide the contempt in my voice.

"No shit? How did that happen?"

"Nathan," I tell him, and he nods like that's the only explanation he needs. "Would you mind grabbing me drinks for the whole group?"

"Even her?"

I think it over for a second before nodding in reluctant agreement. He fills up a tray with beers from the tap, and I take them back to the group. With only one drink left to deliver, I work up the courage to face the she-devil head-on.

She has her back to the group as she stares out into the crowd. I place a gentle hand on the back of her elbow to avoid startling her. "Hey, I got you a drink."

My attempt fails as she jumps and spins to face me. Her abrupt motion knocks the full beer out of my hand, and I'm unable to do anything but watch in horror as its contents spill out onto her.

"What the hell, Morgan?" she screeches.

"I'm so, so sorry, James." I search around us and grab some napkins off a nearby high-top to help clean her off. Without thinking, I try to wipe the liquid off her chest, and she pushes my hands away with a sound of disgust.

"Seriously? You are trying to cop a feel right now?" The rage on her face is clear as day.

"What? No. I was just trying to help. I'm sorry." My cheeks flush as I hold out the napkins to her without meeting her eyes.

"I'm sure you were," she says, her words dripping in venom. She rolls her eyes but doesn't make a move to grab them from me. "Fuck this. I'm going home."

"James, wait." I stop her as she tries to storm off. "At least let me walk with you."

She barks out a dark, bitter laugh. "Fuck off, Morgan."

"It's dark, and you've been drinking. Please let me come with you." I reach for her wrist, but she rips it from my grasp.

"What about this isn't getting through your thick fucking skull? You aren't my dad, and you sure as hell aren't my boyfriend, so you can take that bullshit white-knight attitude and shove it up your ass where it belongs." She turns away, and this time, I don't stop her as she flees the bar.

Chapter 7
James

"Jamie, how the hell could you not tell us about Morgan?" Chelsea ambushes me as I join her and Evelyn at our normal table in the dining hall.

A groan threatens to escape my lips. I should have known they would want to talk about him. Heaven forbid I have a single moment where Morgan fucking Hall isn't at the forefront of my mind. He's like a fungus slowly infesting my home and my mind. How am I supposed to stop thinking about him when his shoes are by the door and his dishes lay unwashed in the sink?

He's everywhere, and now he's spread his spores to infect my friends too. It's beyond infuriating.

"I was hoping he would be gone before I had to," I tell them with a bitter tone.

"Gone? Why?" Evelyn asks. "He seemed nice." Her full cheeks grow pink as she drops her eyes to the table.

"Oh, I'm sure he did," Chelsea teases and pokes her elbow into our friend's ribs. "I saw the fuck-me eyes you were giving him all night."

"I wasn't giving him you-know-what eyes," she mumbles, her face growing even brighter.

For a brief moment, a flash of something ugly rears up inside me. In the three years I've known Evelyn, never once has she shown an interest in anyone, but here she is, crushing on my...I struggle to find the right word for Morgan. My roommate? My nemesis? I'm not sure, but something in me has laid claim. I force it back into the dark, where I can't see it. Morgan Hall isn't mine in any capacity.

"You're one to talk, Chels. When I left, it looked like you were seconds away from sticking your tongue down Nathan's throat."

Her face breaks into a goofy grin as I bring up Morgan's friend.

How did he manage to make friends that quickly? I floundered through my whole freshman year without finding anyone I clicked with. I didn't even meet Chelsea and Evelyn until my sophomore year, but somehow, Morgan found a whole group within a few days. I don't get it. He isn't *that* great.

"Where *did* you run off to?" Chelsea questions.

"Don't change the subject. I want to hear all the details." And I don't want to talk about Morgan; it's bad enough I can't stop thinking about him.

"Well, I went home with him," Chelsea hedges, and her whole face shines with love-drunk adoration.

"Chels," Evelyn gasps.

"Does he fuck as good as he flirts?" I ask.

"That's the thing, we didn't even fool around. Sure, we made out for a bit, but we stayed up for hours talking until we both fell asleep on his couch. Then this morning, he made me breakfast before driving me home." She bites on her lower lip to hold back her growing smile.

"So do you plan to see him again?" Evelyn asks.

She nods, and the grin breaks free. "He asked to take me out tomorrow."

"That's great, Chels," I tell her. At least one good thing came out of running into my mistake. Although, this probably means I'll be running into him more too.

"I really like him," she confesses.

I don't get a chance to respond before my phone rings. They roll their eyes when they hear the familiar sound—Tanner's special ringtone. It's been set that way since eleventh grade when he broke up with me for a week after I missed his calls while I was on vacation with my dad.

I haven't missed one since.

His behavior yesterday makes me want to break that streak. White-hot anger still burns through my veins at the mere memory of how he spoke to me, and my finger hovers to decline the call, but a twinge of guilt holds me back.

"I gotta take this," I tell the girls as I excuse myself from the table.

I swipe to answer but don't say anything as the line connects. If Tanner comes at me with the same attitude he had yesterday, I'm going to hang up.

"Ophie, are you there?" he asks after several seconds of dead air. An edge of desperation distorts his voice, making it more gruff than usual. Hearing it only makes my anger boil closer to the surface.

"Yes." I keep my answer terse, or I'll lose my shit.

"O, baby, I'm sorry."

"For?"

"Yelling at you. Accusing you of bullshit. All of it. I fucked up." He lets out a heavy sigh.

"Yeah, you did."

"Can you forgive me, baby?" he pleads. I can practically hear his pout through the phone. "It will never happen again. I promise."

"Okay." I sigh and lock away all the growing bitter feelings. "Just don't do that shit again."

"Thank you, Ophie." He sounds more like himself again in an instant. "I did want to talk about the roommate, though."

Here we go again.

My eyes roll as I brace myself for what's coming. Maybe this time, he'll be able to talk things through without making an ass of himself.

"I want to meet him."

"What? Why?"

From the tone of his voice, I can already tell how this is going to play out. He's going to show up and do the whole alpha-posturing thing to show Morgan that he owns me. It will be a one-man pissing contest as my boyfriend does everything he can to mark me as his territory. I might as well let him piss on my leg to get it over and done with.

"Is it really that strange that I want to meet the man who's trying to fuck my girlfriend?"

"What the fuck, Tanner? You literally just said you weren't going to be a dick. Morgan isn't trying to fuck me."

"Yet. He hasn't tried to fuck you *yet*, but he will."

"Do you even hear yourself right now? You sound like a crazy person. I thought things were too busy with work for you to come up."

"I'll make time."

His words cut through my heart like a sharpened blade. He couldn't find the time to come visit me, but somehow, he has all the time in the world to come intimidate my roommate. The fight leaves my body on a sagging breath. What's the fucking point? He will probably cancel on me again anyway.

"When are you coming?" My voice takes on a dull, hollow tone.

"I'll be there in two weeks. I have stuff I need to take care of this weekend. His tone is too chipper. He's either missed my change in attitude or is willfully ignoring it. I'm not sure which is worse.

"Okay, I guess I'll see you then." I start to ask about the girls, but he cuts me off before I can get the words out of my mouth.

"I gotta run. I'll talk to you soon. I love you, O."

"I love you too," I try to respond, but the line is already dead.

My head falls back as I let out a groan of frustration. My life has become a steaming pile of shit over the past few days.

"Everything good?" Evelyn asks as I rejoin them at the table.

"Everything is great," I lie, plastering on my best plastic smile. "Tanner just wanted to iron out the details of his next visit."

Chelsea gives me a skeptical look but doesn't push any further. Thankfully, the girls relent as I steer the conversation away from the guys. That doesn't keep the thoughts of Tanner and Morgan from ripping through my head in a cyclone of rage and confusion, though. I can't focus on a word that comes out of my friends' mouths. Not when I can still hear Tanner's harsh accusations, and every time my mind wanders, I see images of Morgan's elusive smile and flashes of the sculpted lines of his naked body.

I excuse myself earlier than I normally would, making a bullshit excuse about pre-semester reading when what I really need is to wipe the last forty-eight hours from my memory.

The whole walk home, my fingers dance along my thigh, itching to purge the storm of emotion the only way they know how. The growing ball of tension only lessens once I step foot into my bedroom.

My room is my oasis. It's the one place I have complete control. Everything is decorated in matching shades of gray and peach, and, more importantly, everything is kept exactly where it belongs—well, almost everything. My art corner, with its easel by the window, is the one blip of utter chaos in my otherwise immaculate space. No matter what I try, I can never get it to fall in line like the rest of my belongings.

I change into ratty clothes and grab my headphones, putting on my most chaotic playlist to match my mood. Muscle memory kicks in as I set my workstation up with a fresh canvas and an array of paints, the familiarity soothing some of my fraying nerves. I don't think about what I'm going to paint. My hands simply go, moving of their own accord as they take my tangled mess of emotions and make them into something beautiful on the canvas.

I fall into a state of zen while I work, and all my worries temporarily melt away. Something starts to take shape from the swirling swaths of color, and my heart drops into my stomach as I recognize it. Immortalized in thick, messy strokes is Morgan Hall and that heart-stopping fucking smile.

Chapter 8
Morgan

The first week of classes was an absolute shock to my system. I've always done well in school, but I don't think undergrad could have prepared anyone for the realities of the first year of law school. The intense workload has overwhelmed any capacity I had to focus on my situation with James. We haven't crossed paths since that night at Cutter's. I haven't been intentionally avoiding her; I just make sure to leave while she is on her morning run and then study at the library until well into the night.

My absence hasn't stopped James from letting me know how terrible she thinks I am. She leaves daily Post-it Notes in the bathroom that nitpick my every move. Unsurprisingly, another one is waiting for me on the mirror as I drag myself out of bed and head for the shower.

Great. Let's see how I displeased the she-devil this time.

I shake my head as I pull it off the mirror and add it to the ever-growing pile in my room. She was the one who wanted us to stay out of each other's hair, and this feels like the opposite of that. I don't think I'm a bad roommate; no one has ever complained before. After a week straight, you'd think she'd run out of things to criticize. At this rate, I'll have a full notepad's worth by the end of the year.

That night, I stumbled back from Cutter's drunker than I intended with an inescapable urge to fish that crumpled scrap of paper from the bin. I don't know why, but I saved it, tucking it away behind the cardboard box that doubles as my bedside table. When I found another note the next morning, it went there too.

I finish getting ready and head to class, and by the time my professor starts quizzing us on the prior day's reading, all thoughts of my roommate and her notes are pushed to the back of my mind. They don't make their way back to the forefront until Karis ambushes me as soon as I approach our normal table in the library.

"So what was it this time?" Trying to guess how I messed up this time has become a bit of a game between her and Nathan. "Did you breathe too loud? Did you put the mugs away with the handles facing the wrong direction?"

"No, he did that three days ago. I don't think she will repeat it again so soon," Nathan adds.

"He put the mugs in the dishwasher wrong last time, not away."

"It's the same thing." Nathan waves a hand at her dismissively.

"Is not," she snaps, the look on her face daring him to challenge her again. Her eyes light up with a manic gleam. I've only known her a few weeks, but I know that look, and I can say with absolute certainty that she will make him pay for it on the mats later if he does.

Learning that my small group of friends all train in MMA and jiu-jitsu together was an unexpected but welcome surprise. I've done various types of martial arts since I was a kid. My parents put me in whatever classes were cheap at the local rec center, and it sort of stuck. I started wrestling in middle school, which eventually led to me receiving an athletics scholarship for my bachelor's degree. Nathan has been relentless in trying to get me to join them at their gym. As much as I would love to, my classes and the cost make it impossible.

"I didn't close the shower curtain good enough," I cut in for Nathan's sake.

"Damn, didn't have that one on my bingo card." Karis relaxes back into her seat. "I think she's running out of ideas. At least you didn't leave the remote on the wrong side of the coffee table this time."

"I'd rather she just leave me be," I grumble.

"But then what would we talk about? Before you, Nathan would just lament about his flavor of the week." Her nose crinkles in disgust.

"How are things going with Chelsea?" I take the opportunity to shift the focus away from me and the she-devil.

"Things are great." Nathan slouches into his seat with a dopey smile, and his sandy hair flops in his eyes.

"Here he goes," Karis mumbles under her breath and pins me with a half-hearted glare.

"I know it's only been a week, but she is something special," he answers, not acknowledging her interruption.

"That's what he always says." Karis rolls her eyes and goes back to studying.

"I mean it this time. She might be the one."

"That girl is so far out of your league, it should be criminal."

"I know," he says with a love-sick sigh, letting her dig slide off him like butter. "I'm inviting her out with us this weekend. Want to hit Cutter's again?"

Karis doesn't even look up as she snarks, "I'm in. Can't wait to see this one blow up in your face."

"Sorry, but I'm out. I've got too much to catch up on this weekend." And I don't want to risk running into James again. "Rain check?"

"Are you still up to meet at Ramsey later for a few rolls?"

"Yes, we are still on for Ramsey."

Nathan decided that if I wouldn't go to Double Teep, he would at least meet me at the university's gym a few times a week for reps.

"We could meet up with Gage if you would come to Double Teep with me. Coach David would be willing to work with you if cost is the only concern."

We've had this argument at least four times over the past week.

"I promise I'll talk to Coach next semester. I just need to find my footing with school first."

Nathan hums like he doesn't believe me but doesn't push me any further. I pull out my laptop and settle in for another evening of staying as far away from James Clarke as possible.

***

Like every night, the small bulb under the microwave is the lone source of light in the otherwise dark apartment when I return. It's the only welcome I ever get. Even the hellhound has stopped reacting when I slip in through the door each night. I'm not sure if James leaves it on out of habit or if she is doing it for me.

Why would she leave it on for me?

It's definitely a habit, or for the dog, but I appreciate it anyway. It's nice not to come back to darkness every day.

I head toward my room and pause to see if there's any light spilling from beneath James's door. Thankfully, the gap is dark. My whole body relaxes, knowing there's no risk of an encounter with the she-devil tonight. I step into the bathroom and glance at the mirror, half expecting to see another note, but it's empty. The tension I've been carrying lessens even more. Those two-note days always wind me up, making sleep more elusive.

I take my time showering and going through my nightly routine. Without the looming threat of James interrupting, I'm able to get in a rare moment of peace. Afterward, though, I pay extra attention to make sure the shower curtain is pulled tight, my toothbrush is put away, the toilet lid is closed, and there is no trace that I was ever here at all. I find her demands excessive, but maybe tomorrow, she won't find fault with my mere existence. Maybe tonight, I can actually do something right in her eyes.

My body is exhausted as the endorphins that remained from my earlier workout flee, and I'm left blissfully sluggish. I chase that bliss, crawl into bed, and slip into what I pray is a night of dreamless sleep.

***

I wake with a gasp, my heart racing and my body drenched in sweat. My hands fumble in the dark, searching for my phone. The display shows what I already knew: it's way too late—or too early, depending on how you look at it. It's 4 a.m., and I know I'm not getting back to sleep anytime soon.

I never do.

I've been plagued by nightmares for over half my life. They are always the same: red and blue lights shining in from behind the curtains on the front windows of our house, a forceful knock on the door, my mother's almost inhuman scream as she falls to the floor as grief overtakes her, and watching the coffin lower into a bottomless pit, feeling like my own soul was going with it. They were worse when I was younger, happening almost every night. Time and therapy helped, but they always come back in unfamiliar environments or when I'm stressed, which means I haven't gotten a full night's rest in over a week.

Resigned, I pull myself off the mattress on the floor and head out to the living room. Watching TV has always been my go-to way to cope. James doesn't know it, but I took her up on her offer to use the living room TV that first night and every night since.

After a few seconds of deliberation, I put on one of my favorite comfort watches, *The Adventures of Sir Lancelot*. I've seen it dozens of times through at this point, but the campy 1950s take on King Arthur and his knights never ceases to amaze me.

Yes, it's cheesy.

Yes, the acting leaves a lot to be desired.

No, it isn't even in color.

It doesn't matter. I love it anyway. Other iterations of the legend do a good job, and I love those too, but none quite capture the magic of chivalry and heroism the same.

The hellhound wakes with a growl as the opening sound of trumpets plays softly through the speakers. This has also become a part of my nightly routine. I realized pretty early that the growls were just for show, but he still hasn't warmed up to me.

I can change that.

The thought hits me like a lightning bolt. James might be a lost cause, but I can make this dog like me. Then at least someone in this house would be happy to see me.

With my quest in mind, I head to the kitchen to look for a suitable bribe. I'm not above buying this dog's affection. I search through the cabinets, careful not to mess up the she-devil's meticulous organization. Even though I'm sure nothing is out of place, I guarantee I'll get a note about leaving things where I found them in the morning. Finding my faults is her superpower.

My fingers itch to ruin it and leave something out where it doesn't belong. Why am I even trying to please her when it's never going to be enough? But I resist the urge; kicking the hornet's nest seems like a bad idea when I have to live with the consequences.

I'm about to give up my search when I find it, the holy grail, a jar of dog treats.

I grab my loot and go sit cross-legged on the floor near where the hellhound rests. He watches me with wary eyes but doesn't growl again. I'm calling that progress. His head perks up as I take the lid off the jar and hold one out to him with a flat hand. I stay still, letting him make the first move. I never had any pets growing up, but I know better than to try to force this, especially with an animal this on edge. That's how you end up with a bitten hand.

I suppose James isn't so different.

She is a scared animal lashing out with anger when she feels threatened. If I'm going to try to salvage this year, I'm going to need to be as nonthreatening as possible and let James lead.

Grover approaches cautiously and sniffs at my hand before devouring the treat in one wet bite. I extend my hand toward him, watching for any signs of aggression, and scratch the coarse fur behind his ear. His tail thumps against the floor, and he licks my face, leaving a trail of saliva.

I think he's sufficiently charmed.

To be safe, I give him a few more treats while dragging my hands through his fur. I don't want to give him too many or make him sick, so I take the jar back to the cabinet where I found it. This time, though, I have a hellhound shadow. My shadow persists even after I get comfortable on the couch again, and he jumps up on the seat next to me, curling up to lay his head on my thigh.

That went way easier than I thought. Maybe James will be just as easy.

I choke on a snort of laughter. *Like that will ever happen.*

I keep petting Grover as I focus back on the screen. My chest feels a little lighter knowing I have one ally in this apartment.

Chapter 9
James

Deep breaths, James. You can do this. The worst he can do is say no.

I raise my fist, poised to knock on Morgan's door, but chicken out. Again. My arm falls back to my side, and I let out a sigh of defeat. This is the third day in a row I've stood outside his door, and it's the third day that I've not followed through. I don't even know if he's in there.

We haven't crossed paths since that day at Cutter's. The daily disappearance of my notes is the only proof I have that he comes home. He's taking my insistence that we stay out of each other's way seriously. I should be grateful. He's doing exactly what I asked of him, but I didn't expect him to be this good at avoiding me.

Or for it to be this lonely.

At least it's been peaceful, or as peaceful as a cold war can be. I'll take careful avoidance over constant fighting any day. It feels wrong to disrupt it. Pushing Morgan away was hard enough the first time, and I don't know if I'll be able to do it again.

I don't have a choice, though. Tanner wants to meet him, and I've put off informing him of this fact for as long as I can. My time is up; I have to talk to him today.

I raise my fist again.

If I don't do this now, I never will. As I'm about to man up and knock, the door swings open. The man I've tried so hard to avoid stands in the doorway, dressed in his normal uniform. He doesn't notice me at first, stepping out into the hall while digging through the backpack slung over one shoulder.

Yelping in surprise, I stumble backward, trying to avoid being run over. That noise catches his attention, and he stops in his tracks—at least, he attempts to. His feet stop moving, but his upper body doesn't quite get the memo. Caught by inertia, he stumbles forward as he tries to regain his balance and barrels straight into me. The impact knocks me off balance, and I start to fall back, but his strong hands grip my shoulders, steadying us both. His hazel eyes meet mine, and a myriad of emotions flit across his face. I'm able to single out a few of them: concern, fear, and something I can't quite place—a flash of heat that causes the butterflies in my stomach to take flight.

As quickly as it came, the moment passes, and his face hardens into an emotionless mask. It's the same expression he wore when I tore into him in the bathroom; the look rips the wings off those butterflies, and they plummet into my gut.

He stands up straight and takes a step back, releasing my shoulders as if they burned him.

"I'm sorry, I was just leaving. I'll be out of your hair in a few minutes." His voice sounds hollow, completely void of emotion. He steps around me without waiting for a response and doesn't look back as he walks down the hall.

"Morgan, wait." I cringe inwardly at the sharpness of my tone. I'm already fucking this up. He ignores me as he continues to walk toward the door.

"Please," I add in a soft whisper. That word gets him to freeze with his hand hovering over the doorknob.

"What do you want, James?" He doesn't turn to face me, but I can see his back tense as if he's bracing for a blow.

"I need to talk to you about something. It's important."

"All right," he sighs and finally turns back around to face me. "What's up?"

He watches me with apprehensive eyes. It's the only spark of life on his otherwise stony face.

"Tanner is driving up for the weekend." I rip the Band-Aid off.

"Is that it?" A small smile pulls at his lips, and he visibly relaxes. "I'm pretty sure you could have put that in one of your notes."

"He wants to meet you. I figured it would be better to tell you that face-to-face."

"Sure, I'm happy to meet him if that's what you want." The last of his indifference slips away, and I feel like I'm talking to the Morgan I met a few weeks ago. My heart does that stupid little fluttery thing at the thought.

"Okay, good, because he is going to be here in, like, twenty minutes."

His eyes flick down to his watch, and his brow furrows. "Will he be here later? Maybe I can meet him then instead. I'm supposed to be at the library with Nathan in fifteen."

"Please, it won't take more than a minute once he's here." *And once he meets you, he should chill out about everything.* Despite my near begging, I can still see the no start to form on his lips. After the way I've treated him, I can't blame him one bit. I wouldn't go out of my way to do things for me if I were him.

"I know you have no reason to do this for me," I say before he can shut me down completely, "but it would mean a lot to me if you did. I promise I'll make it up to you."

I mean it. I'll do damn near anything for him to push his plans back another thirty minutes. I can't offer him anything personal because I don't actually know anything about him. He's practically a stranger who happens to live in my home.

"Fine." He pulls out his phone and sends a quick text before sitting on the couch.

Several minutes pass, but he doesn't say anything else while he waits with me. An almost tangible tension looms in the quiet air. He seems completely unperturbed by the silence, but I can feel its pressure growing, suffocating me, begging for me to break it. Each one of my heartbeats echoes in my ears. Every rhythmic thump marks another second passing by, another second of nothing.

"How are classes?" I ask in a desperate attempt to fill the silence with anything.

"Good." He doesn't look up from his phone.

"Law, right? That must be hard."

"It is." He doesn't give me any more than that, but I do feel a small bit of pride that I remembered something about him. It's obvious he isn't going to entertain my attempts at conversation, and we lapse back into silence.

Time drags as it passes.

Ten minutes crawl by.

Then fifteen.

And then twenty.

I find myself growing more anxious for Tanner's arrival. *He should be here by now.* My leg bounces, keeping pace with the rapidly escalating rhythm of my heart, and my nails carve little crescent moons into my palms. I fight to keep my breathing even, but I feel like I'm gasping for air with each inhale.

"James, hey. Look at me." I didn't even notice that he moved to crouch in front of me. My eyes snap down to his striking hazel ones—pools of green rimmed with gold. His whole face is etched with concern. One of his hands holds my knee in a firm grip, and he gives it a gentle squeeze, becoming my anchor in the raging whirlpool of panic. "What can I do?"

"Meds," I choke out between gasping breaths.

"Where?"

"Bathroom."

He is gone in an instant. Without the feeling of his touch anchoring me, I'm pulled back under the crushing waves. I'm not sure how long he's gone—it could have been seconds or hours—but he brings me a pill and a glass of water, which I swallow back without hesitation. He settles back into that spot between my knees and reanchors me with a steady hand on my thigh.

"That's it, there she is. I need you to take a deep breath for me. Can you do that?" Morgan's voice is soft and low, each word attempting to soothe my rattled nerves. I try to listen, but each breath catches in shallow gasps. He pulls my hand to his sternum. "Do you feel my breaths? Let them guide you, James. We will do it together. Just match my breaths."

It takes several attempts, but I'm able to synchronize my ragged breathing to his, using the steady rise and fall of his chest as my metronome.

"That's it, pretty girl."

I expect him to pull away, but he doesn't. He stays with me, letting me use his body to find my way back down. It takes another few minutes before I feel confident that the worst has passed. The warmth from his chest soaks into my hand, blanketing me with the same comfort of an embrace. As I let my hand fall away, the tight knot in my throat falls with it, settling in my stomach with a heavy weight. He takes that as his cue to get up off the floor, giving my knee one more squeeze before he sits back in his spot on the couch as if he didn't witness me completely fall apart.

"I'm sorry," I whisper.

His head snaps back in my direction, confusion clear as day on his face. "For what?"

"That you had to see that." My hands wave through the air as if that will make what I'm trying to say any clearer. "I know it's a lot, and you shouldn't have had to do any of that."

"Listen to me," Morgan commands. "You never have to apologize to me for having a panic attack. I'm glad I was here to help. If you ever need my help again, I'll be there, just ask. Okay?"

"Okay." I say the word, but it lacks conviction. There's no reality where I let him see me weak again. His lips purse. I'm pretty sure he knows I'm lying to him, but he doesn't push it. He pulls his phone out again and winces.

"Do you think Tanner will be here soon? I was supposed to meet Nathan twelve minutes ago, so I really should be going." He runs his hand through his hair as he stands to move toward the door.

"No, please stay," I plead, jumping up to stop him. I grab his forearm to hold him in place, trying to ignore how right it feels to be touching him again. "I'm sure he will be here any seco—" I'm cut off by the sound of a key turning in the lock.

"Hey, Ophie, sorry I'm late," my boyfriend calls out into the apartment, pushing the door open. His words trail off as his eyes narrow on where my fingers are wrapped around Morgan's arm. I jerk my hand away and take a step back, putting much-needed space between my roommate and me.

Tanner's eyes flash with cold rage, but it's gone almost as quickly as it came. He effortlessly schools his expression, pasting on one of his bright, thousand-watt smiles that I've watched him practice a million times in the mirror. His image is everything; it has to be when his dad is a small-town celebrity. His father is a state commissioner with aspirations of becoming governor.

For as long as I've known him, he has worn the mask of a perfect, devoted son. Even now, he looks the part, wearing clothes that would be more suited for a golf course than a date night in. I'm one of the few people who ever gets to see the real Tanner Nicholson, not just Commissioner Nicholson's son. The real Tanner is the man who dotes on his little sisters and whose perfect day would be spent fishing on the river. It's the man who watched hours of videos to learn how to line dance so he could take me out dancing when I begged to go. I've always loved the unmasked version of him the most, even if I see less and less of him now that the campaign is in full swing.

"Hi, babe." I walk over and wrap my arms around him. He reciprocates, but his focus doesn't leave Morgan. I guess we are doing the alpha-posturing bullshit today. *Great.*

My roommate doesn't take the bait. He simply throws his backpack over his shoulders and extends his hand.

"Hey, you must be Tanner. Great to meet you. James has told me a lot about you. I'm Morgan." It's a bit of a stretch, considering how little I've actually spoken with him over the past few weeks. I cringe inside, hoping he won't take it to mean we've gotten too friendly.

My boyfriend eyes him up for another second before grabbing Morgan's hand in an iron grip. "Tanner Nicholson." He says his name as if it means something. "I can't say Ophelia has had much to say about you."

To Morgan's credit, if Tanner's antics are getting to him, he doesn't show it.

"That's understandable. We don't see each other that often. I spend a lot of time at the library, and I actually need to head that way now. If you are still around when I get back, we can have a beer or two and get to know each other."

"Sure thing." His tone says the opposite. He claps my roommate on the back as he helps guide him out the door. Morgan doesn't spare me a second glance, fleeing the apartment like a bat out of hell, not that I blame him.

The door falls shut, and Tanner latches the deadbolt with an ominous *click*. With that sound, his smile falls and his fury returns with a vengeance.

"What the fuck was that?"

Grover picks his head up from where he had been sleeping to let out a low growl at Tanner's tone.

"What was what? Why are you angry?" I feign ignorance, but my voice sounds wrong.

"You know exactly what I'm talking about. I walk in here and see you with your hands all over that chump. You know exactly why I'm mad."

"That? That was nothing. He was about to leave, and I tried to stop him so you could meet him, that's it. If you had walked in six minutes earlier, you would have seen us sitting on opposite ends of the couch, in silence, waiting for you to get here." And if he had walked in here two minutes before that, he would have seen Morgan on the floor between my legs with my hand on his chest. *Jesus fuck, that would have been bad.* "You asked to meet him. I hadn't talked to him in weeks. I only did it for you."

"You're right. I'm sorry." His anger deflates, and he gives me a sheepish smile. "I overreacted. I just hate that he gets to be here with you all day, every day, and

I'm stuck hours away." He wraps me up in his arms, tucking me into the hollow of his neck. "Forgive me, love."

I sigh, breathing in his familiar fresh, citrus scent, but it doesn't fill me with the same comfort it normally does. I force myself to relax into his hold anyway. I'm probably still unsteady from the roller coaster of emotions I just rode. My equilibrium is off.

"Always."

"So what's the plan for tonight?" He kisses the top of my head and releases me.

"I was going to cook your favorite lasagna, and I thought we could watch that new World War I movie that just came out."

His face scrunches in distaste. "I just drove for nearly six hours. Sitting around is the last thing I want to do tonight."

"Oh." I fight to keep my expression neutral despite the sharp stab of disappointment. Tanner always wants to stay in when he visits. He says he can get more of me that way. "We can eat out and then go out downtown if you want."

"That sounds great, O. Wanna hit Cali-n-Titos, then go to Magnolia's?"

"Sure, sounds good. Let me take Grover out, and then we can go."

I guess I'll have lasagna later this week. It's not like it will go bad in the fridge if it sits unbaked for an extra day. It's also more fun to watch movies by myself. He always gets handsy, and the movie gets forgotten for sex. This will be so much more fun than what I had planned. At least, that's what I tell myself as I grab the leash and rush outside, fighting back tears.

***

Tanner peppers my neck with wet, sloppy kisses while I try to unlock the front door. His hot breath reeks of cheap liquor and the stale stench of cigarettes that he claims to only smoke when he's drinking. That one was new to me. I've never seen him smoke before, and I don't think I like it. Once again, my unsteady hands fail to get the key in the door. I'm sure it would be easier if I wasn't a little tipsy, but it would also be easier if he wasn't glued to me. His hands roam over my body, groping and squeezing as if he's afraid of what will happen if he lets go.

"God, I missed you, O," he slurs. He pulls me in closer to him right as I'm about to get the key in the lock. This is also new. He's never been a binge drinker before. He's always been more of a glass-of-bourbon-after-dinner type of guy, as it has a classier image.

"I missed you too, but give me a second to get us inside." I'm unable to hide the annoyance that's bubbling up, not that he would pick up on my cues at the moment. Thankfully, he relents, letting me get the key in the lock. My reprieve from his overzealous affection only lasts a second. As soon as the door is open, he has me pressed up against the wall, and his lips crash into mine.

I fight back the urge to recoil at the taste of ash and nicotine. His tongue and teeth bash against my own without any finesse. Normally, his kisses would send tingles racing down my spine, but right now, I feel absolutely nothing. I kiss him back, though, and he continues to try to devour me like he's a starving man and my lips are the only thing that can sate his hunger. The evidence that he isn't experiencing the same hesitancy presses up against me, making my stomach clench. This is exactly where I saw tonight going, but for some reason, everything about his touch feels wrong. He lifts my shirt to pull it over my head, and I rip my mouth from his. Without missing a beat, his lips descend onto my neck.

"Tanner...wait...roommate...bedroom," I manage to gasp out between heaving breaths. As soon as I utter the words, I'm lifted into the air. His hands squeeze my ass as he carries me to my room, but his lips never leave my skin. That's all it takes to break past whatever mental block was holding back my arousal. My legs instinctively wrap around his waist, my hands grip his hair, and I seek out his lips with the same passion he has been giving me. He slams me back against the bedroom door, and my feet sink to the floor as his newly freed hands roam my body, trailing up my torso and to my chest. His fingers expertly tweak my nipple in the exact way he knows drives me crazy. I bite my lip to hold back the moan that's fighting to escape.

"Don't hold back, baby," Tanner growls in my ear, "I want that fuckhead roommate of yours to know exactly who you belong to."

A wave of unease washes through me at his words, but I push the feeling down and focus on the feeling of his hands on my skin.

He moves to pull off my shirt again but freezes. A sheen of sweat breaks out on his now-pale forehead. He takes a slow step back, then turns and makes a mad dash for the bathroom. Before I can fully process what happened, the sound of retching echoes off the porcelain toilet.

"Babe, are you okay?" I straighten out my clothes and go to check on him.

"No," he moans before letting out another stream of vomit. He looks so pitiful on the floor, curled up around the base of the toilet. I move to sit next to him and brush back his hair while his body forces him to purge the poison. It doesn't pass quickly; we stay like that until my limbs go numb and he starts to drift to sleep.

Pins and needles shoot through my legs as I uncurl from my awkward position. It takes a lot of prodding and coaxing, but I'm able to get Tanner off the floor and into the bed. His head hits the pillow, and I place a soft kiss on his temple before standing up to get myself ready for bed.

"I really love you, O," he mumbles as I leave. He is unconscious again before I can even respond.

Red splotches paint my skin as I scrub myself to the point of pain under the shower's scalding spray. As if that could somehow pluck out this awful new feeling that has taken root within me. It started small, but as the day progressed, it grew until it bloomed into this ugly tangle of disappointment and resentment toward the man I love. Every logical thought says I should go to join him in bed, but I can't bring myself to crawl under the covers. Seeing him lying there brings those feelings swelling to the surface with a vengeance. My fingers itch to purge my emotions onto a canvas, to expel them the only way I know how, but Tanner's oppressive presence looms in the room, suffocating me. Through the muddled haze of emotions raging through my head, one thought comes through crystal fucking clear.

I need to get out of this room.

I don't look back as I bolt for the hall.

Chapter 10
Morgan

Dear Roomie,

If you are going to use my blankets, make sure you fold them and hang them back up neatly when you are done. Don't just throw them over the back of the couch.

—J

The sound of a door opening down the hall interrupts the low murmuring coming from the TV. I jump at the unexpected noise and turn my head right as James bolts out of the darkness. Skimpy shorts barely cover her ass, and her hard nipples peek through a thin camisole, but that all fades away when I spot her black-rimmed, tear-stained eyes through the damp hair framing her face.

She looks wrecked.

I don't think she's noticed me yet; her frantic eyes are locked on the front door while her chest heaves. I'm on my feet before I have a plan. All I know is I have to fix it.

"Hey, are you all right?" Slowing my steps, I approach with an outstretched arm. I want to touch her and offer her comfort in my arms, but if I do that, she'll flee. Heck, she's already eyeing my hand like it might bite her if she lowers her guard. I run it through my hair and let it drop to my side, halting in place as I do.

"What are you doing out here?" She wipes the moisture from her eyes, but her voice is still steady, biting even.

"Watching TV," I tell her. "I like to come sit out here when I can't sleep."

"Oh." Her eyes lock on the screen, which strobes in the darkness behind me. She moves toward it with ghostlike grace. It's a stark contrast to how she fled down the hall like a bat out of hell. She observes the screen for a moment with a furrowed brow and then turns back to me with narrowed eyes. It's the first bit of life I've seen on her face since she ran out here.

"What the fuck is this *Lord of the Rings* shit?" The disdain in her words is emphasized by the clang of clashing swords.

This is the she-devil I've come to expect. After this morning, her venom doesn't hold the same sting. She's deflecting, trying to make me mad so I forget something was bothering her in the first place. It's exactly what she did that day in the bathroom and at Cutter's, but I won't let her do it again.

"It's called *Merlin*," I tell her and hit pause. I finished my watch-through of *The Adventures of Sir Lancelot* last week and moved on to my second favorite show. "It's a version of the King Arthur legends. This episode is almost over. We can put something else on after if you are planning on staying out here."

"Are you inviting me to hang out and watch nerd shows with you?"

"Or other shows. I mean, it's your apartment and your TV. Inviting you doesn't seem necessary. I'll be out here either way, but I'd like it if you'd stay."

"Why on earth would you like that?" she asks, her voice ringing with genuine curiosity.

Why *do* I want that?

Images of her breakdown this afternoon flash through my head, and that overwhelming need to take care of her floods through me again. That was a whole new James, a vulnerable one with no walls, and seeing that roused something in me. I want to see more of that. More pressing, I want to see what an unguarded James is like when she's happy. I bet she's breathtaking.

"I'd like the chance to get to know you. Maybe patch things up enough between us that we can live together peacefully. I don't think we will ever become friends or anything, but I'd like to get to a place where I can pass you in the hallway without worrying that you are going to accuse me of something crazy or criticize my every action."

"Is that why you've been avoiding me?"

"I haven't been avoiding you. You told me to stay out of your way. I took it literally."

"That's the very definition of avoiding me," she says with an exasperated huff.

"Would you rather have had it the other way? I didn't get the impression you liked me very much." I give her a pointed look, watching her fidget as she mulls over the question.

"Yes. No. Maybe. Fuck it, I don't know. I don't *not* like you. It's just that Tanner isn't happy with this whole situation, and it's easier if I keep away." She flops down on the far side of the couch and throws one arm over her face while looking up at the ceiling.

"Is that why you came out here so upset? Did you fight? I can talk to him if you want me to." I don't know what I would say to him. But the last thing I want is for James to be hurting. If my being here is putting strain on their relationship, I'll need to sit down with Tanner and make sure he knows I'm not a threat to them.

"No. At least not this time."

"But he upset you?" My hands clench by my side. I might need to set him straight regardless.

James pauses for a second, before letting out a deep sigh.

"Yeah, I guess he upset me. I don't want to talk about it anymore. Just put your nerd show back on. Please."

As much as I want to push her further, I bite my tongue. She will tell me if she wants me to know. If I push her too hard, she will be gone faster than I can blink. I resume the show and settle back on the couch, keeping my attention on James out of the corner of my eye.

At first, she watches the screen with predetermined contempt, but it doesn't take long for her to get sucked into the magic of it all. Her face relaxes as she leans forward, watching the drama unfold with wide eyes. A small smile curls the corner of her lips, and the sight flips my stomach.

I can't bring myself to turn my attention back to the episode. My eyes do a quick scan over her, looking for any signs that her fight with Tanner involved more than harsh words. When I don't find any, I relax back into my seat. I don't think James would put up with that type of abuse, but I had to be sure.

As the episode plays on, James becomes more at ease. The tension she was carrying melts off her shoulders. Right as the credits roll and the next episode queues on the screen, my stomach decides to interrupt with a loud growl. That sound breaks the spell she was under, and James turns her focus to me.

"Are you hungry?" she asks. Her voice is soft and riddled with uncertainty. We have reached uncharted territory.

"Kind of," I tell her as my fingers rake through my hair. "Dining halls were closed when I left Ramsey. I'll be fine until breakfast, though."

"Why didn't you get something once you got home?"

"I don't keep any food here." My eyes drop to the floor with the mumbled confession. I can't bear to see the judgment in her eyes. My stipend only goes so far, and it seems wasteful to spend it on extra food when the dining plan has already been covered by my loans.

"Do you like lasagna?"

I lift my gaze back to her in confusion. *Lasagna?* I'm not sure how we got from my financial situation to what food I like.

"I can put some in the oven if you want it," she continues as if that answers all my questions.

"Sure...I mean, yes, I like lasagna. Thank you...I mean, if it isn't too much trouble, that is." I stumble a bit over my words and wince at how caught off guard I sound.

She beams at me, and it lights up her whole face. I think it's the first time I've seen her smile since I saw her dancing at Cutter's, and it's definitely the first time she's ever smiled at *me* like this. If I were Tanner, I would be doing everything in my power to keep that smile on her face permanently. Even with her raccoon eyes and unkempt hair, my she-devil looks like an angel.

"It's not a problem at all," she says, her southern drawl thickening. She gets up and makes her way over to the fridge, and I don't resist the urge to follow her. I'm like a junkie: I've gotten my first hit of her radiant smile, and I'm already jonesing for another.

She opens the door and pulls out a full tray of homemade lasagna, ready to be baked. I lean against the counter and watch her move around the kitchen with practiced ease. For the first time since I moved in, I feel like I'm welcome in this apartment. It doesn't take her long to wrap the pan in foil and put it in the oven, not even bothering to wait for it to preheat.

"Not to look a gift horse in the mouth or anything, but why did you have a tray in there ready to go?" My tone is teasing, but her smile falters and then fades completely. That was clearly the wrong thing to say. James folds her arms in front of her and curls in on herself, turning back into the sad ghost of herself that came out of her bedroom less than an hour ago.

"Hey, please tell me what's going on." I move closer, and this time, I don't resist the urge to reach out and place a hand on her bare shoulder. She stills for a second and then leans into my touch. Warmth radiates from where my skin meets hers.

"I made the lasagna for Tanner," she admits, melancholy coating each word.

"If you made it for him, then why did you give it to me? You didn't need to do that. I wou—"

"No, Morgan," she interrupts, "I made it for him to have for dinner tonight, but he didn't want it." She sucks in a deep breath, and her eyes grow glassy with unshed tears. "I planned a night in for us, something simple. I made his favorite food, and I figured we could watch a movie and spend some quality time together. It's been months since we've had the time to just do nothing together. He started a new job that's been eating all his time, and I did summer classes, so I couldn't go to him much."

The floodgate opens for both her words and her tears. She wipes away the trailing liquid with the base of her palm, smearing the remnants of her makeup even further.

"I know I'm being stupid," she says with a bitter laugh. "He didn't do anything wrong by saying he would rather do something else. We still had fun, or we did until he got so drunk that he ended up spending the night with his head in the toilet. I just wish we could have had more time together. He leaves in the morning, and I feel like I barely saw him."

"You aren't being stupid." But I am as I pull her into my arms. She melts into my embrace, and I hold her closer, whispering reassuring words in her ear and running my hand in soothing patterns along her back as my shirt grows damp with her tears. After a few minutes, her crying quiets and she pulls back. I let her go despite my every instinct to keep her close, and I immediately miss her warmth and sweet, woody scent. She wipes the remaining tears from her face and adjusts her posture, standing straight to be the woman who tore me down the day I moved in.

Her lips open and close again like she's trying to find the right words to say. She will probably apologize for being upset or something equally as unnecessary.

"What movie," I ask her before she can utter a word.

"What?"

"What movie did you want to watch?"

"It's stupid." Her cheeks turn pink as she drops her gaze to the ground.

"Stop saying that," I growl at her, and her eyes widen as they snap back to mine. "Your interests aren't stupid. Your feelings aren't stupid. Now tell me what movie you want to watch."

"It was the one that came out a few months ago about World War I. I really like war movies."

"Go put it on."

"But what about your show? It was actually kind of cool for being nerd shit."

"If you liked it, we can plan to watch it together another time. Right now, you are going to walk into the living room and put on that movie." My commanding tone leaves no room for argument.

"Yes sir," she says and freezes. A deep blush spreads across her cheeks as her eyes grow comically wide, and she scurries off to the living room.

Those two words set my heart into overdrive as it thumps wildly in my chest, and my whole body tightens with awareness. I stall for several seconds, willing my body to calm down, and then join her on the couch, choosing the seat furthest away from her. I've spent too much time in her space today, and it's messing with my head. She gets the movie playing, and like before, she's mesmerized by the on-screen action within minutes. I force myself to watch the movie and not her reactions to it.

Comfortable silence hangs between us. It's so different from the oppressive pressure I felt when we were in the same position before Tanner arrived. The oven's timer beeps, and James pauses the TV while she prepares our bowls. I offer her a soft "thank you" as she places the dish on the coffee table in front of me, which earns me another beautiful smile. I dig in, savoring each morsel, but she barely gets three bites in before she drifts to sleep and lets out a soft snore.

I chuckle and pause the movie so she doesn't miss anything. The couch shifts as I get up, and I wince, not wanting to disturb her, before grabbing the bowl from her hand. There isn't a huge mess, but I clean up in the kitchen and put the leftovers away. Once that's done, I go back to check on James; she's dead to the world, probably exhausted from the whirlwind of emotions she went through today.

Not that I can blame her.

Snagging a blanket off the back of the couch, I drape it over her. A stray piece of hair lays across her face, and I tuck it back behind her ear, letting my fingers trail along her face for this one quick moment.

With a weary sigh, I turn and make my way to my bedroom. This morning, I thought I knew what to expect from my roommate, but now I'm not so sure she's as bad as she made herself out to be.

Chapter 11
James

A small square piece of paper tacked on the mirror causes butterflies to take flight in my stomach.

Morgan left me a note. He's never left me one before.

I was halfway through brushing my teeth when I noticed it, sitting exactly in the spot where I leave him notes of my own every morning—at least I did until last weekend. I haven't had anything to nitpick since then. Maybe he has been more courteous—not that he wasn't before. It was an effort to find a new issue every day—or maybe I just don't want to be a bitch to him anymore.

Things have been good since that night. He's home more, and we sometimes talk if we pass each other in the hall. We aren't friends yet, but things have been friendly enough. It makes his note even more shocking; it's a complete change to the status quo. I don't waste time ripping it down, and the butterflies multiply at the words.

Morgan wants to hang out with me.

He still wants to give me a chance, even after the shitty way I've treated him. I have no idea why—I would have told me to get fucked—but it stirs something inside me all the same.

Do I even want to go down this path?

My gut screams yes, but I know Tanner won't like it. I don't think I'll get this opportunity again if I don't take it, though.

That whole day was a whirlwind of highs and lows, but Morgan was my port of safe harbor through it all. He was my lighthouse and my anchor. It was the best night I've had in a long time, even if I spent half of it crying on his shirt. He made me feel completely safe and actually *seen*.

I was wrong when I pegged him as a judgmental asshole. Hell, I don't think he has a judgmental bone in his body. For the first time in weeks, I felt like I could truly relax and breathe. The guilt didn't hit until the next morning.

We didn't do anything even remotely inappropriate, but Tanner's accusations play on repeat in my head. If he knew I spent the night hanging out with my roommate, he wouldn't hesitate to throw it in my face that he's right—that Morgan is trying to sleep with me—even if it isn't true.

Fuck it.

If I spend my whole life making every decision based on how Tanner will react, I will go crazy, especially if he doesn't give my desires a second thought.

***

My fingers curl and uncurl into tight fists as I wander around the city streets. Each small bite of pain from my nails digging into my palms helps distract me from the ever-growing ball of anxiety in my chest.

I never gave Morgan an answer about tonight.

I told myself that if I happened to see him after class, I would let him know that I was in. I may have also made a quick stop to grab Grover when I knew he was in class, and I've been roaming around to kill time since.

God, I'm such a fucking coward.

For the hundredth time in the past thirty minutes, I pull out my phone to check the time. It's ten till eight, so there's no time left to stall. I walk home on autopilot because if I think about it too hard, I'm going to chicken out again. The door creaks on its hinges as I push it open and find Morgan sitting on the couch, overdressed as always. Bare feet poke out from under his nice pants, and I struggle to stifle a giggle at the sight. His head snaps toward me, and a brilliant smile lights up his face. He runs a hand through his curls and then drops them to his lap, wringing his hands together with nerves, but that goddamn smile never leaves his face.

"Hi." The tentative word breaks the silence.

That's it? That's all he has to say? I open my mouth to tell him exactly what I think of that, but a whispered "Hi" is all that comes from me too.

The awkwardness is palpable, filling the space between us and locking us in place. Neither one of us is quite sure what to do next. This isn't nearly as easy as it was before; now there are expectations.

Fuck, this was a bad idea.

A shrill beeping from the oven breaks the silence and snaps Morgan into action.

"I made us a pizza," he shouts over his shoulder as he jumps from the couch and moves into the kitchen. "I wasn't sure if you were going to join me, but I figured I might as well have food just in case. You fed me last time, so it's only fair. I got us cheese because I wasn't sure what you liked, and cheese is safe. Do you like pizza? If you don't, I can order something else."

His rambling catches me off guard. It's endearing. I don't know his mannerisms or quirks yet, but if they are this cute, I want to learn them.

"Yes, I like pizza."

His smile grows larger at my answer, and I swear my heart does a backflip. Morgan is looking at me like my simple answer made his whole day, and I don't know how to process it other than to smile back.

Tanner has never cooked for me—if you count sticking a frozen pizza in the oven as cooking—and he certainly has never looked at me like that. Especially over something as stupid as confirming I liked pizza. Honestly, who doesn't?

With a few careful cuts, he slices the cheesy pie and plates a few pieces for each of us. That carefree smile never once wavers. He doesn't feel the need to fill the silence, and, surprisingly, I don't want him to. It's comfortable, which is odd; long gaps of silence normally make my skin crawl.

The moment gives me time to get my head on straight and push the feelings Morgan stirred back into the recesses of my mind. I take a centering breath and start to count backward in my head. The coping mechanism works, and my heart slows to its normal rhythm, but this isn't a panic attack. My heart may be racing, but it's in anticipation, not fear.

He carries the plates back to the living room and sets them on the coffee table. Then he takes the same seat he did the other night, as far to the side as he can possibly sit, leaving plenty of room between us. I'm not sure what I would do if he sat any closer; I don't think I could handle it.

"Are you joining?" He grabs the remote and turns the TV on without waiting for my response.

I don't answer but let Grover off his leash and hang it on the hook by the door. Grover immediately trots over to the couch, jumps onto the empty spot next to Morgan, and excitedly licks all over his face.

The fucking traitor. Since when have they been friends? Grover doesn't like anybody but me and Evelyn. He's not aggressive or anything, he just doesn't like most people in his space.

"Hey, boy, missed you today." Morgan scratches behind my dog's ears and accepts the overzealous affection without any hint of annoyance.

My heart melts a little at the sight, but I don't say anything. With Morgan's attention fully occupied, I make my way over to the couch and squeeze myself as far as I can into the opposite corner. Grover starts to calm down, freeing Mogan's hands, but stays glued to his side. My roommate glances at me from the corner of his eye and presses play without a word.

Neither one of us speaks once the movie starts, and we lapse back into the comfortable silence. I make a point of keeping my eyes locked on the screen as the movie plays out, but I'm keenly aware of Morgan's presence. The air between us is charged, connecting us with currents of energy, and my skin tingles with awareness every time he moves to adjust his position, sending waves of goose bumps along my skin.

The credits start to roll, and for the first time since he hit play, I look over at him. He has his bare feet propped up on the table, and Grover has crawled completely into his lap. He pets my dog with a dopey smile on his face, looking happier than I've ever seen him.

Fuck, *I'm* happier than I've been in a long time, and I'm not ready for it to end yet.

"So you said we could watch more of your nerd show another time. I think this counts as another time." I bite my lip as I wait for his answer.

His eyes widen and shine with wonder. "You really want to watch *Merlin* with me?"

"I don't have any other plans." I shrug, feigning indifference. I can't let him see how badly I want this.

"All right, sure." He flashes a blinding smile and grabs for the remote. "I'm going to start us over from the beginning. That way you can get the whole story." The screen comes alive with new movement.

We aren't even halfway through the episode when my phone rings. That sweet sense of serenity is ripped away from me as Tanner's tone plays. I hadn't realized how content I was until every drop of peace is wrung from my body. My gut hardens as a wave of guilt and dread washes over me. For the second time in a few short weeks, I want to hit decline; I want to stay out here with Morgan until I can't keep my eyes open a second longer.

I hold up my phone and try to beg Morgan with my eyes to tell me what to do. Seeing my expression, he winces as his face falls, and a resigned sadness shines in his eyes. Disappointment washes over me as he nods his head toward the bedroom.

I want him to tell me to stay here.

I want him to be an excuse for me not to have to deal with Tanner tonight.

I want him to fight for me, even though he has no right to.

My heart drops into my stomach as I go to answer the call. I cast one more forlorn look in his direction before I enter my room and hit Accept.

"Ophie, baby, I miss you," Tanner slurs too loudly through the phone before I can even say hello.

"Are you drunk?" I try to keep my words from sounding like an accusation but fail. This makes two weekends in a row he's been trashed before 10 p.m., and it isn't like him. He turns the call to video but doesn't hold the phone in a way that lets me see his face. All I can see on the screen is a blur of sideways people and what looks to be a pool as he clumsily moves the phone in his hands.

From what I can piece together from the sparse glimpses, he is at a house party, not a bar. No one there will cut him off when he's had too much to drink.

"A little bit," he admits with a laugh.

"Where are you?"

"Not sure. Went out with some of the guys from the office to blow off steam. Started at a bar, but then one of them knew this guy throwing a party, and here I am."

I'm barely able to piece together the slurred rambling.

"Um...yeah, okay. All right. Are you safe? How are you getting home?" My anxiety starts to climb, and it's apparent in my tone.

"Baby, Ophie, I called because I really, really, really miss you." I can practically hear his pout through the phone. "We didn't get to finish last week, and I miss your sweet pussy. Will you show it to me? Please?"

I freeze at his vulgar request. What the absolute fuck is he thinking. This is a conversation we've had before, and I thought I made my boundary clear: video sex isn't something I'm comfortable with, and I never will be.

Point blank, period.

"What the fuck, Tanner? You know I—"

"Please, baby? I need you right now."

"No. Why the fuck would you even ask me that?" My skin crawls at the thought. I don't even want to hear his voice right now.

"God, why do you have to be such a prude, James? I bet you already fucked that roommate of yours. You can't show me your pussy when it's filled with his cum, right? Fuck you, I'll have to take care of myself, then."

"No. What the fuck? Why don't you just—"

The phone goes dark.

Fuck. Why does he keep doing this? I try calling him back, but he doesn't pick up. I call again and again but give up when I get disconnected on the first ring.

That fucking asshole.

I toss my phone onto my bed and scream into a pillow. Why is he making everything so much harder than it has to be? If he would listen for half a second, he would see how crazy he's been acting, and maybe then he'd realize he has nothing to worry about with my roommate.

Even if I didn't have a boyfriend, the idea of Morgan and I together is laughable. I barely know the man, and as far as I can tell, he's a nerd—a nerd with abs that look like they were carved from stone, but a nerd nonetheless—and I don't date his type. Fuck, I've never been friends with one either, although I was having fun watching his swords and sorcery shit before Tanner ruined it.

As much as I want to, I can't go back out there now. He will know something is wrong, and he'll ask a bunch of questions that I don't feel like answering, but I can't just sit here and wallow either. What I need is a night out with the girls. I grab my discarded phone and call Chelsea.

"Hey, Jamie, what's up?" There's already a slight slur to her words. It's like she's read my mind.

"What are y'all up to tonight? I could use a night out."

"We are pregaming at my place, and then we are going bar hopping. You wanna come with? I thought you were too busy with an essay or something." *Or something is right.*

I didn't tell Evelyn or Chelsea about the weird budding friendship I have going with Morgan; it's still too new.

"Yeah, I finished earlier than I anticipated," I tell her, and Chelsea lets out an excited squeal. She says something to Evelyn, but the words are too muffled for me to make out.

"Perfect. I'll text you the details, and we can meet up in a bit. I'd say give us another hour or so."

"Sounds good, girl. See you in a bit."

If Tanner can spend his nights getting trashed with the guys, I can spend mine with the girls. I take my time getting ready, curling my hair into loose golden waves that cascade down my back and painting my face with dark, moody hues.

The black corset dress and matching wedges complete the vampy look. It's petty, but I want to look hot; I want him to know what he's missing while he parties with his friends.

I'm ready to go when my phone lights up with a message from Chelsea, telling me where to meet her. An errant thought causes my hand to freeze on my bedroom door.

What if Morgan is still out there, waiting?

I don't know what would be worse: him still waiting for me after all this time or finding the living room empty. Both make my stomach turn but in different ways. I shake it off and step into the hall.

The living room is dark, and he is long gone. The empty space takes the wind out of my sails. Part of me was hoping he was waiting for me, that he would stop me from going out and beg me to pick up where we left off. It was a stupid thought. It's been almost two hours since I left him out here. There is no universe where he waits that long for me to come back, but I do wonder if he waited at all, and if so, for how long.

Chapter 12
James

Drinking with the girls was exactly what I needed to forget Tanner's assholery. We move from bar to bar, drinking and dancing, and with each one, my worries about my boyfriend become less and less pressing. I turned my phone off as soon as I met up with Chelsea; I can play the silent treatment too. Fuck him for thinking I owe him anything, and fuck him for being mad I enforced a boundary.

The problem with my drink-to-forget plan is that something has to fill that void in my mind, and that something happens to be my roommate. I've managed to keep most of my thoughts of him locked away behind a carefully constructed wall, but the alcohol has obliterated it like a wrecking ball, and they've all escaped to wreak havoc. They flit between innocent and obscene—the way his dimple pops when he smiles, and every hard edge of his naked body.

My cheeks warm as I shake the image from my head. I can't be thinking like this. Maybe another drink will drive the thoughts of Morgan away too.

"Guys, guys, look. It's Nathan," Chelsea squeals and points across the street.

I look, but it's the man behind him who catches my attention. As if he was manifested by my fucked-up desires. Seeing Morgan kicks up a flurry of excitement in my core. He never comes out with Nathan.

Chelsea has dragged me out a few times so she could meet up with her latest fling, but Morgan is never there. The goth pixie and scary bartender have been around, but no roommate. His absence has been both relieving and disappointing, but I pushed both of those feelings away before I could dwell on them.

Morgan's eyes land on me and trail up my body before landing on my face. My skin heats under his scorching gaze. I know what I'm wearing; I look good, and from the smile on his face, I'd say he agrees. He flashes his hand in a nervous wave, and I mirror the motion.

"Let's go say hi." A car horn blares as Chelsea grabs my wrist and pulls me into the busy street. She flips off the car but doesn't adjust her course. The girl is on a mission. Evelyn follows a few steps behind us, mumbling an unheard apology to the driver.

Chelsea flings herself into Nathan's arms, and he catches her with ease. "Saying hi" must be code for making out in the street based on the way those two are going at it.

Good for her, I guess.

Morgan stares down at me with that stupid smile on his face, and I freeze. A ball of nervous tension coils in my gut. What do I even say? For all I know, he's pissed at me for abandoning him earlier.

"Hi." He echoes his greeting from earlier, and the tension evaporates.

"Hi yourself," I shoot back with a grin.

"So this is what was so important that you skipped out on me? I'm hurt." He covers his heart with an overdramatic flourish of his hand.

"I think you are the one who ditched me. When I came back out of my room, you were gone."

"Oh, I am so sorry, Queen James. Next time, I swear I will wait on the couch for eternity until you are ready to join me again."

"Next time?" I ask him hopefully, dropping the playful banter.

"Yeah, next time. I mean, if you'd like, that is." He runs his hand through his hair, and the smile slips.

"I would. Like to, I mean. Fuck. Yes, more nerd shows, please," I ramble.

"Good." That smile of his finds its place once more.

"We are headed to Cutter's. You ladies want to join?" Nathan asks, popping the bubble surrounding me and Morgan. For a second, I forgot the others were even here.

My immediate reaction is to decline. The way my body responds to my roommate is dangerous, and I don't trust myself this many drinks deep. But Chelsea shoots me a pleading glance, and I hesitate. Fuck Nathan for actually seeming like a good guy and making her happy. I won't let my own issues jeopardize that.

I give her a subtle nod, and she pulls me into a hug with a high-pitched squeal. We make our way down the street, and I can feel my roommate's stare on me the entire journey. His attention makes my spine tingle and heat pool in my core. I sway my hips more than what's natural with each step—might as well give him a show.

To no one's surprise, the goth pixie is waiting when we walk through the doors.

"About time you got here," she shouts over the music.

"We ran into a bit of trouble on the way here," Nathan says and kisses Chelsea's neck, drawing a peal of laughter from her glossed lips.

"Always bringing in the strays." Karis shakes her head and turns her attention to Morgan. "Want to play pool?" she asks with a shark-toothed smile.

"Not particularly…"

She's walking way before the words are out of his mouth. He shrugs his shoulders with a sigh and follows her.

"Oh, this is gonna be good." Nathan chuckles. He leads Chelsea toward the tables in the back, and I follow with Evelyn on my heels.

"Why, is Morgan good at pool or something?"

Nathan throws his head back in a fit of full-bellied laughter. "Good joke." He pretends to wipe a tear from his eye. "You'll see."

I do see. He is fucking terrible.

He goes to make the break shot, and the cue ball spins off to the side without touching the racked balls. Karis cackles, her eyes shining with glee while Morgan's roll at her antics, but there is a hint of a smile on his lips.

"Do you mind if I have a shot?" I reach out for a stick.

"Be my guest, Goldilocks." She thrusts hers into my hand and crosses her arms over her chest as she squints. "Let's see what you can do."

I add chalk to the tip and line up my shot. The motion is second nature. When my dad wasn't deployed, I would spend my summers on the base with him. He made a point of teaching me all the skills he deemed necessary for life, and pool made that cut. A sharp clattering rings out through the bar as the cue connects with the balls in the middle of the table, causing them to scatter, and one sinks into a pocket on the backside. I sink a second and then a third with ease.

Karis lets out a long whistle. "I'm impressed."

I shrug off her compliment, and my attention darts over to Morgan. He's watching me with unguarded awe, and his gaze stirs the butterflies in my stomach.

"Come here," I tell him. He fidgets with his hair for a second before flashing one of his stupid smiles and following my command. "Line up your shot." Like a good little soldier, he does what I ask, and I take a moment to assess his technique. "Here, like this." I step up behind him and wrap my arms around him to adjust his angle.

The butterflies riot.

Thank God my face is hidden from him like this; my whole body flushes. He feels so much bigger between my arms—I can barely reach around his frame. It's overwhelming. *He's* overwhelming. I'm cocooned in his spiced-wood scent and the heat radiating from his body, and it's intoxicating. For a moment, I forget what I'm doing. All that exists is Morgan Hall.

Fuck. Pool.

"Now shoot," I instruct. The cue ball strikes its intended target, sending it careening across the green carpet. It doesn't land in a pocket, but it's an improvement.

"Like that," I praise before jerking away from him. "I'm gonna go get a drink." I'm halfway across the bar before he can respond. The distance doesn't help; the ghost of his body still haunts mine.

"Can I get some whiskey?" I ask the scary bartender.

He's one of the guys' friends, but I've never actually spoken to him outside of ordering a drink. It's for the best. The man is terrifying. He's huge, and the permanent scowl he wears only makes him more uninviting. Mr. Scary Bartender only grunts in response but grabs a bottle from the shelf.

"And something for Morgan, if you know what he likes," I add. He pours my drink and sticks a bottle of beer next to it.

"Thank you." I pull out my wallet, but he stops me with a shake of his head.

"I don't charge friends," he says in a gruff monotone.

"I didn't know we were."

"You live with Morgan. Your friend is fucking mine." He shrugs. "It's close enough."

"Well, I appreciate it."

He nods and turns his attention to another patron.

Maybe this drink will be enough to put thoughts of Morgan and the inappropriate way my body reacts to his out of my mind. It's wishful thinking, but knowing that doesn't stop me from finishing the glass in one long swallow. I'm going to need the liquid courage if I'm going to face him again.

I turn around and recoil; Karis is right behind me, far too close for comfort. The bottle of cheap beer nearly slips from my fingertips as I startle. *When did she even get there?*

She doesn't seem fazed, opting to stare at me with her head cocked and that wide, toothy grin that makes my spine tingle. "You know, Morgan said you were a bitch, but I don't see it."

I'm sorry, what did she just say?

It takes another second for the words to fully register. She just called me a bitch—well, no, she said I wasn't a bitch. *Morgan* called me a bitch. He talked to his friends about me, and it wasn't good. My heart plummets. I'm not sure if I'm more upset that he called me a bitch or that he thought it.

I know I was a bit difficult, but I don't think I was that bad, was I? Our past interactions run through my head like a slideshow, and I cringe. Maybe I do owe him an apology.

I mumble meaningless sounds in acknowledgment and move past the impish woman. The sight of Evelyn cozied up against my roommate's side rips the air out of my lungs. My fingers clench the bottle in my hand as she moves her hand along his bicep and leans to whisper in his ear. I have no right to be jealous, but that doesn't change the fact that I am.

He isn't mine, and he never can be.

I have Tanner, I love Tanner, and I need to stop thinking about my *roommate* this way.

I block out the aching in my chest and join Chelsea and Nathan. Evelyn deserves this; Morgan is a really great guy, and they will probably be very happy together. This is a good thing. Plus, he will be even more off-limits if he's dating someone else, and maybe then this stupid crush will die. His gaze finds mine, and I give him an encouraging thumbs-up and take a sip of the beer that was supposed to be his.

For the rest of the evening, I hang back with Nathan and Chelsea. Karis comes back over and spends most of the night bickering with her friend. It's a near-constant back-and-forth of threats, insults, and swear words. Despite the words flying from their lips, this seems to be fun for the two of them. Mr. Scary Bartender—Gage, as Karis tells me—joins in on their antics in the brief moments he can escape the stream of customers. It's the first time I've seen something that even resembles a smile on his face. The trio mostly ignores me, but every time Gage comes over, he brings me a drink too.

Evelyn and Morgan rejoin the group after playing through several of the worst games of pool I've ever witnessed. Morgan slips out of Evelyn's hold on his arm but hovers near her.

"Do you guys want to come to the game with us next weekend?" Chelsea asks.

"I'm in," Nathan says, then plants a kiss on the top of her head. "Sounds like fun."

I cast a glance toward Morgan as excitement bubbles in my chest. Georgia football is one of my favorite things, and it's the perfect opportunity to push him and Evelyn closer together. The excitement has absolutely nothing to do with how I'll get to spend more time with him too. His eyes meet mine, and he studies them for a moment before responding.

"I've never been to a football game. As long as you don't mind explaining things to me along the way, I would love to go."

"Absolutely. We are going to have so much fun." Evelyn wraps her arms around him in a giddy hug. He reacts with a stiff one-armed side hug, but his attention is still on me. I give him a small nod and a smile, and he flashes one right back.

We stay at Cutter's until last call and are eventually forced out into the cool night air.

"Let me walk you home," Morgan says. "It will be awkward if you don't. People will think I'm stalking you or something."

His joke is terrible, but I don't put up any fight. We walk together in silence, but Karis's words from earlier buzz around in my head.

"Do you really think I'm a bitch?" I ask as we get about halfway back to the apartment, and he freezes with his mouth agape.

"What? No. Why would you think that?" His hand takes that all-too-familiar path through his hair.

"Karis said you did."

"She said *what*?" His voice takes on a hard edge I've never heard before. "You aren't a bitch, James. I never thought you were." He says it with such fervor, I'm incapable of doing anything but believe him.

"But I did act like one," I tell him, "I'm sorry."

"No, I'm sorry. I clearly said something that put that impression in her head, and that was a mistake. I'll talk to her about it."

"It's fine...as long as you don't think I'm a bitch now."

"I think you are pretty great." Pink stains his cheeks at the confession.

"Good." I resume walking, and he falls in step beside me. We don't say anything else as we finish walking home.

As soon as I'm alone in my room, I remember exactly what drove me to go out in the first place. My gut hardens with dread as I pull my phone out and turn it back on. The screen brightens with life, and a notification pops up with a chirp.

It does it again.

And again.

The notifications seem to arrive in a never-ending wave. My dread only deepens with each new message, but it's nothing compared to the weight that settles once the phone falls silent.

Seventeen missed calls and forty-eight unread texts. All of them are from Tanner.

Fuck.

I wasn't expecting it to be this bad.

Missed call

> O, I'm sorry, babe

> Please pick up the phone

(3) Missed calls

I'm really, really sorry

Answer the phone, O

I know I messed up, just talk to me, please

Please, O, you are killing me

(2) Missed calls

James, answer your phone

(2) Missed calls

Babe, I'll change

I won't push you again

I love you, please answer your phone

The texts continue like that, getting more and more desperate as the hours passed without a response. I don't listen to the voicemails; I already know they'll all be Tanner drunk off his ass, alternating between begging for forgiveness and demanding I answer him in the same breath.

I'm about to turn the phone back off when another call comes through. *Fucking read receipts.* He was probably waiting for me to open his messages.

I take a deep breath and answer the phone. Might as well get this over with.

"Baby, I'm so fucking sorry. I'll never ask you to do that again. I was drunk and an asshole, and I'm sorry. Please forgive me, O." His desperate apology rings out before I can utter a hello. He at least sounds more sober.

"I'm tired. Can we talk about this in the morning?"

He may be sober, but I am not, and I don't trust myself to have this conversation like this.

"I'm sorry. Please just tell me we are okay. I love you. Please tell me I didn't ruin us."

My heart melts at the raw anguish in his voice, and my anger melts away with it. "Tanner, love. We are fine, I promise. I love you too. I just went out with Chelsea and Evelyn tonight, and I'm tired. Let's talk about this more when we are both rested and sober."

"Okay. I love you, babe. I really am sorry."

"I know. I love you too. I'll talk to you tomorrow."

I hang up the phone with a hollow feeling in my chest. We are fine, right? My head tells me yes, that it was just a fight, and he's apologized for it—it's not even the worst fight we've had—but my words lacked their normal conviction. Telling him everything is fine feels like a lie, and my heart agrees.

I love him, but am I happy?

I shake the thought away as quickly as it came. Of course I'm happy. He's the love of my life. It's practically a fairy tale, so how could I not be happy? I keep repeating that mantra in my head as I get ready for bed, not stopping until I actually start to believe it.

I'm just drunk, and the alcohol is confusing me.

But all it takes is a sticky note on the bathroom mirror to knock over that house of cards.

Dear Roomie,

I had a lot of fun tonight, both at the apartment and at Cutter's. I don't think I ever told you how beautiful you looked tonight. Do you want to pick up where we left off next Friday, maybe around 6? I'll get more pizza.

-M

I clutch the note to my chest, and my reflection stares at me with a stupid smile on her face. With butterflies fluttering with renewed vigor, I grab my notepad and scrawl a response.

Dear Roomie,

Sounds like a plan. Let's get wild and try pepperoni this time.

-J

Next Friday can't come soon enough.

Chapter 13
Morgan

Dear Roomie,

I'm stopping by the store later. Do you need me to grab anything?

—J

I've never really understood team sports or why getting drunk is a requirement to enjoy them. My friends aren't an exception. The sound of glasses clinking rings through the apartment as Nathan, Chelsea, and Karis take their third shot of tequila in the kitchen.

I wasn't expecting to have a full house this morning, but James conspired with our friends to organize *this*. They call it pregaming; I'm not sure what I call it yet.

Evelyn and Chelsea showed up first, with champagne and a spread of pastries. I can at least respect their attempt to disguise day drinking as brunch. It was Nathan and Karis who brought the liquor.

I, for one, have no desire to get drunk at 10 a.m., and I think James feels the same. She has spent the morning joking and laughing with her "girls," but she's had the same can of hard seltzer in her hand since they got here.

Evelyn sips on a mimosa from her spot on the couch next to me. She's too close for comfort; her leg is pressed up against mine, and she keeps trying to catch my gaze from under thick false lashes. I've made small talk with her but don't let the conversation go any deeper than that. I don't want to lead her on. She seems like a nice girl, and she's cute, too, but I'm not looking to start a relationship or a fling. Even if I were, only one woman in this apartment draws my attention to her like a moth to a flame, and she is wholly and unequivocally unavailable.

I swirl the now-warm beer around in the bottle without taking a sip. It's all I can do to keep my eyes from drifting over to my roommate. She's all dressed up in a red dress and heels, and her hair has been meticulously curled into long blond waves. Apparently, there is an unofficial dress code for games. She filled me in on it all this morning: you either dress up like you are going out or wear jerseys, no in between. James and her friends fall in the first category.

I don't get it. Wearing heels to go stand on concrete steps for the next three to five hours seems like the opposite of a good time, but even Nathan is dressed up more than normal, wearing khaki shorts and a polo.

A siren's song of laughter spills out from the kitchen, and I'm unable to resist its pull. My eyes snap over to my roommate, and she catches my gaze with a soft smile.

"All right, finish your drinks. It's time to go," she says loud enough to get everyone's attention. She doesn't follow her own instructions. Instead, she moves over to the sink to pour her drink out, and I follow suit, moving up behind her to dump mine as well.

"Not your thing?" I ask. She jumps at the sound of my voice and stumbles back against my chest. My empty hand grips her bare shoulder on instinct to help steady her.

"I love football," she says, leaning into my touch instead of pulling away. Warmth grows in my chest at the unexpected move. "I also like to go out with the girls. I just don't feel the need to mix the two."

"I can understand that. I don't know much about football, but I'm not a fan of drinking this early."

"I'll make you a football lover, trust me. It's impossible to go to a UGA game and not come out a fan for life."

"That's a pretty serious claim, but I trust you."

She beams at me and rounds up the rest of the less sober crowd. They follow her out the door and down the street like little drunk ducklings. Campus is the most crowded I've seen it; the streets are packed with fans adorned in red and black, and every lot is full of people camped out around the trunks of their cars with TVs, grills, and lawn chairs. James marches down the street, smiling as bright as I've seen her as she takes in the charged atmosphere around the stadium. She's in heaven. Every so often, she glances back at me and smiles a bit brighter when she meets my stare. I can't help but smile back, her enthusiasm infectious.

Nathan and James push ahead of the group to find us a spot in the student section. It's crowded enough that we have to split into two rows. I squeeze in between Karis and James, while the other three stand on the row behind us.

"Evelyn, switch with me," James commands and all but shoves her into the space at my side before moving to stand behind me.

"Hi." Evelyn blushes and glances at her feet.

My face starts to fall, but I mask my disappointment. She isn't the woman I was hoping to spend the day with.

"Hey." My fingers run through my hair. "Are you excited for the game?" I ask. It's better than standing around in awkward silence.

"Eh." She shrugs. "Football is Jamie's thing. I only come along to hang out with her and Chelsea."

"What is your thing, then?"

"I don't know. I just go along with what they want to do."

"Well, what do you do when it's just you?"

"I guess I like to volunteer." She brushes a lock of chocolate-brown hair behind her ear and bites her lip. "What's your thing?"

I don't get a chance to respond. On a cue that I miss, a hush falls across the crowd, and everyone turns and points to the southwest corner of the stadium. I look around at the rest of my group and see they clearly know what's going on.

"Just point," James whispers in my ear, her unexpected nearness causing a wave of chills to move across my body. I turn my head enough to get a glimpse of her nearly bouncing on the stands with excitement. Indulging her, I point, and her excitement only grows.

The silence is cut by the sound of a lone trumpeter playing the opening bars of the "Battle Hymn of the Republic." The rest of the marching band joins in, and the song is overlaid by a man giving a speech while a montage plays on the scoreboard's large screen. The song and video come to an end, and the crowd goes wild, and despite not knowing what exactly just happened, I go crazy with them. The band continues to play through their pregame routine, and the crowd only grows more rowdy.

"That's my favorite part. No other tradition compares. Not here, and not at any other school." Her breath caresses my ear with the rasped words.

"That was something else." I can't say why, but the experience has my heart pounding in my chest and my skin covered in chills. I can see why she loves this so much; I don't think I've ever felt so connected to a crowd.

The game kicks off, and everyone's attention is drawn to the field—even mine, despite not understanding what exactly is happening. James spends the whole game leaning over and talking in my ear as she explains each play, who all of the players are, and what terms like *flag* and *first down* mean. She is so patient with all my questions and lack of understanding. At some point around halftime, Evelyn gives up on trying to make small talk with me, and James takes her place at my side to continue her play-by-play of the game.

I think she was right about making me love football. It would be impossible not to fall in love with anything she is this passionate about.

"As long as the other team doesn't score in the next three minutes, we win. But they have possession," she explains as we switch to defense.

The minutes tick by, agonizingly slow, and the other team moves closer and closer to the end zone. With each play, and each time our defense fails to stop the opposing team's drive down the field, she grows more tense. As the game enters its final minute with the other team still in possession of the ball, she grabs my hand in a death grip.

We both watch the field, completely invested in the game. The opposing team's quarterback pulls back his arm and throws the ball to his teammate waiting in the end zone. She sucks in a sharp breath and squeezes my hand even tighter. The throw looks good as it spirals through the air in a perfect path toward its intended target. Right before he can catch it, though, one of our players materializes out of nowhere and intercepts the ball.

A bright squeal of excitement cuts through the roar of the crowd as James launches herself at me. Her arms fly around my neck, and I catch her on instinct. I don't quite know how to react, but her joy is contagious, so I pull her closer and spin her around. Laughter spills past her plush lips, and she holds on even tighter. The subtle scent of her vanilla perfume blossoms in the air as her hair fans out in a golden wave. Reluctantly, I place her feet back on the ground and let her go. She tightens her embrace for a second longer, burying her face into my chest. When she looks back up at me and finally lets go, her cheeks are stained red, but her face is still radiating joy.

I've always thought James was beautiful, but I don't think she's ever looked as beautiful as she does now—carefree and smiling, with her guard completely down. The world around us freezes as I get lost in her mossy eyes. In this moment, all that matters is the smile on her face and the light in her green gaze.

"Hey, Morgan, we are going downtown to celebrate. Wanna come?" Nathan claps me on the shoulder while keeping one arm firmly around his girlfriend's waist. The abrupt words break whatever spell James has me under. Evelyn glances toward me with clear hope in her eyes, but my attention strays back to the enchantress who has me at her mercy. I'll do whatever she wants to do. He reads my face and rolls his eyes but turns to her as well.

"What about you, James?"

"I think I'm gonna pass. I've got a paper due on Monday that I haven't done nearly enough work for, so I'm gonna call it a night."

"I think I'm going to call it a night too," I tell my friend, and a twinge of guilt sparks in my chest as Evelyn's face falls. It's not enough for me to change my answer, though. "Mind if I walk back with you?"

She smiles at me even brighter than before. "Not at all. I guess we will see y'all Monday."

James motions for me to follow her, but my friend puts a hand on my shoulder to stop me. He pulls me away from the group, leaving even Chelsea behind.

"Dude, you know she's not available, right?" he asks, his tone more serious than I've ever heard before.

"I know. It's not like that. We are barely even friends."

"You sure as hell don't look at her like a friend, and y'all definitely seemed more than friendly earlier." He casts a disapproving look in my direction.

"I swear, just friends. I know she has a boyfriend, and I'm not going to get in the way of that. But she's actually pretty cool once you get past the spiky shell."

"Whatever you say, man. I hope you know what you are getting yourself into." He waves me off and moves to wrap Chelsea under his arm again. With a quick wave, I hustle back over to James and fall in step at her side.

"Do you really have a paper?" I ask once we're out of the chaos.

"Yes, but it's mostly finished," she replies with a playful smirk. "I could use a night in, though." Her face twists in pain, and she reaches down toward her feet. "Goddamnit. I always hate this part. I put on the heels and think I look cute, but my feet are dead by the time I have to walk back."

She pulls off her shoes, exposing her blistered feet. Groaning, she starts to walk again, wincing with each barefooted step.

"Wait. Let me give you a ride back." The words spill out of my mouth before I can think them through, but I can't let her walk back barefoot and in pain. Crouching to her level, I command, "Get on my back. Your chariot awaits, Queen James."

She looks at me oddly for a second before jumping up, wrapping her legs around my waist and her arms around my neck. Her head drops to rest on my shoulder, and I'm suddenly hyperaware of everywhere her body touches mine. The whole way back, I'm focused on the heat radiating off her body and the way she clings to my chest. I swear it's the longest twenty-minute walk of my life. We get odd looks from strangers as we pass, but it's worth it to hear her laughter that rings out the entirety of the trip.

"You go change. I'll take Grover out, and then we can watch something if you want." I put her down at the front door and fish the key out of my pocket.

"That sounds great." She beams up at me, and I try to shake off the sinking feeling that Nathan may be right.

Chapter 14
Morgan

I'm so stupid.

I need to get this crush under control before I fall for her and break my own heart in the process. But that's impossible when every thought is filled with James: her voice, her laugh, her fiery anger, and her infectious joy. Rationally, I know we are nothing more than roommates, and I am okay with that. However, rationality doesn't stop my heart from racing when I see her or my dick from hardening with every one of her carefree touches. Each moment I get to spend with her, I feel like I'm learning more, peeling back layers, and getting to know the real her, and I really like the person I'm meeting.

The sky is washed red with the glowing lights from the stadium, and the streets are flooded with fans celebrating the win. It's not the peaceful atmosphere I imagined when I grabbed the leash and fled. This walk was supposed to clear my head, but all it's done is muddy it further. I glance at the time and mutter a silent curse as I realize I've already spent way too long trying to figure it out.

Steeling myself, I walk back into the apartment and find James already waiting on the couch. She's changed into her pajamas, wiped off her makeup, and thrown her hair up into a messy bun on the top of her head. There are two tumblers and a bottle of nice-looking whiskey sitting on the coffee table in front of her.

"Want a drink? This feels like a more acceptable hour." She watches me with her eyes wide and her cheeks flushed.

"Sure. Thanks." I slip off my shoes and join her.

"So I was thinking we could play a game." Her voice quavers, and she drops her nervous stare to her hands, which fidget in her lap. "I don't know you that well and was thinking we could play truths. It's like truth or dare, but we can only ask each other questions. If you don't want to answer, then you have to drink."

It sounds like a terrible idea.

I shouldn't agree to it—I know where games like this lead—but James looks up at me from under her lashes and catches her lower lip between her teeth, and I find myself agreeing against my better judgment.

"Sure, you go first." I need her to set the tone of how personal this is going to get.

"So what's with the nerd shows? Why do you like *Merlin* so much?"

A breath of relief passes my lips. This is an easy one.

"It's not just *Merlin*. I love anything having to do with Arthurian legends and Camelot and the Knights of the Round Table. They are stories of people going off and fighting evil and defending the innocent. That's all I've ever wanted—to be someone who fights for justice and is moral and good."

"Is that why you chose law school?"

"I think it's my turn to ask a question," I tease, but the question sends a ripple of dread through my chest. She pouts a little but doesn't argue. "What's your major," I ask her. It's a little crazy to me that I've lived with her this long and don't know that, but we didn't get off to the best start.

"Finance, but I feel like I tried them all. I wasn't passionate about any of them, but I had to settle on something. That's why I need this fifth year to finish it up. So is that why you want to be a lawyer?" She jumps straight into her question without taking a breath.

I pick up my drink and down half of it in one go, ignoring the burn as it travels down my throat. Her face drops; she probably thinks I'm drinking to avoid the question. That isn't it. I'm going to answer her, I just need to build up the courage to do it. Several silent seconds pass while I try to figure out exactly how I want to tell her this story.

With a heavy sigh, I break the silence. "Maybe a little bit, but not really." My voice comes out too even, too hollow. She sits up straighter at the shift in tone. "My sister was seven years older than me. I'm pretty sure my parents meant for her to be the only child, and I was an accidental kid. I have no proof of that besides the age gap, as my parents never made me feel like I was a mistake. Her name was Laura, and I absolutely idolized her. Never once did she make me feel like I was the annoying little brother. She always let me tag along with her and her friends. She was the best big sister a kid could ask for."

I pause and finish off the rest of the whiskey in my glass. She fills it again without speaking. Her gaze drills into me, burning a hole in the side of my face, but I can't bring myself to look at her. I can't bear to see the pity in her eyes that everyone has when they learn about Laura.

"Was?" Her small voice cracks on the lone word.

I nod as my eyes start to burn. "Yeah, was." I bring the warm liquid to my lips once again.

"I was twelve when she died. Laura was nineteen and about to finish her first semester of college at Wayne State. My parents were so proud of her. *I* was so proud of her. She had gotten an academic scholarship and was the first person in our family to go to college. She thrived there. Really, truly thrived. That night, she had stayed at the library to study. It was late and it was dark, but her dorm was only a few blocks away, so she decided to walk. On the way back, she was struck and killed by a car while crossing the street. She did nothing wrong. She was using the crosswalk, and she had the walk signal. The driver ran a red light and didn't see her until it was too late."

"Morgan, I am so, so sorry."

I risk a glance at my roommate and find tears flowing down her cheeks. My eyes dart back to my hands; the thin thread of control I have on my emotions will snap if I keep watching her cry.

"The driver was rich and connected." The floodgates have opened, and the story pours from my lips, but my voice is a hollow reflection compared to the feelings raging inside me. "His BAC was over 1.0, but he got a plea deal. A fucking plea deal, James." I drop my hand, slamming the whiskey down on the coffee table harder than I meant to, startling both of us. Grover lets out a low growl at the sound. My hands twist together in my lap, and I take a deep breath to try to get my anger back in check.

"At the end of it all, he only got a slap on the wrist. The judge ruled that he had to pay my family one hundred thousand dollars and be on house arrest for six months while attending weekly AA meetings. Laura's life was only worth one hundred thousand dollars to the court, and the man who killed her got to spend six months in his multimillion-dollar mansion doing whatever it is rich people do. That's why I decided to go to law school. I want to become a judge so I can make sure men like him get actual justice when they ruin good people's lives."

My voice cracks, and the tears I've been trying to contain spill over. James reaches over and grabs my hand, and her warm fingers trace patterns along my knuckles. The gentle motion soothes the festering edges of the old wound. Silence hangs between us, only broken by the occasional sound of the choked sobs I try to repress as I regain my composure.

The sobs soften to sniffles, and I wipe the remaining tears from my face. Over a decade later, the grief still hits as hard as it did the night I learned she died. The only thing that's changed is that the periods of still water between each crushing wave increase as time goes on.

I'm sure this isn't how she saw this game of hers going. Of course I've gotta kill the mood before we had the chance to actually get to know each other. I should have taken the drink and been done with it, but I wanted her to know. I just hope I didn't ruin things.

"What do you think you would be doing if you found your passion?" I ask, my voice still raw.

"You don't have to—"

"No," I interrupt her, "I want to keep playing, and it's my turn to ask a question."

She mulls it over for a moment, her teeth biting into her bottom lip while she thinks.

"I'd be an artist," she finally says. "My first major was graphic design, but I struggled with digital art. Painting is my favorite medium, but my dad wouldn't let me switch to fine arts. He said that as long as his benefits were paying for my school, I wasn't going to waste them on a useless degree. So I switched to education, then biology, and then journalism. Before I knew it, I was a junior with no direction. I made one last switch and decided to apply to the Terry School of Business, and I got in. I don't love finance, but I'm good enough with the numbers, and I will have lots of opportunities when it comes time to look for a job."

"Are you any good?" My brow raises in a challenge.

"I think it's my turn to ask a question." She mirrors my words from earlier with a tentative laugh. "What's your favorite pizza? Don't tell me you are one of those boring people who only likes cheese or pepperoni." She tries to keep her tone light, but there is a hesitancy to it that wasn't there before.

The abrupt change in tone leaves me dumbfounded for several seconds, and I burst into a fit of laughter at the absurdity of it.

"Probably Hawaiian," I tell her between chuckles. "What about you?"

She wrinkles her nose in disgust, making her face scrunch in a way that is strangely adorable.

"Pineapple on pizza? That's disgusting. Putting a point in the red-flag column for that one. If you had made a Hawaiian pizza the last time we did this, I would have turned around and left. I'm easy: mushroom, pepperoni, and olive for me."

She joins me in carefree laughter, and all the looming tension is banished. Her radiance burns through the gloom, and it looks like my demons have finally met their match.

"You are one to talk about bad taste. Olives, really?" I mime gagging. "I can do pepperoni and mushroom, but the olives ruin it for me."

"*What*? They're the best part. Nothing beats the savory taste of a freshly warmed olive."

"I think we need to agree to disagree on this one. It just keeps getting worse every time you speak. How do you feel about meat lovers?"

"Nope, it's my turn to ask a question."

"Come on, can we not pause the game for the good of finding a common pizza order?" My tone is deadly serious, which sends James into another fit of bell-like laughter, and my heart skips a beat in my chest.

"Fine, fine, you win. Yes, I like meat lovers, and BBQ chicken is also really good."

I take mental notes of her order before asking the most important question of all. "Where do you order your pizza from?"

"Domino's, but Pizza Hut will also do."

I nod in approval and let out an overdramatic sigh of relief. "All right, you pass. If you had said Papa John's, I might have moved out."

She lies back on the couch, clutching her stomach, completely overtaken by her laughter. I swear the lights in the room dim. Everything dulls in comparison to the way she glows.

"What was your last relationship like?" she asks, catching her breath.

"I'm gonna pass," I say as I reach for my drink. I have no intention of bringing the mood down again.

"Boo, you are no fun." She throws one of the decorative pillows my way. "Your turn."

"This may break the rules, but will you show me some of your art?"

"You want to see it?" James jerks back up to sit straight as a rail. Her voice shakes, but her eyes light up.

"Is that your question?" I can't help but tease her. This version of James, this insecure girl sitting on the couch, is so different from the girl who confronted me in the kitchen on my first day here. She stares up at me with joy glittering in her eyes, and I swell with pride knowing I put it there.

"Yes, James, I would love to see your work."

She springs up off the couch and stumbles her way to her bedroom. The sounds of pages rustling and furniture thumping drift out from the open door. A few minutes later, she rejoins me in the living room with her arms full of different books and places one with a blue canvas binding in front of me.

"Look at this one first."

I pick it up and thumb through it, careful not to rip or smear any of the pages. The first book is full of still-life drawings from around campus, made with a dark fine-point pen. As I finish looking through the book, she hands me another. I take my time looking through each page, spending those extra few seconds to appreciate the artistry. It's clear she has put a lot of time and effort into every piece.

Each book offers something different: some are full of brightly colored portraits, and others are hastily drawn outlines. There are several drawings of Grover, Tanner, and her friends mixed in throughout the pages, and I'm surprised to find drawings of Nathan, Gage, and Karis toward the back of one of the books. I flip to the last page and gently close it. Disappointment shoots through me when I don't find any drawings of me, but I swallow the feeling back down. This isn't about me, this is about her art, and it is good. Really, really good.

"James, I don't know what to say." I pause for a second and her face falls.

"You hate them, don't you?" She begins panicking before I can finish my thought, haphazardly collecting the sketchbooks into a pile. "This was a mistake. I never should have shown you these. My dad is right. I will never make it as—"

I grab both her shoulders, forcing her to look at me and stop her frantic ramblings.

"They are amazing. No, *you* are amazing."

She freezes completely and ducks her head toward the ground, but I catch a glimpse of pink on her cheeks before she can fully hide her face.

"Thanks," she mumbles at her feet.

"I think it was your turn to ask a question," I prompt her, trying to draw the light back out of her.

We fall into an easy routine, quickly abandoning the drinking rules in favor of getting drunk, and the one-question-at-a-time rule is abandoned not too long after. At some point, the game turns into genuine curiosity and a desire to truly get to know each other. Between the alcohol and the late hour, the conversation comes to a lull, but I don't want this to end. I can't let this end when there is no guarantee that I'll get it with her again. I rack my brain to find any excuse to keep her out here with me.

"Do you want to see another of my favorite shows?" It's a shot in the dark, but it's better than nothing. She gives me a sleepy but enthusiastic nod, so I move to fiddle with the TV. It takes longer than it should due to the alcohol in my system, but I'm able to get the first episode of *The Adventures of Sir Lancelot* playing on the screen.

"How is this even nerdier than your other nerd show," James asks through a yawn.

"Shh, just watch."

She listens to my order, leaning back to get more comfortable on the couch. I don't know who initiates, but we drift closer and closer as the episode progresses, drawn together by some magnetic force until our thighs touch in the center of the couch. The air between us buzzes with electricity, making me keenly aware of her smallest movements. Normally, this is where a guy would pretend to stretch so he could drape his arm over his girl's shoulder. That isn't the play here. There is nothing like that happening between my roommate and me. But no matter how many times I tell myself that, the roaring of my heart in my ears never lessens.

The pictures on the screen fade into the background as my focus locks in on the woman beside me. My throat tightens and my whole body freezes as her head droops and comes to rest on my shoulder. Before I can get a question out, a quiet snore passes from her lips.

A sharp pang of disappointment rocks through my chest at the sound. Of course she is only sleeping. Even if this was intentional, I shouldn't let her do this. I should wake her up and help her get to bed, but I've been ignoring a lot of *shoulds* when it comes to James Clarke, and this is no different. Wrapping my arms around her, I pull her closer, adjusting our position so we're both lying down and her head is on my chest. For one brief second, the world stops spinning around us, and everything is right. The heat from her body soaks through the layers of our clothes, creating pleasant pinpricks along my torso. She snuggles in deeper as if she's chasing more of that feeling. I mute the TV so it doesn't wake her but leave it on so the flashes of light from the screen still illuminate her face. I drink in her features, knowing I will never get a moment like this again.

This is wrong.

She is going to wake up tomorrow and see this as a mistake, but I am too selfish to stop her from making it. So I watch her in silence, committing every inch of her in this peaceful state to my memory. My eyes grow heavy and burn as I fight sleep. I would give anything to live in this moment forever, but sleep eventually pulls me under, and for the first time since I moved into this apartment, I don't dream.

Chapter 15
James

Morning comes, and with it, a sense of serenity. My consciousness hangs in that delicate space between awake and asleep, that limbo where you're aware of your surroundings but not what they mean. I float in that peaceful state, only truly aware of an all-encompassing warmth that wraps itself around me in a tight embrace. It's the type of warmth that feels like drinking hot cider while sitting on a porch swing on a chilly fall night—the type that feels like home.

I burrow in closer, inhaling the woody scent that floods my senses as my face presses against a solid wall of heat. The wall shifts and groans, and then I'm encircled in molten iron bands.

Wait, walls don't move or groan like that.

The thought breaks through the half-asleep haze and brings me to a full state of alertness. I crack my eyes open, only to find my face buried in a chiseled chest. It's not the chest that would make this whole situation okay—not Tanner's chest—but Morgan's. He lies underneath me, dead to the world, with his arms wrapped around me, locking me in place. I try to pull away, but his vise grip tightens against my escape.

Jesus fuck, James. How did you let yourself get here?

I search through my memories in a desperate attempt to figure out how I ended up asleep in my roommate's embrace. The roommate who is most definitely not my boyfriend. I've woken up in Tanner's arms more times than I can count, but never once has it felt like this.

Why the fuck hasn't it ever felt like this?

A wave of nausea rolls through me at the thought, and panic constricts my lungs, reducing my breaths to shallow gasps. I need to get away from here—no, away from *him*. His once-comforting embrace now feels like a cage. But I fight the urge to thrash until I'm free from his grip, because seeing him awake will only cause me to spiral deeper. Sucking in a breath, I count backward from ten. I do it again, and then again, matching my count to the beating of Morgan's heart until my panic subsides enough for me to think things through.

With slow, controlled movements, I disentangle myself from Morgan's arms. A deep frown mars his sleeping face at the loss of contact, and he reaches out at the empty space, letting out a small, distressed sound, before rolling back into a deep sleep. That noise skewers my racing heart. I want nothing more than to curl back up with him and put the smile back on his face, but I can't.

That isn't my place. My place is by Tanner's side.

Guilt tears through me, causing any semblance of control I had to snap. I sprint to the safety of the bathroom and sink down onto the cold tile floor. Questions race through my head, coming so quickly that I don't have the chance to fully process one before another takes its place.

Is this considered cheating? Should I tell Tanner? Am I a bad person? Why the fuck did he not go to his own bed? Why did his arms feel so much like home?

I restart my counting, but I'm too far gone for it to have its intended effect. My breaths come too quickly, and my heart beats the same. Every feeling I've been repressing pushes against my crumbling defense, threatening to consume me.

Fuck it, I'll give myself five minutes—five minutes to fall apart and let myself be weak, but then I am going to get my shit together and face the day head-on.

As soon as I give myself permission, the floodgates open, and the riptide of emotion drags me under. My body shakes as angry, confused tears pour down my face, and it feels as though my heart is going to explode in my chest. Those five minutes pass, and I'm able to stop the tears. I didn't actually think that would work, but I am able to regain control over my breaths and pull myself off the floor.

With puffy, red-rimmed eyes and sleep-mussed hair, I look like absolute shit, but it's nothing a little well-placed concealer can't fix. I throw on my normal running clothes and head toward the front door, careful not to wake my roommate. The state of my normally immaculate living room causes me to recoil in disgust. Nothing is where it's supposed to be. Mementos of a night that needs to be forgotten decorate the space, reminding me of my bad decisions. It takes everything in me to fight the urge to clear it all away, but I do, forcing myself out the door to start my morning run with Grover.

The brisk autumn air is exactly what I need to shake away the remaining sense of gloom. I push myself harder than I normally would, setting a brutal pace from the start. Each cold breath of air and cramp in my side is a deserved punishment for the actions that got me to this point. No matter how many times I run through it in my head, I can't trace back the route that led me to wake up in my roommate's arms. I hate him, or at least I did hate him, but now I don't even know what I feel.

That's a lie.

I like Morgan. I don't know when my brain decided "Hey, we like him now," but I can't deny that I do. There's no pressure with him; I can be myself without having to mask parts to fit what's expected of me. With my friends, I have to be Jamie, the girl who drinks a little too much and loves to party with a smile on her face. With Tanner, I have to be Ophelia. Ophelia is the girl living a storybook romance with her high school sweetheart. She is the perfect girlfriend who will turn into the perfect wife. Ophelia cooks and cleans, and she is always happy to say "yes, dear" while making sure all of Tanner's needs are met—physical and emotional.

But with Morgan, I get to be James. I get to be emotional and combative without fearing his reaction. I can get too excited about dumb things like football and war movies, knowing he will never ridicule me for it. Somehow, this man has not only wormed his way into my life, but he's become my safe place, and it scares the living fuck out of me.

My pace slows to a crawl as my body reaches its limit, and I start the journey home on jelly-like legs. I make it back to the apartment but pause in front of the door. The shadows of my earlier panic start to creep their way back into my mind.

What if he is awake? What if he wants to talk about whatever the fuck last night was? I'm not ready to have that conversation, but I don't think I ever will be. If he wants to talk about it, though, I will; I owe him that much.

With a resigned sigh, I push open the front door. My focus darts over to where I left Morgan, only to find the couch empty. Not only is he gone, but the apartment is spotless. Any lingering evidence of the previous night has been wiped away, and all that remains in its place is the subtle scent of Clorox wipes. That smell is normally a comfort, but it causes a pang of disappointment to pulse through me.

Maybe he is just as desperate to erase what happened as I am.

That's a good thing, or at least it should be. I can't tell anymore.

A block of orange sticking to the wall catches my attention as I turn to put away Grover's leash. The bright Post-it Note stands out against the dull white like a beacon, drawing me in. My heart freezes for a split second before taking off in my chest, and I pull the piece of paper down. My thumb runs in small zigzags over the familiar scrawl before I build up the courage to read the message.

> Dear Roomie,
>
> I never understood the appeal of football until I saw the joy on your face while you watched it.
>
> Your sketches are wonderful, by the way. I know your dad is just trying to be practical, but he's wrong. You have more than the talent needed to succeed. I would love to see some of your paintings, if you ever feel like sharing.
>
> —M

I take in the words, reading through them a second time to be sure that my eyes aren't playing tricks on me. They don't change on the second pass or the third. My eyes start to sting with the familiar prickle of tears. I wipe them away, but that doesn't take away the budding sense of awe that fills me.

Morgan likes my work. No, more than that, he believes in my ability to succeed.

No one—not my dad, not Tanner, not even my Grandma Anne—has ever expressed that much confidence in my dreams.

Clutching the note to my chest, I scurry toward my bedroom and rummage through my collection of sketchbooks, running my hands along each of their well-worn spines until I find my current favorite—the one I didn't show him last night. I find it, flip to one of the more recent pages—a quick sketch of him lying on the couch with my dog—and squirrel the note away.

Tanner won't like it, but I'm not about to throw away the words of someone who believes in me.

As if summoned by my thoughts, my phone rings with that fucking cursed tone. I slam the sketchbook closed and toss it back on the pile. It's a stupid reaction—it's not like he can see it through the phone.

"Good morning, my love," I answer with fabricated cheer.

"Hi, babe." My boyfriend's voice only increases the guilt that's been eating away at me all morning. He sounds sober, which is a relief. Our calls have been a game of roulette lately, and more often than not, I lose.

"What are you up to?"

"We are headed to brunch with some of the other families from church," he says, completely unaware of the guilt toiling in my gut or the way my traitorous heart pounds in my chest. "I've got the twins in the car, and they are dying to talk to you. Mind if I put you on speaker?"

Talking to them is what I need right now. Nothing beats the sound of their voices on a shitty day. Those girls are a balm to my soul, two pieces of my heart that are always missing.

"Yes, please. I miss them so much." Something clicks on his end, and my ears are filled with the excited squeals of "Ophie."

"Hi, girls. I love y'all. How has school been? Tell me all about it."

"It's so good," Kinsley starts to gush, "I thought Mrs. B was gonna be scary, but she's actually kind of cool. She has a reading corner and lets us go there if we don't have any homework, and it has so many books." She draws out the *O* sound to emphasize her point. "Maya is in my class, and we made friends with a new boy named Jack. We all play together at recess, and Mrs. B lets us do group work together."

"That's great, Kins. What about you, Rae?"

"School is okay," she says in a dejected tone. It's a stark contrast to her twin's enthusiasm.

"Just okay?" I ask, pressing further. It isn't like her to be sullen. She's always been my little Rae of sunshine. "Do you not like Mrs. B?"

"She's in Ms. Mckenzie's class," Kinsley says, answering for her.

"Oh." The girls have never had different teachers before. Raelyn has always been the quiet one, the one who follows, happy to support her sister in all her schemes with a smile on her face. This must be rough for her, but it will be good for her to learn how to do things on her own. "Tell me one thing you like about Ms. Mckenzie's class."

"She has a class bunny named Fish," she tells me after thinking it over for a moment, then lets out a small giggle. "It's a silly name."

"That it is." I laugh with her.

"All right," Tanner interrupts. "As much as I love talking to my three favorite girls, we just parked, and Mom is already waving us inside. Girls, go inside with Mom, and I'll meet you in a few minutes." Their disappointed grumbling is masked by the sound of car doors opening and closing.

"How is Raelyn handling everything? No bullshit," I ask when the car is quiet again. He lets out a sigh, and I can picture him slumping down in his seat the way he always does when he doesn't know how to fix something.

"It's been rough. Dad said she hasn't been herself. I'm worried about her, but I know this is a part of watching them grow up. I've been trying to make a point of doing something special with her, separate from combined twin activities, when I find the time."

"They are lucky to have a brother like you."

"They are lucky to have you too, Ophie. We miss you."

"I miss y'all too. Only two weeks until I'll be home for the fundraiser."

"I can't wait. Shoot, Mom is summoning me. I've got to go before she drags me out of this car. Love you, talk soon."

"I love you too."

Chapter 16
James

The heels of my shoes catch in the cracks of the cobblestone streets, making it impossible to walk without stumbling. I have to hold Tanner's elbow to stay upright, but he isn't complaining, as having me cling to his arm only improves our image. Our love is something straight out of a storybook, and tonight, more than ever, we look the part of a prince escorting his princess to the ball.

"You're late," Tanner's mom chastises as we walk into the historic hotel's lobby. Despite the biting tone of her words, the warm, welcoming smile never falters. Unless you heard her speak, you wouldn't be able to tell she was upset; Mrs. Nicholson's mask is that flawless.

"Sorry, Mom. Time may have gotten away from us a bit." He pulls her into a hug and places a respectful kiss on her cheek.

Once he lets her go, she grabs both of my hands and gives me an appraising once-over.

"You look lovely, Ophelia." She would think that; she picked out the dress. Not that I'm complaining. The burgundy trumpet gown is beautiful.

"Thank you, ma'am. My stylist is quite talented," I tease. Mrs. Nicholson laughs and pulls me in for a quick embrace as well.

"Go mingle while you can. Dinner will be starting soon." She shoos us into the ballroom.

"You really do look beautiful," Tanner whispers in my ear.

My heart swells, and I turn my head to give him a chaste kiss. I could say the same about him, but I'd never hear the end of it if I called him beautiful. He is beautiful, though, with his perfectly tailored suit and meticulously sculpted golden hair. The dark cherry lip print is the only thing out of place on him, and he makes no move to wipe it away. His icy eyes melt into shimmering pools as he smiles down at me with a rare genuine smile.

This right here, this is the man I love.

I smile and try my best to wipe away the mark I left.

"You should wear this for me again and let me paint you."

"Ophie..." he says, and his face pinches. That fleeting smile fades from his lips, and the glimpse of my best friend goes with it.

"What? You used to always sit for me." My closet back at Grandma Anne's is full of paintings I've made of him over the years. Even back when they were truly atrocious, I could never get myself to throw them away. It felt wrong, like I was throwing him away.

"When we were kids, sure. I don't have time to waste while you play artist anymore, and you won't either once you get a real job."

Oh.

Right.

120

I keep my face locked in a faux smile despite the crushing waves of disappointment wreaking havoc in my chest. It was stupid of me to ask. Over the years, he has made his opinions on my hobby clear—it's a waste of time. At some point along the way, it became something we don't talk about, but that doesn't stop me from hoping that one of these days, things might be different.

I wonder if Morgan would sit for me.

I've painted him more times than I care to admit over the past two months—especially since the night we went to the game—but I can never get the shape of his curls quite right or the shadow of his dimple on his crooked smile.

I shake off those intrusive thoughts.

"Why don't you introduce me to some of your coworkers," I suggest.

He nods and leads me toward a group of young guys in suits that are clearly off the rack. They look like children playing dress-up compared to the glitzy elegance of the donors here tonight.

I'd much rather spend the night with the twins, but the Nicholsons didn't think this was an event they should attend. Instead, they get to spend the night with Grandma Anne and Grover while I'm stuck listening to Chads and Brads reminisce about the "glory days." At least Tanner seems to be having fun.

Mr. Nicholson's voice breaks through the dull hum of chatter, thanking everyone for coming and asking everyone to find their assigned seats for dinner. These fundraisers are always my favorite of the political events I get dragged to. The meals are typically to die for—for the price per plate, I wouldn't expect anything less.

Tanner wraps his arm around my waist and guides me over to our table. Like always, we are with his parents, which means all eyes will be on us. The remaining seats at the table are already filled with familiar faces: Joseph Harris—Mr. Nicholson's old business partner—and his two children, Jacqueline and Owen. Those three are as much Tanner's family as his flesh and blood. The Nicholsons aren't a large family—no grandparents, no cousins; it's just him, the girls, and his parents—but the Harrises were always around.

"Uncle Joseph," he greets, reaching his arm out to shake Mr. Harris's hand, but the man pulls him in for a hug.

"It's good to see you, son." He releases him and turns his attention toward me. "Ophelia, you look breathtaking as always."

Smiling graciously, I thank him and find my seat. Tanner catches up with Mr. Harris and Jacqueline, talking far too quickly about the technical aspects and financials of a business I've had no reason to learn. The other Harris looks as entertained as I feel, but he has no qualms about sprawling in his seat and playing on his phone.

I wish I could relax and play on mine, but I have a role to play. I'm "Ophelia James" now, doing my best impression of Jackie O meets Kate Middleton. The weight of every eye in this room bears down on me, waiting for me to make a mistake. The pressure is almost unbearable, but no one else at the table seems to feel it.

The waitstaff brings out the first course, and my stomach rumbles as the aroma of tonight's meal drifts out of the kitchen. I hadn't had a chance to eat today; I left Athens before dawn to drive the five hours to Savannah and started getting ready for the evening as soon as I made it to Tanner's apartment. Normally, I would have driven down on Friday and spent the night with Grandma Anne or Tanner, but I didn't want to miss out on nerd night with Morgan.

A sharp elbow digs into my side, pulling my attention back to the conversation. Tanner gives me a pointed look.

"Uncle Joseph asked what your plans are for after graduation," he says with a tight smile. My face grows hot, and I bite the inside of my lip to keep from snapping at him. I take a steadying breath to try to regain my composure.

Come on, James, channel your inner Michelle Obama.

"I'm still figuring that out," I tell them with an artificial smile. "I've still got most of the year to figure out what I want to do."

Jacqueline lets out a huff of laughter.

"Do you have a problem with that?" I snap.

"No problem," she says with a bored expression. "I just think it's cute you are pretending to look for a job when we all know you're going to end up either working for the campaign or with me at Niarris."

Pain shoots through my fist as I clench the fork and imagine stabbing it into her smug face while I fight to control my breathing.

"There's no shame in that," she continues like she isn't aware of the fuse she's lit and how dangerously close I am to detonating. Tanner's worried eyes bounce between us, but he doesn't say anything—doesn't jump to my defense or try to shut her up. He just sits there, bracing for the explosion. "Tanner and I both work for our parents. I'm sure Owen will, too, once he graduates. You are set, James. Embrace it. There is no need for you to go through the motions pretending otherwise."

I'm fucking speechless.

I think the rest of the table is too.

Jacqueline goes back to eating her salad like nothing happened while the rest of us sit in stunned silence. The servers come around with the next course, breaking the tension, and Mr. Harris and Mr. Nicholson resume their conversation. The others follow suit, except for Owen, who hasn't looked up from his phone once.

The food looks delicious, but my appetite is gone. While the others eat, I move pieces around on my plate, fighting to keep my face pleasant. I can bitch about her to Tanner later—it won't be the first time.

A Chad and Brad from earlier come over to chat with my date, and he excuses himself to go with them after polishing off his fourth glass of bourbon since we've sat down.

Fan-fucking-tastic. I hate these stupid events.

He doesn't return for another thirty minutes, well after dessert is served. He swaggers back over with a Cheshire grin, slides back into his seat with a slight stumble, and throws his arm over the back of my chair.

"Do you want to get out of here," he whispers in my ear while pawing at the exposed skin on my shoulder. The sour stench of alcohol coats his breath, making my empty stomach turn. I nod, and he practically drags me out of my seat.

"Mom, Dad, thank you for the wonderful evening, but Ophie and I need to head out."

I give his parents an apologetic smile as he leads me out of the ballroom.

He is on me as soon as the door closes behind us. His mouth crashes into mine and his hand seizes my waist. The taste of burnt tobacco and liquor makes my stomach churn, and I stiffen. His hand roams higher, pawing at my clothed breasts, which snaps me out of the daze. The last thing I want is to be groped in a hotel lobby. I shove his chest, and he relents with a chuckle, but his eyes continue to rake over my body with unbridled heat.

"I've got a surprise for you," he says, his voice thick with lust.

"I swear to God, if the surprise is your dick, I'm going to kill you."

He throws his head back and laughs again. It's a euphoric sound—unrestrained and unlike anything I normally hear pass his lips.

"No, baby, it's not my dick. You can have that anytime you want it." He pushes his erection into my hip and nips at the skin of my neck. "I got us a room here tonight," he rasps into my ear and grabs my hand to lead us through the hotel, not stopping until we reach a room on the top floor.

"Open it," he tells me, placing the key card in my hand.

The door swings open, revealing not just a room but a suite. The large four-post bed in the center of the room immediately catches my eye. It's easily the largest bed I've ever seen, and it's curtained with a canopy of sheer fabric, creating a romantic air. The atmosphere is only heightened by the trail of rose petals leading toward the bed and a small sitting area directly across from it. A chilled bottle of champagne and a bouquet of red roses sit in the center of a small table in front of a couch, and the whole room is lit with dozens of flameless candles.

My heart swells and tears prickle in my eyes. I cover my mouth with my hands, and I'm unable to do anything beyond choke out an emotion-filled "Tanner."

"Surprise, baby." He wraps his arms around my waist from behind and leads us into the room, kissing my neck the whole time.

"How? Why," I stutter as I take it all in. He's never done anything like this before. Hell, I had to buy my own corsage for prom. Twice.

"Because I've been an ass lately, and I'm sorry. I love you. So fucking much."

My heart aches with how much I love this man. Words fail me, so I turn in his hold and mold my lips to his. It's a soft kiss. Completely unhurried as I nip and suck on his bottom lip. Tanner grabs my ass and pulls me flush against him, and a low moan escapes from his throat.

"Wait." He pulls away, and I let out a soft wine. "I wanted to wine and dine you first."

"We already ate." I pull his head back to mine and leave a trail of wet kisses along his neck.

"Fine. Wine and dessert, then." He untangles himself from my hold and crouches in front of a small fridge, pulling out a black cardboard box.

"I got you chocolate-covered strawberries," he says with a proud smile.

I'm powerless to do anything more than kiss him again. He guides me over to the sitting area and doesn't take his lips from mine as he lowers me to the couch.

"Sit, eat." He opens up the box and holds out a strawberry for me. I bite into it, letting the sweet juices spill down my face, and he has to bite his lip to hold back a groan.

"You're killing me, Ophie." He loosens his tie and pulls off his jacket as he stands to pour us champagne, then brings me a glass of bubbling liquid and sits beside me with one of his own.

His glass is empty before I have a chance to sip mine, and he pours himself another.

"So what are the plans for Frat Beach?"

Frat Beach?

What?

The abrupt tonal shift short-circuits my brain. How can he go from romancing me to travel plans with no transition?

"Frat Beach"—aka "the world's largest outdoor cocktail party"—is the unofficial pregame event for the Georgia-Florida game. Every year, the University of Georgia plays Florida State at a neutral site near the border, and every year, college students flock to the beaches of St. Simon's Island, regardless of whether they have tickets to the game or not. It's close enough to home that Tanner always joined me and the girls to party on the beach.

"There aren't any plans yet," I tell him, and his shoulders stiffen.

Fuck.

"It's three weeks away. At least tell me you booked a hotel," he demands, all of the playfulness replaced by a chilling rage.

A shiver of unease travels down my spine and pools in an icy block of fear in my gut. This isn't like him. I inch away from him, moving closer to the edge of the couch. He only grows more tense as each second passes without a response.

"No," I finally answer in the most even tone I can muster. "I didn't get tickets to the game this year, and I wasn't sure if you would be able to go with work. I can start looking—"

"Goddamnit, James!" The glass flies from his hand and explodes into a sparkling spray of glass shards and champagne as it hits the wall.

A scream rises in my throat, but I choke it down before it can pass my lips. Screaming might set him off even worse. Fuck, I have no idea how to navigate this. I've never seen Tanner display anything remotely close to this rage. The man in front of me is a stranger—a hostile invader in my boyfriend's body. I shove myself into the furthest corner of the couch and try to keep my breathing even despite the frantic beating of my heart.

"There's no way you're getting a hotel three weeks out," he rants and jumps to his feet. He paces back and forth in front of the table in short, rapid bursts. He doesn't look at me, though, which is good. I don't want his attention when he's acting like this.

"I'll talk to my dad's assistant and see if she can find us something that wouldn't normally be available," he continues to ramble. "We need two rooms, right? Your girls coming too?" His manic gaze snaps back to me, and I curl even deeper into the couch.

"Yes," I whisper. My eyes burn with pooling tears, but I refuse to let them fall.

"Hey, baby, what's wrong?" His voice softens as he crouches at my feet with a frown. He reaches out to brush a strand of hair back from my face, and I recoil, which only causes his face to fall even more. "Don't worry, Ophie. I'm gonna fix it, and we will have a great time."

"Okay, Tanner." I force a smile on my face, and he relaxes back onto his heels.

"What should we wear? I don't want to do the whole group thing with your friends again this year."

Costumes. Right. The game falls on Halloween weekend.

I rack my brain for ideas, but the only thing I can think of is Morgan. I wish he was here—actually, no, I don't. Tanner would lose his shit if Morgan was here—I wish I was home with him. Morgan would never act like this. He would keep me safe.

"We could do a Ren Faire thing?" The words come out like a question, not a statement.

"That's lame." He brushes my idea to the side, then jumps back up to his feet and resumes pacing. "I've got it," he says after a few moments, and a wide smile grows on his face. "We could do JFK and Marilyn Monroe."

"Don't you mean Jackie O?"

"No, Marilyn is way hotter. Let's plan on that."

"Okay, Tanner."

He freezes, studying my face for a moment before he sighs and drops back on the couch beside me. "I'm sorry I yelled." He cups my face in his hand. "Do you forgive me, O?"

"Of course." My voice shakes, but he doesn't seem to notice.

"Good." Discomfort slithers down my spine as he places a gentle kiss on my forehead. "I love you, Ophie."

"I love you too," I respond instinctively.

"Go shower," he tells me, "I'll join you in a bit."

He doesn't need to tell me twice. On autopilot, I flee to the safety of the bathroom, strip out of my dress, turn on the shower, and step under the freezing spray. Only then do I let the tears fall.

Chapter 17
Morgan

Dear Roomie,

Have you ever watched Band of Brothers? It's one of my favorites. Maybe we can watch it after we finish Merlin.

—J

Hot sand surrounds me with each sinking step I take, creating uncomfortable friction between the cheap rubber flip-flops and the soles of my feet. I didn't even own flip-flops until Nathan forced me to buy a pair yesterday.

"I don't know why I agreed to come with you guys." This so-called Frat Beach is living up to its name in all the worst ways. The sea of red and black collegiate wear is peppered with random bursts of color from the more festive among the crowd. They neglected to mention that this doubles as a Halloween party.

"You came because you love us," Nathan slurs as he throws an arm around my shoulder.

"No, he came because he owes us," Gage corrects.

"How do I owe you?"

"You never come out to Cutter's anymore. If I didn't know better, I'd think you were avoiding us." He isn't wrong about me not going out. I don't have much free time, and I would rather spend the time I have eating pizza and watching "nerd shows" with James. Not that I would tell them that.

"He's just avoiding you, Gage." Karis reaches up to tap her middle finger on his chest with a coy smile. "We see Morgan all the time."

"She's right," Nathan adds. "We study together almost every day and try to fit some gym time in at Ramsey a few nights a week. You're the odd one out, man."

"We could all get gym time if he would stop dragging his feet and join us at Double Teep."

"I'm seriously considering it for next semester," I tell him, but Gage only grumbles; he's heard it all before. "You can always get a day pass to join us at Ramsey."

"And spend time surrounded by undergrads? No, thank you."

"Oh, that's rich coming from you," Karis mocks. "Why the fuck are you here, then?" She gestures out to the writhing mass of drunk students that surround us. "This is the definition of surrounded by undergrads."

"Sure, but someone has to keep your crazy ass company when Nathan ditches us for the redhead and Morgan starts making goo-goo eyes at the roommate from hell."

"Her name is Chelsea," Nathan starts to protest at the same time I argue, "I don't make goo-goo eyes."

From Gage's smirk, I'm pretty sure we just proved his point.

"So you're telling me that if you saw them right now, you wouldn't run off to join them?" He pauses and folds his arms across his chest, doubt written on his face. We both deny his claim, which only causes him to raise a skeptical eyebrow. "Prove it, then," he says, turning us both toward a familiar trio.

I notice Chelsea first; her fiery hair whips wildly in the wind, standing out like a beacon against the blue horizon. She dances freely, with Evelyn by her side. The two of them are dressed in the beachwear approximation of Disney princesses—Chelsea as Ariel and Evelyn as Belle. It takes a second pass to find James in the crowd. She's withdrawn from the group, staring out over the horizon with her arms wrapped around her waist. Her shoulders curl around her in a protective shell, making her seem meek, but the stark white dress she's wearing doesn't allow her to hide.

Alarm bells ring through my head. James is a lot of things, but meek isn't one of them.

Without any thought of Gage's teasing, I start to make my way toward her, needing to make sure she's okay.

"Unbelievable," Gage scoffs, and I freeze mid-step. Nathan keeps walking toward the girls, blindly throwing a middle finger up at him over his shoulder as he goes.

"Come on, old man. Let the kids have fun with their women. I'll buy you a drink, and we can meet up with them later." Karis grabs Gage's elbow and leads him toward the nearest bar. He says something in return, but I can't hear it over the crowd. She continues to poke at him as they walk away, and even without hearing, I can tell they fall into their normal playful bickering.

The pair disappear into the crowd, and my gaze falls back on James and her friends. Nathan's got Chelsea wrapped up in his arms while they dance carefree near the shore, and Evelyn dances alongside them. James drifts off to their side, removed enough from them to seem disconnected but not far enough away to be her own entity. She's a melancholy moon, orbiting their bubble of happiness.

This time, my journey to join them is uninterrupted. Nathan gives me a small nod in acknowledgment but doesn't move away from Chelsea. I'm not sure what to do next. Do I approach James and ask her to tell me what's wrong? Do I ask her to dance? Hesitation holds me hostage, and I get caught in an orbit that mirrors James's. I try to catch her eyes, but she refuses to look up and meet mine.

The soft touch of a hand on my bicep pulls my attention back to the group. Evelyn is looking up at me, hope shining through in her honied-brown eyes.

"Hey, Morgan. I'm really glad you're here." She bites on her lower lip and glances down at the ground to hide her blush, but she doesn't let go of my arm.

"Oh...I...hi." My hand makes a pass through my hair as I stumble over my words. "It's good to be here. It's been fun."

"That's good. Fun is good. I'm also having fun..." She lets out a nervous chuckle and looks up at me from under her eyelashes. "I-I was wondering if you would maybe like to dance with me," she asks, the words coming out in one long nervous stream. Her hand trails along my arm, and the sharp edges of her nails dig into my skin, causing it to crawl with goose bumps. I have to fight the impulse to jerk my arm out of her grasp.

This is flirting, right? How do I deal with flirting?

"I...uh...sure," I agree, and the look of pure joy that overtakes her face is like a punch to the gut. Everything about this feels wrong, but I don't know why. Putting my reservations behind me, I let her lead me out toward our friends and dance.

She moves with that same fluid grace that she displayed the first time I saw her at Cutter's. It's a stark contrast to the normal timidness I expect from her. She seems like a whole new person when she dances, and I've got to admit that confidence looks good on her. My own movements are stiff and clumsy in comparison. I try my best to keep up, but it's clear I'm way out of my element here. She doesn't seem put off by my lack of skill, though. She is all smiles as she guides me through it.

Racking my brain, I try to remember anything I could use to start a conversation, but nothing comes. I know we've talked before, but my brain is short-circuiting. Between James's behavior, Evelyn's advances, and trying not to make a fool of myself by tripping over my feet, there isn't any room left for me to remember how to make small talk. Thankfully, she doesn't let me flounder for too long.

"I've noticed you haven't been coming out with Nathan much lately."

It really isn't much to go on, but I'll take what she gives me.

"It's hard to find time to go bar hopping with my classes. Plus, that's not really my scene."

"That's a shame. I've missed having you around." She wraps both her hands around my neck and pulls her body flush against mine. My hand grabs her waist on instinct, and she beams up at me. "Maybe we could find something to do together that's more your scene, then." She all but whispers the words in my ear as she grinds against me.

Did she just ask me out?

I stumble over her feet, and she pulls back, ungluing herself from me. It gives me a second to think over her offer. She's cute, and she's a nice girl, but there's something missing.

She isn't James.

I don't know where the thought comes from, but it sinks its barbed claws into me and refuses to let go. The sharp realization makes everything crystal clear, and disgust coils deep in my gut, not at her but at myself. I wrench myself away from her hold. Indulging her attention feels like the coward's way out, like I'm stringing her along. It's not like James will ever be mine, but it's unfair to Evelyn to entertain the idea of dating while I'm pining after someone else.

"I don't know if that's a great idea," I tell her, then grimace at the look of disappointment that flashes across her face.

Her focus shifts to something over my shoulder. I turn to follow her gaze and find my roommate watching us with cutting focus. The remnants of melancholy still seem to hover around her, but she's standing taller, more sure of herself, more like the James I know. If looks could kill, my she-devil would have murdered us where we stand. Evelyn looks between us both for several seconds before she comes to the same realization I had just a moment before.

"Oh, I see," she says, stepping back to make the space between us even larger.

"Evelyn, I'm sorry. It's not—"

"No, it's fine. I totally get it," she interrupts.

"There is nothing to get. She's with Tanner, and—"

Evelyn lets out a bitter laugh. "She deserves better than Tanner. Did you know he stood her up today?"

"He did what?" My tone is sharper than intended, but I can't contain the spark of rage that her words ignite. That explains why James currently looks like a hollow version of herself.

"He was supposed to meet us at the hotel hours ago but hasn't shown." Her face scrunches up for a second, as if just thinking about the man puts a bad taste in her mouth. She shakes it off and gives me a nudge in James's direction. I start to reply, but she cuts me off with a shake of her head. "Go talk to her."

I give her a small nod and make my way over to James. Wariness shines in her expression as she tracks my approach; she's like a rabbit caught in a predator's sights, readying itself to flee at a moment's notice. Disappointment pangs in my chest. One of these days, she will learn that I'm not her predator, and that she could never be anyone's prey. Until that day comes, I'll keep doing what I can to reassure her there's no wolf waiting to strike underneath this wool.

"Ariel, Belle, and..." I pause to try to figure out what exactly she is supposed to be. My gaze roams over her white dress and coiffed blond locks. "...Marilyn Monroe? That is an interesting combo."

She huffs and turns her attention to the ocean.

"Hey, I'm sorry. I was only joking around. You look beautiful, James." My words tumble out in a rush. Two sentences in, and I'm already messing this up. I want to cheer her up, not make things worse.

"No, it's fine." She lets out a long sigh but turns back to face me. "It's just...I'm only...It wasn't..." She stumbles over her words, never finishing a thought.

"It was Tanner's idea, right?" I supply, and her eyes narrow as her shoulders fall.

"You know about that?" she questions in a small voice.

"Evelyn told me he didn't show up. I put the costume thing together on my own."

"Oh." She turns back toward the ocean, eyes glistening.

"It was stupid of me to bring it up. I'm sorry he did that to you." I keep my arms locked at my side, fighting back the urge to grab her and pull her close.

"You aren't the one who stood me up." She palms away the tears from her eyes, scowling, and her spine steels as she looks at me again. "I don't want to talk about Tanner."

"Okay then, we won't talk about that."

The conversation stalls.

James turns back toward the water, watching the waves crash against the shore. Normally, these little moments of silence between us are comfortable, but her gloomy aura taints it, causing it to bear down on me with oppressive weight.

"You know, this is my first time seeing the ocean." The words come tumbling out without any thought. Her head snaps toward me, disbelief shining through her glassy stare.

"How the fuck have you never seen the ocean before?"

"I've never had the opportunity," I say with a shrug. "I grew up near the Great Lakes, so I've been to the beach, but the one we always went to was more rocky than sandy."

"This is a terrible first beach experience," she says, sounding appalled. "Come on, I have an idea." She grabs my hand and starts to pull me away from the crowd. I should pull my hand away, but, for the first time since I laid eyes on her today, James is smiling. So I let her drag me along, and I savor the feeling of her hand in mine.

"Where are we going?"

"For a walk. Now shut up and trust me."

I shut my mouth and follow behind her.

The crowd thins as we move away from the party's epicenter. Seeming satisfied with the distance she's put between us and the horde, James stops, kicks off her shoes, and steps ankle-deep into the surf. Even after she lets go of my hand, I'm haunted by the ghost of her touch.

A few stray golden strands flutter in the gentle breeze as she walks in front of me with her attention fixed to the shallow tide. She's like a dog on the hunt for its quarry; I half expect her to freeze and point in a direction once she catches its scent.

"What are you do—" I start to ask, but she lurches forward, reaching into the water just as the words pass my lips.

"Looking for this." Her face glows with pride as she holds her hand out to me, displaying a pile of sopping sand littered with tiny bits of seashells that have been eroded by the waves.

"A handful of sand...?" I try and fail to mask my confusion. I only just got that smile on her face, and I'd hate to kill it now. But she simply laughs, and the sound loosens the knot that had settled in my gut.

"No, it's a shark's tooth." She plucks a tiny black speck out of the silt and drops the shiny triangle into my hand.

"From an actual shark?"

"No, it's from an imaginary shark." She rolls her eyes and lets out another bubble of laughter. "Of course it's from a real shark."

"Well, excuse me for asking," I say in mock offense, but she can tease me all she wants if it keeps her happy. "We don't have sharks back in Michigan. Is the water even safe?"

"As safe as a large body of water can be." She shrugs and turns her attention back toward the tide. "Growing up, anytime my dad was stationed near the ocean, he would take me out to find cool shells or shark teeth when he had free time. I've got a jar full of them in my room back home that we gathered from all over the country."

"People look for Petoskey stones around the lakes," I tell her. She cocks her head and looks back in my direction with her forehead pinched. "Fossilized coral," I explain, "Laura always said they were overrated. She collected sea glass instead."

"Tell me something else about you," she demands with a playful glare.

"Like what?" I can't think of anything about me that is worth sharing that she doesn't already know. She knows more about me than anyone else; the others don't even know about Laura. It isn't a story I like to share.

"What's your favorite color?"

"My favorite color? Why do you want to know that?"

"Because I don't know it, and I feel like I should. Friends know each other's favorite colors."

"Is that what we are, James? Friends?" The words come out sharper than I intend them to, honed by the bitter bite of resentment, and my tone catches me off guard. She makes me feel a lot of things, and resentment isn't one of them, but coupled with the word *friend*, it rips its way to the surface. It's not because I want to be more than friends—or, more accurately, I am not resentful of only being her friend despite my feelings—the resentment stems from the fact that, until now, friendship hasn't been on the table.

James turns to face me, her eyes narrowed and simmering with heat. The look causes unease to churn in my gut, and my back stiffens as I brace for the impending verbal lashing. She moves closer, invading my space. The nearness forces her to tilt her head back to look at me, but she leaves enough of a gap between us that our bodies don't touch. Her hardened expression softens, but the heat in her gaze only grows. My heart rate climbs, the thrumming so intense I wouldn't be surprised if she could hear it. I'm enthralled by her presence; any rational thought I could have is eclipsed by *her*.

She places her hand on my bicep, and my skin lights up with pinprick tingles at her touch.

"I'd like to be," she says, squeezing my arm with a soft smile.

She'd like to be what?

It takes another second for my brain to break through whatever spell she cast. We were talking about being friends, and sharks, and colors.

"Purple," I blurt out, "but not royal purple. The softer type, like a lilac-y purple."

Her bottom lip catches between her teeth in an attempt to hold back a grin. She resists for a moment before she laughs, and a radiant smile lights up her face.

"What's so funny?" I try to keep my face serious, but her smile is contagious.

"Lilac-y purple isn't a color. It's just called lilac. Saying lilac-y purple is like saying maroon-y red or aqua-y blue." She lets out another peal of laughter.

"Fine, Miss Color Expert, what's your favorite color, then?"

She slams her mouth shut, locking her lips in a tight line, and stares up at me with mirth.

"Come on, now, it's only fair," I prod.

She doubles down on her refusal, shaking her head back and forth in defiance. Then she takes a step back, drops her hand, and takes off running down the beach. I run after her, closing the distance in a few long strides, and catch her waist in an iron grip, pulling her flush against my chest. Unbridled laughter rings out as she kicks her legs in the air, squealing as I spin us around in a circle. The fabric of her dress flares with the momentum, painting a white swath against the blue horizon.

I place her feet back on the sand and pull away. Her breaths match mine, coming fast and heavy. She turns to face me, her whole face radiating joy, and I'm once again struck by her beauty.

"Do I get my answer now? I caught you fair and square."

"Do you promise not to laugh?" she asks, her forehead creasing in consideration.

"Why would I laugh?"

"I don't know. I laughed at yours, so it would only be fair."

"James, I promise—no, *pinky* promise—that I won't laugh at your favorite color." I keep my tone as serious as I can and hold my pinky out to her. She bursts into another fit of laughter but links hers with mine.

"My favorite color is a very specific shade of terracotta," she says. Her attention drifts back toward the horizon, seeming a million miles away. "It's a color that only lives on the horizon for a few minutes while the last rays of sunlight fade away. It's kind of a sad color, the color of a dying day, but I can't help but look on at it in awe when I am lucky enough to catch a fleeting glimpse."

Her shoulders stiffen, and she grimaces in anticipation.

"That is a beautiful color," I tell her and place a hand on her shoulder. She sighs and leans into my touch.

"We should head back to the others," she says with resignation. Her tone mirrors my feelings. I have to fight to hold back the instinctual "no." Everything in me wants to keep her here, with me, for a little while longer.

Instead, I give her shoulder a final squeeze and start to move toward the other students, while she walks beside me in tranquil silence

At the edge of the crowd, she freezes in her tracks. I turn to check on her and find her face pale and mouth agape. I track her wide-eyed gaze back into the horde, and lead forms in my stomach. Tanner is watching us with fury burning in his glare. I don't trust the look on his face, and I certainly don't want her to deal with his ire, especially now that she is feeling like herself again. He doesn't get to stand her up and then treat her like the bad guy for having fun without him.

"I'll go calm him down. Wait here for a second." I start to step toward him, but her arm whips out, stopping me.

"No, I-I'll deal with this." Her voice quakes as she speaks. "Go back to Nathan and the others. I'm sure we will catch up with y'all later."

"James, I—"

"Just go, Morgan," she snaps.

Unease gnaws at me as I watch her join her boyfriend. She tries to hug him, but he blocks her attempt, snarling something at her in response. He grabs her arm, and she visibly recoils.

A hazy red clouds my vision.

I stalk toward them, but Tanner meets my glare from over her shoulder and smirks before pulling her deeper into the sea of people. My heart takes off in my chest, and I break into a run to catch them. By the time I join the throng, they are gone.

The unease grows, solidifying into a heavy knot in my chest as my fingers make a pass through my hair. I don't know where to go or how to make this right, but I need to make sure James is safe.

Without a better plan, I book it back to where I left our friends. The knot loosens some as I catch sight of them still dancing. Karis and Gage have joined the group, Karis dancing while Gage hovers off to the side. I pivot my path and beeline toward the intimidating man.

He raises an eyebrow at my near-frantic approach, his mouth opening to speak, but I cut him off.

"I need your help," I manage to say around short, gasping breaths.

Gage stands a little straighter, his forehead furrowing at my demands. He places an arm over my shoulder and pulls me further off to the side, flashing Karis a reassuring smile when she gives us a questioning look.

"All right, what's up?" His tone is no-nonsense.

"Tanner showed up, and James went with him."

"And? He's her boyfriend, that's expected."

"I just have a really bad feeling about it," I say, pushing my hand through my hair. "He looked really mad, and I think he might have hurt James. She winced when he grabbed her arm."

His eyes bore into me as he studies my face. He's going to say I'm being stupid, that this isn't my place. I try to convey how serious I am about this, and he must see it because he nods and turns back toward our friends. He makes eye contact with Nathan and flicks his head back. Without any hesitation, he breaks away from the girls and joins us.

"All right, Morgan, explain the situation to Nathan as we walk. Let's go save your girl."

Chapter 18
James

P ain blossoms under the vise-like pressure of Tanner's fingers as they dig into the exposed flesh of my upper arm. He wrenches me forward, dragging me through the sea of students congregated on the beach. Splotches of red and black blur past my vision, creating a swirling, expressionist image of hedonism at its peak. No one spares me a second glance as we pass, too self-absorbed to notice my silent pleas, or maybe too drunk to realize what they mean.

His grip is unrelenting as he maneuvers me through the throng of people. He drags me behind him with strides longer than I can match, forcing my body to contort into an awkward angle with my feet lagging behind the rest of me. I jerk my shoulder back, attempting to dislodge his grasp, but he clamps down harder. A small whimper escapes my lips, and only then does his grip relax, but he doesn't release me completely.

It's as if his hold is on both my body and my mind, but as he eases off my bruising shoulder, the binds that kept me locked in shock break, setting my fury free. How dare he think he can treat me like this? Never in the fifteen years I've known him has he put his hands on me in an unwelcome way. Even as a kid, he was always gentle to the point it was almost insulting. He got even worse once we started dating, always treating me like I was made from glass. It's such a contrast from now that I don't even recognize the man in front of me.

Sand gives way to pavement as he continues to haul me further from the beach and into the public parking lot. I plant my feet, stop dead in my tracks, and jerk my arm again, this time with enough force to pull it free from his steely claws.

"What the hell, Tanner?" I shout, my outburst catching the attention of a few drunken stragglers.

The stranger wearing my boyfriend's skin whirls around to glare at me, his eyes alight with a manic intensity that looks alien on his face. His lips curl into a sneer as he stalks toward me, radiating malicious energy. My heart takes flight in my chest, beating hard enough to break free from the confines of my rib cage.

For the second time in twelve years, Tanner scares me.

I take a step back.

Then another.

I go to take another step, but my retreat is blocked by the cold frame of a stranger's SUV. He is on me in an instant, slamming his hand into the metal near my head, boxing me in.

"Shut the fuck up," he snarls through clenched teeth. He doesn't raise his voice; he doesn't need to—the loathing that drips from every word sends a spear of icy fear through me in a way shouting never could.

"You don't get to say shit," he continues, looming over me further. His eyes bore into me, his pupils so dilated that only the barest hint of his icy blue irises peeks out from behind them. "What the fuck were you doing with the roommate?"

"With Morgan? I wa—"

"Don't fucking lie to me!" This time, he yells, punctuating his words by slamming his hand on the car, inches from my head. He turns away from me in one erratic, sweeping motion and starts to pace. "I saw you with him. I saw you *touching* him," he seethes.

"Tanner, love, I promise you nothing was happening. We were just talking. We are friends, and I talk to my friends." My voice quakes, but I keep my tone calm otherwise. I reach my arm out and take a hesitant step forward like I would if I was approaching a stray dog. That's what he feels like right now, a feral beast lashing out without discretion. I can't find a trace of the man I loved at all.

"I told you to shut up," he roars, whipping back around to focus his attention on me. As he spins, something dislodges from his pocket and is flung into the air.

Time seems to slow as I watch it arc through the air and hurtle to the ground. He doesn't notice, too consumed with slinging vitriol in my direction, but his words fade into white noise as my focus narrows in on the small plastic baggie full of white powder lying on the asphalt.

"Is that cocaine?" I ask, holding my voice calm and level against the white-hot rage ignited by the drugs. He knows—he fucking knows—how I feel about this. "Are you fucking high right now?" My rage burns through the paper-thin mask of calm, making my voice shrill.

That snaps him out of his coke-fueled ranting. He looks at the bag and then up at me, his eyes widening in abject horror as the color drains from his face, and he glances away from my scorching stare.

"Ophie...I...baby...it's not what it looks like." He refuses to meet my gaze as he stumbles over his words.

"It looks like a fucking bag of drugs," I shout, and he recoils. At least he has the decency to look halfway ashamed of himself.

"Baby, it's only a little coke," he whines. "It helps with stress, and all the guys at work use it to help blow off steam."

"I...I can't do this right now." The tidal wave of anger recedes almost as quickly as it came, leaving devastation in its wake. An aching void consumes my heart and takes its place. "Please, just go. I'll stay with Chelsea tonight. We can talk when you are sober."

"O, just let me explain." The desperate edge to his voice causes the hairs on the back of my neck to stand on end. He lurches at me, reaching out to grab me again, but I step away from his touch. I don't want him anywhere near me right now.

"Is everything all right here?" Morgan asks, his tense tone making it sound more like a warning than a question. He's flanked by Gage and Nathan, the three of them wearing matching scowls as they approach us. Morgan comes closer than the others and tries to angle his body in front of mine.

That spark of manic intensity reignites in Tanner's eyes. He turns toward Morgan and cocks his arm back, but my roommate is oblivious, his focus entirely on me. I want to warn him, but I freeze, unable to do anything but watch as Tanner's fist crashes into his unsuspecting face. He stumbles back but regains his footing before he falls. Blood starts to well from the fresh cut on his lip. A cruel smile grows on Tanner's face, and he rears back for his next attack.

A scream catches in my throat. That hollow void inside me grows solid, filling with lead. It's a paralyzing pressure, rendering me unable to move or speak or even breathe.

Gage steps in with catlike grace and catches Tanner's arm before he can do any more damage.

The constricting pressure lessens enough that I can suck in a gasp of air, but I can't fill my lungs. My breathing grows frantic, coming in short, erratic pants, matching the furious hammering of my heart. A high-pitched ringing resonates in my ears, and dark shadows circle my vision, causing everything to seem so far away. I lose the world around me: Morgan, Tanner, love, drugs, blood.

None of it matters.

Not when I'm dying.

My legs give out from under me, and gravity pulls me to the ground in a heap. I'm vaguely aware of my surroundings, but everything feels indistinct, like the remnants of a forgotten dream. A few sensations slip past the haze—the soft caress of a hand on my cheek, a familiar voice calling my name, the smell of spiced wood drifting past my nose—but nothing is able to break through the cloud of all-consuming dread.

The world turns on its side as I feel my body being lifted off the ground. I'm enveloped in a protective warmth, and I turn into it, burrowing my face into that same woody scent. The sound of a car door shutting registers through the fog. My body is shifted around again, and then I'm surrounded by a low, steady thumping. I focus on it, using it as a metronome to count the time in between breaths.

Five beats in.

Hold for two.

Five beats out.

Repeat.

The beating is my lighthouse in the storm, guiding me toward the safety of the shore and helping each breath come easier than the last. A gentle hand runs over my hair in soothing strokes; I'm not sure if it's a new sensation or one I'm just now becoming aware of.

I pull my head out of the darkness and find that my refuge is actually the hollow of Morgan's neck. The creases that mar his face relax as his watery eyes roam over my face, taking in every detail. He lets out a small breath and pulls his hand from my hair.

"There she is," he says, wiping the drying tears from my face with his thumb. The touch is almost reverent, and I lean into it, embracing the comfort it brings.

"Wh-what happened? Where are we," I ask, my voice still raw.

He cradles me against his chest, holding me in his lap in the back seat of an unfamiliar sedan. I shift, turning to sit up straight on his thighs, and find Karis behind the driver's seat. She watches us through the rearview mirror, her eyes narrowed on me in Morgan's lap. I meet her stare, and she raises an eyebrow in challenge. We hold each other's stare for several seconds before I avert my gaze to the road.

"We think you had a panic attack," Morgan starts to explain. "It was pretty bad." He takes in another shuddering breath. "I was really scared. You stopped responding to us. It was like we weren't even there. I tried to talk you through it like I have before, but you didn't register a word that I said. I looked for your medicine, but I couldn't find it. I asked Chelsea about it after Nathan went to get her, and she looked at me like I was crazy. Are they back at the hotel? Do you still need them?"

"No. I-I didn't bring them with me." My eyes fall to my lap.

"Why not?"

"I didn't want anyone to see them." I hate showing this weakness to others, and now everybody knows just how broken I am. *Fuck*. With any luck, they will think this was a one-off. Tanner's actions were bad enough to warrant it.

"Where are we going?"

Thankfully, he lets the subject drop, but there's a hit of disapproval written on his face.

"We decided it was best to get you out of there. We are on the way to your hotel now."

"What about Tanner?" My heart rate jumps again. "I-I don't want to see him tonight. I can't. I-I—"

"Shh, don't worry about him." He rubs small circles on my back. "We are going back to Chelsea and Evelyn's room. Gage was calming Tanner down when we left, but you don't need to worry about him tonight."

"Okay." The tension flees my body, and I melt against him. His arms wrap around me, holding me close. I should move to the seat beside him, but the comfort of his embrace is too enticing, so I stay like that the entire ride to the hotel.

We are both flung forward as Karis slams her foot on the brake in front of our destination. Morgan's arms tighten around me, which keeps my face from hitting the back of the seat.

"All right, Blondie, this is your stop," Karis says. She turns around in her seat and holds out her hand. "I take cash, credit, or firstborns as payment."

"Thanks for the ride," Morgan tells her, rolling his eyes. He opens the car door, and I crawl out of his protective hold.

"Call me if you need anything," she yells as he follows me out. The car is moving before Morgan takes his first step away.

He shakes his head and mumbles something under his breath before leading me into the hotel and through the maze of identical hallways. It's all a convoluted blur around me, and if it wasn't for the warm fingers threaded through mine, I would get lost in the monotony of it all. Those tiny sparks of tingling heat are my lifeline, keeping me grounded until we stop in front of the room that must be the girls'. He fishes the borrowed key card out of his pocket and opens the door.

The room is generic—nothing more than two beds and a midsized TV. The only thing that sets it apart from any other hotel room is the art on the walls having a vaguely beachy theme. The door swings closed behind us with a resounding *click*, and he drops my hand. He peers around the room, looking at everything but my face. With a sigh, he runs his hand through his hair and tugs on his bottom lip with his teeth. Blood pools as the barely healed cut reopens under the tension and drips down his chin in a steady stream.

"Morgan, your face..."

He tries to palm away the blood but only succeeds in smearing it across his face.

"Crap," he mutters, gazing at the fresh red streaks on his hands. He goes into the bathroom, inspecting the damage in the mirror, and I follow him.

"Let me look." I nudge him to sit on the closed toilet seat, and I'm hit with a sense of déjà vu; it wasn't too many months ago we were strangers in the same position. If someone had told me then that the random person I found online to be my roommate would weasel his way past my walls so quickly, I would have laughed in their face, but in only three months, he has done exactly that. This man has carved out a place in my heart for himself as my friend, my defender, and under different circumstances, maybe something more. I shake my head, trying to fling that thought from existence. There is no use dwelling on what-ifs.

"We don't have a first aid kit here, but at least let me clean it up," I tell him, kneeling to inspect the small wound. Seeing it makes my throat tighten. It's my fault he got hurt, being it was my boyfriend who acted like a fucking

Neanderthal. As an array of emotions slams into my chest, I wet a washcloth and use it to clean the blood from his chin—it's the least I can do to make up for what happened.

"You don't have to—" he starts to say, pulling away from my touch.

"Please, let me do this," I cut him off with a plea. He nods, and I continue my work, moving from his face to his hands. "I'm really fucking sorry he did this."

"It's not your fault," he reassures me, but the words do nothing to soothe the gnawing guilt. "Tanner should be the one apologizing. He's the jerk who sucker punched me."

"This isn't like him. He would normally never do something like this." I rush to his defense on instinct, but the words feel wrong, causing my gut to twist. My mind flashes to all the moments over the past few months where I've thought the same thing. A bitter laugh bubbles past my lips; maybe I don't know him at all anymore.

"Actually, fuck that. I'm done making excuses for him. He hasn't been the man I grew up with for a while now. I think he was high. A baggie of cocaine fell out of his pocket before you walked up. Drugs are a hard limit for me. He knows this, but he did it anyway." My voice cracks as the competing emotions war within me. I didn't know it was possible to be this sad, angry, and guilty all at once.

"Are you okay?" Morgan catches my hand between his, stilling the mindless wiping. He stares at me, his eyes so bright that the hazel shines like gold.

"No," I choke out. He stands, guiding me up with him, and pulls me into a bone-crushing hug. I bury my face into his neck and squeeze him back, soaking in his warmth.

"What can I do to make things better?"

"Is there any way we could watch your nerd shows here?" I ask, my words muffled by the embrace. He lets out a small chuckle, and his chest vibrates, erupting chills across my skin.

"I think I can figure something out."

He releases me and guides me toward one of the beds, clearing away the mess of clothes and cosmetics that the girls left in a sprawling heap. The white sheets are rumpled, clearly having been slept in. I cringe internally at the disheveled state of things, but he starts reorganizing the bedding without me saying a word. Seeming satisfied with his work, he flops down on top of the freshly made bed and pulls out his phone.

"We will have to make this work," he says, waving the device in his hand.

I crawl onto the bed next to him and lie down, leaving several inches of space between our bodies. That gap feels charged, the air electrified, and the hairs on my arm stand on end. I'm acutely aware of where we are and what Morgan is to me—or, more accurately, what he isn't—but only part of me cares. I know I'm crossing lines, but they are lines that might not exist come morning, and that thought only feeds the other part of me—the one that wants nothing more than to crawl back into the comfort of his embrace.

He holds out his phone so we can both see the screen, but the picture is so tiny that I still have to inch closer. And then I do it again. Currents of tingly shock waves erupt across my skin as my arm brushes up against his. He looks at me, his face flush and eyes dilated, and his tongue darts out to wet his lips. My breath catches and my heart rate picks up again, but for the first time today, it isn't panic that drives the spike.

"Come here." He opens his arms, inviting me to move closer.

His words break the growing tension, and heat rises in my cheeks. I take him up on his offer and try to ignore the feeling of rightness that comes as my head meets his chest and his free arm wraps around me.

Episode after episode passes by in a blur, but I'm too focused on the distracting touch for the stories of knights and wizards to draw me in. Sure fingers trace small circles on my back, drawing me deeper into his warmth with each deliberate path. Shadows envelop the room as sunlight fades from the window, and my eyelids start to sink as well. I do everything I can to fight sleep, but, as always, sleep wins. The last thought that passes through my head as I drift into unconsciousness is that I never want this moment to end.

***

Morgan is gone when I wake up.

My stomach sinks as I feel around the cold bed, looking for any remnants of the comfort from the night before, but find nothing.

Disappointed, I sit up and look around the room. At some point in the night, Chelsea and Evelyn stumbled back to the hotel room and passed out in the bed beside mine. Did Morgan leave before they got back, or was their arrival what drove him away? They weren't supposed to have to share a bed this year, but I had to go and ruin that for them. A surge of nausea twists in my gut, urging me out of the bed. Cursed fragments of yesterday's events bombard me, and without my knight in shining armor here to ground me, the churning grows.

I flee toward the door, keeping my steps quiet, but freeze when a piece of hotel stationary wedged in the frame catches my attention. The note is my lifeline. With desperate hands, I snatch the paper and read over the words, and like magic, the heaviness in my gut evaporates.

Dear Roomie,

I thought it was best that I didn't stay the night, but I couldn't bring myself to wake you up when I left. You looked so peaceful, and I couldn't ruin that, especially after the day you had. Yesterday was rough, I know that. Heck, I felt it. If you need to talk about it or anything else, you know where to find me.

Thank you for showing me the beach. Maybe one day I can take you to look for sea glass on the lake shore.

M

Taking a deep breath, I clutch the note to my chest. Somehow, he always manages to say the exact right thing, or maybe it's the right thing because it's coming from him. Maybe he didn't go too far. He needs to know how much yesterday meant to me. I push open the door to find him, but the familiar sight of my boyfriend—*ex-boyfriend?*—sitting in the hallway stops me in my tracks.

Tanner is curled in on himself, with his head tucked in on top of his knees, still wearing his stupid costume from yesterday. To be fair, so am I, but his American-flag swim trunks and suit jacket look even more ridiculous when he's moping on the floor.

As the door swings shut behind me with a loud *thud*, his head snaps up, and he stares at me with red-rimmed eyes. He looks wrecked; his hair is flat and greasy, and dark bags have made themselves at home under puffy eyelids.

"Ophie..." His voice cracks as he scrambles to his feet.

"What the fuck are you doing here?" I spit the words at him, the protective armor of rage slipping into place.

"Ophelia...baby...please talk to me. I'm so fucking sorry." He reaches for my wrist, and I pull away before he can touch me. The bruises on my arm are still too fresh for me to trust his fingers. He flinches but doesn't make any moves to touch me again.

"Baby..." he rasps out. "Please don't leave me over this. I can't lose you." His eyes grow glassy with unshed tears.

"You know what happened to my mom. You know how I feel about drugs. Give me one good reason why I shouldn't walk away right now," I say through clenched teeth.

"Because you would be throwing ten years down the drain over one mistake. Fifteen, if you count the years before I got up the nerve to finally ask you out." He chokes on his words as tears start to spill over. "You wouldn't just be giving up on me, but my whole family. The twins don't even know what life is like without you in it. Please, please just talk to me before throwing it all away."

His pleas break through my defenses, and my anger starts to deflate.

"Fine. Answer me honestly, and we will see."

He nods, so I ask *the question*, even though I already know the answer.

"Were you high yesterday?"

"Yes." His head hangs with his solemn answer.

"Was it cocaine?"

"Yes."

"How long?" When he doesn't respond, I ask again, my anger springing back in full force. "How fucking long have you been using, Tanner?"

"I don't know," he mumbles, "a few months? Around the time I started working at the campaign office."

Fuck. That's almost a year.

How the fuck did I not see it. I feel like the rug has been pulled out from under me, but it took the ground with it, and now I'm hurtling down into an endless abyss.

"Why?" I ask, my voice coming across calmer than I feel, too calm for the storm raging in me.

"I don't know. The guys at the office had it one night when we went for drinks after work, and I tried it."

"Was it worth it?" I ask with that same steely calm. Fury whips inside me, begging to be let free, but I don't lash out. I can't even look at him without feeling my stomach roll.

"Not if I lose you," he says, his voice wavering as the tears start to fall in earnest. "Please say I didn't ruin us." He falls to his knees in front of me. "Baby, I'm begging you. I promise I won't touch the stuff again. I will do anything as long as you stay mine."

Looking down at him, I feel nothing but disgust, but he's right about a few things. I would be throwing away way too much if I ended it now. His family, his sisters: they are too important for me to give up on. If he is serious about never using again, I think I can forgive him, in time. I have to. I can't let a few months of mistakes overshadow a decade of good.

"Fine, but if you touch that shit again, it's over."

His arms wrap around my waist, constricting me as he buries his face into my stomach. "Thank you. Thank you. I love you, Ophie. I'm so sorry." Tanner utters the phrases like a mantra as he clings to me. Prickles of unease crawl across my skin, but I don't pull away. Instead, I clutch the crumbled note to my chest like a lifeline as my throat grows thick with tears of my own.

Chapter 19
Morgan

Dear Roomie,

You will not believe what happened in my Econ class yesterday. We were, like, halfway through the lecture when a girl a few rows in front of me spilled her coffee all down the back of the guy in front of her. He was understandably pissed but wasn't listening at all when the girl tried to apologize. He made such a fuss about it, the professor let us go early. So I guess thank you, Mr. Douche Canoe, for getting me out of class early.

Have you ever had anything like that happen?

—J

James hasn't talked about what happened at the beach. Really, she hasn't talked to me at all. Our schedules seem almost cosmically misaligned; it's been almost a week since the incident, and without fail, if one of us is coming, the other is going. If it weren't for the daily notes, I'd think she's been avoiding me. But every morning, something waits for me on the bathroom mirror, either asking me about my day or telling me about hers. Yesterday, the normal orange sticky note was replaced by a piece of notebook paper that she taped to the mirror and filled both sides with the details of her night out with Chelsea and Evelyn. Today, though, the note is short, but it's enough to send my heart into overdrive.

The note joins my collection, and I leave the apartment feeling lighter than I have in days. The walk to class passes in a blur, my head too busy running through tomorrow in my head a million different ways.

Will things be different now?

I don't know what to expect after what went down last weekend, but something has to have shifted. No one walks away from something like that with everything staying exactly the same.

My phone rings, breaking me from my daydreams, and my chest tightens at the name on the screen. With a heavy sigh, I answer the call.

"Hi, Mom." The manufactured cheer in my voice rings hollow.

"Hi, baby." The familiar soft rasp of her voice soothes an ache in my chest that I had learned to ignore. "I've missed hearing your voice. You never call anymore. How are classes? Have you made many friends? Have you met anyone special? Tell me everything, it's been too long."

"I've missed you too." The growing thickness in my throat chokes the words. I try to shrug away the sudden wave of melancholy, focusing on answering her questions instead of how much I wish I could tell her these things in person.

"Classes have been good. Tough, but good. I've made some friends, they also train and have been bugging me to join their gym," I tell her.

"What about a special someone? I'm sure there are lots of nice girls in your program."

My eyes roll, and I fight to suppress a groan. I love my mom, but every phone call turns into an inquisition.

"Sorry to disappoint you, but no, I haven't met anyone special." Technically, that's a lie, but my mom doesn't need to know I'm hung up on an unavailable woman. Sometimes, meeting someone special isn't the issue. It's everything that comes after.

"I swear, every time we talk, it's like I'm on trial," I tease.

"I wouldn't have to ask so many questions if you would call your poor mom sometimes," she jokes back, but the words skewer my heart.

"I know. I'm sorry, Mom. I promise I'll call more," I lie again.

Hearing her voice is too hard. It reminds me of everything I've missed over the past few years. I think she feels the same because she only calls every couple of months now. Maybe she just got tired of me not answering.

"I know you're busy with school," she says, giving us both something to blame when I inevitably never call. "Do you have any plans for your birthday? I hope those friends of yours are throwing you a party. You only turn twenty-five once."

"Yeah, we have plans." The lies keep coming. It's difficult to make plans when I haven't told anyone about my birthday. I'm sure if they knew, they'd drag me out to Cutter's, but that would ruin my plans of locking myself in my room and pretending the day doesn't exist.

"That's good. I wish we could be there for it."

"I know, me too. How's Dad?" Normally, I wouldn't bother to ask, because the answer is always the same, but I'm that desperate to change the subject.

"He's fine, been taking extra shifts at the warehouse, but that's nothing new. He misses you, even if he doesn't say it."

"I miss you both too. I better get going, though, my lecture is about to start."

"All right, call me soon. I love you, Morgan. Stay safe."

"I love you too, Mom."

***

Athens wasn't built for the rain. The city floods, transforming streets into rivers and staircases into waterfalls. Even with a rain jacket, the pools of water soak through my shoes, and the bottoms of my pants get more and more drenched with every step I take toward the apartment.

Thoughts of dry clothes and a hot shower evaporate as I push the door open. For the first time in days, James is at the apartment when I return. She's sprawled out on the couch, lying on her stomach while she works in one of her sketchbooks, and she flashes me a brilliant smile that makes my heart skip a beat. My hands dart to my hair in a fruitless attempt to get the damp curls into a presentable state.

"Hey, stranger," she greets me, pulling her headphones out of her ears.

Grover gets up from his bed and comes to greet me as well, with a toy in his mouth and his tail wagging, and I'm struck with an overwhelming sense of rightness. It's as if a piece of me I didn't know I was missing returns, slotting itself back into the empty space in my heart.

"Hey," I rasp, my voice thick with the unexpected wave of emotions. I clear my throat, pushing the feeling away, and walk over to stand behind her. "What are you working on?"

I glance at the sketchbook, but she slams it closed before I'm able to get more than a short glimpse of the graphite lines on the page.

"Nothing," she says, her face growing pink.

"Nothing? Doesn't seem like nothing," I tease, and her blush deepens.

"It's not done yet," she says, sitting up and clutching the book to her chest.

"Fine," I concede, "but I want to see it when you're ready."

"Okay." She flashes me another small smile and tucks a strand of hair behind her ear. "Did you get my note?"

"Which one," I tease. James narrows her eyes into a mirth-filled glare. Her lips are turned down in a pout, which feels more petulant than forceful. I can't hold back my laughter. She's too cute when she's trying to be intimidating.

"Yes, I got your note this morning." I place my hand on her bare shoulder and give it a gentle squeeze. James stiffens under my touch for a moment before leaning into it, letting out a small hum of satisfaction as she does. My thumb traces a small circle over the curve of her arm, brushing against the yellowing marks Tanner left on her skin. Chills erupt across her sun-kissed skin at the contact. "I didn't expect to see you here tonight, though."

"Grover hates the rain." She turns her whole body toward me and sits on her knees, facing the back of the couch.

My hand falls away, and I wish it could take those bruises with it. Her pupils dilate as she stares up at me, catching her bottom lip between her teeth, and the look shoots straight through me.

I am overwhelmed by the sensation of *James*. Her presence is palpable, an electric aura that magnetizes the air, drawing me to her. I take a step back out of sheer need; otherwise, I'll lose myself to her pull.

"So?" she asks. Her tongue darts out, moistening her lips, and my eyes track its every movement.

"So, what?" My head is hazy, drunk off her.

"My note," she says, but the words are meaningless to my addled mind. "Are we on for tomorrow? I haven't gotten your response yet."

"Oh, tomorrow..." I swallow deeply. "I'd love to if you're still free."

She beams at me, her smiles only adding fuel to the fire raging inside me. "I'm still free," she says and then bites her lip again.

"We could move it to tonight if we're both around," I suggest, and her face falls.

"I actually have a video call date with Tanner tonight..." Her eyes drop to her fingers as she picks at a loose piece of fuzz on the sofa.

All of the building heat is doused in an instant, extinguished by the cold shock of her words. It's a fight to keep the sneer off my face, and I have to bite the inside of my cheek to keep my expression neutral.

We both still bear the bruises from his behavior, yet he's already back in her good graces. It's sickening. My fingers graze the still-healing cut on my lip, and she winces. At least she realizes how this looks. I didn't have illusions that she would dump her boyfriend and come running into my arms—I'm not an idiot—but the James I thought I knew, the one who stared down a complete stranger and let him have a piece of her mind, has too strong of a backbone to go crawling back to the man who keeps hurting her.

"I'm gonna go dry off," I tell her, my voice hollow. I shake my head as I step away from her, still trying to wrap my head around the fact that she forgave him.

"Morgan, wait...let me explain." Her voice shakes, and she gets up from the couch to follow me. I quicken my pace, reaching my door before she can even move around the couch.

"There's nothing to explain," I tell her as I step into my room.

"Please..." Her desperate plea breaks some of my resolve.

"There is nothing you can say that could help me understand this." My words are harsh, but there's no venom behind them. "He *hurt* you. He assaulted me. He's lucky the cops didn't get involved, or he'd be looking at charges for battery and possession. I just thought you would be smarter than—you know what, never mind. I'm not doing this." I raise my hands in surrender and step back into my room. "Have fun on your date." The door slams behind me, echoing through my too-empty room with a resounding *bang*.

I sink to the ground with my back to the door and drag my hand through my hair with a heavy exhale. The unmistakable sound of James's soft cries bleeds through the walls, and my gut twists while my heart aches, but this isn't on me. I didn't tell her anything she didn't already know. My head hits the door as I stare up at the ceiling. I can't sit here and listen to *that* and not try to make things right, but there is nothing I can do, not this time.

With a sigh, I pull out my phone and shoot a quick message off to Nathan asking him to meet me at the gym. My clothes are still dripping, but I don't see any point in changing only to get soaked again, so I grab my gym gear and flee from the apartment without waiting for Nathan's reply.

***

"Again," Nathan commands as he repositions the sparring pads for my strikes.

Sweat drips down my face, stinging as it rolls into my eyes. I wipe it away with the back of my arm and roll my shoulders, squaring up with the pads. We've been working on this combo for the last twenty-five minutes, and I can't get it right.

My fists fly in what should be a familiar pattern, but my timing is off *again*, and Nathan's pad glances off my forehead as I miss the dodge *again*.

"All right, I'm done," I growl as I rip my gloves off and hurl them across the small training room. They slam into the mirror-lined wall and bounce onto the padded floor.

Nathan watches my outburst with a raised eyebrow. He takes off his pads with a deliberate lack of haste and grabs a towel to wipe the sweat off his face. I wish I had thrown my gloves at him instead.

"Are you ready to talk about what's been bothering you?" he asks, dropping to sit on one of the aluminum benches.

"Nothing is bothering me," I grumble. Nathan doesn't justify my obvious lie with a response, merely raising a skeptical eyebrow instead.

With a sigh, I join him on the cold bench and brush my sweat-soaked curls back from my face. Of course he's picked up on my mood. I've been off my game all evening, though I was hoping he'd let me take it out on the punching bags instead of wanting to talk about it. We sit in silence for several minutes before I finally spill what's been eating me up inside.

"James is still with Tanner. After everything that happened over the weekend, she forgave him." I shake my head, still unable to understand it.

"So?" he asks. His voice is serious, and his face is locked in a neutral mask.

"What do you mean 'so'? *So*, James is still with the guy who punched me in the face and left bruises on her. *So*, he could hurt her again. *So*, she's making a huge mistake." My voice rises with each sentence. How can he sit there so unbothered by this? He was there—he saw how that monster acted.

"Morgan, man," Nathan says, clapping a hand on my shoulder. "This is going to sound harsh, but you need to hear it: James and Tanner's relationship is none of your business."

His words hit me like a slap in the face, and I physically recoil. I open my mouth to protest, but he shakes his head, cutting me off.

"I get the frustration, I really do. Tanner is a grade-A douchebag, but that doesn't change the fact that James is a grown woman who can make her own choices."

"But he might hurt her again," I argue.

"Yeah, he might," he agrees with a nonchalant shrug that makes my fists clench. "But he might not. Either way, she has to make this decision for herself. She doesn't want or need you to save her. If you want to be her friend, be her friend, but you can't be her friend if you are going to act like a jealous asshole."

"I'm not jealous, I'm worried. Tanner's dangerous. I can't stand by and watch him hurt her."

"So you are going to alienate her further by acting like an ass? What happens when she actually needs your help, but you've pushed her so far away, she won't ask for it?"

The fight drains out of me in an instant.

He's right.

She doesn't need my judgment, but she will need a friend in her corner when Tanner inevitably screws things up again.

He must sense the shift. "Good. Are you ready to go again?" He claps me on the shoulder and stands back up, reaching for the pads.

The aching in my shoulders says no, but I shake out the tension and grab my discarded gloves off the floor anyway. This time, when I throw the combo, the movement is effortless. Nathan's pad breezes over my head, just a hair's width away from where my face was less than a second ago.

"There he is." A toothy smile fills his face as I finish the drill, and the ghost of my smile grows to mirror his. "Again?" he asks, and I nod.

We fall into an easy flow after that, running through our normal drills before sparring for a few rounds. My muscles are weak as I make my way back to the apartment, but my resolve is stronger than ever. I'm going to be whatever it is James needs, even if it tears me apart inside.

Chapter 20
James

The aroma of bleach permeates the bathroom, stinging my eyes while I scrub down the grout in the shower. I welcome the burn, though; it means the chemicals are working. The world around me is silenced by the chaotic music blaring through my headphones, leaving me to get lost in my own little bubble. I wipe the tile in time to the aggressive beats, and my hips sway to match.

I'm dancing more than I'm cleaning as the song builds to the breakdown, my quest for cleanliness all but forgotten. The beat drops, and I twirl but freeze when I find Morgan watching me from the doorway.

"What the fuck, Morgan. You scared the shit out of me," I snap, jerking my headphones out of my ears.

He doesn't flinch at my tone—hell, the only indication that he's heard me is that his eyes lose a bit of their glassy sheen. I guess maybe he wasn't watching *me* after all.

He looks awful.

There's no trace of the perfectly put-together Morgan Hall in the man standing in front of me. It's the middle of the afternoon, but he looks like he just rolled out of bed the morning after going on a bender. His hair is a wild rat's nest of uncontrolled curls, and the bags under his eyes have bags.

More unsettling than the fatigue on his face is his choice of clothing. I don't think I've ever seen him dressed down—even his pajamas are always a perfectly coordinated set. This impostor in front of me, though, is wearing ratty sweats that are too short, ending in the middle of his calves, and a white T-shirt with a large stain across the front.

He has been...*off* since everything that went down at the beach. We've still hung out and had a couple of pizza nights over the past few weeks, but he hasn't been himself. He's been more withdrawn, barely giving me a reaction when I talk shit to poke his buttons, and he never asks me questions anymore. It's like he's there physically, but his mind is somewhere else. Even then, his behavior has been nothing like *this*.

Something is very wrong.

"Jesus, are you okay?" I climb out of the tub and reach out, needing to hug him.

"I'm fine," he says, rearing back to sidestep my touch. His voice is empty of emotion, and his eyes reflect the same hollowness. "I'm sorry I scared you, but I knocked. I just need to use the restroom, and then I'll be out of your hair."

"Seriously, you look like shit." I move to fully block his path. He has made me talk through my issues more times than I'd like to admit, so there is no way I'm going to let him get away with keeping his own bottled up now that the situation is reversed. "What's wrong?"

He stiffens and narrows his eyes at my blatant disregard. It's the first time I've seen a glimpse of the man I know buried beneath this hollow shell since he walked in here.

"It's nothing. I'm fine," he grits out between clenched teeth. "I just really need to pee."

"Don't lie to me." My hand falls to my hip, and I meet his hardened stare with one of my own. If he thinks he can lie to me, he's got another thing coming. "Tell me what's wrong with you, and the bathroom is all yours, or we can both just stand here. Choice is yours."

"James, I'm not in the mood to play games," he snaps, then looks to the ceiling and takes a deep breath in. "Please just let me use the restroom."

"You have about thirty seconds before I turn the water on. So make this easy on both of us and tell me."

It's childish, I know, but it's the only thing I can think of to convince him to tell me what the fuck is going on.

"James…" he says with a frustrated growl, his whole body growing stiff with his rising frustration.

"Time's up." I whip my hand toward the sink handle to make good on my threat. He catches my wrist before I can turn the knob. Despite the rigid tension in his fingers, his grip is soft against my skin, almost tender.

"Fine, you win." He lets out an exasperated sigh. "It's my birthday. Are you satisfied? Now will you *please* let me pee in peace?"

"It's your birthday?" I stare at him, absolutely dumbfounded. How could he not tell me that? Why is it such a bad thing?

A steely glare is the only response he gives me.

"Okay, okay, I'm leaving," I concede, maneuvering around him toward his bedroom door. "But we aren't done with this conversation."

I pull the door shut behind me as I slip into his room. My focus roams around the space that has mostly remained a mystery to me, and my face falls into a frown.

His room is practically barren. Almost nothing has changed since the first time I stepped foot in here; the boxes have been unpacked since then, leaving the floor clear of clutter, but it doesn't feel like anything actually came out of them. There is nothing here that gives me the impression that this is Morgan's space, no personal touches that make this anything more than a place for him to sleep.

The shower turns on in the next room, and I roll my eyes. Morgan is stalling. He can take as long as he wants, but he isn't getting out of this conversation; I don't care if I have to camp out in here all day.

Why didn't he tell me it was his birthday? And why does it seem like such a bad thing? If I had known, I could have made today better for him.

Fuck it, the day isn't over yet. I still can.

It doesn't take long for the seed of an idea to take root and grow in my head. It's the perfect mix of cheese and camp that I know he will love. Excitement pumps through my veins as I pull out my phone and purchase tickets for later tonight. It's not like he gets a choice in the matter; he is coming with me whether he wants to or not, and he is going to have a good birthday, goddamnit.

Satisfied with my plans, I settle in to wait for him. There isn't anywhere for me to sit, though. The air mattress on the floor is the only real furniture, and that is a loose interpretation of the word. I could sit there, but it feels wrong, like I would be crossing a line by invading one of his most vulnerable and intimate places, so I pace around the small room instead.

The minutes crawl by agonizingly slowly. We might miss our plans if he doesn't hurry the fuck up.

Finally, the door opens.

"So—" I freeze when my gaze lands on the half-naked, soaking-wet Morgan standing in the doorway. The only thing keeping him decent is the old towel precariously wrapped around his hips.

My breath catches at the sight, and my heart speeds up, bouncing around erratically in my chest. He freezes too, his eyes growing wide as he notices me.

A drop of water falls from his hair onto his neck, and I watch it, entranced, as it glides along the hardened angles of his body. It catches on his collarbone, hanging for a moment before rolling onto his chest. I swallow and bite the inside of my lip as it continues to move lower, hugging every defined line of his abs before disappearing into the band of fabric around his hips.

My body feels like it's stuffed full of fireworks, both hot and tingly all at the same time. I knew Morgan was hot, hell I've seen him naked, but he's never affected me quite like this. My mouth waters at the sight of the carved V poking out from the top of the towel.

"Um, James...?" he questions, his face an alarming shade of pink. His voice snaps me out of my lust-addled haze, and I turn my back to him, my own blush rising.

"I...Uh...Sorry..." I trip over my words, trying to find a way to apologize for molesting him with my eyes.

"Just stay there, I'll change real quick," he says, followed by the rustling of him moving around the room. Despite the temptation, I keep my eyes locked on the blank wall.

"Okay, I'm decent."

I turn back around but can't bring myself to meet his eyes. What do you even say in a situation like this? Sorry I saw you naked again? Next time lose the towel? *Get a grip, James.* This is about helping your friend, not your hormones.

"So, yeah. Happy birthday," I tell him, my words sounding as uncentered as I feel. "Do you want to tell me why that has you in such a foul mood?"

He lets out a heavy sigh and flops down onto the air mattress, burying his face deep into the pillow.

"Not particularly," he mumbles into the fabric.

I sit on the edge of the bed beside him, so close I can feel the heat coming off him in waves.

"Hey..." My voice is thick with concern as I place a hand on his back and rub my thumb in small figure eights. The tension in his shoulders eases at my touch, but he still doesn't answer me. "Please tell me what's wrong."

"I hate my birthday," he says with a sigh. "And Thanksgiving, and Christmas, and any other holiday that falls in between. My birthday is the start of the worst forty-three days of the year."

"Why?" I've always loved the holidays; it's hard for me to see how they could be the source of his distress.

"It's complicated."

I let out a small hum but don't push him any further. He will open up if he wants to.

"Do you have plans tonight," I ask, only as a courtesy. Even if he did have other plans tonight, they have been overruled.

"No," he grunts out.

"Good, because you do now," I tell him with exaggerated cheer. "You have forty-five minutes before we need to leave. I would say dress casually, but you're you."

I stand and flee into the hallway before he has a chance to argue. Forty-five minutes isn't much, but it should give me enough time to go to the store to get the rest of what I need for tonight.

***

As I pull into a spot in the parking lot, the car fills with my boyfriend's ringtone. I don't hold back my groan; it feels like I've been hearing that sound nonstop since the blowup at the beach. Tanner has been more attentive in the past three weeks than he had been combined in the three years prior. He calls me anytime he gets a chance, even if it's only for a few minutes, to check in or update me about his day. From what I can tell, he has been true to his word and has stayed sober; time will tell if he keeps that up.

I could let this one go to voicemail—it's not like I didn't talk to him this morning. Ignoring him will only start a fight I don't have the time or energy for, so I answer the phone with a sigh.

"Hey, Tanner." With a tight jaw, I wedge the phone between my cheek and my shoulder and grab a shopping cart.

"Ophie." He says my name like a prayer. "I've missed your voice. What are you up to?"

"Yeah, missed you too." The hollow reply falls from my lips as I walk into the store. "I'm just grocery shopping."

It's close enough to the truth that I don't feel an ounce of guilt for lying. He has apologized more times than I can count for everything that went down that weekend, except for attacking Morgan. It isn't as if he's been claiming that he was in the right, he just hasn't acknowledged it at all.

"So close to the break?" he questions. "Speaking of, I had a thought. I could come pick you up if you want. I may drive up to Athens on Monday, and then we can ride back down together on Tuesday after your classes. It would give us some extra quality time together, and then I can drive you back up next weekend and maybe spend another night at your place."

"I don't think that's the best plan." My face scrunches in disgust at the idea, but I'm able to keep the feeling from leaking into my voice. I've gotten more "quality time" than I needed the past few weeks. We've talked multiple times a day, and he's even asked to start doing video calls at night until we fall asleep. It's just like freshman year when we first became long-distance, only it was romantic then. Now it feels like a hassle and is a bit cringey.

"You would have to take off work, plus that's almost nine hours of extra drive time for you. It isn't practical."

"You're right," he concedes, "I just miss you."

"I know, but it's only three more days."

"I can't wait," Tanner says. "Did you want to do a date night tonight in the meantime?"

"I can't, I have plans with Chelsea tonight and won't be home until late." Another lie easily slips past my lips, leaving no trace of guilt.

"Oh," he says, sounding crestfallen. "Well, I hope you have a good time."

"Mhm," I hum into the phone, only half listening while grabbing what I need from the shelves.

Tanner could talk forever if I let him. He only needs the occasional sound of acknowledgment and he will continue to ramble on, relishing in the sound of his own voice. I stay on the phone and let him prattle on while I finish my shopping. I don't actually hear a thing he says, too focused on my roommate and making sure tonight is perfect for him.

"Hey," I interrupt him, "I'm at the register. I've got to go. Talk to you tomorrow?"

"Yeah, of course. I love you, baby."

"Mhm, love you too."

Chapter 21
Morgan

James drives as though the speed limit is merely a suggestion. My knuckles are white from gripping the overhead handle as we barrel down the highway in her truck.

I'm pretty sure she's trying to kill us.

In one quick jerking motion, she flings us into the next lane without signaling. My stomach flips with unease, and I clench my eyes closed. I'd rather not see this death coming.

Chaotic, heavy music blares from the speakers, so loud that it rattles the windows with its bassy thumping. She dances along with the beat, wiggling around in her seat while she screams out the lyrics, completely oblivious to my discomfort. It would be adorable if I wasn't sure it was going to get us killed.

"Hey, James…" I try to get her attention, but my words meld into the chaos.

With a sigh, I turn the knob to lower the volume. She shoots a glare in my direction, and the car starts to veer into another lane before she jerks the wheel back to center the car.

"What the hell, it was about to hit the breakdown."

"Sorry." I slump back in my seat with a huff. "I just wanted to ask where we are going."

"Be patient, we are only ten minutes out." The annoyed press of her lips loosens into a gentle smile.

"Can you at least give me a hint," I plead.

A mischievous smile plays on her lips as she shakes her head, and she drops one of her hands from the steering wheel onto my thigh. That small touch has my pants tightening.

"Don't you trust me?" Her lithe fingers squeeze my thigh once before she pulls her hand away.

"Y-yes," I stutter, swallowing back the growing moisture in my mouth. "I trust you."

"Good. You are going to love it," she tells me as she maneuvers the car toward the exit ramp.

The conversation lapses, but she doesn't turn the music back up. After a few more turns, we pull into a practically abandoned parking lot.

"You brought us to a mall?" I ask, but she doesn't give me a response as she keeps her face forward. There's no hiding the grin that lights up her face or how her eyes are glowing with excitement, though. That look brings my shriveled heart back to life with an erratic thump. Her smile would have been enough to make my birthday better. The rest of this, though...this has to be a joke. I can't think of any good reason she would bring me here. It's not just any mall—it's one of those malls that is practically empty, even on a Saturday. I half expect to see a tumbleweed roll across the parking lot.

She parks the truck in front of what has to be the largest fishing store I've ever seen. It's built to look like a giant log cabin that's been picked up and glued to the side of the otherwise uniform building.

"Seriously, what are we doing here?"

"You'll see," she says, getting out of the cab.

I shake my head but follow her into the store. She moves with a purpose, clearly having been here before, but I slow my steps, trying to take in what must be the redneck Mecca.

"Come on, we are going to be late." She laces her fingers through mine, dragging me into the heart of the mall, and I have to quicken my pace to keep at her side.

For one brief moment, everything feels right.

James is holding my hand.

The feeling of warmth is frozen solid as the thought chills me to my core.

James most definitely shouldn't be holding my hand, and I most definitely shouldn't be letting her.

I start to pull my hand away, but she comes to a halt.

"Happy birthday, Morgan." Whipping around, she beams up at me with a smile so bright, it rivals the sun. "Wait here. I'm going to go pick up our tickets."

I look around to see where she's brought us. In the middle of the line of storefronts, a large castle gate stands out, and while it's clearly what we're here for, I don't know what *it* is.

"Are you ready?" James asks as she joins me again, now with tickets in hand.

"What is this place?" My voice echoes my inner awestruck wonder as she leads me through the entrance. A woman dressed like she should be at a Renaissance fair takes our tickets and gives us blue paper crowns.

"Medieval Times," James says as though that answers all my questions.

Past the entrance, the building is transformed into a castle courtyard. I have to stop for a moment to take it all in, the child in me overwhelmed and ecstatic. It's hard to believe that just a few seconds ago, I was in a rundown mall.

"Do you like it?" There is a slight quaver in her voice. It's the only indication she's given all day that she might be nervous too.

"I don't actually know what *it* is, but yes." I'm already moving toward a display of swords and other weaponry.

A small laugh tinkles past her lips, but she follows me as I roam around, taking it all in. There's never anything but joy and a smile on her face as she watches me nerd out.

My roaming is interrupted by a man in a squire outfit announcing the start of the show. They usher in the crowd based on the color of their crowns, eventually getting to blue. As we pass through the large doors, my attention is immediately drawn to the enormous throne that sits on a balcony overlooking a sand-filled arena. The rest of the room is divided into a wheel of colors that correspond to our crowns.

The lights dim, the show starts, and I'm enthralled.

I barely register the servers coming to deliver food and drinks to go along with the performance, too focused on the display in front of me. Six knights battle for glory in a tournament of skill. They start with a series of games that display their physical abilities and precision before moving into a joust, which transitions into one-on-one combat. It's as if all of my favorite shows have come to life in front of my eyes. I find myself cheering along with the rest of the crowd, even when our knight is defeated by green's. At least ours wasn't the one who betrayed the queen.

The show comes to an end, and my cheeks ache from how much I've been smiling. James doesn't rush us out the door, letting me scour the gift shop even though we both know I can't afford to purchase anything.

She watches me with an expression I can't quite place, her emerald eyes shining and her lips curving into a smirk as I look at the swords and dragon statues in the glass cases. Her smile grows when I catch her gaze, causing my heart to flip over in my chest. Mine matches, a toothy grin I couldn't restrain if I wanted to.

Together, we walk back through the desolate mall toward her truck. The sky is dark, the sun having slipped past the horizon while we were inside. James doesn't turn her music back on as we start the drive back toward Athens, leaving us to sit in a peaceful silence.

I stare out the window, watching the world blur by with a full feeling in my chest. Today was something I never could have hoped for. Through sheer force of will, James managed to make today okay—no, she made today great.

We pass the exit for Athens, and I sit up a little straighter in my seat.

"Where are we going?"

"You didn't really think that's all I had planned, did you?" she says with a smirk.

"I don't need anything else. Today was perfect. I have no idea how you managed to organize that on such short notice."

"You might not need anything else, but you are going to get it." The corner of her lip twitches upward, but she doesn't give me any more details.

With a resigned sigh, I settle back into my seat and pay more attention to where we are going. The truck bounces as we turn down a long gravel road and stop next to a large field. She jumps down from the cab and then roots around in the back seat, looking for something.

"Are you coming?" she asks, grabbing whatever it is she was looking for and taking it to the bed of the truck.

I unbuckle my seat belt and scramble to get out of the cab to follow her. Crisp fall air bites at my nose and cheeks. I definitely didn't dress to be out in this weather.

She doesn't look my way as I approach, too busy arranging a pile of blankets into a nest in the bed. She gives a satisfied huff and nestles into the pile, wrapping herself in them to fight the cold. I stand there, frozen and unsure. This feels like a bad idea, like a repetition of past mistakes, only this time, we don't have the excuse of alcohol to blame. She must feel my hesitation because she sits up with a raised eyebrow and pats the space next to her, inviting me in. I hesitate for another second but climb into the truck and lie down, leaving as much room as possible between the two of us.

"Did you enjoy the show?"

"It was great. How did you know I would like it?"

She lets out a full-bellied laugh, shaking her head as if my question is the most ridiculous thing she's ever heard.

"Morgan, I think one of the first things you ever told me about yourself was how much you love this stuff. Literally every show we watch together has to do with knights and damsels in distress. It's pretty obvious. This summer, I'll take you to the Renaissance Festival. You will love it too."

My stomach gives a small twist at her words; she's still planning on seeing me this summer. Even after this whole roommate thing ends, she wants me around. The chill of the night vanishes from the warmth that builds in my chest.

"You're right, that was a dumb question." I run my hand through my hair as my cheeks warm. "So, what's the plan now? Where are we?"

"This is Habersham Farms. Grandma Anne is friends with the owner, and he lets me come by whenever I want, as long as I give him a little heads-up. It's one of the darkest places in the Athens area, and there's almost no light pollution here. I thought stargazing could be fun, although if you hate it, we can leave." She bites her lip and looks down at her hand when she finishes rambling.

"This is amazing. Thank you, James, for everything." I lie back with my arms behind my head and watch the sky. James was right—the stars out here are stunning. I've never seen so many dotting the sky.

"Can I ask you a question?" she asks in a small, hesitant voice.

"Sure," I tell her with a sigh. I have a feeling I know where this is going.

"Why do you hate your birthday?" Her voice is barely above a whisper.

I let the silence hang between us for a moment before answering just as quietly. "Because it's lonely."

"Why?" She turns on her side to look at me fully, propping her head up on her arm.

My focus stays locked on the sky. This isn't going to be an easy conversation, and I don't think I'll be able to get through it if I can see my pain reflected in her eyes. I want to tell her, though, and that shocks me. For the first time, I want someone to know everything about me, good and bad, and I want to know the same about her.

"I didn't always hate my birthday or the holidays," I start with a heavy sigh. "Growing up, we never had a lot, but my mom and dad always went out of their way to make everything feel magical.

"For birthdays, Mom would always bake us a homemade cake—lemon for me and chocolate for Laura. Dad would leave work early and bring us a box wrapped in newspaper. We knew what was in the box—it was the same every year—but that didn't stop the excitement. We always got a new book and either a puzzle or board game, and after dinner, we would open the new game and play together from dinner to bedtime."

A wistful smile forms on my lips at the memories.

"Christmas mornings, our stockings were always full of candy, and the presents seemed to overflow from under the tree. Looking back, it was only four or five packages each, but to us, it was a lot. They were all addressed 'from Santa,' even after we were way too old to still believe in him. The gifts were almost always clothes or other necessities, but that didn't make us appreciate them any less.

"New Year's was always my favorite, though. Mom, Laura, and I would spend the days leading up to it making decorations out of newspaper and glitter. We would order pizza and play games while we waited to watch the ball drop on TV, and when it did, Dad would tell us to make a wish, not a resolution.

"But things changed after Laura died." My voice cracks as my throat constricts.

"Oh, Morgan," James gasps. She reaches over and places a hand on my chest. "We don't have to talk about this. I'm sorry I brought it up."

"No, don't be sorry." I cover it with mine and start to move my thumb in small circles on the back of her hand. "I want you to know these things about me, even if they hurt to talk about."

"Okay," she whispers.

"After she died, I tried to hang on to the joy, but nothing was the same. Dad stopped coming home early, and he never brought another newspaper-wrapped package. Mom still made me a cake every year, but I only wanted chocolate after that. Dad started taking more overtime, especially around the holidays, so Mom and I would work old puzzles together, just the two of us.

"Mom tried to keep the Christmas spirit alive, but everything was always tainted with sadness. The first Christmas after she died, Mom had already bought her gifts, so they sat there unopened all day. As morbid as it sounds, it became a tradition. Laura's stocking was always full, and Mom and I bought her a new gift each. Dad said we were acting ridiculous, but I think he appreciated her being there with us in spirit. New Year's Eve is the one that died when she did. Mom and I didn't see the point without Laura there pushing us to make bigger and better decorations.

"I didn't truly start hating the holidays until college. I got a scholarship to a school across the country, and I didn't have any other options financially. I made some friends there, and when my nineteenth birthday rolled around, they wanted to take me out to celebrate, but I was miserable the whole time I was supposed to be having fun. All I wanted was to be back in Michigan, eating a chocolate cake and doing a puzzle I had already solved more times than I could probably count.

"When the break for Thanksgiving rolled around, I couldn't afford to fly back. My roommates all went home, and I was truly alone for the first time in my life. The same thing happened for Christmas break that year, and the cycle continued. I went home over the summer that first year, but I started taking summer courses after that.

"After undergrad, I joined the Peace Corps. It was totally my decision, and I don't regret it at all, but this is now my seventh birthday in a row that I've spent alone, and this will be my seventh Thanksgiving, my seventh Christmas, and my seventh New Year that I'll spend isolated from the ones I love."

My vision swims as my tears gather, turning the sky into a swirling sea of starlight. Steeling myself against her pity, I finally turn to look at the woman who has me wrapped around her fingers. Tears pour down her face in unrestrained rivers, but there isn't any pity in her eyes—sadness, yes, but without any of the underlying judgment.

Without any warning, she sits up and crawls out of the back of the truck. I sit up to watch as she digs through the back of the cab again, then returns with a small foam cooler.

"I wasn't sure what you would like, so I got a few different options," she chokes out around a suppressed sob. She pulls out several plastic containers with single slices of cake in varying flavors.

"It's probably nowhere near as good as your mom's..." She trails off, placing the chocolate slice in my hand, and the dam holding my tears back breaks.

James pulls me into an embrace, tucking my head into her neck as my tears flow. She runs her fingers through my hair while I let the tidal wave of emotions rip through me. After what feels like a lifetime, my tears slow, and the weight lifts from me, leaving me feeling freer than I have in a long time.

I pull away from the comfort of her arms, wiping away the remnants of my grief with the back of my hand.

"When did you have time to plan all of this?" I ask her, grabbing the box of cake.

"Well," she says, lying back down to watch the stars, "I booked the tickets while you were in the shower, and then I ran to the store in those forty-five minutes you had to get ready."

"Why?"

"Because no one deserves to be alone on their birthday."

Her words stun me into silence, but they leave my heart feeling full in my chest.

I finish my slice, lie down beside her, mirroring her position, and embrace the peace that she brings me. My body relaxes, completely at ease.

"I'm cold," she mutters, shifting closer to me.

Every inch of my body tenses as she drops her head onto my chest, all my tranquility shattered by her motion. I wouldn't be surprised if she could hear my heartbeat pounding at her touch.

This is a bad idea. A really, really bad idea.

But I ignore all rational thought and wrap her in my arms, pulling her closer to me.

"Thank you," I whisper into her hair, and despite all better judgment, I place a soft kiss on the crown of her head.

She burrows even deeper into me, and we lie there for hours. No shooting stars cross the darkened sky, but I make a wish anyway. It's the most selfish one I could possibly make. I wish that James Clarke would somehow be mine, because I am so in love with this girl, and I think it's going to destroy me.

Chapter 22
James

"R eceive from thy bounty, through Christ our Lord. Amen."

A chorus of "amen" echoes from around the table as Mr. Nicholson finishes blessing the food and everyone starts to dig in. The spread is immaculate, like something straight out of a magazine. Tanner's mom would vehemently deny it if asked, but she's outsourced the meal every year since his dad was elected commissioner.

The low hum of conversation picks up around the scraping of silverware against China. I push the food around on my plate, barely eating it. Like every year, the food is delicious, but I have no appetite today. How could I when I know Morgan is completely alone back home? Well, not completely alone. I left Grover with him to keep him company. I told him that Grover hates long trips and made it seem like he was doing me a favor, but in reality, I couldn't stand the thought of leaving my roommate alone.

The twins, who I'm sandwiched between, don't share any of my reservations. Their plates are piled high with more mashed potatoes and rolls than they can possibly eat in one sitting. They chatter back and forth to each other with childish exuberance. The rest of the table is locked in a discussion about Mr. Nicholson's campaign, which is about as interesting as watching paint dry.

An errant foot brushes up against mine, but I ignore it; between the Nicholsons and the Harrises, the ten-seat table is stuffed to its maximum capacity, and legroom is scarce. The second brush, though, catches my attention. The invading touch moves up my calf in a slow caress, and I fight to hold back a grimace. Across the table, Tanner gives me one of his rare carefree smiles, one that is a little too gummy and squeezes his eyes into wrinkled lines. It's the smile that normally makes my insides melt, but I feel nothing, not even a tiny spark of heat.

I force myself to smile, contorting my face into a hollow reflection of his shining adoration. It's nothing more than an echo of what used to be—an artificial replica of former feelings.

The room starts to spin around me as I'm blindsided by a moment of perfect clarity.

I'm not in love with Tanner anymore, and I don't think I have been for a while.

The drug use, his outburst at the fundraiser, the violence he displayed at the beach: those are only the vibrant blooms that grow among the tangled hedges, drawing attention to what's gone wrong. The roots of it all go much deeper. My resentment is anchored in the soil in a gnarled, twisted mass that can't be removed without killing the plant.

I drop my gaze to the table, unable to bear the weight of his stare. My heart shatters, splitting into a million tiny shards that rip me to shreds. I can't breathe, not with my lungs in ribbons.

"May I be excused?" I don't wait for a response as I push away from the table.

Tanner tilts his head as a crease forms between his brows, and that carefree smile slips from his face. He starts to get up to follow me, but I stop him with a shake of my head.

Restroom, I mouth with my best attempt at a reassuring smile.

His lips curl down into a frown, but he lets me leave and settles back in his chair to resume his conversation with Owen.

My chin is held high and my breaths are shallow but controlled bursts as I flee, but the second I'm out of sight, I collapse in on myself as a sob racks through my body. The path to Tanner's bedroom is familiar, and my tears fall in earnest as I cross the threshold into the place that holds so many memories. I don't know why I thought coming here would be a good idea. It's an unsullied artifact from better days, a time capsule holding the mementos from when things were good and we were happy. So much happened in this room over the years, so many firsts took place here. It's only fitting that my heart breaks for the first time here too.

Sinking to the floor, I'm overwhelmed by the barrage of emotions. My aching heart beats with such force, I think it's going to burst. I can't catch my breath around each choking sob, and my vision starts to swim.

I need Morgan.

My phone is like a lead weight in my palm. It would be so easy to call him; with the push of one button, I could have the comfort of his voice in my ear. I know without a shadow of a doubt that if I called, he would answer, and that he would talk me through this without any complaints, but that isn't fair to him. This holiday is already hard for him. What kind of person would I be to add to his troubles?

A shitty one—one who isn't worthy of the unconditional support he's shown me time and time again.

So I don't call him, no matter how much my heart begs me to, focusing instead on the times he's helped me through this before. I hear his voice in my head setting the rhythm for my breaths, feel the ghost of his touch grounding me, and search for that sense of serenity that I find when I'm in his arms.

The well of tears runs dry and my heart rate slows along with my breathing. The pain in my chest is still present, but it's a duller ache, eclipsed by growing guilt.

I'm going to have to break Tanner's heart. There's no way to avoid it.

The idea of hurting him is worse than my own heartbreak. Despite his flaws and how things have been between us lately, I've loved him for half of my life—I still do, but not in the way that matters, not anymore.

Dragging this out any longer than I have to would be cruel to both of us. I just have no idea how I'm actually going to do it. There is no way I can break up with him today—not on a holiday, not with his whole family around.

Stifling my sniffles, I pull myself off the floor and try to clean myself up. My face is a swollen, splotchy mess, but I do what I can to hide the evidence of my breakdown and head back into the hallway.

Boisterous chatter floats up over the banister from below, bringing with it a festive aura that clashes against my looming melancholy. From the sound of things, the gathering has migrated from the dining area to the living room, transitioning from dinner to the traditional post-feast drinks.

A flash of movement catches my eye from across the hall. I adjust my course, tiptoeing toward the twins' bedroom. No one else should be up here. Mrs. Nicholson would tan the hides of any of her children if they disrespected their guests by sneaking off on their own. Heaven knows that, growing up, Tanner and I were on the receiving end of her punishment more than I care to remember. She must be going soft, though, because Raelyn is sitting on the floor, playing with her dolls without a care in the world.

I tap my knuckle against the open door to catch her attention. "What are you doing up here, Rae?"

She looks at me from under wet lashes with wide, red-rimmed eyes, and the ghost of a smile pulls at her lips before fading back into a sullen frown. My heart lurches.

"Playing," she mumbles as her face drops back to the ground.

"Alone?" The floor creaks as I move to sit with her. "Where's Kinsley?"

"She said dolls were for babies and that she wanted to stay with the big kids, like Jacqueline." Her nose turns up into a sneer as she says the name, and I'm inclined to agree with the sentiment.

"Dolls aren't for babies," I tell her, reaching out to grab a doll of my own. "Can I play with you?"

Her eyes light up as she nods with enthusiastic vigor. I let her lead as she walks me through the complex, overly dramatic storyline she's come up with for her toys. The dejected kid I found disappears, and in her place is the joyful, creative one I love so much. I wish she could stay like this forever, ignorant of the heartbreak and pain in the world, but that's not life. All I can hope for is that after things end with Tanner, I'll still be able to be there for the girls as they grow up.

"So this is where you both snuck off to," Tanner says with an amused chuckle from the doorway.

Speak of the devil and all that.

She abandons her toys and jumps up with an excited shout of "Tanner" when she notices him leaning against the doorframe, watching us with a reverent smile. He places a glass tumbler of amber liquid on the dresser and meets his sister halfway, scooping her into his arms and swinging her around in circles while she squeals in delight. He sets her back on the ground and kneels down to her level, tucking a loose strand of hair back into place behind her ear.

"What are you doing up here, Raels? Mom has been looking for you," he says in a soft tone.

"I was playing with Ophie," she says, dropping her eyes to her feet and twisting her hands together.

"Hey, head up, kiddo." He places a gentle finger under her chin and guides her eyes back up to meet his, then gives her a reaffirming smile when she does. "Did you have fun? I know you haven't seen her in a while."

"It was lots of fun." Her voice rises with enthusiasm. "There were dragons and spies and a princess."

"Did the spies slay the dragon?" he asks, giving his full attention to her rambling.

"No, the princess and the dragon were friends."

"Of course, that makes much more sense," he says, nodding seriously. "I hate to break up the fun, but you should run along before Mom finds you up here."

She lets out an annoyed huff but listens to her brother and runs out of the room. Tanner shakes his head, but there's nothing but affection on his face. He stands back up to his full height and walks over to where I'm still sprawled on the floor.

"Spies?" he asks, extending a hand to help me off the ground.

"Honestly, that's news to me. I thought we were playing pop stars." I take his outstretched hand, and he lifts me to stand in front of him, my chest mere inches from his. It's too close, too personal. Fresh nausea churns in my gut; I don't want him touching me. I try to pull away but stumble over the dolls littering the ground. Tanner wraps a hand around my waist to steady me, and he stares at me with an intensity that makes my skin crawl.

"You disappeared earlier," he says, his voice barely above a whisper.

"Sorry, I wasn't feeling well." I take a step back, and Tanner drops his hand, letting me retreat. His face flashes with a look of pain, but it's only there for a brief moment before it reverts back to the same mask of intensity. My arms fold in front of my chest, acting as a barrier between myself and his energy.

"Are you okay? I knew I should have followed you." He squeezes the back of his neck while he rambles.

"I'm fine. It was just a headache. I went to lie down in your room, and it's mostly gone now." Guilt claws at my heart, but what's one more lie added to the pile.

"If you say so," he says, but he doesn't sound convinced.

Letting out a heavy exhale, he goes to grab his glass, taking a large drink of the liquid inside. My face pinches with a grimace. *Of course he's drinking.*

When he sees my expression, his face falls and his shoulders slump. "Fuck, O, it's not what it looks like." He starts to bring the glass over to me, but I stop him.

"I never said you had to stop drinking. That was never the issue." The disdain in my voice says otherwise.

"Taste it, please," he pleads, holding the glass out to me. With a resigned sigh, I grab the tumbler and take a sip, bracing for the burn of whiskey, but that's not what washes over my tongue. I almost choke on the unexpected sweetness that overwhelms my taste buds. Tanner's face relaxes when it's clear I've made the connection.

"It's apple juice. I-I've been sober for almost a month." He turns his attention to the floor, unable to meet my gaze with the confession. "I meant what I said at the beach. I'm never touching any of that shit again. Not when it almost cost me you. I've been going to meetings and everything."

"Oh." That's all I can say when my heart is breaking all over again. How can I break his when he's trying so hard to make things right? What if that ruins this for him? What if he relapses because I decide to be a bitch and leave him while he's struggling?

I can't do it. Not now, not when it's the holidays, not when his sobriety is still so new.

"M-my parents don't know." He rubs the back of his neck again. The nervous tick so unlike the man I know, I don't even know how to react.

"Thank you for telling me. I'm proud of you." I really fucking am. I just wish everything didn't have to fall apart first for him to take this step.

"Thanks, Ophie." His cheeks pinken. "I love you so much. I'm sorry things got as bad as they did before I got my head out of my ass." He sighs and his shoulders relax, as if getting that off his chest lifted a physical weight off him. "Do you want to come back to my place tonight? It's been too long since we've gotten to spend time together, just you and me. I know I fucked it up last time, and I won't make that mistake again."

"I...uh...I'm..." I hesitate, stumbling over my words.

It's only another month. What's a few more days to make sure he's in a stable place before I fuck up his whole world. I take a deep breath and let it out as a heavy sigh.

"All right, sure, that sounds great."

Chapter 23
Morgan

Athens is a ghost town when classes aren't in session. During the semester, these streets are flooded with students, but I only see a handful of people as I walk Grover around the barren campus. It's unsettling, and for the first time since I moved here, I feel truly alone.

All of my friends traveled back to their hometowns for the holidays—even Gage took advantage of the slow season to visit his mom in Boston. I had plans to spend the week getting ahead on classwork, binge-watching TV, and not stepping foot outside of the apartment, but James ruined those plans when she asked if she could leave her dog behind with me. She insisted that I was doing *her* a favor by watching him, but I know she left him behind so I wouldn't be alone. It's the same way I know the untouched pan of "leftover" lasagna was her way of making sure I had something special to eat for Thanksgiving yesterday. With each thoughtful gesture, I fall a little bit harder for her.

I pass by Sanford Stadium as I lead us back toward the apartment, then do a double take as I catch sight of a familiar face walking in my direction. Evelyn scurries down the sidewalk bundled up in a thick jacket and hat with her arms wrapped around herself. As she gets closer, she notices me standing there, frozen like an idiot on the street corner, and she freezes as well. Her eyes grow comically large for a moment before a wide smile forms on her frost-reddened face.

"Hi, Morgan," she says as she walks over to join me, then crouches to greet Grover as well.

"Hey. What are you still doing in town?"

James didn't mention that any of her friends would be here over the break.

"I could ask you the same thing," she says with a pointed look.

"As much as I'd love to go home, it just wasn't feasible this year," I tell her, leaving out the rest. She nods with a look of gentle understanding.

"Athens is home for me now. There's nowhere else I'd rather be," she says before peering at our feet. Her tone makes it easy enough to read between the lines—there isn't anywhere else for her to go.

"So where are you running off to?" I try to direct the conversation away from home lives. I don't think it's something either one of us wants to delve into.

"I'm heading to my car, but my parking spot is all the way on the east side of campus, and the buses aren't running today. I don't normally mind the walk, but today had to be the day the temperature decided to drop." She hugs herself tightly, tucking her hand into her armpits as she shivers. It isn't *that* cold—at least compared to what I grew up in—but she is layered up like she's about to traverse the Arctic.

"Where are you headed? I've got nothing else to do today, and my car is way closer. I can give you a ride."

"I can't ask you to chauffeur me around," she protests, "I've got a perfectly capable car."

"I promise you, you would be doing me a favor. It's been a lonely couple of days, and I'm glad to see a friendly face."

She studies me with narrowed eyes for several seconds, and then her face relaxes into a warm smile.

"All right, it's too cold for me to argue. I'm on my way to the Labre Mission, a homeless shelter I volunteer with." She turns and starts to walk up the hill toward the apartment, and I fall into step beside her. "You know, if you are really that lonely, you could volunteer with me. Jamie told me you spent some time with the Peace Corps. I think this would be right up your alley."

The knowledge that James talks to her friends about me makes my stomach flutter. She doesn't tell me much about her friends, though. Nathan talks about his girlfriend all the time, but the quiet brunette is still mostly a mystery. She had mentioned her volunteer work before, but I filed that information away and forgot about it. My mind is too occupied with thoughts of my roommate to give attention to anything else.

"I'd love to," I tell her, and she does a double take as she trips over her feet.

"You would?" she asks, her voice incredulous.

"Of course. I'm not doing anything else today." And I've been slacking off when it comes to donating my time. Between classes, studying, and making time to work out, I only have a precious few hours to spare in the week, and I've been selfish with them, using them to drink with my friends or waste the night away with James.

She beams at me and walks with a newfound bounce in her step as we near the apartment.

"Let me take Grover inside, and then we can get going," I tell her.

She follows me inside but waits for me in the lobby. I hustle up the stairs, taking them two at a time, and spend less than ten seconds inside the apartment. I only stop long enough to unhook Grover from the leash before I make my way back down.

"Where to?" she asks as I exit the stairwell.

"My car is only a block up the street. Let's hurry so you don't freeze."

We make it to the car, and she lets out a small yelp as cold air blows from the vents.

"Sorry, the car is old. It will warm up in a bit. You're going to have to navigate," I tell her, "this piece of junk doesn't have Bluetooth, either. I do have several CDs, though, if you want to listen to something other than the radio." I motion to the book of discs I've collected over the years.

"Radio is fine," she tells me.

We lapse into an awkward silence that hangs in the air as the music plays softly in the background. My companion's attention is fixed on her jacket as she picks at the pilling wool and rolls the bits of lint into tiny balls between her fingers. The discomfort of it all makes me miss James more than I have all week.

"So," she says, breaking through the tension, "how are things with Jamie?"

The question catches me so off guard, I nearly choke on my own saliva.

"Things are..." I trail off, unsure how to answer. "I'm sure you heard that she forgave Tanner." I have to hold back a scowl as the bitter words coat my tongue.

"I did," she says, and her face falls into a deep frown. "I was hoping she would be smarter than that."

"Yeah, so was I," I bite out.

"I'm sorry. I know you liked her. If it makes you feel any better, I was hoping she would choose you." She reaches over and puts her hand on my arm.

"I don't care about that," I tell her, ignoring the unwanted feeling of her touch.

It's mostly true. I'm not delusional—I know James wasn't going to drop her long-term relationship for the man she just met a few months ago. That was never even a thought that crossed my mind. I simply don't want her to get hurt any more than she already has.

"I'm worried about her," I clarify. "You didn't see how he was acting that night. He was unhinged and hungry for violence. I saw the bruises he left on her, and I felt the ones he left on me. James was terrified." The memories blur as I shake my head, trying to clear away the growing cloud of anger.

"I shouldn't have brought it up, I'm sorry." She pulls her hand away and averts her eyes toward the road.

"Has he always treated her like that?" I can't hold back the question that's been eating me alive since that night. Has she been putting up with Tanner's mistreatment this whole time? The thought makes my stomach churn and bile rise.

"No," she says in a small voice. "He's always been a little oblivious, but he always treated Jamie well enough. Things changed after he graduated last

December. I'm not sure what triggered the change, but he started acting more erratically, and James started to withdraw."

I can make a pretty confident guess on what drove the change, but that's not on me to explain.

"Thank you for telling me that," I tell her with a grimace. It's easier to see why she would stay with him if the behavior is new.

Evelyn hums in acknowledgment, but she doesn't look in my direction. She keeps her attention locked on the road ahead.

"Take a left at this stop sign, and it's the second building on the right," she says abruptly. Her voice lacks any of the emotion it held before.

I nod and follow her instructions, parking in the crumbling lot in front of an even more decrepit brick building.

"Are you okay?" I ask her before we exit the car.

She blinks and shakes her head before she looks at me again. "Yeah, I'm great," she says, her smile returning. "Are you ready to go?"

"Yeah, let's go," I tell her, choosing to ignore her odd behavior despite my instincts.

Evelyn climbs out of the car, and I follow her inside. She introduces me to the Mission's leader, Sister Margaret, who, using a no-nonsense tone, instructs us to "go be useful in the kitchen." We spend the afternoon prepping produce for a stew and cleaning up a growing pile of dishes. I'm surprised to find myself having fun. Evelyn isn't the most talkative, but we fall into a comfortable rhythm with each other. Even more surprisingly, my unrequited feelings barely cross my mind while we work.

"That wasn't too bad, was it?" she asks as we leave hours later.

"No, that was actually pretty great," I tell her.

"Great enough that you'd want to come with me again tomorrow?"

"I would love to, Evelyn."

Chapter 24
James

Dear Roomie,

I think this last painting might be your best work yet. I have no idea how you do it, James. You somehow manage to put a tiny piece of you into everything you make. It's magical.

-M

Everything aches—my knees, my arms, my back. Hell, even my head as the scent of bleach burns my nostrils. But I don't let that stop me as I continue to scrub the linoleum floors, moving in time to the music blasting through the apartment. Morgan *should* be doing the same in the bathroom. I should probably go check on him, just to be safe. We need this place spotless.

With the floors finished, I move to clean the stovetop and catch a glimpse of the time. *Shit.* People should be showing up in half an hour. While I was driving back from Grandma Anne's I had the realization that while I couldn't help him go home for the holidays, I could make sure he got to celebrate them with people who loved him, even if the timing was a little off. I just didn't realize how much work would need to go into getting the apartment ready to host what Nathan has dubbed "Friendsgivmas." Morgan insists the place is fine but didn't put up much of a fight when I sent him to deep clean the bathroom this morning.

The sound of bare feet padding across the floor catches my attention, and I pause mid-wipe to turn toward the hallway.

"Morgan Hall, don't you dare step on these floors that I just cleaned. They're still wet," I chastise. He freezes with a sheepish look on his face, his foot hovering centimeters over the glossy floor.

"How am I supposed to cook if I can't come into the kitchen?" he asks with a small smile and places his foot back down on the hallway carpet. It's a good question, and he might have had a point if I didn't literally just finish mopping.

"Wait until they are dry, and then you can come in."

He rolls his eyes but doesn't move from his spot as I make my way out of the kitchen, climbing over the counters to avoid the wet patches.

"I'm going to get ready and grade your work." I shoot a quick wink in his direction as I pass. Despite my playful tone, I dip my head into the bathroom to see if I'll need to do another pass. He did a pretty decent job, but I still do another quick wipe down of the sink and toilet to be safe.

I throw on a nicer outfit and add a quick coat of mascara to my lashes before a sweet, spicy aroma floats down the hallway, drawing me back to the living room. The sight of him cooking on my freshly cleaned stove sets my spine on edge. I knew he would need to use it, but I hate seeing my work be ruined so soon.

A knock on the door saves me from the festering panic, and I open it to find Chelsea and Nathan, who's holding a large aluminum pan wrapped in a layer of foil.

"Is that the bird?" Morgan calls out from behind me. He washes his hands before stepping out of the kitchen to greet our first guests, placing a hand on my shoulder as he stands behind me in the doorway, crowding my space. It takes every ounce of my willpower not to lean further into his touch.

It's so domestic—the cooking and the cleaning and greeting our guests together at the door—but everything about it feels so right, and that scares me. I can see it in my head, a future where this is the norm. Morgan is a lawyer, and I've found a job that I love—something that bridges the gap between my art and what makes sense financially—and we host parties like this for our friends all year round. We stand in the doorway together, just like we are now, but he pulls me into his side, holding me close while we greet our guests, dropping quick kisses to the top of my head whenever he thinks they aren't looking. At the end of the night, we will say our goodbyes together, and once the door closes, he pushes me up against the door and—

I shake my head to clear away the thoughts. It's not a path I can go down, at least not yet. After winter break, I can entertain these feelings, once I've broken things off with Tanner. I definitely feel *something* for my roommate, but I haven't let myself explore those feelings. Now that things with Tanner are as good as done, I can't ignore my growing attraction or how right being with Morgan feels. We haven't crossed a line, not really. I've toed it—have stood right against the edge—but I haven't crossed it. I want to, though; the desire is an ache deep within my chest that has only grown stronger as time goes on.

A gentle squeeze on my shoulder pulls me out of my head, and the subject of my fantasies guides me away to let our guests through. Over the next twenty minutes, our small apartment fills with both friends and food. We fall into a natural rhythm, wordlessly communicating as one of us answers the door while the other stays behind to entertain our guests.

When the oven timer dings, I retrieve the pies while Morgan chats with Gage and Karis. The mouthwatering smell hits me full force as I open the door; the trio of pies inside are golden brown and crisped to perfection. This skill was a surprise. What other secret talents has he not shared? If I have my way, I'll get to uncover them piece by piece.

The pies nearly slip through my fingertips as I turn and see the picturesque scene that awaits me in the living room: Morgan and Evelyn sitting side by side on the couch, heads bent together as they talk. Dread tightens around my throat. Since when have they been close?

Every interaction I've seen them have replays in my head, and none of them have ever been like this. Morgan was always polite but never showed any signs of being interested in her—not the way she did him.

My friend says something that causes Morgan to throw his head back with laughter, and my teeth clench. I'm so fucking stupid. He was never into me; this fantasy I've built in my head is nothing more than one-sided infatuation.

"Turkey's carved, let's eat," Nathan calls out from the spot he's claimed in the kitchen.

Everyone gets up and, somehow, in the chaotic flurry of movement, manages to make their plates and find seats between the island counter and cramped table.

Throughout dinner, the seeds of my jealousy grow into an ugly, writhing mass in my chest. I seethe in my seat as I watch Morgan from where he is squished between Evelyn and Gage at the counter. He leans in close to look at something on her phone, and my eyes narrow. Did I do this? Did I put this into motion before I realized how much he would mean to me?

Fuck.

I should be happy for them. Evelyn deserves someone who will treat her right, and he will. That doesn't change that seeing them together makes me murderous.

The rigid toe of Chelsea's high heel stabs into my shin, and I let out a soft grunt of pain that snaps Morgan's head in my direction. I'm surprised he was able to hear the small sound over everything else, but I wave him off with a reassuring smile, and he goes back to his conversation.

"What the fuck was that?" I hiss at Chelsea once his attention is no longer on me.

"Why the fuck are you staring at Evelyn like you want to drown her in the gravy?"

"Am not," I huff, and she rolls her eyes.

"Girl, if you glared any harder, she might catch fire where she sits," Karis pipes in.

"Fine, I was. So what?" I cross my arms and sit up straighter in my chair.

"*So*, what the fuck happened? Because you weren't acting like this earlier, and I know Evelyn didn't do shit to you." Chelsea sits up as well, meeting my defiant posture head-on.

"She's jealous, boss," Nathan says as casually as he would talk about the weather, not bothering to pull his attention away from the tower of food in front of him. Chelsea's eyes widen and her jaw falls slack.

"I'm not jealous," I argue, but my protest sounds weak even to my own ears.

"You are so jealous, it's not even funny," Karis says, and then turns to Chelsea. "The two of them have been circling each other all semester. You've just been too dick blind to see it."

"Wait...what?" Her mouth gapes open and closed as she stumbles over her words. "How am I just now finding out about this?"

"It's true." Nathan wraps his arm around her and pulls her in, kissing her on the cheek. "Morgan's had it bad for James for months, and your girl here has been stringing him along the whole way." He narrows his eyes with his cutting words, and my cheeks grow hot.

"But what about Tanner? Are you finally leaving that waste of space?"

"There is nothing going on between me and Morgan"—*yet*—"and Tanner is an issue I'd rather not get into right now. Can we talk about this later?" I give her a pleading look, and after a moment, she sighs and relaxes her shoulders.

"Fine, but we are talking about this."

I nod in agreement, and she drops it.

"Don't worry about those two, Goldilocks," Karis says, clapping me on the shoulder. "Morgan's only got eyes for you."

"Well, I'm stuffed," Nathan says, loud enough for the whole room to hear. "Is it time for Christmas?"

Gage grumbles something I think is supposed to be a sign of agreement, and that seems to be the cue everyone was waiting for. Morgan and our friends get up and clear away their messes. I don't get up, though. Instead, I take the moment to watch my friends as they live out their chaotic moments of merriment. Chelsea chastises Nathan with a playful smirk, and he swoops her up into his arms, peppering her neck with kisses as he spins them both around. On the couch, Gage and Karis are locked in a quiet but intense conversation. Karis throws her hands around as she talks, nearly knocking Gage across the face. He manages to duck out of the way, and a hint of his rare smile pulls at the corner of his lips. Even Grover has found his person with Evelyn. He is blissed out while she showers him with affection from her spot on the floor. The apartment feels more like home now than it ever has before. The only thing missing is Morgan.

The back of my neck tingles with awareness half a second before Morgan reaches around me to grab my plate from the table.

"Go join them." Warm breath brushes past my ear, the deep timber of his voice causing goose bumps to blossom over my skin. "You've done enough today. I've got this."

He's gone before I can protest, moving back to the kitchen to clean up from our meal. I don't know the last time I've been able to sit back and enjoy a party that I've hosted. God knows Tanner has never helped with any of the hosting duties; getting him to show up was a hard enough task.

"Jamie, what movie are we watching?" Chelsea asks.

I decided it was best to forgo any sort of gift exchange for the Christmas part of Friendsgivmas. At first, it seemed like the obvious thing to do, but the more I thought about it, the more wrong it felt. Morgan doesn't care about material things—he misses his family, and no twenty-dollar Secret Santa gift is going to give him that. I eventually landed on doing Christmas movies with the gang, but I never got around to picking what movie we'd watch.

"Before she says anything, *Die Hard* isn't a Christmas movie," Nathan interjects.

"Oh, come on"—Karis rolls her eyes in exasperation—"and *Paul Blart: Mall Cop* is?"

"Both of you, knock it off." Karis's and Nathan's heads snap toward Gage as he cuts off their arguing. "We have this argument every year, and they are banned, so no point in getting into it now."

They both let out petulant huffs but let the matter drop.

"We could watch *The Grinch*," Evelyn offers.

"Animated or Jim Carrey?" Karis asks, directing her focus toward my more reserved friend. Evelyn blanches under the almost predatory intensity of the sharp woman's stare.

"Um...Jim Carrey..." Evelyn mumbles, her tone raising in a way that makes it sound more like a question than a statement.

"Good choice." Karis flashes her a toothy smile. "I vote *Grinch*."

"Fine, I guess we can watch that." Nathan sighs. "But it's no *Paul Blart*."

Gage and Chelsea nod in agreement, and Morgan rejoins us while I'm setting up the movie, dropping an arm full of pillows and bedding onto the floor in front of the couch.

Once everyone is settled, Morgan turns off the overhead light and settles into his nest of blankets at my feet. His head rests in the small gap between my knee and the arm of the couch, a few short inches away from my hands. My fingers itch to close the gap and bury themselves in his silky curls.

I don't think any of us truly watch the movie; it's impossible to with Karis and Nathan interjecting every few minutes with their best quippy one-liners. The two of them feed off each other's antics, and it's not long before the rest of us join in, trying to one-up and get the most laughter out of each other.

It's the most fun I've had in a long time.

The credits roll, and everyone lapses into silence for the first time since it began.

"This was great, Jamie," Evelyn says, stretching as she stands from her spot on the floor, "but I should head out. I've got a final tomorrow and need to get some last-minute cramming in."

Evelyn grabs her things, and Morgan walks her to the door. The thorny tendrils of jealousy lash out as they stop to talk for a few moments longer at the threshold, and I actively have to fight to prune back its sharp vines. Karis and Gage follow behind her not too long after, leaving Chelsea and Nathan as the last ones remaining.

"Are you sure there's nothing we can do to help?" Chelsea asks as I try to herd her toward where her boyfriend waits by the cracked door.

"No, Morgan already cleaned up the kitchen. Plus, you did more than enough by bringing the turkey."

"Well, thank you for having us. We had fun." She pulls me in for a tight hug.

Nathan echoes her sentiment, and they finally make their way into the hallway. Morgan shuts the door, and the soft *click* of the latch resounds through the now-silent apartment, signaling Friendsgivmas's end.

I let out a heavy sigh of relief and sag on the couch, the tension melting from my shoulders as the last remnants of my anxiety dissipate. He picks up the last of the trash from around the living room without breaking our tranquil bubble of silence, then drops down on the couch beside me, mirroring my sprawled posture.

Grover's pitiful whine bursts the moment of peace and brings me back to reality. The party might be over, but my plans for tonight aren't. There's still one more holiday for us to celebrate tonight.

"Would you mind taking Grover out for me?"

He nods as he moves to grab the leash and clips it onto Grover's collar.

"Be right back," he says, slipping on a pair of ugly foam shoes and flashing me one of his brilliant, dimpled smiles before walking out of the apartment.

He pulls the door shut behind him, and then the heavy *thunk* of the deadbolt latches into place. I stay frozen in place as I watch the door, but my body tenses like a coiled spring.

One second passes.

Then another.

Yet another ticks by, and I'm convinced he isn't about to turn around and walk back through the door anytime soon. I shoot up from the couch in one explosive burst of movement and dart to my room to collect my secret stash of supplies. My room looks like a carnival just came through, and not in a fun way. The floor is littered with the assortment of multicolored balloons I've blown up over the past few days, and long strands of paper chain garland sit in neat stacks near my bed. The growing disarray has been eating at my sanity over the past few days, but it will be worth it if it brings him joy.

He doesn't know about these plans. Everything has to be perfect before he gets back, and that could be five minutes or thirty, depending on Grover's mood.

With no time to waste, I grab balloons by the armful, kicking some out into the hallway as I wade back and forth to scatter them throughout the living room. Once I finish with the balloons, I collect the delicate paper chains and drape them over the blades of the ceiling fan above the couch. It's tacky as fuck, and Morgan will love it.

I pull up a video of last year's New Year's Eve ball drop on the TV and grab the last bag of supplies—the one that takes my plan to a whole new level of cheesiness—spreading its contents over the coffee table. The lock turns in the door, and I throw myself back onto the couch, picking up a plastic noisemaker in the process. He starts to walk through the door but freezes as I blow into the small device, filling the apartment with a loud trill.

"Surprise!"

He surveys the room with wide eyes, his lips curling into a smile as he takes in the chaos. "What is all this?" he asks, shutting the door and letting Grover off the lead.

"We did Thanksgiving and Christmas already, now it's time to celebrate New Year's Eve."

"James…" he says, his voice thick with emotion, and his eyes take on a glassy sheen.

My heart swells, and I have to shove back the unexpected surge of emotions his reaction summons.

"Come sit." I pat the spot next to me on the couch in invitation. "I got us hats and noisemakers, and even those stupid glasses with the year number on them." My arms wave over the coffee table, emphasizing the collection of overpriced junk I bought to make today special.

He ignores it all as he takes the seat beside me, his gaze locked on the floor. He places one of his hands on my knee, giving it a gentle squeeze before moving his thumb in soothing circles, although this time, I don't think the motion is meant to comfort *me*.

"James, seriously," he says, still refusing to look at me. "Thank you."

"For what? Throwing a party?" I ask with a forced laugh.

"No." He lifts his head, and his eyes blaze with an emotion I can't place. "Thank you for going through all this effort to try to make the holidays better for me. Thank you for letting me into your home, no matter how much you didn't want to at first, and letting me live life with you these past few months. More than that, thank you for making this place feel like home for me. That isn't something I've had in a long time."

"Morgan…" My voice cracks as the lid I had on my emotions snaps. I reach out to grab his hand, turning his palm to lace my fingers through his.

I'm not sure if it's his words, or if my conversation with Nathan earlier opened my eyes, but something clicks in my head—I know that look on Morgan's face.

It's love.

Morgan Hall loves me…and I love him too.

He may have found his home here in Athens, but somehow along the way, *he* has started to feel like mine.

"Sorry," he says, clearing his throat. "I didn't mean to derail your plans. What's next?"

"Ball drop," I choke out, motioning toward the TV.

"Okay, then," he says, his face relaxing into an easy smile. "Let's ring in the New Year."

I hit play on the video, but neither one of us looks at the screen. The hosts prattle on about something and start counting down the final minute, but it's nothing more than a hum of noise in the background, my attention locked on the man beside me. He's sitting so close that our bodies seem to meld into a single point of molten heat where he presses against mine, and his eyes are filled with such unbridled adoration that my heart nearly bursts in my chest. His tongue darts out, moistening his lips, and I want nothing more than to close the gap between us and find out exactly what they would feel like against mine.

An eruption of celebratory noises blares from the video.

"Happy New Year, James," he says with a bright smile. "Make a wish."

God, I wish I could kiss him right now. My body yearns to be closer to him—to feel all of him. It's a magnetic pull that I'm barely able to resist. *Why am I resisting?*

Fuck wishes.

I lunge forward and press my lips against his. It's like grabbing hold of a live wire; shock waves of electricity pulse throughout my body, building unquenchable heat in my core. He is unresponsive to my touch. Until I run the tip of my tongue across his lips, which snaps him out of his paralysis. He lets out a groan and pulls me onto his lap, deepening the kiss as he meets my tongue with his own. I tangle my fingers into his hair, pulling him even closer as I grind down on him. I can feel him harden beneath me, creating the perfect amount of friction to send my need for him into overdrive.

"James..." He tries to pull his mouth away from mine, but I chase his lips, refusing to let him go. He gives in, and his hands move up my body, finally exploring, finally touching me in ways my body has been craving. I move my hands from his hair and snake them under his shirt so I can do some exploring of my own. My fingers meet his heated skin, tracing along his defined abs, but it isn't enough. I start to unbutton his dress shirt, and he goes rigid, grabbing my wrists in one of his large hands.

"We can't do this," Morgan says, sounding pained.

Why the fuck can't we?

Nothing has ever felt more right than this. I ignore his protest and try to kiss him again, but he dodges my attempt, leaning away with a frustrated groan.

"James, stop," he commands, and I go still in his lap. "What about Tanner?"

"I'm breaking up with him," I tell him, sounding just as sure about the decision as I feel in this moment.

"Breaking up, as in future tense?" he asks, keeping my hands locked in his tight grasp.

"Yes," I admit, "I'm waiting until after the holidays to do it, but I made the decision over the break."

His face falls, and he lets out a disappointed sigh. He releases my hands and grabs my hips, pulls me from his lap, and places me back on the couch, then slides to the far end, putting as much distance between us as possible.

"It was wrong for us to do this," he says, his breaths coming in heavy pants. "We can't do this again."

Despite the reluctance in his voice, the rejection stings. My shoulders slump and my face grows hot with shame. A lump forms in my throat as tears pool in my eyes.

"James..." His voice is strained. He starts to reach toward me but pulls his hand back and runs it through his hair with a sigh. "Please don't cry. It's not that I don't want this. Believe me, I do, but this can't happen while you're in a relationship. I won't be the other man."

I bite my lip and nod, holding back the tears threatening to spill over.

"I'm doing it before I come back for the spring semester." My voice is resolute. "Just a few more weeks."

"Okay, then. A few more weeks."

Chapter 25
Morgan

"**M**erry Christmas, Morgan!"

My mom's voice crackles with static as it sounds from my aging laptop speakers. She and my dad are crowded together on the screen, their webcam catching them at an awkward angle that has me looking up their noses. Her smile is how I always remember it: slightly too large and radiating warmth. But the creases on her face have grown deeper since the last time we video called, and the crow's feet by her eyes are even more pronounced. Thick streaks of gray now color her curly hair, which used to be the same shade of chestnut brown that Laura and I shared. My dad looks like another man completely; his hair has thinned, his once work-hardened body is more slender than I remember, and the skin of his face hugs his jaw- and cheekbones, making him appear gaunt.

It's a cruel reminder of how much time has passed and how much time I've missed. I hate seeing them like this. It's worse to watch the slow progression of their aging in sporadic snapshots than it would be not to see them at all, but my mom always insists that we do a video call for Christmas so she can see my face, and I can't deny her that.

"Merry Christmas." The cheer in my voice rings false to my ears, but I doubt my parents pick up on my mood. My mom is too happy to see me to notice the underlying current of melancholy, or maybe she's also faking it. My dad, on the other hand, would have to engage in the conversation to notice that something was off, and that isn't going to happen anytime soon.

"Did you get your package?" my mom asks. "The post office said shipping could be anywhere from three to five days, so I sent it a week ago in case there were any delays. You know I don't trust those delivery times anymore, not since I tried to mail that blanket I was working on to your aunt Carol, and it got lost for weeks. Their quality has been going downhill these days—"

"Yes, Mom, I got your package," I interrupt. She could ramble on forever if I let her, and I'm sure my dad has already heard this story three times too many.

"Well, why didn't you say so? Go get it, I want to see you open it."

I fight the urge to roll my eyes, grab the small box from the spot I had it stashed in, and bring it into the webcam's view. She smiles even wider, urging me on, and I carefully cut through the tape with one of the kitchen knives. Inside is another package wrapped in festive paper. It sags in my hand as I pull it out, the thin covering starting to tear under its weight. I push the box to the floor and sit the wrapped package in my lap, preventing it from tearing further. With careful fingers, I find the pieces of tape holding it together and break them apart, revealing a navy sweater.

"Thank you," I tell my parents, holding it up so they can see it from their screen. "I love it."

"You're welcome, honey. I just wish you could be opening it here instead." She doesn't mean for them to hurt, but the words are like a stab in my chest. I'd give anything to grant her that wish.

"I know. Me too. I think I might be able to visit next year, though. If I get a job over the summer, I should be able to afford the ticket."

"That would be wonderful." She beams, clasping her hands in front of her chest. "We miss you."

"I miss you too." Probably more than they realize.

"What are your plans for today? Making cookies? Christmas movie marathon?"

"I've actually got plans with a friend who is still in town. We are going to do some volunteer work at a local homeless shelter."

Evelyn and I have been going to the Labre Mission every day since winter break started. I thought things might be weird after what happened at the beach, but she's never given any indication that she still has romantic feelings for me. It's been fun—as fun as cleaning dishes and doing laundry can be—and I've enjoyed getting to know her better; I should have done it earlier. The work has also been a welcome distraction to keep my mind off James and what life might look like when she gets back in two weeks.

"That sounds like something you would do," my mom says with a soft smile. "I'm glad you have friends there to keep you company."

I let out a small hum of acknowledgment and cut the conversation short before she can press for more details. "I should probably get going. We are scheduled to be there in less than an hour."

"Oh, okay." Guilt stabs me in the stomach as her face falls in disappointment. "Well, we love you. Call us again soon."

My dad grunts, which I guess is his way of saying he agrees.

"I love you too," I say and hang up the call, letting my head fall back against the couch as the facade of Christmas crumbles.

A heavy silence falls over the empty apartment, a stark reminder of how empty this place feels without James here to fill it. The air is stale, and the overhead lights emit a dingy sort of glow, nothing like the warm radiance I normally feel when I'm here with her. She's the heart of this place—the very thing that breathes life into our home.

And now she's gone, sucking all that life away with her.

She didn't even tell me goodbye before she left, opting to let me know she was gone with a Post-it on the mirror that said she would miss me and see me in January.

For the first time since she stopped using the notes to nitpick my behavior, seeing the words on the paper caused dread to pool in my gut, which has only hardened into a festering mass of doubt and anxiety. I would have liked to have said goodbye and seen her off before she disappeared for three weeks.

Especially after *that* kiss.

The kiss that somehow managed to change everything and nothing all at the same time, completely shattering my worldview while also bringing everything clearly into focus. The kiss we still haven't talked about. The kiss that's been playing on a loop in my head, burning me alive on the inside ever since.

I would be spiraling now if she hadn't left something else for me along with the note: a simple envelope, sealed with the stain of a pink glossy kiss. The words "Don't open until Christmas" are written on the front in that looping script I've come to cherish. The envelope has been taunting me for the entire two weeks she's been gone, begging me to open it and reveal its secrets, but I've respected her wishes and waited, impatiently counting down the days until I could rip open the flap and find out what she left inside.

It's Christmas now, and there's no time like the present.

With newfound excitement, I head to my room and grab the now-creased envelope from under my pillow. The barest hint of her sweet vanilla perfume wafts from the paper, so faint I'm not certain I'm not imagining it. My fingers twitch, itching to open it, but my hand stalls as it catches on a gap under the flap.

What if this is nothing and I've hyped it up in my head so much that I'll be disappointed?

What if this is her way of telling me to forget about what happened between us?

I wouldn't blame her if she did. The kiss was a mistake, a moment of impulsivity on her end that would be best left in the past, and I would leave it there if she hadn't insisted that things would be different between us when she gets back. Those emotion-laden promises made under the cover of darkness destroyed any chance of me seeing it as a single moment.

Ruminating on it isn't going to make things any clearer, and neither is leaving the letter unopened. I tear through the paper and pull the contents out.

Dear Roomie,

Merry Christmas!

I wish I could spend some of today with you, watching our shows or working on a puzzle or something, but I can't. That doesn't mean I've forgotten about you or that I'm not thinking about you today, because I am. You are always on my mind.

I debated waiting on doing this until I could see your face when you opened it, but I have a surprise for you. Go to my room and open my closet. You will know what you are looking for when you see it.

I'm going to miss you, Morgan, or I guess I already do miss you. I know it's only a few weeks, but I already can't wait until I'm back home with you. I'm sorry I left without saying goodbye, I just knew that if I saw you, it would make leaving even harder.

Enough sappiness, go get your surprise.
I'll see you soon.

Love J XO

I run a finger over the word *love* as a knot forms in my throat, and I brace against the tsunami of emotions that rips into me.

God, I miss her.

My chest is hollow without her here. James is my heart, and I need her to come home so I can be whole again.

I tuck the note back into the envelope, placing it in the small box that holds the rest of my collection, and follow her instructions. A large wrapped box sits on the floor of her closet; festive paper hugs the cardboard underneath with razor-sharp edges, and a bright ribbon encircles it with an oversized bow stuck dead in the center. It's wider than it is tall, which makes it awkward in my arms as I carry it to her bed.

Even though she hasn't been here in weeks, her presence is still palpable. The air seems to buzz, alive with the remnants of her energy. I should take the box and leave, but I can't pull myself from this space if I tried. Her scent envelops me as I sit on her soft, cushiony bed, and it feels like coming home.

I open the box, and my heart grows fuller. Inside is a beautiful painting in a style I've come to recognize as uniquely hers. The painting is of us: me as a knight, Grover as a dire wolf, and James as our queen, who is bestowing the knight with a symbol of her favor.

My fingers run across the textured surface, needing to feel that this is real and that my eyes aren't deceiving me. All of my feelings for her—all of the love—bubble to the surface and overwhelm me completely. If she were here now, everything I said about mistakes and Tanner would be nothing more than meaningless words; I'd make her mine regardless.

I don't know when she would have had time to paint this—judging by the details and size, this took her time. Definitely more than I'm worth. Especially since I didn't get her anything. I haven't gotten anyone anything in so long, it didn't even cross my mind. She won't be home for over a week, though, so I still have time to rectify that and find something for her that's as meaningful as this. *No pressure.*

A soft knock on the door signals Evelyn's arrival and shatters my moment of tranquility. I head toward the door to meet her, but my mind is still on the woman hundreds of miles away.

Chapter 26
James

The Nicholsons' home glows from where it sits at the end of the long driveway, standing out like a beacon among the marshland trees and hanging moss. The sight should be cheery, especially with the abundance of perfectly positioned white Christmas lights that adorn the front of the house and wreaths that sit in every window. But it feels ominous as I walk up the all-too-familiar path for what will likely be the last time. Dread weighs down on my shoulders with each step forward, every instinct in my body screaming at me to run, but I keep moving forward like a moth drawn toward its own beautiful destruction.

Tanner's house has always been intimidating. The first time I came over, I begged my grandma to take me back home. I was convinced that it was the wrong place, or that he had invited me over as a joke. The waterfront house dwarfs the small two-bedroom ranch we lived in down the road and any of the places I lived at with my dad on the bases. There was no way I was supposed to be there. Seven-year-old Tanner running out of the house, beaming at me with a gap-tooth smile, is the only reason I stayed, and over the years, the house lost most of that edge and started to feel like home.

It doesn't feel like home now, though.

Cars line the driveway in packed rows, the clear work of hired valets. The annual Nicholson holiday party gets more elaborate every year, and with Mr. Nicholson's campaign for governor in full swing, this is bound to be the biggest one yet. I spent Christmas morning with Tanner's family, and we've already gotten our actual celebrations out of the way. This event, which always takes place the Saturday after Christmas, is purely a political affair, and I'm here to play my part, one last time. Once the last of the guests leave, I'm going to pull Tanner aside and end things once and for all.

I step onto the porch, and my heart starts to accelerate as panic claws its way through me. My breath catches, and I squeeze my eyes shut as I count in my head, trying to stave it off. Morgan's face pops into my imagination, his voice counting alongside mine as he has so many times before. With him in mind, I'm able to pull myself together. No matter what happens tonight, I'll be going back to him in just a few days, and that makes everything worth it.

The door swings open seconds before my fist makes contact, and I'm met by a flurry of blond curls and high-pitched squeals as Kinsley and Raelyn throw themselves at me as if I wasn't here a few days ago. They talk over each other, filling me in on everything I've missed, and all I can do is hug them tighter as my eyes grow wet with unshed tears. There's no promise that I'll ever get to do this again after today. Tanner is going to hate me, and they might too. Even if they don't, Tanner might not let me be in their lives after this. Out of everything, that's what scares me the most.

"Ophie, that's too tight," Raelyn whines, so I let them go.

"Sorry, I just love you both so much." I wipe the tears away from my eyes before they can notice and plaster a smile on my face. "Let's go inside. I need y'all to show me where the best food is."

They each grab one of my hands and lead me into the house. I'm met with an air of sophistication that I've come to expect from these parties, and it never fails to make me feel out of place. A towering fir, gilded in golden ornamentation, stands as the focal point in the main entryway, and Mr. Nicholson's guests gather around it in small groups while waitstaff move between them with silver plates of hors d'oeuvres and champagne. I grab a glass, drink the bubbly liquid in one gulp, and place it back on the tray to grab another before the server can move.

Tanner's face emerges through the sea of unfamiliar faces, and a large smile breaks across his lips when he notices me. He dashes away from his group and crosses the room, never once taking his eyes off mine. Even now, I can admit he looks fucking good in his tailored suit, the picture-perfect model of a politician's son.

"O, you look stunning." He gives me another appreciative once-over and pulls me in for a chaste kiss.

My cheeks flush, both from his compliment and the attention drawn by the PDA. I always feel underdressed at these things; the emerald-green dress Mrs. Nicholson chose feels plain compared to the luxurious designer gowns many of the women are wearing.

"Thank you. You don't look half bad yourself." I try my best to keep my tone light, but just looking at him causes my heart to pang. It's hard to see his smile knowing I'm going to kill it in a few hours.

"Not half bad?" He feigns offense with a teasing tone. "You wound me, Ophie. I got dressed up just for you, and you don't even appreciate it." He wraps me in his arm, burying his face into my neck, and whispers, "I guess you'll just have to appreciate me getting undressed later."

I freeze under the wrongness of his touch, but Tanner is oblivious to my discomfort. He pulls back, dropping another kiss on my lips, one that doesn't stir anything inside me like kissing Morgan did. Kissing Morgan was a lightning strike against the rod of a skyscraper—an electrified inevitability. With Tanner, there's no spark, no heat. Looking back, I don't know if there ever was. Even at its best, kissing Tanner was a small shock of static, still electric, but nowhere near the same magnitude. Now it's nothing more than the cold touch of damp skin.

"Hey, girls." Tanner crouches to talk to his sisters at their level. "Why don't you go play with some of the other kids. I promise I'll bring Ophie back in a little while, and you can play with her then."

The girls nod and scamper off to wherever the rest of the children have been banished. Mr. Nicholson runs on a platform of family values, but kids aren't necessarily the best thing for this sort of atmosphere. The sounds of children playing would drown out the ethereal renditions of Christmas melodies coming from the small string ensemble playing next to the tree.

He grabs my hand and parades me through the house, introducing me to all of the people who were deemed important enough, or more likely rich enough, to get invited to this year's soiree. I smile, putting on a well-practiced mask, and play the expected role of demure and polite girlfriend, but every word spoken passes by me unheard. It's not like any of this will mean anything to me tomorrow. I'll never have to see any of these people again or spend my night being a version of myself that doesn't actually exist at a pointless party in order to please donors.

Morgan would hate this.

I hate this.

The night passes by in a blur of endless small talk and smiling for the cameras who wanted "a real, candid look at the Nicholson family." Through it all, Tanner never once leaves my side, keeping a hand glued to me like I might disappear if he lets me go—and I just might. At least the food is good, and the champagne flows endlessly from the silver trays.

We near the center of the room again, joining his parents in front of the tree. For the first time tonight, Tanner grabs a flute of champagne for himself. *So much for his sobriety.* My eyes narrow on the offensive glass. He must pick up on the venom in my gaze because he has the audacity to look sheepish. I open my mouth to ask him what the hell he's thinking, but my words die on my lips as he grabs a knife from the tray to tap against the glass. The high-pitched tinging rings throughout the room, and the chattering of guests ceases. Even the musicians stop playing to observe. He places the glass back on the tray and clears his throat as he turns back to the crowd.

"I just wanted to take a moment to thank everyone for coming out to spend the holidays with us." He flashes a thousand-watt smile, slipping into his politician's son persona. It's a seamless transition from the man I grew up with into one I barely recognize. "I know it means a lot to me, and my dad, that you are choosing to spend your evening here; however, that's not the only reason I gathered your attention.

"I also wanted to thank my wonderful girlfriend for being here today," he says, turning back to face me. His features soften from the plastic perfection he was projecting only moments before. "She is the glue that holds my very soul together, and this family wouldn't be the same without her."

Every eye in the room locks in on the two of us, and I freeze, keeping my fictitious smile in place even while my heart drops out of my stomach. A camera flashes in an all-too-pointed reminder that my every action is being recorded and scrutinized.

"You are the best thing that has ever happened to me." Tanner squeezes my hand and turns back toward our audience. "For those of you who don't know, I met Ophelia when we were just seven years old. Believe it or not, she was an absolute menace. She never listened to instructions if she didn't think they were right, and she was the first to throw a punch if she felt wronged. I was in awe of her but was too scared to approach her. Luckily, I didn't have to, because when Jack Caldwell was making fun of me on the playground, she marched right up to him and punched him square in the face. I knew then and there that she was the girl I was going to marry someday."

Oh, fuck no.

Please tell me he isn't about to do what I think he is. If any god is listening, please strike me down where I stand. Death is better than this.

I'm powerless to do anything but stand and watch in abject horror as he pulls out a velvet box from his jacket and drops to one knee in front of me.

"Ophelia James Clarke, my beautiful and fearless Ophie, there aren't enough words to describe how much you mean to me. You are my best friend, my soulmate, the source of joy in my life, and the reason I strive every day to be the best version of myself so I can be the type of man you deserve. I know I'm not always perfect and that, sometimes, I mess things up, but I promise you I will spend the rest of my days trying to make up for my failings. I love you more than I've loved anyone, and I can't go another day without making sure you and the world know it. So will you marry me, O? Will you make me the luckiest man who's ever lived by giving me the honor of calling you my wife?"

No.

The room around me starts to spin as I grow light-headed. The pressure of dozens of waiting eyes bears down, throwing me even more off balance. I scan the room, looking for any familiar faces to ground me.

No.

Raelyn and Kinsley stand apart from the crowd, staring up at me with hope-filled eyes.

No.

Mrs. Nicholson wipes away a tear, and Mr. Nicholson looks at the two of us with pride shining on his face.

No.

That's it. There is no one else here for me. No Grandma Anne, or Dad, or any of my friends from school. It's just me, Tanner's family, and a slew of local bigwigs who will eat this shit up. That godforsaken camera flashes again, capturing this cursed moment.

No.

By sheer force of will, I move my head and actually look at the ring in the box. The ring itself is beautiful but gaudy beyond all belief. The large center diamond is surrounded by a halo of smaller stones, making the ring bulkier than it has any right to be. I try to imagine it on my finger, but the picture never comes.

No.

I think about Morgan and the promises I made to him before I left. A tear runs down my cheek, followed by another as I mourn the love that never got a chance to be. I don't even bother to hide them; everyone else will attribute the tears to joy.

"Yes."

Chapter 27
Morgan

The wheel of the cheap plastic lighter spins, but my shaking fingers kill the spark before it can grow into a flame.

"Come on," I mumble under my breath, struggling as I try once again to light the wick of James's favorite candle.

The flame *finally* comes to life in my hand, filling the air with the smell of sweet caramel and fall spices as the wax starts to melt, adding the final touch to the atmosphere I've spent all day trying to create. A vase of roses and a small wrapped box sit on the coffee table, sticking out against the backdrop of the otherwise immaculate apartment. I spent the morning cleaning it from top to bottom, only to do it again as soon as I was done. The repetitive task occupied my hands and kept my mind from fixating on her and what the future might hold for us.

James should be home by now. The sun set hours ago, draping a blanket of cold winter darkness over the city. It's late enough that even the streets have grown quiet, but there hasn't been any sign of her.

I fluff the pillows on the couch, adjusting their position for the twelfth time, trying to get them perfectly straight. My fingers itch with the need to call her, to make sure she is okay, but I fight it. The last thing she needs after Tanner is to have me breathing down her neck.

The sound of a key scraping against the pins of the lock paralyzes me where I stand.

She's home.

My heart skips a beat and takes off in my chest, urging me back into action, and I run my fingers through my hair in a desperate attempt to fix the unruly mop of curls. Time slows as the door swings open, and my breath catches in my throat when I see her. It's like the piece I've been missing these past few weeks slots back into place, restoring the world to full color when I had been living in shades of gray.

The blissful feeling of relief only lasts a moment as I take all of her in before it crashes down around me. James looks like a ghost of herself standing frozen in the doorway. She looks through me with swollen red eyes, but there's no spark of life in them. Her hair is just as lifeless as it hangs in dull clumps around hunched shoulders. It's like the woman I love has been completely eclipsed by despair. Each piece would be worrying on its own, but all together, it's a flashing red warning that something is really, really wrong.

She trembles in the doorway, not moving and not saying anything. I take a step toward her, and she recoils, the small motion piercing my heart.

"Hi." The whispered word is all I can manage.

That breaks her out of her trance. She stumbles forward, dropping her bags and Grover's leash as she closes the front door and hurls herself at me. I'm able to get my arms around her just as she collapses against me with a heaving sob.

"Morgan," she chokes out through gasping breaths.

"Shh, I've got you, pretty girl," I tell her, pulling her in close.

She only cries harder, fully falling into me as her legs give out beneath her. My heart aches to see her like this and not be able to do anything but hold her while she shatters. I murmur soothing words into her hair between barely there kisses until her sobbing slows and her breathing evens out.

"I-I need to tell you something," she says. Her tone holds the same solemn severity of a death sentence. Like a doctor telling you there's nothing else they can do. My stomach rolls as I brace myself for the impact of whatever it is she says next. I don't know what those words might be, but I'm certain they're going to destroy me.

"Tanner proposed," she whispers against my chest. "I'm engaged."

Her words strike true, piercing into my heart, creating fractures that splinter into tiny pieces until there's nothing left but shattered fragments. I pull my arms off her, recoiling from the burn of her toxic touch, and take a step away. She doesn't even try to hold herself up as she resumes sobbing in earnest, sinking to her knees in front of me.

I don't watch her fall; I can't. I'm too numb, and I don't look at her as I step around her toward the front door, slipping on a pair of shoes and collecting my wallet and keys along the way.

"Wait, please stay," she begs as my hand starts to turn the knob, and as much as I hate myself for it, the sound of her pleading stops me in my tracks.

"For what?" I snap through clenched teeth.

A chaotic tangle of rage, confusion, and pain breaks past the initial emptiness of shock, and the emotions catch me off guard with their intensity. I need to get out of here, or I am going to say things or do something I might regret.

"Please just talk to me." She scrambles to her feet, wiping away the still-falling tears as she takes a step toward me. The light catches on the sparkling stone that now adorns her finger, and my nonexistent heart manages to break apart even further as my chest caves in. My back hits the door as I flee from her approach, and she freezes.

"What is there to talk about?" A bitter laugh falls from my lips; it's a sound that I don't recognize coming from my lips. "You went home, Tanner proposed, you said yes, and now you are engaged. All the talks of leaving him and plans for our future were just empty promises that got thrown to the curb when something bigger, better, and shinier came along."

"It isn't like that..."

"Then what's it like, James?" My voice comes out louder and angrier than I intend, not quite a shout, but it causes her to flinch all the same. I take a deep breath to rein in the raging storm of emotion before continuing in a more even tone. "Please, enlighten me on how you went from 'I'm breaking up with him' to 'I'm marrying him' over the course of a few weeks. That isn't something you decide on a whim."

"I don't know," she sobs.

"You don't know?" Another incredulous laugh escapes my lips. "You agreed to spend the rest of your life with someone and you don't know how or why you decided to do it? I don't even know what to say to that. Just answer me this, are you happy? Is this what you want?"

"I don't know," she wails, falling back into a fit of sobs.

"Okay." All the fight drains from my body. "Good luck figuring it out, but I can't be here while you do. For what it's worth, all I want is for you to be happy. So congratulations. Tanner is a lucky man."

I turn and walk out the door, no longer listening as she pleads for me to stay, then pull the door shut with an almost silent *click*. That action brings the reality of the situation home. The door to any possible relationship with James is now firmly closed and locked behind me. I've been such an idiot to think this was all going to work out and that she was going to choose me. Nathan was right from the beginning—she was never going to be mine. He is never going to let me hear the end of this.

I don't have a destination in mind as I take to the streets, letting my feet guide me in their aimless wandering. The cold bite of January air pierces through the thin layers of my clothes, growing more unbearable with every minute that drags by. Its sting is the only thing that keeps me from sinking completely into the hollow, empty feeling growing in my chest. Returning to that apartment tonight isn't an option—I would rather sleep on the street than face her again—but I need to find somewhere to go.

Despite the noticeable lack of students, the glowing neon signs that litter the window fronts declare the bars are open, marking Cutter's as the clear choice for where I might find refuge, or at least something to help me forget this waking nightmare. The familiar sight of Gage behind the bar should be a relief, but I don't feel anything, not even a pulse of gratitude as he hands me my favorite beer as I sit down at the counter.

"You look like shit." He crosses his arms and gives me another, more thorough look over.

I don't bother responding to that as I drink down the bitter liquid like it's water and drop the empty glass back to the counter. He puts another in front of me before I even have time to ask for it, but he doesn't lose the appraising look in his eyes. This one I sip slower, and he relaxes out of his tense stance.

"Seriously, Morgan, are you okay?" He doesn't bother trying to hide the sound of his concern.

"No," I tell him honestly, my voice void of any inflection.

He doesn't push me to elaborate, but he doesn't need to. The scrutiny of his gaze does all the work for him.

"James is getting married." My heart shatters all over again as I say the words out loud, as if verbalizing it somehow makes it more real.

"Fuck." He grabs a bottle of vodka and pours me an overfilled glass.

"Yeah. Fuck."

The clear liquid burns my throat, but that doesn't stop me from draining the glass. The pain is a welcome distraction from the gaping hole in my chest.

"Look, I'm not great at this shit, but I know you have feelings for her. I was rooting for you two. I'm no Nathan, but if you want to talk about it, I'm all ears."

"She kissed me before she left for break." The words spill past my alcohol-loosened lips. His eyes widen a fraction, but his face doesn't betray his response any more than that. I hadn't told anyone about what happened between us after they all left the party. For as right as that kiss felt, it came with a layer of guilt that I couldn't shake, so I kept it as my own sordid secret.

"She kissed me, and she told me she was leaving him. She told me that when she got back, we could finally explore what an *us* might look like. I'm an idiot because I believed her. I really, truly believed her." My voice cracks as the emotions start to overwhelm me again.

"When she got ho—" I choke on that cursed word. I was wrong before. That apartment sure as hell isn't my home. "When she got back to the apartment, I was expecting her to be mine, but I knew right away that something was wrong. The worst part, though, is that even while she was actively destroying my heart, she had the audacity to lean on me for her support and beg me to stay."

"Fuck, I knew she was a bitch, but I didn't think she was that heartless."

"She's not a bitch." I jump to her defense on instinct. He gives me an incredulous look, and I drop my head to the sticky bar top with a deep sigh. "I can't go back there tonight."

"You can stay with me for as long as you need." He claps a hand on my shoulder and fills my glass, leaving the half-full bottle with it.

It's empty by the time we leave.

Chapter 28
James

Morgan never came home last night.

I waited for him in the living room, not willing to risk missing his return, but it never came. My swollen eyes fought to stay open until they grew too heavy and sleep dragged me under. When I woke up and there was no sign of him, a pit of dread formed in my stomach. That pit has only grown deeper as the morning dragged on.

Where is he?

He took the news worse than I anticipated. It's not like I thought he was going to jump for joy, but I didn't think he would leave me, either. Watching him walk out that door was a blow to my mangled heart, but that look on his face—the steely scorn honed by heartbreak—eviscerated it. I need him to come home so I can fix this—fix us. If he would just stop and listen to me, I could explain everything. I'll just tell him...I'll make him see that...

Fuck.

This is all so fucking fucked.

A loud banging against the front door causes me to jump.

Morgan?

I'm on my feet before my brain finishes processing the sound. Did he leave without his keys? Where did he stay last night? Is he going to forgive me? What do I even say?

As I open the door, any hopes that had started to grow are sucked back into the black hole swirling in my gut. Nathan looms on the threshold, his face set in a stony mask that I would sooner expect from Gage. Chelsea hovers a few steps behind him with pursed lips and a furrowed brow.

"What ar—"

Nathan doesn't let me finish or even look in my direction as he pushes his way into the apartment.

His arm slams into my shoulder as he passes, knocking me off balance. The move is so unlike him, I'm unable to do much more than step aside while my brain tries to reconcile Morgan's friend with the man in front of me. Chelsea follows him inside, mumbling a soft apology before she drops her eyes to the floor. Grover growls at Nathan's aggressive intrusion, and the sound snaps me out of my momentary stasis.

Rage rises within me, greeting me like an old friend as it wraps me in its protective embrace. I fall into the feeling, letting it envelop me in its molten ire, creating an all-too-familiar armor that burns away all other emotions.

"What the absolute fuck do you think you are doing barging into my apartment uninvited?" My words are dripping with venom as I hurl them at the intruder.

"I'm here to get Morgan's things." His tone is too controlled, too even, and an octave lower than normal. The curl of his lip, paired with the vein throbbing in his temple, gives away how close to the surface his own anger is residing. He turns toward me with a sneer, squaring his shoulders in a mirror of my aggressive posture. "Is that going to be a problem, James?"

He's seen Morgan?

The first crack forms in my armor at the mere mention of his name.

A million questions spring to my head. Is he okay? Where is he? When is he coming home? Getting his things? Is he even coming home?

He has to come home.

Fuck him for thinking he can end things like this, and fuck him for thinking he can simply walk away and send his friend to come pick up his shit.

My anger grows hotter, and any fissures that might have existed are filled and welded shut.

"Yeah, that's gonna be a fucking problem." My hands find purchase on my hips, and I stand a bit taller.

"Jamie…" Chelsea says my name as if she's already resigned herself to my inevitable blowup.

"No," I snap, turning toward her. "If Morgan wants his things, he can come get them himself."

"Jesus Christ, woman," Nathan shouts. "I knew you were a piece of work, but I didn't think you were this much of a cunt."

"Don't talk to her like that," she snaps at her boyfriend and glares daggers at him as she comes to stand at my side.

"Oh, here we go." He throws his hands in the air with an exaggerated sigh. "Of course you're going to take her side." He directs his attention back toward me with hate-hardened eyes.

"Listen," he growls through clenched teeth, "I got woken up in the middle of the night by a call from Gage asking me to come down to Cutter's to help deal with the mess you created, and I haven't had a chance to go back to sleep since. I'm fucking tired, James, and I don't have any patience for your bullshit. So here is what's going to happen: I'm going to go to Morgan's room, pack him a bag, and then I'll get out of your fucking hair. If there is any part of that black heart of yours that actually cares about him, you'll let me do this. Don't you think you've hurt him enough?"

He crosses his arms and waits. I open my mouth to respond, but the words die on my lips.

He's right.

I'm the one who fucked everything up. Morgan doesn't deserve any additional pain, especially by my hand. I've already done enough damage.

"That's what I thought," he says with a scoff.

I don't stop him this time as he turns and storms down the hallway. My friend looks between me and his retreating form with wide eyes and a slack jaw. She looks like she wants to say something or maybe chase after him, but she doesn't do anything more than stare.

Morgan's door slams shut, the force of it sending shock waves through the walls, causing the hanging frames to rattle and shake. The sound cracks through the air and dies within the same abrupt burst of energy. Silence looms in its stead, leaving nothing but the roaring of my pulse in my ears. It's a tangible, heavy weight bearing down on all sides of me, constricting the very breath in my lungs.

"Jamie, what the hell is going on?" Her whispered question cracks through the soundless vacuum like a whip.

"Tanner proposed." My voice is void of emotion. There's no trace of the heartache or dread those two words fill me with on my tongue, but there's no joy either. Getting engaged should be one of the happiest moments of my life, not whatever the fuck this is.

"Oh." She cocks her head to one side and recoils. She shakes away the initial shock and focuses back on me. "And you said yes?" she asks as though she's trying to put together a puzzle but can't make the pieces fit.

"Of course I said yes." I hold out my hand to show her the sparkling manacle on my finger. From the moment Tanner slid it on my hand, I've wanted nothing more than to rip it off, but I can't bring myself to do it. The gaudy bits of metal and stone are too important of a reminder of the promise I made and the ones I've broken.

"Oh." Her face pinches as she processes the news. After a moment, her face relaxes and is masked with false cheer. "The ring is beautiful. When did this happen? How did he do it? Why didn't you tell me?" She asks the questions that I would expect, but they ring hollow.

"He asked me at the holiday party, and things have been so hectic since that it must have slipped my mind."

The lie slips easily past my lips as I mirror her facade. A shitty lie is easier than the truth. The truth that I spent the past several days locked in my room, barely eating, while I mourned the future I thought I would have with Morgan. The truth that I didn't tell her because speaking the words out loud would make them real, and more than anything, I wanted them not to be. The truth that I don't want this but have no idea how to break things off with Tanner now that I've promised myself to him.

She studies my face for several seconds and pulls me into a tight hug.

"It's going to be okay, Jamie," she whispers into my hair.

We break apart at the sound of a door slamming against the wall from the hallway.

"What the fuck is this?" Nathan storms down the hallway with a box in one hand and an all-too-familiar canvas in another. I cringe as he tosses the canvas that I spent countless hours perfecting onto the couch without care. He turns over the box, pouring dozens of tiny orange scraps of paper onto the coffee table.

Morgan kept them?

My heart fills and breaks all over again. *Of course he kept them.* Looking back, it's easy to see just how oblivious I was to his feelings. Love was present for every moment between us—through every tear and every smile, every touch and every instance of restraint. It's love that I've never once deserved.

He drops the box to the floor and rips one of Morgan's precious mementos from the table.

"Dear Roomie, Can you take Grover out when you get home? I need to go by office hours, so I'll be getting back late. Pretty please? I'll even watch extra nerd shows with you to make it up to you. J"

His face twists into a sneer as he spits my words back at me. He crumples the note, throws it off to the side of the room, and picks up another.

"Dear Roomie, I passed the exam. I couldn't have done it without your help studying. Seriously, Morgan, thank you. I'm picking up carryout to celebrate. I should be home around eight, and I expect you to have our shows queued and ready to go. I'll grab your normal order. J"

"I gave Morgan shit for falling for you, but you've been leading him on this whole time. It's no wonder why he couldn't get past his crush. You sunk your claws in and claimed him when you had no right to. It's fucking cruel, James. But this, this takes the fucking cake." He holds a familiar letter in his clenched fist and shakes it in my direction. I know those words. I could recite them from memory if he made me.

"*I wish I could spend some of today with you.*" His voice raises an octave in a harsh imitation of my own. "*You are always on my mind. Love, James,*" he sneers. "What did you think he was going to take from this?"

"I-I..." I love him, but those aren't words that can leave my mouth; no words do. I don't have it in me to fight him anymore. Not when I deserve the verbal lashing.

"That's enough, Nathan," Chelsea snaps, wrapping a protective arm around me. "She gets it. Morgan's sad, and you're mad. Well, she's going through something too. You've got his stuff, now let's go." She never wavers from her low, even tone, but each word is resolute. Her steely gaze bores into him. It's a challenge, the look daring him to defy her.

For several seconds, the pair stay locked in their silent standoff. He is the first to break. He grabs the stuffed duffel and storms toward the door without another word, slamming it behind him as he finally leaves. Even with him gone, the tension in the room is palpable.

"Just...call me if you need anything, okay?" Chelsea lets out a deep breath and follows her boyfriend out.

The first tear falls as the door clicks shut. Over the past few days, I've learned that particular reservoir is fathomless. I can't tear my eyes from the notes that litter the small table, surrounding the vase of roses and the small package that has sat there untouched since last night.

The roses aren't red—that would be too impersonal. No, Morgan managed to find some in a perfect shade of blood orange, one that almost captures the color of the sky as the last of the daylight fades away, one that he knew I would love.

I never even got to thank him.

I'm sure whatever is in that box is just as perfect, but I won't open it until he comes home and I make things right between us.

I tuck his notes back into their box and carry them to his room with the intention of leaving them there for safekeeping, but once I cross that threshold, all of my willpower flees. Without any forethought, I crawl onto that half-deflated mattress and tuck one of his pillows against my chest. His scent is a comfort that fills a small part of the emptiness he's left inside me, but it doesn't stop my tears from falling even harder.

Chapter 29
Morgan

The ceiling fan in Gage's living room spins above me, its blades creating a hypnotic illusion that pulsates with each rotation.

It's always on.

The consistent view from my makeshift bed on his couch has been one of my few sources of comfort over the past few weeks. I'm not sure exactly how long it's been since *she* ripped my heart out and tore it into tiny little pieces—the days have all blended together in a monotonous blur of sorrow and self-loathing—but those spinning blades have been my constant companion through it all.

"All right, enough is enough. Get your ass up." The light flares to life above me, blinding me, as Gage barks out his command.

I scramble to sit up as the dark stars fade from my vision. He stands near the hallway in his Double Teep branded shorts and rash guard, with a gear bag over each shoulder. He studies me from under his heavy brow, the rest of his face locked in a tight expression. The weight of his judgment bears down on me, making the days-old grime and oils that coat my skin and hair feel even heavier, but I haven't been able to make myself fix it. Outside of dragging myself to class and making sure I don't fall behind, I haven't had the motivation to do much of anything except lie here and watch the never-ending spinning.

"You've got fifteen minutes, and then you're coming with me." He tosses one of the bags to me, but it bounces off my chest and hits the floor.

Gage doesn't say a word. He just watches me with that same assessing gaze; the weight of his scrutiny is enough to get me moving. The fifteen minutes pass by on autopilot. I shower and change into the gym clothes he provided, and he hovers nearby, making sure I don't crawl back into my nest of sadness. Satisfied with my newly freshened state, he ushers me out the door and to his car.

The gym's parking lot is abandoned save for Karis's bike and Nathan's car. The absence of others doesn't seem to faze my new drill sergeant. He grabs both of our bags and continues to corral me up the steps and to the door.

I've listened to my friends talk about this place for months, but I'd never made the trip out. They've asked me again and again to join them, but I always brushed them off and told them I didn't have time because of classes. It was a lie, though. I didn't have time because I wasted every free moment I could muster with *her*.

The small warehouse space isn't anything special: a front desk, locker rooms, a wall lined with benches, and three fenced-off areas padded with foam matting in shades of black and green. Chill music plays over the sound system, but it isn't loud enough to cover Nathan and Karis's bickering as they fight to take each other down on the center mat.

"Where is everybody else? Isn't there a class," I ask him.

"Nah, Coach said we could use the mats for some private training time," he says, clapping a hand on my shoulder.

"And to knock some sense into you," Nathan pipes in.

The momentary distraction is all Karis needs to catch her foot around his ankle and take him to the ground. Within seconds, she has him locked in an arm bar, and Nathan taps with a huff, which draws a gruff chuckle from Gage.

"Still getting your ass kicked, I see," Gage teases. He drops his bag on the bench and joins the other two on the mat.

"I was going easy on him this time, too," Karis says with a smirk.

"Oh, please, I don't think you could go easy on someone if they paid you to," Nathan says, still lying on the floor.

I watch my friends in their carefree playfulness, and regret bubbles up in my chest. For the first time since I've met them, I feel like an outsider to their group, a hanger-on with no real connection, and it's my own fault. I pushed them to the side in favor of chasing an impossible, selfish desire and shot down every attempt they made to include me along the way. I was such an idiot, and I still am because, as much as I've tried, I'm still hung up on *her*, and I've still been pushing them away in favor of my self-pity.

"Hey, Morgan," Gage shouts over the music, "come warm up. It's about time you show me what you can do."

I drop my bag next to his and step onto the mats. Nathan pulls himself off the floor in a fluid motion and drags me into a hug.

"It's good to see you, man," he says, releasing me. "Things haven't been the same without you around the past few weeks."

I don't know how to respond to that. Another wave of guilt and regret washes over me, leaving me paralyzed in its wake. My mouth starts to open but snaps shut again. Do I apologize for being a horrible friend, not just these past few weeks, but from the beginning? Do I thank him?

"Less talking, more training," Gage says, saving me from having to figure it out.

I shoot an appreciative glance in his direction, but his face is locked into a serious mask. This Gage standing in front of me isn't my friend but my coach, and any trace of friendliness is gone, replaced by the seriousness required to do the job.

"All right, let's start with a jog to warm up. Karis, you lead." He turns the music up even louder and switches it to something with more energy.

She follows his command without hesitation, and Nathan and I follow suit. Gage pushes us harder than I've been pushed since my coaches back in undergrad. The three weeks I've spent sedentary didn't prepare me for this. I'm already panting for breath by the time our warm-ups end, and I don't have time to recover them before he instructs me to spar with Karis.

She kicks my butt. She is quick, ruthless, and knows how to make herself heavy. That's one of the best things about this sport—skill matters more than size, and she has that in spades. It doesn't help that my focus keeps drifting back to things I'd rather not think about—a certain blond she-devil and the cage she's keeping my heart in on the other side of town. Karis takes advantage of my distraction, and it's submission after submission until the timer goes off. My frustration starts to grow, and I'm not given a second to simmer as Nathan takes her place and the timer starts again. This should be easier—he doesn't have anywhere near the same amount of training that Karis or I have—but the cycle continues, and my frustration only builds each time I'm forced to tap out.

Gage keeps rotating my friends, never giving me a chance to breathe, and never letting me have the reprieve of bag work. Thirty agonizing minutes later, my body aches, my muscles feel like jelly, and I'm too tired to think of anything more than what I'm doing right now. But the pain brings clarity, and at some point along the way, I fall back into my normal rhythm, going sub for sub with Karis and falling into flow rolls with Nathan.

"Break. Good work, guys." Gage's voice drops back into its normal, softer tone as Coach Gage slips away and my friend returns.

I drop back to the mat in a sweaty heap, and Nathan is right there with me, gasping for air. Even Karis sinks to the ground on wobbly legs.

"What the fuck, man?" Nathan says between gulps of air. "I signed up for private practice and an intervention, not boot camp."

He only shrugs in response and joins us on the floor. It takes another second for Nathan's words to fully process. *Intervention*? Is that why he dragged me out here?

"What's Nathan talking about, guys?"

The three share a look, their eyes shifting from me to each other with unmasked unease.

"We wanted to talk about James," Karis says, biting the bullet.

Her words cause my chest to tighten and a knot to form in my gut. No, not words. It only takes one—James.

It's the first time I've heard her name since I wandered to Cutter's after my heart shattered. It hurts too much to think about, and no one has dared to mention her until now.

"What about J—her?" I fight to keep my voice even, to not let them see just how under her spell I am.

"You can't even say her name," Nathan says as he pulls himself up to sit. "It's not healthy. I know that bitch played with your heart, but you can't let her win by letting this destroy you. You need to go back there and show her that she fucked with the wrong guy."

"No," Gage says at the same time I mumble, "She's not a bitch," which only gets eye rolls from Nathan and Karis.

"What Nathan is trying to say"—Gage gives our friend a pointed glare—"is that it might be time for you to face her so you can get some closure and move on."

"Fuck closure, I'm on Nathan's side. I think you should get revenge." Her eyes light up and her lips twist into a cruel smile. "I've got the perfect plan if you want to—"

"No," I interrupt her and drag myself off the floor. "No revenge. No schemes. I don't want that, and there's nothing to get revenge for. James didn't owe me anything. It's my own fault I went and fell in love with her." I cringe as the words I've kept locked away fall from my lips without any restraint.

"Ah, fuck, man." Nathan shakes his head with a scowl. "I knew you had it bad, but I didn't know it was *that* bad. I didn't even know you two were that close until I went to get your stuff, which we are going to talk about at some point. I can't believe—"

Karis launches herself at him, covering his mouth with her hand as she knocks him back to the floor. "What our dear, idiot friend meant to say is, we are sorry you are going through this, and we respect your decision to not seek revenge, even if we don't agree with it. But if you did want to get back at her, you can always—"

"For fuck's sake," Gage growls, putting a stop to their antics. "Can the two of you grow up for five minutes? This is about Morgan, not you."

Karis lets go of Nathan, and they both mumble out sheepish apologies.

"What we wanted to say was, while you are welcome to stay with me for as long as you need, you have a home, and you shouldn't let one woman drive you from it. You don't need to talk to her or be her friend, but go home and show her that she didn't break you. Don't let her take anything else from you."

His words make sense, but they do nothing more than cause the knot in my gut to grow; the weight of it drags my whole body down as I sink into my shoulders. Do I want closure? Sure, although I'm not entirely sure what type of closure she could realistically offer. I would like to apologize for how I acted when she told me, though, but that all hinges on me going back.

He squeezes the back of his neck with a sigh. "The longer you put this off, the more you are going to build her up in your head as some sort of unconquerable beast you'll never be able to slay. You don't even have to spend any time at the apartment except to sleep. Study with Nathan and Karis, come hang out with us at Cutter's, and finally, stop dragging your feet and join us here at Double Teep. Coach David has already agreed to waive your fees in exchange for working the front desk a few hours a week. You have plenty to keep you busy, but you aren't going to be able to move on until you stop being a coward and face her."

He's right.

King Arthur and his knights wouldn't hide away in the castle when the kingdom was under attack. No matter the enemy and no matter how stacked the odds were against them, they would face it head-on.

"Okay." It's time to face my demon.

***

The apartment is a disaster.

Out of every scenario that played through my head on the way here, I can't say that any of them included the apartment being anything less than immaculate, but it's piles of dirty dishes, empty bottles of whiskey and wine, and the sour stench of trash left to ripen that greet me when I walk through the door. The combination causes my stomach to churn—not only because of the pungent smell or molding plates but because of how out of character this is for James. Alarm bells blare in my brain that something is very wrong here, with her, but I ignore the gnawing sense of dread by sheer force of will.

James isn't mine to worry about. She never was.

With a sigh, I close the door behind me and set my duffel down on the floor next to it. Someone has to clean up this mess, and from the looks of it, that person is going to be me. I start to make my way toward the kitchen to grab a bag to start collecting her trash, but my journey is interrupted by my favorite hellhound skulking out of the darkened hallway that leads to our rooms. Grover freezes with his ears pinned back against his head and his tail low when he sees me in the kitchen, and he lets out a soft whine.

"Hey, boy. I missed you." A lump forms in my throat, and the unexpected swell of emotion nearly chokes my words.

His ears perk up at the sound of my voice, and his tail beats against the wooden doorframe with vigor. He rushes toward me, letting out a series of excited, high-pitched yelps, and I drop down to my knees and brace myself for the onslaught of relentless kisses. Laughter bubbles up in my chest as his warm tongue laps at my face. It feels foreign on my lips; it's the first time I've laughed since I left. I scratch behind his ears, and he sinks to the floor, rolling over to give me access to his belly. My heart starts to grow in my chest, kicking to life for the first time since it was broken.

"Grover, what's gotten—oh." The sound of James's voice washes over me like a wave of icy water, washing away the budding sense of euphoria and transforming my heart into a useless, frozen block.

In that short moment of joy, I had nearly forgotten about the monster that lurked in the shadows, the very reason I'd put off returning.

She stands in the mouth of the hallway. Dim light pours out from the now fully opened doorway to her room, surrounding her in a halo of golden light. It looks like she's handled the past three weeks about as well as I have. Dark circles surround her dull, lifeless eyes, and her hair is piled into an unkempt nest on the top of her head. Despite it all, she is still the most beautiful woman I've ever seen. *My devil disguised as an angel.*

Her face looks sunken in, her cheekbones more pronounced, and her clothes hang off her baggier than they should.

Has she been eating enough?

No. I shake my head to clear away the thought. That is something firmly in the "not my business" category. She has her *fiancé* to worry about things like that now.

That word forces bile to rise in my throat, leaving a bitter taste in my mouth. Seeing her like this, like a hollow shell of the woman I knew, destroys the monstrous image I built in my head. There is no dragon to slay or demon to banish, just her and me—two broken people trying their best given the circumstances.

Just like that, all the anger and resentment I've been harboring melt away.

That doesn't mean things can go back to being how they were. I don't blame her for the decisions she's made, but I can't be her friend. That would only be setting myself up for more heartbreak. I understand what Gage meant by closure, though; the weight of the past three weeks finally lifts from my shoulders, and I feel like I can finally breathe.

"Morgan..." She whispers my name with an almost reverent edge. "You're back."

"Yeah." I stand up from the floor and brush away the layer of dust that clings to my pants. "I'm back."

She stumbles forward into the room, reaching out for me, and her eyes shine with renewed life. I'm not sure if she's trying to hug me or just make sure I'm really here, but I don't stick around to find out. I maneuver back out of her grasp and run a hand through my hair, ignoring the stab of guilt that shoots through my heart at the crestfallen look that passes over her face. The look is fleeting as James steps back, straightens her shoulders, and schools her features into a mask of indifference.

It's a mask I know well.

I've seen her don that protective armor time and time again, and I know it means she's preparing for a fight. Like a wounded animal, she lashes out when she's in pain, but I won't give her that satisfaction. Not this time. I can't promise that my words won't hurt her, but I won't fall into the trap of feeding her reactions.

"For good?" she asks with a detached tone, and I can't get a read on what answer she's hoping for.

"Yeah, for good," I tell her, my voice steady with conviction.

There's more I want to say. I practiced the script the whole way here. My plan was to say my piece and give her space to digest it, but the words die on my lips when I realize what she's wearing.

That's my shirt.

She's wearing an old Arizona State T-shirt my mom got me before I left to start my undergrad program. I had forgotten about that shirt. It's been abandoned in the bottom of a box since I graduated, but somehow, she not only found it but decided it would be the perfect thing to wear today. It does look perfect on her, even though it's riddled with holes and has a large stain across the front. A wave of possessiveness surges through me, but it's caught in the riptide of my self-loathing as rapidly as it arrives.

This is why we can't be friends. There's no version of this where I can have a platonic relationship with her, not anymore. She's a drug, and I'm an addict. No matter how many times I've tried to quit her, I fall off the wagon at the slightest temptation. All it took was one hit and she rewired my brain—and heart—making it believe she's something vital to my very existence. The only way to get clean is a complete detox and separation from any source of temptation.

"Good." A small smile tugs at the corners of her lips. She lets out a breath, and the tension falls away from her shoulders. "I missed you. We should talk. I don't like how we left things before."

"No, James." The knowledge that I'm about to kill the hope shining in her eyes causes my heart to ache. My eyes fall away from hers, focusing on the wall behind her head instead to make this easier. "There is nothing for us to talk about."

"Wh-what do you mean? Of course there is. We need to—"

"No." My voice is stern, but there is no malice in it. "I'm here because this is the apartment I pay to live in, but whatever it was we had before—call it friendship or something more, it doesn't matter—that's over. We will go back to just being roommates, and I'll stay out of your hair."

"Morgan, no." Her voice cracks, and my heart breaks with it. "Don't say that. I-I need you. There's no reason we can't still be friends. Nothing's changed."

"That's a lie, and you know it," I scoff. "Everything has changed. I'm not doing this to hurt you, but this isn't something I'm willing to negotiate on."

"Morgan..." My name falls from her lips in a desperate plea.

"Please." I interrupt her attempt to dissuade me with a whispered plea of my own. "If you ever cared about me, even just a little, you'll respect this boundary. Please, James, don't make this hurt more than it already does."

Silence hangs between us for several seconds while she contemplates, and my breath stalls in my lungs.

"Okay," she says, the softly spoken word resonating with harsh finality, and this time, she's the one to walk away.

Chapter 30
James

Dear Roomie,

I miss you. You're finally home, but you've never felt further away. I don't know what to do. I fucked everything up and don't know how to fix it.

Please tell me I can still fix it.

I don't want to marry Tanner, but how do I end things now? I wish you would talk to me. You would be able to figure this shit out.

I love you, Morgan. Please don't give up on us now.

—J

Mrs. Nicholson insisted on hosting an engagement party for us, promising it would be a "small, intimate affair." Tanner loved the idea and spent the past seven weeks coordinating with her to get all of the details perfect, and I...I didn't have it in me to care about venues or color schemes.

It turns out, small and intimate doesn't mean any less extravagant.

My fiancé's face shines with pride as he parades me around the trendy riverfront loft, but I'm numb as he introduces me to friends and coworkers I've never heard of. His arm is locked around my waist, keeping me glued to his side while he drones on about things I can't force myself to care about. It's not like I need to care about them; as long as I keep my features locked in a pleasant mask with a demure smile, Tanner is happy.

Tanner is happy, and I am...here.

Present and accounted for.

Although, despite this being my own engagement party, I doubt that my presence was necessary at all.

The guest list is sorely lacking in familiar faces. To everyone here, I am Tanner's fiancée—not James, barely even Ophelia—just another piece of the carefully designed decor to sell the illusion of picture-perfect storybook love. They see what they want to see: childhood sweethearts moving to the next stage in the natural progression of love, the prince who found his princess. But what they don't know is that the princess's heart longs for a knight instead.

"I've got a surprise for you." Hot breath brushes past my ear, sending a rolling wave of disgust through my body. My shoulders tense, but that's the only outward indicator of how repulsive his touch has become to me.

"A surprise?" I can't fully hide the quaver of dread in my voice. The last few of his surprises haven't been good.

"Look behind you."

I do as he asks, bracing for the worst, and my heart skips a beat in my chest.

"Dad..." The word comes out strangled as emotions overwhelm me, and my vision grows cloudy with unshed tears.

The room goes quiet, watching our reunion like we're here to be their source of feel-good entertainment for the week. I'm sure a few people have their phones out recording. A spike of bitter resentment spears through the cloud of my joy. Even if bringing my dad here was done with the best intentions, there's no denying that Mr. Nicholson's campaign will benefit from the positive media.

If I were a stronger person, I'd fight against it and not give them the spectacle they want, but it's been ten months since I've seen him, and I've missed my dad. I pull myself out of Tanner's grasp and fling myself across the room. Dad catches me with ease as I all but jump into his arms, and the floodgates holding back my tears open.

"Hey, kid," he whispers, crushing me to him in a tight embrace.

I cling to him as I sob into the crevice of his neck. Everything I've been bottling up—all the pain and heartache—hits me with the force of a truck the second I'm in the comfort of his arms. To everyone else, this scene looks like a girl who is happy to see her active-duty father, but in reality, it's a girl looking to her dad to make everything better.

It takes several seconds, but I'm able to regain control over my emotions and, with considerable effort, slip my mask back into place. I pull away from the hug and wipe the tears from beneath my lashes.

Tanner walks over to join us, sticking one hand out to greet my father while wrapping the other around me in that possessive embrace.

"It's good to see you, sir."

My dad's eyes roam over the two of us, the look assessing and critical. The smile that graced his face when I first saw him fades away into a hardened scowl.

"Likewise," he responds, but his tone says it's anything but. "If you don't mind, I'd like a few minutes to catch up with my daughter. Alone."

Tanner's fingers twitch, digging into the flesh of my hips for a split second before he releases me.

"Of course, sir." He flashes one of his plastic smiles and saunters over to one of the many groups of strangers milling around the room.

Dad nods toward a door and leads me out to the deck that wraps around the building and overlooks the river. Normally, the vibrant mix of orange and gold

248

hues filling the sky would be a sight that would make my heart sing—it's so close to the color I told Morgan about on the beach—but I don't feel anything as I step out into the brisk February air. I walk over to the railing and lean against it, looking out over the shimmering water. My dad steps up beside me, letting several moments pass by in serene silence as the sun continues to sink further below the horizon.

"Ophelia, what's going on here? What's wrong?"

My first instinct is to lie to him, to try to sell him the same story I've sold to everyone else—the lie that I'm happy, the lie that everything is fine. That notion dies before the words can even form on my lips. I can lie to the world, but never to him.

"Everything," I whisper, dropping my gaze down to my hands. The sun's rays catch on my diamond ring, mocking me with the sparkling reminder of how fucked everything has become.

"Oh, kiddo." He drops an arm over my shoulder with a sigh, tucking me into the comfort of his side. "I'm gonna need more specifics than that. As much as I've always tried to make you believe otherwise, I can't actually fix everything."

"I don't want to marry Tanner."

Saying those words aloud feels like I've dropped a bomb. I brace for the inevitable destruction and the violent aftershock that is sure to follow.

"Okay, don't marry him," Dad says like it's the simplest thing in the world. The lack of anger or judgment leaves me reeling; I had been prepared to face shock waves but didn't even feel a breeze.

"It's not that easy," I protest.

"Of course it is. If you don't want to marry him, then you don't, end of story." His tone doesn't leave any room for arguments, but that's never stopped me before. He makes it sound so easy, like I could turn and walk away, and everything would be fine. I want to believe him—everything would be so much simpler if I did—but the oversized diamond is a noose on my finger, dragging me back to reality.

"I already told him I would."

That's the crux of the issue. I knew what I was committing to when I told him yes, despite that being the last thing I wanted, and I've made peace with what my future entails. There are too many things in motion for me to back out now. The engagement announcements have already been sent out to all of the Nicholsons' friends and colleagues, and there was even a story in the local paper gushing about our "storybook romance."

The ring seems to grow tighter on my finger. I twist it around to try to relieve some of the pressure, but it does nothing to lessen its choke hold.

"A ring isn't legally binding." My dad eyes my fidgeting hands with a deep frown. "And if you are having any doubts, it's better for everyone to end things before it is. It's probably going to hurt, believe me, I know, but it will hurt so much more if you wait for what should be a breakup to become a divorce."

"What about his family? His sisters? How would this look for his dad's campaign?" My voice takes on a frantic edge as I grasp at the loose strings of my unraveling argument.

"None of that matters. The only things that need to be taken into consideration are you and Tanner, and if you want to spend the rest of your life with him."

Fuck. He's right. He's *always* right.

The looming, oppressive sense of doom that's shadowed my every move since I uttered that cursed "yes" is driven back by my father's guidance.

"I thought you liked him," I argue, but there's no weight behind it, not anymore.

"What I like is you being happy, and that look on your face when I walked in there? That was not the face of my daughter when she's happy. Tell me I'm wrong."

"You aren't. I'm not happy." I stand straighter as I admit aloud the things I've already known.

"Then that's that. It doesn't matter how much you love him—"

"I don't," I interrupt with sharp vehemence.

"Don't what?"

"I don't love him. Not anymore."

My dad pulls back to look me over, his face awash with a look of horror. "Why did you say yes, then? Oh God. You aren't pregnant, are you?" he growls. "I'll kill that pretentious fucker if he knocked you up."

"No! I'm not pregnant," I reassure him. The mere thought of being bound to Tanner in that way sends chills of disgust rolling through my body. "I've known for a while that I needed to end things with him, but it was never the right time. I had planned to do it after New Year, but then he went and proposed, and there were so many people, and so many cameras, and his family all looked so happy, so I said yes, even though everything in me was screaming at me to say no."

"He hasn't hurt you, has he?"

"No, nothing like that." It's not entirely the truth, but I don't see the point in reopening old wounds. I pause for a moment, debating whether or not I should bring up my other problem, the one that's been eating me alive since it walked out of the apartment and out of my life.

"I met someone else," I admit with a wistful sigh. "I know it's wrong, but every moment I spent with him made me realize how much was missing between me and Tanner, and that I deserve more than to settle for good enough just because it's familiar."

"You love him." It isn't a question.

"I do. I never meant to fall in love with Morgan, but I did. I love him so much, and I ruined any chance I had at being with him." My heart aches in my chest at the thought of him, and tears fill my eyes. "He won't even look at me. It's like I'm a ghost living beside him, and it fucking hurts. I don't know what to do, Dad. I don't know how to fix us."

He sighs and pulls me into a tight hug. "I can't help you win his heart or make amends, but you can't start until you end things with Tanner once and for all."

"You're right. After the party, I'll—"

"No, no more stalling. You are doing this now." He releases me and moves back toward the loft. "I'll go let him know that you need to talk to him, and I'll be waiting on the other side of the door to back you up if you need me."

"Okay," I tell him, but he's already gone back inside.

The last of the sunlight disappears below the horizon, painting the sky with the star-speckled indigo of twilight. I slip the sparkling shackle off my finger and steel myself for this past-due conversation, drawing on the shadows to give me the strength to do the thing I could never do in the light of day.

"Hey, babe, your dad said you wanted to see me," Tanner says as he steps out to join me on the porch. I turn away from the railing to face him, and for a moment, I'm struck with a pang of bittersweet nostalgia. The carefree smile and joyful gleam in his eyes make him look so much like the boy I was in love with for so many years, and this is the last time I'll ever see him like this. It doesn't last long; his face falls as soon as he sees the solemn expression on mine.

"We need to talk." I don't beat around the bush, and my tone doesn't leave much room for ambiguity. Despite the growing lump in my throat and the heat behind my eyes, my words sound steady and decisive.

He flinches, his hackles raising knowing where this conversation is going. "Ophie, baby," he pleads, "don't do this."

"I'm sorry." *I really am.* "I can't do this anymore. I can't marry you." I hold the ring out to him in the palm of my hand. His eyes flit between it and my face, and a myriad of emotions dance across his features before he straightens his shoulders and hardens his expression into an icy mask.

"This is because of *him*, isn't it?" His nostrils flare and his lips curl into a hate-filled sneer. "The roommate."

"No—" I start to lie but catch myself. If there was a time to be one hundred percent honest, it's now. I owe him these truths, even if they are painful. Even though this is the end, I respect the fifteen years of history between us enough to give him that. "Not entirely."

"How long have you been fucking him?" He is eerily calm, but his tone is honed with bitter sharpness.

I think I'd rather have the burning rage. At least I know what to do with that.

"I'm not fucking Morgan," I snap. As much as it stung, he was right to reject my advances. At least Tanner won't have that to hold over me when all of this is over.

"This"—I gesture between us with my free hand—"would have happened with or without him. Let's be real, things haven't been good between us for a while. You prioritized your dad's campaign and your image over me time and time again, and I can't remember the last time I felt like I could just be myself around you. We could have worked through that, but you broke us the second you decided drinking and drugs were more important than us. We were over then. It just took me a while to figure that out. All Morgan did was show me how it is I deserve to be treated in the meantime."

"I'm sure he has shown you plenty." He barks out a bitter laugh. "I should have beat the shit out of him while I had the chance. But really, James, it's a low fucking blow playing the addiction card. I know I fucked up there, but I apologized, and I got sober *for you*. If that was really the problem, you should have ended things then instead of stringing me along for months while fucking your roommate behind my back. So go ahead, place all the blame on me if it makes you feel better, but we both know this is happening because you are a cheating whore."

Each of his words is a carefully crafted blow, a cold and calculated dismantling of my defenses, pulling all the bottled rage and resentment out from below the surface.

"I've never had sex with him!" My anger explodes out of me from the pressure of it all.

"Fine, you didn't fuck him. But tell me to my face that you don't have feelings for him."

I can't.

"That's what I thought." Tanner shakes his head and grabs the ring out of my hand. He starts to retreat but hesitates, deflating as a look of anguish flashes across his face for a moment before the cold mask returns. "Get fucked, Ophie."

He turns and walks back into the party.

My shoulders slump as all of the fight leaves my body, and uncontrollable laughter bubbles up past my lips. That's how Dad finds me, laughing like a lunatic in the starlight.

"Are you okay?" he asks, placing a hand on my shoulder.

"I'm fine," I say around gasping bursts of laughter, and the truth is, I'm more than fine. *I'm free*.

"Let's get you home before that asswipe does something stupid." My dad ushers me down the staircase and away from the life I woke up thinking I'd be trapped in forever. I'll figure out how to navigate my relationship with the twins later. Right now, I just want to go home.

When Dad said home, I knew he meant Grandma Anne's small cottage, but that's not home to me anymore. My heart yearns to be back in Athens with Morgan. I've wasted enough time already. I don't want to waste a second more without him.

Chapter 31
Morgan

The stagnant air inside Double Teep is thick with the sweat that pours from our exhausted bodies. As if it wasn't already hard enough to breathe through the humidity, Gage traps my face against the damp canvas of his Gi, stealing my breath entirely. I tap to the pressure seconds before the buzzer sounds, signaling the end of the round.

"Good work, guys. I'll see you next week," Coach David calls, dismissing the class.

I lie in a gasping heap on the mat while the other gym members move around me to gather their things. It's only been a month since I started training at Double Teep with my friends, and it's been a wake-up call to just how out of shape I let myself get since undergrad. I used to have practice like this twice a day during the wrestling season, and I may have thrown myself into training at Double Teep with that same intensity knowing full well the half-assed sparing I did with Karis and Nathan last semester wasn't enough to prepare me for it.

They were right to bring me here, though. The extra time away from the apartment, away from James, has been good for me.

"You coming to Cutter's tonight? Gage is working." Nathan offers me a hand and pulls me off the floor.

"Yeah, I just need to hit the showers first."

He didn't need to ask. We both knew I'd be at Cutter's tonight, with or without the invitation.

"All right, cool." He claps me on the shoulder and starts toward the door. "See you in a bit."

The single-stall shower in the gym's tiny locker room isn't ideal, but it's preferable to an unnecessary stop at the apartment. I go there to sleep, that's it.

Avoiding James has been easier than I thought it would be. Between the three of my friends, shifts and classes at Double Teep, and my school obligations, I haven't had to look hard to find things to occupy my time. She has respected my request and hasn't tried to force me to talk to her again. The few times our paths have crossed, she was polite but did not push for anything beyond the type of pleasantries you would expect from a distant acquaintance. Despite it being exactly what I asked for, every shallow interaction makes my healing heart ache, but at least it's healing.

An hour passes, and my muscles still burn, but I'm at least clean and presentable as I push my way through the sea of drunken students who have taken to the streets in packs. It's not even eleven, and the streets already reek of stale booze and urine—the smell of a typical Athens weekend.

There is a small line outside Cutter's, but the bouncer at the door ushers me past with a nod. He doesn't even ask for my ID. I guess he's seen it enough over the past few weeks that I'm a regular now.

Cutter's is packed with writhing bodies, making finding my friends a challenge. Our normal spot at the bar is taken by a group of girls brandishing a sign declaring that the blond wearing the crown and sash just turned twenty-one, and the birthday girl has her sights locked on Gage. It isn't surprising. To his utmost annoyance, he gets targeted for those stupid birthday bucket-list dares fairly often. I think they like the challenge. His face is pinched in a scowl that would have most sane people fleeing, but the birthday girl isn't getting the hint. I'm sure Karis will drive them away soon enough.

I shake my head with a small chuckle and push through the crowd to find a high-top to hole up at for the night. If I decide to get a drink, I'll need to fight my way through the crowd, but mediocre beer doesn't seem worth the effort—it's not like I'll drink much of it anyway. Nathan or Karis can bring me something if I get desperate, but that's not why I come here in the first place. After firing a text off to my friends to let them know where to find me, I lose myself in mindless scrolling.

"Morgan?" A familiar feminine voice cuts through the roaring din of the bar.

I turn and find Evelyn a few feet away. She beams at me like finding me here has made her whole day. I don't know why she'd look at me like that. She should hate me. After everything happened, I stopped responding to her invitations to volunteer with her, and eventually, they stopped coming. Our budding friendship was pruned before it had a chance to grow roots.

"Hey, Evelyn." My tone is light, but a pit rapidly grows in my stomach. If she's here, that can only mean James is nearby. I scan the room but don't see any sign of her friends. "No James or Chelsea tonight?"

"No, it's just me. Cutter's has been blacklisted since, well, you know..." Her face flushes as she casts her eyes down.

I do know.

Beyond my falling out with James, Nathan and Chelsea broke up at some point while I was still locked in the haze of sorrow and self-pity. I didn't even find out until I caught him making out with some girl in the back of the bar and let him know exactly what I thought of his behavior. He let me give it to him, too, and once I was finished telling him how despicable he was, he calmly filled me in on everything I'd missed.

It wasn't my proudest moment and only emphasized how awful of a friend I've been to him.

"No, Jamie went home for the weekend. She had her big, fancy engagement party last night, and Chelsea...wasn't in the mood to go out tonight."

"Oh." I didn't even know James was gone.

Last semester, she kept me updated on every single aspect of her day in the notes she left for me. I didn't think I would miss seeing those pieces of paper as much as I do. Every morning, the empty space on the mirror breaks my heart all over again. You'd think I'd be used to it by now, but it hasn't stopped hurting. I think I preferred it when the notes were scathing criticisms compared to their absence.

"I was hoping to run into you, actually," she says, moving closer into my space.

"You were looking for me?" Why on earth would she do that?

"Yes." She pauses for a moment to bite on her lower lip. "You disappeared on me. I wanted to make sure you were okay."

A month ago, I would have said no. Nothing was okay while my shattered heart was still bleeding, but I've picked up the scattered shards and stitched them back together, creating a patchwork version of the organ. The fresh scars still fester from time to time, but the wounds have mostly healed, and the constant stabbing pressure has lessened to an occasional dull throb.

Now I *am* okay.

"I'm good," I tell her, earning a soft smile. "Nathan and the gang have been keeping me extra busy. They should be around here somewhere."

Her face falls at the mention of my friends.

"I'll leave you to them, then." She starts to turn away, but I place a hand on her shoulder to stop her, giving it a gentle squeeze.

"I'm sorry I ghosted you like that." I pull my hand back and run it through my hair with a deep sigh. "I'll be honest, I wasn't okay for a while there, but things have been better lately. It's not an excuse, but I don't want you to think you did something wrong. I actually really enjoyed hanging out with you over break."

She puffs up under my praise, her face glowing with the blush that fills her cheeks.

"I liked it too." She glances down at our feet and twists a chocolate-colored strand of hair between her fingers. "Does that mean things with Jamie are..."

"In the past," I tell her firmly. "We aren't even friends anymore."

258

"Okay. Good," she says, rolling her shoulders back to stand straighter. The muscles in her jaw tighten as a look of steely determination flashes in her eyes.

I don't have time to process the change before her soft lips find mine. My body reacts on instinct, matching the pace she sets. Her tongue traces along my bottom lip, trying to deepen the kiss, and I part my mouth to grant her access.

The kiss is...fine.

Evelyn knows what she's doing, and her plush, full lips were made to be kissed, but I feel nothing from it. There's no spark, no heat, only the soft touch of her lips on mine.

She pulls away and refuses to meet my gaze.

"That was..." Nothing I can say will eliminate the awkward tension in the air.

"Weird," she supplies with a breathy laugh.

"Yeah, weird," I agree, letting out an uncomfortable chuckle of my own.

"I'm sorry." She covers her red face with her hands. "I don't know what came over me. Forget I did that."

"Consider it forgotten." My fingers run through my curls as we lapse into an awkward silence.

"Listen, I'm gonna—" Her words are cut short by Nathan's shout of "Morgan" as he and Karis spot us from the other side of the room.

His arm is wrapped around the birthday blond from earlier, and her whole group follows him and Karis over.

Fantastic.

Karis looks about as pleased as I feel with the situation. She passes me a beer and joins me at the table, glaring daggers at the drunken girls who have glued themselves to Nathan's side. Evelyn scoffs and rolls her eyes at his antics, and I'm inclined to agree with her assessment.

"Who's the chick?" His words are far more slurred than they should be at this point in the night. I look to Karis for some clue as to what exactly is going on, but her focus is locked on our friend.

"That's Evelyn, you fucking idiot." Karis slaps his arm with the back of her hand. "James's friend."

"Oh." He looks Evelyn over slowly, practically undressing her with his glassy eyes. Her face pinches, and she shifts behind me, blocking his view. "Hi, James's friend."

"Hey, fuckhead, eyes up here." Karis snaps her fingers in front of his face, breaking his lewd perusal. "She's off-limits. Have your fun with Barbie and the bimbo squad."

He rolls his eyes with an overdramatic sigh but directs his attention back to the blond hanging on his side.

"Hi, Morgan," Karis says without looking at me. Her narrowed eyes are locked on the woman behind me, shining with a predatory glint that always means trouble.

I rest an elbow on the tabletop and drop my head into my hand. There's nothing I can do to stop whatever chaos these two have decided to sow.

"You look like you could use a drink. Come on." Karis grabs Evelyn's wrist and drags her toward the bar. Evelyn shoots a wide-eyed glance in my direction as she disappears into the crowd, leaving me alone with Nathan and his entourage.

"I-I think I'm just gonna go," I say into the air.

Nathan isn't paying any attention, too busy making out with the birthday girl while her friends cheer them on. I drop the untouched beer onto the table and slip through the room, back into the frozen night. The crowds of students thin the closer I get to the apartment, but the sounds of mindless revelry don't dissipate until the door to the lobby falls shut behind me.

I unlock the door to our apartment and walk in expecting darkness, but I'm met with the blinding light from the overhead fan. James is sitting on the couch, and for the first time in a while, she has a healthy glow about her. She smiles when she sees me, her face lighting up with the radiance I fell in love with.

The sight is a bullet to my heart.

She wasn't supposed to be here.

She stands and starts to approach but freezes after taking a step toward me. She twists her hands together in front of her and sucks on her bottom lip. There's something off about her appearance, I just can't put my finger on it. I run my eyes over her again and curse myself for relishing in committing every curve of her body to my memory. It takes me a moment, but I finally notice what's different.

She's not wearing her ring.

What does that mean? Did she finally leave Tanner? If she did, does that even change anything?

My mind reels with the possibilities.

"Morgan, we really need to talk," she says before I've had a chance to finish processing it all, and just like that, the fragile peace I built over the past few weeks crumbles around me.

Chapter 32
James

Dear Roomie,

I did it. I left TANNER. I'll see you soon.

Love J

After seeing my dad off at the airport, I broke traffic laws to get back to the apartment—to Morgan—in record time, only to find myself alone for hours, with nothing but my anxious thoughts to keep me company. I don't know what else I expected. It's not like Morgan is ever even home anymore.

He's perfected the art of avoiding me.

That knowledge didn't stop hope from building in my chest. Hope that maybe this time would be different, that somehow he would just know on some instinctive level that I needed him, and he would be waiting for me with open arms when I walked through the door.

The deafening silence that greeted me when I entered the apartment took that hope and tore it into tiny little pieces, destroying the fantasy reunion I built up in my mind.

So, instead, I've waited.

I scrubbed away the layers of grime I let accumulate, and once there was nothing else to clean, I paced circles through the living room. The shadows of dusk chased away the sunlight and spread their inky tendrils into the sky, bringing forth the veil of night. I watched it all pass, not daring to go anywhere else in case he came back and managed to slip into his room undetected. My feet grew tired hours ago, forcing me to rest on the couch, but even still, he hasn't come home.

Is this the new normal for him? Has he found somewhere else to spend his nights? Is it a woman? Has he moved on already?

I've done my best to respect his wishes; I've left him alone and let him live like a stranger beside me, no matter the cost to my sanity. It hurts the most when something good happens and my first thought is "I can't wait to tell Morgan," only to remember that he doesn't want to hear it. I still write it in the notes, though, ones that he will never see. In those moments, I can at least pretend that I never fucked things up.

I just need him to come home so I can try to make things right.

The sound of the deadbolt turning in the door is the sweetest sound I've ever heard.

All of the air catches in my lungs as I watch that door open and my greatest desire step through. My God, he's a sight for sore eyes. He's dressed in his normal pair of slacks and a button-down, with his hair hanging around his glasses in a mop of unruly curls. I don't know why, but I expected him to look different—be different. Maybe it's because I feel different on some fundamental level, but he's still just my Morgan.

A smile forms on my face as I take him in, and my heart flutters, matching the beating of the butterflies' wings in my stomach. I spring to standing, desperate to fling myself into his arms, but the look on his face stops me in my tracks.

He doesn't want me here.

My gaze drops to the ground as I fidget with where the ring used to burden my finger. I didn't think this far ahead. Every fantasy ended with me throwing myself into his arms and everything clicking back into place. I didn't plan for a conversation.

"Morgan, we really need to talk." I cringe as the unplanned words leave my lips. It's so similar to what I told Tanner yesterday, but the intent behind them couldn't be more different.

"James..." He sounds pained as he runs a hand through his hair.

That simple motion squeezes my chest, and the weight of just how much I've missed him crashes down around me. I was so fucking stupid for letting him go, for prioritizing everyone else's feelings over my own. With any luck on my side, I'll be able to make him see that.

"I don't know if that's a good idea. It's late, and I'm tired." His attention darts between me and the refuge of the hallway.

"Please." I put every ounce of emotion I have into that choked plea. He isn't walking away from me again. I won't let him.

His shoulders sag as the fight leaves him, and he gives me a small nod. Unable to resist his thrall any longer, I close the gap between us with tentative steps and grab his hand, guiding it to cradle the side of my face. He shudders as I lean into his touch, and his thumb caresses my cheek. The motion is so subtle, I doubt he's aware he's doing it, but it sends a wave of electricity through my body, erupting goose bumps across my skin.

"Thank you." I lower our hands, keeping them locked together as I guide us to the couch. He follows without a word. I can't bring myself to let go, even after we've both settled on the cushions. Having his hand in mine feels too right.

"I ended things with Tanner." The words tumble out of me in one long breath. My teeth catch my bottom lip between them, preventing anything else from spilling out while I wait for his response.

He presses his thumb to the back of my hand, giving me a wistful smile before he pulls his hand out of my grasp and places it on his knee.

"That's good. I'm proud of you, James."

That's it? Does he not realize what this means?

"Don't you see? We can be together now like we talked about before." I reach for his hand again, but he moves it away. It's a fluid movement, subtle even, but it's clear he's avoiding my touch.

"No we can't," he says, dropping his eyes to look at anything but me.

His rejection is a physical blow to my chest, and my paper heart crumples from the force of it.

"W-what do you mean we can't? Of course we can. Tanner isn't an issue. It will be just like we talked about. I'm so sorry it took me this long to figure it out. I should have ended things with Tanner at the beach, but I was a coward. I fucked everything up and kept making the wrong choices, but I'm making the right choice now. We can finally be together. There isn't anything holding us back anymore." My voice takes on a hysterical edge that only grows with each uttered phrase.

"I know." His lashes flutter as they fall shut, and a look of absolute anguish mars his beautiful face. His chest heaves as he fights for composure, and when he opens his eyes again, they're steeled. "I'm what's holding us back. I can't—won't—do this with you, not now."

"Why not?" A hot lump forms in my throat.

How can he be doing this to us?

"I don't want to be your rebound."

My *rebound*?

I'd laugh if my world wasn't crashing down around me. There is no universe where what this man means to me could be reduced to that. Does he really think so little of what's between us? Does he not realize how much I love him?

"You wouldn't be," I tell him, but those three words are different from the ones threatening to bubble up and spill out of me. I'm not ready to say them yet, not when he still might leave me after.

"Yes I would. You've barely been single for a day. Jumping from one relationship into the next isn't what you need."

"What I need is you." My hands reach out for him again without conscious thought, drawn in by whatever spell it is he has me under.

"No it isn't." He moves before my fingers make contact, jerking away and running his hand through the tangled mess of curls to keep it out of my yearning grasp. "What you need is time to process everything that's happened and heal from it."

"But—"

"No buts. If I give in now, there'll always be a nagging doubt in the back of my head that you are only with me because I was a safe place to land, not because you wanted to be with *me*. I'm not saying no forever, but right now, this can't happen."

All of yesterday and this morning passed by without me shedding a single tear, but this is my breaking point. My breath hitches as I'm overcome with a heaving sob, and hot tears spill over my lashes. He places a hand on the side of my face, cradling it in his palm, and wipes the falling tears from my cheek with his thumb. A glassy sheen covers his hazel orbs, making them look like liquid amber under the warm glow of the overhead light.

I didn't think the dingy bulb had the ability to cast this sort of illumination, to make someone glow, but the golden hues reflect off Morgan's tortured features, creating the perfect balance of darkness and light, painting him as the paragon of righteous self-sacrifice. My fingers itch to immortalize the image on canvas: *The End of a Good Knight*.

He drops his head toward mine, and the gleam is eclipsed in shadow. For a moment, I think he might kiss me—no, I'm certain of it. His eyes are locked on mine as his lips descend. Even through my tears, my heart swells in anticipation. That bubble of hope in my chest bursts as his lips stop short, and he presses his forehead against mine, shifting his hand to rest in my hair.

"Don't cry, pretty girl," he pleads. "You're breaking my heart."

"Well, you're breaking mine," I accuse.

"I know." His expression shifts, pinching in pain, and he lets out a deep sigh. "I'm so sorry, James."

We stay locked like that, breathing each other in, until my tears run dry. The moment passes by, feeling like a millisecond and an eternity all wrapped up as one.

The brush of his warm lips on my forehead as he pulls away simultaneously sends electric currents racing through my body and pierces through my already mangled heart. He leaves me there, alone on the couch, but this time, for some reason, it doesn't feel like he's running away, at least not forever. It's a tactical retreat, one so we can regroup and come back together stronger.

He pauses in the doorway and turns back to face me, opening his mouth as if to speak before closing it again with a small shake of his head, and he slips into the darkened hallway.

I just need to give him time. I can do that. As much as I hate it, I think he might be right. My heart needs room to breathe so that all this pain that's been festering doesn't grow stale and stagnant in my chest, poisoning it and leaving it uninhabitable for the love that wants to grow there. For him, I can be patient.

Chapter 33
James

Dear Roomie,

Grover made a friend with the tiniest little puppy today. Watching them play was ridiculous. I thought for sure Grover would crush them, but he was nothing but gentle and patient.

I'm trying to be patient too.

How much longer will you make me wait? What will it take for you to trust that what I feel for you is real?

Love J

Outside, rain falls in heavy sheets, battering against the window of Chelsea's apartment. Its constant droning covers all other sounds, creating the illusion of complete isolation. It's as if the brick-walled living room exists outside of normal time and space.

Or maybe it's me who's disconnected.

Loneliness and I have become well acquainted over the past three weeks. I've been an island adrift in an empty sea.

Evelyn and Chelsea know something is wrong, but they haven't had the time to grill me for answers. They've both been too busy figuring out their post-grad plans. I'm grateful for that. I don't think I have it in me to try to explain my relationship with Morgan to them—or how I fucked it all up.

Every time I think about him, my heart pangs with a familiar dull ache. He's been home more often since I broke things off with Tanner, but he still keeps his distance. I didn't know I could miss someone I see every day, but I miss him so much it hurts; I miss our nerd show nights, I miss doing school work together at the tiny kitchen table, I miss finding his notes in the bathroom, I miss spending hours talking about anything and everything that came to our heads, and more than anything, I miss seeing his smile and knowing I was home.

The only thing I don't miss is my asshole ex-fiancé.

Going from talking to him every day to never talking to him at all was jarring, but the sadness never came. I grieved that relationship long before it was over, so when the final nail was hammered into the coffin, there was nothing left to mourn. The twins are a different story, though. Their absence cuts me clear to the bone. Tanner hasn't let me talk to them. He claims I lost that right when I threw a decade of commitment in his face. I claim he should shove my foot up his ass, and the conversation typically devolves from there.

He is handling the breakup about as well as I thought he would, which means he's turned into a vindictive ass. If it wasn't for the girls, I would block his number and be done with him, but I'm not giving up on them. They might not be blood, but they are my sisters too.

A pillow hits the side of my face, yanking me out of my pensive brooding.

"Are you even listening, Jamie?" Chelsea asks with a huff.

"What? No. I'm sorry, can you repeat that."

She shakes her head and rolls her eyes at my response. "I said I got invited for a second interview at Galvtek this week."

"Really? That's awesome. I'm sure you're going to blow it out of the water."

"I hope so. I've deferred other offers for the off chance Galvtek will hire me."

"They would be fools not to."

She is going to kick ass and take names wherever she ends up, but the thought of her leaving sucks. Evelyn too, although she is still waiting to hear back from several schools before she makes her final decision on her graduate program. Regardless, both girls are on tracks that will lead them out of Athens, leaving me completely alone.

Well, alone except for Morgan, but as it stands, that's the same thing.

He told me he needed time, but at this point, I'm not sure if that will ever be enough. I might have done irreparable damage.

"Have you figured out what you're doing yet?" she asks.

Shit.

I haven't given any thought to my post-grad plans. As much as I loathe to admit it, Jacqueline was right. I had been coasting by on the assurance that I would have a position waiting for me at Niarris. I can confidently say that option doesn't exist anymore.

I hadn't even thought about that. *Fuck.* It's mid-March, and I haven't even started applying for jobs. I'm so fucking fucked. I've been so caught up in the shit show that is my love life that I've neglected my future.

My dad is going to kill me.

I need to get my resume together and start applying, but I can't go too far. I won't leave Athens, not when there's still hope for Morgan and me.

"No, not yet," I admit with a grimace.

"Where have you applied?"

"I haven't," I tell her and look out the window again. I don't want to see the disappointment on her face.

"Jamie," she admonishes.

"I know. I know. But after everything with Tanner"—*and Morgan*—"it just slipped my mind."

"Well, let's put some applications in now." She straightens up from her reclined spot on her favorite chair and grabs her laptop. "Do you have access to your resume?"

"No."

"That's fine. I can write one for you pretty quickly if you tell me the information. Evelyn, will you help put together a list of potential employers?"

The next two hours pass by in a daze as Chelsea takes charge of my floundering future. Between the three of us, we're able to put in a couple dozen applications. I know it's not enough, but it's a start, and her version of my resume is better than anything I've ever put together.

I'm really going to miss them next year; I don't know how I got so lucky with my friends.

The rain slows to a gentle patter and eventually stops completely as the sunlight dims. The sky remains covered in a blanket of looming gray clouds, threatening to unleash another downpour. Evelyn and I gather our things and move toward the door. With any luck, we'll make it home before it gets too dark or the sky opens back up.

We only make it a few steps into the hallway before Evelyn stops me by placing her hand on my forearm.

"Jamie," she says, then sucks her bottom lip between her teeth.

As I turn and face her, she drops her gaze to her feet.

"I-I need to tell you something," she all but whispers. Her hand falls away from my arm and joins her other to fidget in front of her chest.

"Jesus, you sound like you're about to tell me you killed someone. Just spit it out, it can't be that bad." I laugh off her odd behavior, but it sends a shiver of dread down my spine and into my gut.

She swallows and steels herself to meet my stare. "I kissed Morgan," she blurts on a single breath before peering at the floor again.

"You did what?" I snap and jerk away from her as if the words were a slap.

Jealousy rears its ugly head, but this time, the beast is bolstered with the fiery breath of my rage. How could she do that when she knows…she…fuck. I never told either of them the extent of my feelings for him. I've not been subtle—she wouldn't be apologizing otherwise—but never once did I say "Hey, guys, I'm in love with Morgan, so back off." She would never do something like that if she knew it would hurt me. I never had a right to lay claim to him anyway, not when I was still with Tanner. That doesn't keep her confession from hurting; it does, however, soothe the raging beast enough that I no longer want to claw at her face.

"I'm so sorry, Jamie," she rambles. "I was a bit tipsy, and you were engaged, and Morgan said anything between the two of you was over because of the whole Tanner thing, so I figured I would shoot my shot. It was beyond awkward. No sparks, nothing…"

"Evelyn—" I try to stop her stream of words, but she keeps going.

"We both agreed it was best if we forgot it ever happened, but I couldn't keep it from you. Especially not now that you're single. I'm so sorry, Jamie. I—"

"Evelyn. It's fine," I say, and I'm shocked by how much I actually mean those words.

"Really?" She looks up at me with a glassy but hopeful stare.

"Yes. Like you said, I was engaged. Morgan and I weren't even talking to each other at that point."

"But—"

"I promise. I'm not mad."

It's a lie. I am mad, just not at either of them; all of my anger is directed at myself. I'm the one who screwed everything up and lost Morgan before he was ever mine. If I could go back in time and do things differently, I would have ended things with Tanner at the beach. Dragging things out only hurt everyone more in the end.

"Oh." Her face pinches for a moment before she shakes it off and gives me a tentative smile. "Good. How are things with Morgan?"

"Complicated," I sigh. "He said he wants to give me time to heal."

"What do you want?"

"Him." I don't even have to think about it. The only thing I want is his forgiveness and for things to go back to the way they were before. I would take friendship. Anything is better than not having him at all.

"Oh, Jamie. I'm sorry."

"It will be fine. I'm being patient. I have to have faith that things will come together in the end."

I've repeated those words to myself more times than I can count, but at this point, I'm not sure if they are true. I don't know what happens when the princess strays from the words written on the page. Her happily ever after was promised with the prince, not the knight, and now that she's gone rogue, nothing is certain. All I can do is pray that she's still the hero in this tale because the villain never gets true love in the end.

Chapter 34
Morgan

The muffled sound of James's voice resonates through the apartment. Her exact words are obscured by her bedroom door, but the fury behind them isn't lost. Grover lies outside her room with his nose pressed into the crack above the floor. There's a momentary lapse in her shouting, and his soft whimpering fills the silence as he paws at the door.

"Hey, boy, what's going on?" I discard my school bag on the island counter and crouch at the entryway with an outstretched hand, beckoning him to me.

He slinks over with his ears pinned and tail tucked between his legs, and he pushes his wet nose into my palm with another worried whine. I scratch behind his ears for a few seconds before straightening back up to my full height and moving closer to the source of the noise.

The smart thing to do would be to leave it alone, but I've never been able to do the smart thing where James is concerned.

My steps are light as I sneak down the hallway. Her words start to come into clearer focus as I near her room. I hear a clear "Goddamnit, Tanner" seconds before she lets out a frustrated shriek, and something hits the wall with a loud *thud* that causes both of us to jump.

Why is she talking to him? When I asked for time, I had hoped she would use it to heal, not go crawling back to him after a few weeks.

I guess that answers the question of how much I actually meant to her.

Silence hangs in the air. It feels fragile, and I hold my breath, worried that the smallest exhale might crack it. It only holds for a few moments before it's shattered by an anguished sob.

My heart lurches at the sound of her broken cries, and my hand is on her doorknob before I've thought through the action. Every fiber in my being is screaming at me to go in there, to comfort her. But I freeze before I can turn the handle.

I shouldn't do this.

Opening this door now would be like opening Pandora's box. It would be the end of any time I asked for, and everything I'd locked away would escape into the world. I'm not ready for that, especially not now when something is still going on between her and Tanner. I drop my forehead to her door with a sigh and let go of the handle.

James doesn't need me to save her. Letting her figure this out on her own is the right thing to do.

I drag myself away and head to my bedroom, repeating that mantra under my breath. Her sobbing bleeds through the walls, haunting me even here.

To hell with it.

I grab a notebook and pen and scratch out a quick note on my way to our shared bathroom. Her cries are louder here, each heaving sob another stab in my chest. I slide the note under the door with a small knock and wait, listening for her response.

Are you okay?

Her sobbing is broken by a softer sniffle as the paper crinkles on her side of the door. The padding of her feet on the old carpet as she moves away travels through the wood separating us. Time seems to stand still while I wait for her response. The seconds tick by, and it becomes clear she isn't going to respond.

I don't know what I was thinking.

I try to ignore the heavy feeling in my chest as I turn to walk away. Suddenly, the paper slips back under the door, stopping me in my tracks. I pick it up, and her short message confirms what I already knew.

No, Not Really.

I sink down to the cold tile with my back to the door between us and pen my response.

Talk to me about it. Please. Maybe I can help.

Do you KNow why I stayed with TaNNeR as long as I did?

Because you loved him? Because he was the safe option? Because you were scared of what your life might look like if you followed your own heart instead of killing yourself to please others?

I don't write any of those things, though.

No.

He's got two sisters. They are twins, only nine years old. I love those girls as if they're my own flesh and blood, and I was terrified that if I left, I would never get to see them again. The thought of losing them was so much more painful than anything else, so I stayed, and I put up with the bullshit until I was a hollow shell of myself.

In the end, I was right. TANNER won't let me talk to them. It's been five weeks since I've been able to see them or hear their voices, and it fucking hurts. Today is my birthday, and all I wanted was to talk to them, but TANNER won't let me.

Shame floods me as I read the note. I'm such an asshole. How could I not know any of this? About the girls or that today is her birthday. What other vital information have I neglected to learn?

Why didn't you tell me?

I can hear her bitter laugh from the other side of the door.

when? I tried to explain things to you when I got back from break, but you walked out on me. And even when you came back, you shut me down before I had a chance to explain.

Her words send a fresh wave of self-loathing through me, so potent that my face twists in a grimace. I'm just as much to blame for things souring between us as she is, maybe even more so. I should have seen how much she was struggling too. If I hadn't let myself be blinded by self-pity, I could have prevented all this heartache.

I'm sorry, James. I'm so, so sorry.

I never should have walked away from you. I've wanted to apologize for how I acted that night from the moment the door closed behind me, but I was too much of a coward to actually do it, so I'll say it now. I'm sorry. I'm sorry for letting my anger get the better of me. I'm sorry for blaming you when I wouldn't let you even explain. I'm sorry for ignoring you these past few months. I'm sorry for it all, pretty girl, and I'll tell you every day if I have to.

I take a steadying breath and send my truth under the door. Putting those words on paper is easier than saying them out loud.

I'm the one who is sorry. This could have all been avoided if I treated you the way you deserved in the first place. I'm sorry for all the times I took you for granted, and all the times I lashed out at you when you were nothing but kind. I'm sorry for putting everyone else's feelings above yours time and time again. You deserve better than that. Of course I forgive you, Morgan. I just hope that maybe one day, you can forgive me, and we can go back to how things used to be.

I miss you, and I need you in my life. Can we put all this shit behind us and start over?

There aren't adequate words to explain to her that there's nothing to forgive.

Deal.

My body slumps against the door as all the tension I've been holding on to over the past few months flees. Something brushes against my back, catching my attention, and I turn to find her fingers poking out from under the door, wriggling around against the white tile in search of something. I tuck my arm behind my back, resting the edge of my hand in her waiting grasp, and she curls the tips of her fingers around my pinky. I'm helpless to fight the goofy grin that takes over my face.

We are going to be okay.

It might not be today or even next week, but there's no doubt in my mind that we will be able to figure it out together. I don't care how much time it takes for James to be ready, she will be worth the wait.

I don't know how much time passes, but it's long enough that my legs start to go numb.

James is the first to pull away. The absence of her touch sends a pang of longing through me. No amount of her will ever be enough. I pull myself off the floor with a groan and stretch out my stiff limbs as I head toward my room. The sound of paper sliding against the floor catches my attention, stopping me as I'm halfway out the door. A smile tugs at my lips as I pick up the note and read it, and then I read it again.

My heart swells and bursts with a wave of joy that crashes through me, but as it recedes, something else is left, a nagging dread that this is all happening too soon. It's only been a month since she left Tanner. Has she actually had the time to heal? Can she really love me when it feels like only yesterday that her heart belonged to somebody else?

I clutch the note to my chest and walk into my room, not giving her a response. A few moments pass, giving me time to fully process what she told me, and one thing becomes glaringly obvious.

I'm making a huge mistake.

Walking away again is the coward's way out, and I'm done being a coward.

I turn around and walk back through the bathroom, not giving myself the time to think through my actions, and push open her door without knocking.

Her bright, swollen eyes widen at my sudden intrusion, but then her face relaxes into a brilliant smile. God, I've missed that smile. She looks better than she did a month ago. Her radiance has returned, and she glows against the mundane backdrop of her room. This woman holds my heart in the palm of her hands, and she has for far longer than she will ever know. If she wants it, it's hers. I'm all in.

I hold the note out to her, my hands shaking with nerves, and ask, "Do you mean it?"

Chapter 35
James

I slide the written confession under the door and wait.

One moment passes, and then another. By the third, my heart breaks. He isn't going to respond.

The sound of his retreating steps breaks through the roaring static of blood echoing in my ears. Of course he ran away. If I had any tears left, they'd be flowing, but all that's left is an empty void in the pit of my stomach. I guess this is it for us.

Some fucking birthday.

The cheap plastic carpet fibers dig into the skin of my exposed thighs, leaving a map of irritation on my legs as I peel them off the floor. My body aches from being in the same position for so long, but I didn't notice the pain until the soothing balm of his presence was ripped away.

I only make it halfway to my bed before the door behind me swings open, revealing my roommate looking every bit as out of control as I feel, with his eyes wild behind his glasses and his curls disheveled. It's easy to picture him sitting on the other side of the door, running his hand through his hair the way he does when he's uncomfortable. The sleeves of his button-down are rolled, and the top few buttons are undone, exposing the toned muscles in his forearms and the tops of his collarbones. The rest of him is just as disheveled, with the shirt untucked and his bare feet sticking out from under his wrinkled khakis. He looks perfect. I can't help the smile that breaks out across my face. Morgan is here. He didn't run.

"Do you mean it?" he asks, his voice shaking as much as the outstretched hand that holds my confession.

"More than anything." I put the full depth of my feelings into those words.

"Say it." His commanding plea is thick with emotion.

"I love you, Morgan Hall." The weight of the world lifts off my shoulders at the words, leaving me feeling lighter than I have in a long time.

"Again," he pleads.

"I love you."

He crosses the room in a few long strides, wraps an arm around me, and crushes his lips to mine. His kiss ignites fireworks throughout my body, sending sparks of white-hot pleasure to my core. I gasp at the feeling, and he doesn't hesitate to take advantage of the opening, coaxing my tongue with his own. My fingers weave into his hair, pulling him closer as I take control of the kiss. He gives in readily, mirroring my movements but letting me set the pace.

Hot breath caresses my face as he pulls away and tries to catch his breath. Annoyance flashes through me. Now is the time for kissing, not breathing. I chase his lips, desperate for another taste of him, but he moves far enough back that my hands fall from his head. His gaze finds mine, those hazel eyes shining with uncensored adoration.

"I love you too, James Clarke."

"Say it again," I tease.

"I love you," he tells me over and over, peppering my face with quick kisses between each reverent declaration.

His lips catch mine again, which pulls a soft hum of pleasure from my throat. Without breaking our kiss, I grab his hips and pull him with me as I take the final few backward steps toward my bed. My thighs hit the mattress, and I let myself fall back, bringing his weight down on top of me. Heat blazes through me as my fingers trail up and work his shirt buttons open, giving me unrestricted access to the hard plane of toned muscles underneath. Goose bumps spring to life under my fingertips as I brush them over the hard surface of his abs, and he lets out a hiss and pulls away.

"James, wait," he pants. I ignore him, moving my lips to his neck while I continue exploring. His eyes fall shut, and he takes a deep breath to regain his composure. "We should take things slow." The pain in his voice sounds like he would rather do anything but.

I bite down on the curve of his neck, earning a small moan from this infuriating man. How dare he pretend he doesn't want this as badly as I do when his hard length is pressing into my thigh.

"We *have* taken things slow. I've wanted this—you—for months. Please don't make me wait any longer," I beg, still tracing my fingertips along each line on his stomach as they inch closer to his waistline. "Please."

Groaning, he brings his lips back to mine with more hunger than before. His tongue clashes against mine in a battle for dominance, no longer content to sit back and let me lead. The change of pace is unexpected but not unwelcome. That doesn't mean I'm going to give in easily. He snakes one arm between my back and the mattress and the other under the curve of my ass as he pulls me to him. I match his fervor, wrapping my legs around his waist and clawing at his back. Salty sweat dances across my taste buds as I lick and suck on his neck while he moves us further onto the bed. A startled gasp is ripped from my lungs as he lets me go without warning and I drop onto the center of the mattress, hitting the soft cotton with a *thud*. He hovers over me and runs his eyes down my body in unashamed appreciation. The heat in that look sets my body alight, and my chest and neck flush.

"So beautiful." Hot lips find my collarbone, leaving fiery pinpricks in their wake as they trail toward the low-cut top of my camisole.

He slips his hands under my shirt and pulls it over my head, leaving my breasts completely exposed. Cold air turns my nipples to hard peaks, and he doesn't waste a second capturing one with his mouth. A whine of pleasure is ripped from me as he works his tongue and teeth in tandem to tease the rosy bud.

"Morgan, please." My words are a mix of a moan and a plea. "I need you to touch me."

I try to grind my aching pussy against him, but I can't find the angle to get the friction I so desperately crave. Sparks of need dance in my center as he chuckles around my nipple.

"I am touching you," he teases, his breath against my damp skin painting me with goose bumps. His mouth descends again, giving my other nipple the same blissful treatment he gave the first.

"That's not what I mean." I squirm under his touch, desperate for something to relieve the building ache between my legs.

"Patience, pretty girl." Mischief dances across his smirking face.

Oh fuck. Never in my wildest fantasies was my nerdy roommate this much of a tease.

His mouth falls back to my body, placing unhurried kisses down the length of my torso as he drags his hands down my sides. The languid pace only adds to my desperate hollow ache.

If he doesn't go faster, I'm going to lose my mind.

Finally, his fingers find their way to the waistband of my sweats. In my desperation, I lift my hips to help him go faster. I don't care if it makes me look easy, I need him inside me. A shiver racks through my body as he pulls them off, leaving me completely exposed. With nothing covering me, he drinks in my naked form. I should be feeling self-conscious. Hell, I'm lying here naked while he's still fully clothed and on his knees, but I don't—I can't. Not with the way he's looking at me. He stares at my body with the reverence of a man worshiping at the altar of his goddess.

No one has ever looked at me like that before.

It's enough to send another wave of pleasure through me, the walls of my pussy tightening in an aching reminder of how empty I still am. I need his cock to fill me more than I need air to breathe. I might actually die without it.

"Morgan, I swear to God, if you don't—"

He shuts me up with another burning kiss.

Static short-circuits my brain as he touches me for the first time, dragging his fingers through my damp folds, gathering the pooling liquid, and circling my clit. Dear God, his touch is everything I hoped for and more. I cry out as he pulls away from my lips, taking his fingers with him. The absence of his touch makes my whole yearning body ache.

He holds up his glistening fingers, and his tongue slips out from between his swollen lips, licking them clean with a deep moan. Another pang of molten heat floods my throbbing center. I don't think I've ever seen something that erotic in my life.

"Yeah, I'm going to need more of that," he muses as he hoists one of my legs over his shoulder and brings his mouth to my pussy.

His tongue teases my opening before it moves up to focus its attention on my clit. Stars explode throughout my body as he eats me with relentless devotion. My hands find their way into his hair again, pulling him closer as my orgasm builds.

"Holy fuck," I gasp around my breathy sounds of pleasure. He chuckles but doesn't falter. A finger circles my entrance and slowly pushes its way inside, and I groan as he curls it against my walls. He repeats the motion once, twice, and then I explode. Shock waves of bliss roll through my spasming body, and more wetness gushes out of me.

My release shines on his face as he pulls away and gives me a devilish smile. I scramble up to my knees and catch his lips for another searing kiss. The tanginess of my ecstasy coats my tongue, which only enhances his heady taste.

"Off," I command between kisses while tugging at the still-buttoned shirt. He breaks our connection, getting off the bed to follow my instructions, and with quick fingers, he works the shirt open, throwing it to the side before doing the same with his pants. Not for the first time, my roommate stands bare in front of me, but this time, I can appreciate the view.

He crawls back into my bed and kisses me again as he guides me to lie back against the mattress. The need to feel him is more than I can handle. I reach out and stroke his thick length, loving the way his entire body shudders from my touch.

"James..." He moans my name and buries his head into the crook of my neck. The more I stroke him, the more precum leaks from his swollen tip until I bring him to my soaking entrance.

"Wait," he says, pulling away. His eyes are wide and alert without the haze of lust clouding them. "I don't have a condom."

Fuck condoms. I've waited too long to let something like that get in the way now. Birth control is covered, and I trust him. No, it's more than just trusting him. I want to feel him without anything in the way the first time he makes love to me—because that's what this is. Love. Not some causal fling or a one-time fuck.

"I've got the implant. I'm okay without one if you're comfortable with it. I'd rather feel all of you."

He stills for a moment, weighing his options, and for one terrible second, I think he might walk away again. Those worries melt away as he catches my lips again and pushes into me. Blazing heat fills me inch by inch. The slow pace is agonizing as it reignites my already smoldering nerves. I could come again from the feeling of him inside me alone.

"I love you," he whispers against my lips, pulling his hips back to thrust into me again. His mouth never leaves mine as he falls into a gentle rhythm. Every stroke rubs against the sensitive spot inside me, bringing that familiar building of pleasure to the surface. There's no urgency in the way he fucks me, no race for release. It leaves me simultaneously drowning in pleasure but desperate for more.

"Please, I need more," I beg him. It's a miracle my words are half coherent with how bliss-drunk my brain feels.

"I won't last long like that, beautiful."

"Please. Please, Morgan, please fuck me harder. I need it. I need *you*," I ramble as I beg.

He groans and pulls back to switch our position, sitting back up on his knees to put both my legs over his shoulders. His next thrust is deeper, hitting new nerve endings that send sparks through my body, and he quickens his pace. I couldn't hold back my moans if I tried. He snakes a hand around to play with my clit, and I fall back over the edge. My pussy clamps down around his cock, pulsating with my orgasm, and he follows me, filling me with his cum.

He lowers my legs with delicate care and lies down beside me, tucking my still-shaking body against his chest. The sweat coating my skin grows cool while he holds me in his arms, and my mind is blissfully clear. Nothing matters except being here with him—being home. Barely there kisses pepper my hair while we recover. After a few minutes, he pulls away and climbs out of the bed. I scramble up to sit, watching as his naked ass retreats into the bathroom.

Where does he think he's going?

I have half a mind to follow him. Who does he think he is blowing my mind like that and walking away?

The sound of water flows from the bathroom, and he returns with a washcloth in hand. He drops back down between my legs, reaching for my oversensitive flesh.

"W-what are you doing?" I shuffle back and grab a blanket to try to cover myself.

He tilts his head and gives me an incredulous look from under a raised brow.

"I'm cleaning up our mess."

My cheeks grow hot and red at the prospect. Sure, he's now acquainted with my most personal of places, but, for some reason, having him clean me outside of the heat of passion feels too intimate.

"It's okay, I'll just do that later."

"James." He grabs one of my hands and rubs his thumb in soothing circles. "Please let me take care of you."

Sincerity shines in his eyes, and I find myself nodding and opening my legs back up to give him access.

"That's a good girl," he hums, mostly to himself. The words send a new wave of arousal through me. Holy hell, does this man know how to push my buttons. He wipes away the remnants of our combined release with deliberate gentleness, each touch acting as a caress to my sensitive folds. When he finishes, he throws the cloth off to the side, crawls back in bed beside me, and cradles me with my head on his chest.

"Thank you, James," he says as he strokes my hair.

I'm not sure how much time passes while we lie like that, but one question eats at me the longer we do.

"Hey, Morgan?" My tentative words are barely more than a whisper. He gives me a content hum of acknowledgment and continues to run his fingers through my hair. "What does this mean?"

At that, he pauses.

"It means whatever you want it to mean. I spent way too long fighting my feelings for you, and I'm done. So I'm all in. What that looks like is up to you. We will take this at your pace."

A dopey smile overtakes my face. This man is my home and my heart. He is it for me, and it's about time he realized it too.

"I'm all in too." I seal the declaration with a kiss over his heart.

"Happy birthday, James." His arms tighten around me as he murmurs into my hair. "How do you want to celebrate?"

"Celebrate? I thought we just did."

My body shakes from the force of his laughter. "You know that's not what I meant."

"Hmm." Several ideas roll through my head, but my mind keeps jumping back to one. "Nerd shows and pizza?"

"We have all the time in the world to stay in and watch TV. I want to take you out, like on a real date."

My stomach flutters at the thought.

I can picture us walking down the Athens streets hand in hand while we talk about everything and nothing all at once. We won't have any of that awkward first date energy; how could we when I feel like I was born with his name on my soul? First, we will get dinner and maybe stop somewhere for a drink before we head home for the night and spend it wrapped in each other's arms. It will be perfect because it will be us, it just won't be tonight.

"You can take me out tomorrow. I want to spend tonight doing my favorite thing with my favorite person. Please, for my birthday." I turn to look at him, giving him my best pleading eyes.

"If that's really what you want," he says, resigned.

"Thank you." I give him a bright smile. "Would you mind if I take a quick shower?"

"Of course not, take your time. I'll be here when you're ready."

"You know you could join me." I bite my lip, not hiding my less-than-innocent intentions.

"Don't tempt me, pretty girl. If we start that again, we'll never make it to the living room."

"Doesn't sound like a problem to me."

"Go," he growls playfully, giving me a gentle shove.

"Fine." I place a quick kiss on his unsuspecting lips as I get out of bed and head to the bathroom.

I'm never going to get enough of him.

I speed through the shower, barely pausing long enough for the water to warm up, and half-ass my way through an already heavily modified version of my normal routine, only really worrying about drying my hair. He's still in my room when I finish, although he must have gone back to his room at some point because he's changed into pajamas and tidied his curls. He doesn't look up at me as I waltz in, his gaze too focused on the canvas in front of him.

My heart plummets.

The painting on the easel isn't one I ever wanted him, or anybody else, to see. It's been my companion over the past month on those late nights when I couldn't sleep because the thought of *him* haunted my thoughts. The canvas is awash with golds and tawny browns that have come together to immortalize the moment of his self-sacrifice in intricate detail. It must be strange to see the look of your anguish reflected back at you.

"Morgan..." I clutch my towel tighter to my chest and take a step in his direction.

He's going to hate me. I took a private moment between us and immortalized it in pigment and oil. How could he not hate me after that? He turns his attention toward me, his eyes blazing with emotion.

"James, this is—"

"I know, a violation," I cut him off before he can say anything else. "I'm sorry."

"What? No, don't be sorry. This is amazing."

"Really?"

"Of course it is." He walks over and pulls me into a tight hug. "Were you worried I wouldn't like it?"

"No. Yes. I was worried you wouldn't like being the subject of my art. It's not like I asked for your permission."

"You can paint me any time you want. I'll even model for you if you want me to."

"Really?"

"I'd wear a silly costume and stand there for hours if it made you happy."

"I was imagining something with a little less clothing…" I pull out of his grasp and head toward the door, dropping my towel onto the floor as I step into the hallway. The sound of my boyfriend's clumsy fumbling follows me a heartbeat later, drawing a joyful burst of laughter from my lips.

Some fucking birthday indeed.

Chapter 36
Morgan

James whirls around her bedroom in a flurry of frantic energy, dressed only in her underwear with a towel piled high around her hair. I watch her from the bed, awestruck by her radiance as the midafternoon sun trickles in from the window, bathing her in an aura of light. It's been a little over a month, and I'm still reeling from the fact that, somehow, this beautiful woman is mine.

Her space has become mine too. I've spent every night with her in this bed since her birthday. She about had a fit when I mentioned going back to my own room, so my saggy air mattress has become nothing more than an oversized dust collector. My clothes have started to migrate over as well.

"Get up. We're going to be late," she calls out from the closet without turning around.

Clothes fly over her shoulder without care as she searches through the racks. A shirt hits my face, blinding me as it hangs off my head. I pull it off with an amused smile, just in time to see her spin around and storm out of the closet with a huff.

As she passes by the bed, I wrap my arms around her bare waist, halting her path of destruction.

"Breathe, pretty girl," I say and kiss her exposed midriff. "We still have over an hour before we need to meet your dad and grandma."

"That would be great if I could fucking find my dress," she growls.

"Your dress is hanging next to the dryer with your cap and gown, exactly where you put them last night so you wouldn't have to look."

"I'm an idiot," she says, relaxing into my hold.

"No you aren't. You're just nervous. Today is a big day." I continue to pepper her back with soft kisses.

"I love you," she tells me. Those three words cause my heart to swell and skip a beat.

"I love you too. Now go finish getting ready." It takes effort, but I release her and give her ass a light smack.

The most precious tinkling laugh fills the air as she heads toward the hallway, swaying her hips with each step. I climb out of bed once she disappears from my view, and go through my own routine of getting ready. At some point during my shower, James joins me in the bathroom. I don't even notice her until I open the curtain and find her in front of the mirror working on her hair and makeup. She smiles at my reflection and moves over to give me some space. It's so simple, so domestic, yet it causes a swell of emotion to wash over me, leaving me awestruck yet again. I join her at the small countertop, and we get ready together, moving in a silent dance we both seem to instinctively know the steps of. I'd expect that kind of nonverbal communication after years, not weeks, but I can read her like I've been doing it my whole life.

✳✳✳

High heels clack against the sidewalk as I walk hand in hand with my girlfriend down the crowded campus streets toward the student center. My girlfriend. Even after several weeks, I still expect to wake up on Gage's couch and find this has all been a dream. If it is a dream, I won't complain. These have been the best few weeks of my life.

Golden sculpted waves bounce with each of her determined steps toward the plaza. They shine against the bright red of her dress. That's another UGA tradition she taught me—red dresses for graduation. She will put on the full polyester costume later, but for now, she only has the cap pinned in place.

The closer we get, the faster she walks, dragging me along behind her. A gust of cold AC breezes past us as the doors slide open, and she leads us through the crowd and into the atrium. Her eyes scan the room over and over again until something catches her focus, causing a brilliant smile to light up her face. She drops my hand and half sprints across the room with a squeal, throwing herself into the arms of the man I can only assume is her father.

James's father is intimidating.

There's no other word that would come close to describing him. She's told me so much about him but left out how huge he is. He easily dwarfs me, both in width and height. Even if I were to ignore his size, he would still be terrifying. He carries himself with a hardened edge that would be enough to make most sane people wary. The steely look on his face softens some when he notices his daughter, but it doesn't do anything to quell my rising unease.

His eyes meet mine from over James's shoulder and narrow into a hardened glare. I swallow back my nerves and join them.

"Dad, this is Morgan, my boyfriend." She pulls out of his embrace and steps back to stand at my side.

"It's nice to meet you, sir." I extend my hand, and it's a miracle that it remains steady.

He looks me over with an appraising stare, leaving me feeling vulnerable and exposed. I must meet whatever criteria he was searching for because his face relaxes back into what must constitute a neutral expression for him. That isn't saying much—the look would make Gage seem outright friendly on his worst days.

"You too. Ophelia has told me a lot about you." Her father shakes my hand with a bruising grip, and I have to bite my cheek to keep the grimace off my face.

"Only good things, I promise." She plants a kiss on my cheek, which earns a scowl from her dad. "Where is Grandma Anne?"

"She should be around here somewhere." He looks around the crowd. "She saw a coffee shop near the entrance and disappeared as soon as I took my eyes off her."

My girl laughs and shakes her head, the fondness she has for her grandmother shining through the movement.

"Let's go find her before she gets into too much trouble." Her fingers lace through mine as she leads us back toward the door we came in. "The last thing we need is Grandma Anne hopped up on caffeine during the ceremony. She will talk both of y'all's ears off if you let her, and you'll miss the whole thing."

"Speak of the devil," her father mutters as an older woman pushes her way through the crowd with a tray full of drinks.

I can see the resemblance to her granddaughter in her features. They have the same high cheekbones and the same arrow-straight bridge of their nose. Give it a few decades, and I could see James looking nearly identical.

"Jamie-girl, let me see you." Grandma Anne shoves the cardboard drink carrier into my unsuspecting hands and pulls her in for a hug.

"Grandma, it's only been a few months."

"A few months too long, in my book," her grandma chastises. "And you must be the new boyfriend I've not heard nearly enough about."

"Morgan Hall, ma'am. It's a pleasure to meet you."

"Cute and polite. What is it you do here, Mr. Morgan Hall?"

"I'm in law school, ma'am."

"A lawyer." She quirks an eyebrow. "This one is a catch, Jamie."

"Grandma..." A pink tinge grows on her cheeks, and she gives me an apologetic look.

"Fine, fine. Let's go eat. I'm starving anyway." She turns toward the building's café without waiting to see if we are following. The action is so like James, I can't help but smile.

"Morgan, be a dear and pass out those coffees, would you? I wasn't sure what you would like, so I went with something extra sweet. Figured you'd need it after spending too much time with this one." She nudges James with her elbow and laughs.

"Thank you, ma'am. Sweet is great." I pass the drinks around and take a sip of the syrupy liquid, grimacing at the offensive taste.

We find a table, and Mr. Clarke grabs us food from one of the restaurants built into the complex. I am more than happy to fade into the background while James catches up with her family over dinner. It's clear how much she loves them, and how much they love her in return. A twinge of homesickness stings in my chest. I can't wait until our roles are reversed and she is the one meeting my parents for the first time. I'm sure my mom will love to spend hours showing her all the pictures of me as a kid and telling her every embarrassing story she can think of.

By the time we finish our meals, it's time for her to join the rest of the graduating class in the stadium. She clings to my hand as we walk over to the student entrance with her family. She never lets go, not even as her grandma fusses over her, straightening her cap and gown and making sure there are no smudges of lipstick on her teeth.

"I'll see you guys on the other side," she says with a nervous smile. "Dad, be nice, and Morgan, don't let him get to you." She squeezes my hand one last time and disappears into the mass of shiny black gowns.

"Why don't you go find us some seats, Mom? I'd like to have a private chat with the boy," Mr. Clarke says as soon as his daughter is out of sight.

"Don't go too hard on the boy. Jamie clearly likes this one." She pats my cheek and walks off toward the stadium entrance, leaving me alone with the man I'm pretty sure wants to kill me. He claps a hand on my shoulder and pulls me in the opposite direction.

"Let's take a walk."

This is it. This is how I die. I gulp around the knot in my throat and let him lead me. We walk in silence for a few minutes, not stopping until the crowd is thinned down and no one is watching.

"So, Morgan, what exactly are your intentions with my daughter?"

I stumble over my feet, bringing us to a standstill on the sidewalk. "I'm sorry...intentions...what?" I sputter.

"You heard me. Are you playing games with her heart, or are you in it for the long haul? Because if it's the first, you better figure your shit out real quick."

The accusation knocks all the nervous energy out of me. My spine straightens, and a rare burst of anger boils under my skin.

"Excuse my boldness, but I don't think mine and James's relationship is any of your business," I tell him through clenched teeth, fighting to keep my tone neutral.

"*Ophelia*," he emphasizes her given name, which makes my jaw clench even harder, "is my daughter. Therefore, it's exactly my business."

"With all due respect, *James*," I emphasize in the exact same way, "is a grown woman who is capable of making her own judgments. She knows where we stand, and that's all that matters."

"She just got out of a serious relationship. Don't you think it's a little soon for her to be jumping into another?" He folds his arms across his chest and looks down on me like he's already won the argument.

I won't back down, though. Not on this. He might hate me, but I won't let him bully me away from his daughter so he can control her life. I stand even taller and meet his cold glare head-on.

"Yes, and I told her as much, but I also realized I was wrong to try to be the one to tell her when she was or wasn't ready. Ultimately, it's up to her to decide, and for some miraculous reason, your beautiful, talented, hurricane of a daughter decided that she loved me and I was what she wanted.

"So I'll tell you what I told her, not because I think you are owed this information, but because I'm not ashamed of how I feel about her. I'm all in. I love James with my whole heart, but what our relationship looks like is entirely in her hands. I'm never going to push her for more than she is comfortable with, and when she says she's ready for something, I'm going to take her at her word. Is that enough to put your mind at ease, sir?" I can't keep the sarcastic sneer off that final word.

Mr. Clarke's eyes widen a fraction as he seems to look at me in a new light. His posture relaxes, and his whole demeanor shifts as his shoulders sag and his face calms.

"Call me Reed, son," he says, clapping me on the shoulder again, but this time in a way that feels more friendly than imposing.

"I'm sorry, but what's happening," I ask, dumbfounded.

"I'm sure Ophelia has told you, but due to the nature of my work, I can't be around as much as I would like to be. I missed the signs when things started to go bad with Tanner. Hell, I didn't even know things had gone bad until I saw how miserable she was at that engagement party. I felt like the most sorry sack of shit dad in the world. But in the same breath that she tells me about all the heartache she was going through, she tells me about another man, the roommate who stole her heart, and her whole face lit up talking about you. Then, a little while later, she calls and tells me she's dating the roommate, and I knew I had to see it with my own eyes, to make sure you weren't going to hurt her even more than she's already been hurt."

"I don't appreciate being tested," I tell him.

"I know, but I won't apologize because I'm not sorry. One day, you'll have a kid of your own, and you'll know exactly the lengths a father would go to protect his kid."

I bite the inside of my lip to keep myself from saying more.

"Let's get going. The ceremony will start soon," he says.

I nod and let him guide me back toward the stadium. We join Grandma Anne in the stands, and she gives us both a strange look as we approach but shrugs it off without saying anything on the matter.

Commencement isn't the most thrilling of events. Even as the sun sets behind the large screen in the west end zone, the air remains hot and humid. Speaker after speaker drones on, giving the graduation class words of encouragement for their futures and highlighting the groups who have excelled academically. I don't pay a bit of attention to the words said; instead, I search the rows on the field until I find the woman who holds my heart. It isn't too hard—she painted her cap, and I would recognize her style anywhere. Seeing Chelsea's wild mane of fiery hair next to her might have also made things easier.

The hours drag by. Individual names aren't even called due to the sheer number of students graduating. Eventually, the school's president declares that the class is officially alumni, James switches the tassel over to the opposite side, and fireworks shoot into the night sky.

Students and spectators alike start to stream out of the stadium. I send a quick text to James to let her know where to meet us and lead her family to the designated spot. Only a few minutes pass before a blur of gold and black throws herself at me. I wrap my arms around her as she catches my lips in a blistering kiss.

"Hi," she says as she pulls away, her face glowing from the force of her smile.

"Hi," I mumble back like a love-sick fool with my brain completely short-circuited. "I'm proud of you."

"We all are," Reed says from behind me, and I release her, dropping her feet back to the floor.

She rolls her eyes but turns toward her family, still smiling with the radiance of the sun. Chelsea and Evelyn came with her; Chelsea has a large group of gingers in tow, but Evelyn is completely alone. I walk over to her while my girlfriend stays locked in a final conversation with her dad and grandma before they leave.

"Congratulations," I say to Evelyn, causing her round eyes to widen.

"Thank you." She regains her composure rather quickly. "You've got a little something..." She gestures to my face with her hands.

I reach up and rub the back of my hand across my face, which comes away with a streak of red lipstick. It's going to take more than my hand to get that off, but if this is the consequence of kissing my woman, I'll take it happily.

"I'm happy for you," she says, and after a beat, she adds, "and Jamie. I mean...I...I'm just glad you guys figured it out." Her cheeks grow pink, and she drops her gaze to her feet.

"Thanks. What's next for you after this?"

"I'm actually getting my master's here next fall."

"So that means the only one we're losing is Chelsea," James says, wrapping an arm around my waist.

"But I'm still here tonight," Chelsea adds as she joins our circle. "So let's go party like we never can again."

The girls mutter their agreement, and we head toward Cutter's.

Chapter 37
James

Dear Roomie,

I figured it was time to do something with my old bedroom, so I converted it into a studio for you. Go check it out. I hope you love it.

Love M

The crowd at Cutter's is as rowdy as I've ever seen it. The tiny bar is packed like it's game day, with graduates and their families alike, but the air buzzes with a different type of energy. People are partying like it's the last chance they'll get, and for many people, it will be—at least in Athens. It's a strange mix of nostalgia, melancholy, and euphoria all packaged together to create an almost manic atmosphere. It's the end of an era; the so-called best days of our lives are officially behind us. Tomorrow starts the next adventure, where we are thrust into the real world without a parachute. So tonight, we do the only thing we can—we drink.

"Shots for the graduates," Karis yells over the chaotic thrum of music and conversation. She squeezes between the over-packed bodies, holding a tray with three full shot glasses and two empty ones. "Courtesy of the ugly bastard at the counter. Gage says congratulations, by the way."

The aforementioned man is currently drenched in sweat as he works to keep the swarm surrounding the bar satisfied. This place was so full when we got here, we weren't able to secure our normal spot at the bar and had to make do with gathering around one of the scattered high-tops instead.

"Sorry, Morgan, I drank yours on the way over. Figured you wouldn't mind," she adds with a devilish smile.

His laughter vibrates from where he stands pressed against my back.

"I'll remember that next time you ask me to save you the last donut," he teases, which draws a pointed glare from the tiny woman.

I grab one of the glasses and swallow back the fiery liquid. Chelsea and Evelyn do the same.

"What the heck was in that?" Evelyn sputters. Her face grows red as she coughs around the burn. "Pure alcohol?"

"Don't know, didn't ask. I just said to make it strong."

"Well, it was definitely strong," she mutters.

"So where is life taking you ladies next? I know Blondie isn't going anywhere, especially now that she and Morgan are a thing, but what about you two?" Karis turns her attention to my friends, and I lean back into my boyfriend's hold.

I'm only half listening as the pair fill Karis in on the details that I've already heard a million times. My focus is on the man behind me. I can't see him, but his fingers trace patterns on my exposed arm, sending chills through my body. That has been my favorite change—there is very rarely a time when he isn't touching me in some capacity.

Those gentle brushes of his skin against mine have become my lifeline when everything gets to be too much for me. He might treat me like a queen, but even the best relationship won't magically make my anxiety go away. When the worst of it comes, he holds me and helps me breathe through it, his touch grounding me in a way I could never manage on my own. It's a good thing, too, because we have spent more than a few nights together in bed with him holding me while I cry. Tanner has stayed firm on keeping the girls out of my life.

But fuck that asshole.

That's a fight for another day.

I blink away my growing melancholy. "Want me to go get us some drinks?" The music is so loud I have to tilt my head to keep from shouting.

"I can go get them," Morgan offers, but I shake my head.

"No, you stay here. I need to use the restroom anyway."

He lets out a discontent hum but kisses the top of my head and releases me.

"Be right back," I tell him as I pull away, and push my way across through the crowd.

The restrooms are tucked away in an alcove in the back corner of the bar. Thankfully, the line isn't too long. I've seen it wrap out of the hallway and down the wall before. It only takes a few minutes for me to get in and finish my business, and then I'm making my way back to our group. I'm about to cross over the threshold into the main area when someone grabs my wrist, halting my steps.

The hairs on the back of my neck rise as my chest grows cold with unease. I yank my wrist out of the unwanted grasp and swing around to face whoever was stupid enough to touch me.

"Easy, James. I didn't mean to scare you," Nathan says with a carefree smile, holding his hands up in the air beside his head.

If I didn't know him better, I'd buy the cheerful facade he's trying to sell, but I can see the cracks below the surface. His eyes are shadowed by dark circles that aren't normally present, and his jaw is tight behind the fabricated smile. There's a wild spark in his eyes I don't trust; it's the look of a desperate man, and desperate men are dangerous.

"If you didn't want to scare me, then you shouldn't have grabbed me in a secluded hallway," I seethe and step away from him, not daring to turn my back.

"James, wait, please," he pleads, but he doesn't grab me again. At least he isn't a complete idiot.

"What the fuck do you want?" I'm regretting my decision to hear him out before he's even opened his mouth.

"I wanted to apologize for the way I spoke to you that night, and I guess for grabbing you just now too." He fidgets with his hands in front of him, the confident mask crumbling away.

"Why couldn't you have done that literally any place else," I snap.

"Because you're always with Morgan."

"And you never told him how much of an ass you were that night, did you?" The pieces of the puzzle snap together in my head, painting this whole interaction in a clearer, more pathetic light.

"No, I didn't." He deflates even more. "And he would probably hate me if he knew, especially now."

"Why is that my problem?" I cross my arms in front of my chest and let my inner bitch rise to the surface.

"You're right. It's not," he says with a sigh, "but you are his girlfriend, and I'm his best friend. We both love him in our own ways, and I know you don't want to see him hurt. Making him choose between us would hurt him, even if the choice would be easy."

"Fine," I begrudgingly agree. As much as I hate it, he isn't entirely wrong, and it's not like we can continue to avoid each other forever, not with Morgan connecting us. "So what do you propose, then?"

"A truce, and more importantly, an apology. I was out of line with the way I spoke to you. I could try to blame the lack of sleep, or getting caught up in the emotional high of the day, but I won't even try to make an excuse for my behavior. I'm just sorry it ever happened. If you can bring yourself to forgive me, I would like to start over. We might not ever be friends, but I hope we can at least be friendly, for his sake."

All the fight in me fades. I can do friendly, or at least not hostile, if it will make my boyfriend happy. It helps that I can see the sincerity shining through his eyes.

"Okay, we can start over."

A smile forms on his lips—a real one, not the facade from earlier.

"Thank you. You wouldn't be able to maybe help me get a moment alone with Chelsea, would you?"

"Oh, fuck off, Nathan," I scoff, and this time, I do leave him standing alone in the hallway.

I catch Gage's eye as I make my way to the bar, and he has both drinks ready for me by the time I make it up through the crowd. He doesn't even have time for me to thank him before someone else demands his attention. My friends are still locked in an animated conversation with Karis as I return. Whatever she's talking about has her fully engaged, swinging her hands wildly, somehow taking up more space than should be possible with her tiny frame. Without interrupting, I slip back into Morgan's waiting arms. He drops a kiss on the top of my head like it's the most natural thing in the world, and butterflies stir in my stomach.

I hope it never stops feeling like this.

"Your ex is here," I whisper to Chelsea once it's clear the others are focused on whatever Karis is saying.

Her nose scrunches as she looks around the bar. "Where did you see him? Karis and Gage promised he wouldn't be here tonight."

"He ambushed me near the bathrooms."

"Of course he did," she scoffs and rolls her eyes. "I'll go see if I can find him and make sure he knows exactly how unwelcome he is." She starts to move, but I place my hand on hers to stop her.

"That's exactly what he wants. You are better off ignoring him."

She thinks it over for a moment, and I can see the resolve harden in her eyes.

"I'll be right back," she says, then heads toward the bathroom alcove.

"What was that about," Morgan murmurs in my ear.

"Just boy troubles, nothing you need to worry about." I lean into him and press a kiss against his jaw.

I shift my focus back to the conversation, growing more relaxed with every sip of my drink. He absentmindedly rocks to the music, moving me with him to the beat. It's the perfect way to end my time as a student here, my favorite place with my favorite people. At least it would be if Chelsea returned.

The minutes tick by without any sign of her, and my unease starts to build in my stomach. I should tell Morgan about what happened near the bathroom. Maybe he can go look for his friend and check on mine. As I open my mouth, Nathan storms through the building and out into the warm night air. Morgan, Evelyn, and Karis all watch his exit with varying degrees of concern and confusion written on their faces. Even Gage looks dumbfounded from behind the bar.

"Does anyone know what that was about?" Karis asks as Chelsea maneuvers her way back through the crowd to join us at our table.

Her porcelain skin is flushed and her wild hair more disheveled than normal. I quirk a questioning eyebrow, and she gives me a subtle shake of her head. Message received loud and clear: don't ask now.

"I guess that explains that," Karis adds, giving Chelsea a look that pretty much mirrors what I'm burning to ask, specifically what the fuck happened back there.

"Are you all right?" Evelyn asks. At least one of us is able to be a supportive friend right now.

"Just peachy," Chelsea answers with a saccharine smile.

"Are you sure? I can go talk with Nathan if he's bothering you," Morgan offers, eyeing the door his friend went through.

"No, it's fine. He wanted to talk about us, but I told him there was nothing to talk about, and he left," Chelsea lies. I doubt anyone else but Evelyn picked up on it, though.

"Ouch," Karis says with a hiss. "Didn't sugarcoat it, did you?"

"I didn't see any reason to. I'm moving to Texas in less than a week. Even if we did talk things out, there isn't a future for us."

"That's valid." A rare glimpse of fleeting compassion crosses Karis's face. "This sounds like it calls for another round of drinks," she declares and saunters over to the bar, no doubt to fill Gage in on the gossip.

She returns with another tray, this time with enough drinks for everyone, with some to spare. The rest of the night passes by without any more unwelcome intrusions. The drinks keep flowing, and no one brings up Nathan again. I get more and more tipsy with every drink, and my hands roam over Morgan's body with a mind of their own.

"All right, pretty girl, let's get you home." He catches my wandering hands before they end up somewhere indecent.

Home sounds perfect.

He helps me to the door, keeping an arm firmly around my waist the whole way. I stumble over the cracks in the sidewalk in my high-heeled death traps, but he doesn't let me fall. The world spins slightly, leaving me unsteady on my feet. I may have had a drink or two too many. My ankles wobble again, and he pauses to sweep me up into his arms.

"You don't need to carry me," I argue, but my body tells a different story as I sink into his hold.

"Just relax. We will be home in a few minutes."

"Okay," I tell him in a whispered slur. My eyes start to drift shut against his chest. "I love you."

"I love you too, James," he says, placing a soft kiss on my forehead.

I'm asleep before we cross over the threshold, but that's okay. I was home the second he held me in his arms.

Epilogue - Morgan

In the nearly empty apartment, the songs blaring from James's speaker warp and echo to an almost unrecognizable state. She doesn't seem to mind—as long as it's loud and bassy, she's content—but the unnatural sounds add to the festering sense of wrongness that bubbles under my skin. With each frame I stow away into the filling boxes, that churning grows. My feelings aren't mirrored in my girlfriend. She dances around the kitchen without a care, individually cocooning each mug in a layer of bubble wrap before placing it in a labeled box.

It's all so different from the day I moved in. My shabby boxes weren't labeled, and there was no method to the madness in which I shoved them into my car. They just had to fit. Looking at the neat stacks of boxes, it's clear there's no way everything would fit in that old hatchback now. I remember seeing that picture of James—not knowing who she was—and thinking that her boyfriend was the luckiest man in the world. I was wrong, though; I am. That photo was replaced with one from the first time we went to the Renaissance Festival together, and over the past two and a half years, our walls became packed with photos of our adventures.

I hate that they're getting packed away. Each time I put a photo in a box, my gut churns with unease. I know the fear is unfounded—we are moving across town, not putting them away forever—but the act feels wrong.

The biggest difference from the day I moved in is my relationship with my roommate. I never would have guessed the she-devil who stood in the doorway and told me where to stick it would be the love of my life, but she is. I knew within that first week of us being together officially that I was going to marry her. After everything that happened with Tanner, I've been careful not to push her too quickly. I also wanted to finish school first. That didn't stop me from asking my mom for Nana's ring the first time I took her up to Michigan to meet my parents. I asked Reed for his blessing a few months later, but I've been holding on to the ring, waiting for the right time.

Joining her in the kitchen, I wrap my arms around her waist. She melts into my touch, pressing her entire body against mine with a content sigh. Even now, my heart still flutters with her causal affection. I nuzzle my face into the side of her neck and squeeze her tighter.

"I'm done in the living room," I murmur into her hair. "Where do you want me next?"

"Where I want you will only slow us down," she says with a laugh as she grinds her ass against me. She twists to face me and places her arms around my neck. "Where I need you is a different story. Do you think you could start on our clothes?"

"Of course, pretty girl." I can't resist the urge to pull her in for a kiss.

I mean for it to be chaste, but she isn't having that. She threads her fingers through my hair and deepens it, licking and biting at my lips until I grant her the access she desires. This woman is a siren. It only takes one hit of her addictive touch, and I'm painfully hard. Wrapping my hands under her ass, I lift her and place her on the counter. She hooks her feet around my legs and pulls me in closer, grinding her hot core against my throbbing erection.

This is not where I meant for this to go, but it's not surprising. I don't think I'll ever be able to get enough of her. As much as I'd love to bend her over this counter one last time and fill her until we're both seeing stars, we don't have time for that.

I should be a saint for having the willpower to pull away. Our breaths mingle in the space between us as I try to fully regain my self-control.

"If we don't stop now, there's no way we'll get everything packed by morning." Those words are painful to say.

"Fine, go," she says with an adorable pout. "We can pick this back up later."

"I'm counting on it."

I shoot a wink in her direction before I disappear down the hallway. The task in front of me is more daunting when I'm looking it in the face. I'll start in the closet. The bulk of the clothes are in there, and hangers should be easier than digging through the drawers. There isn't any method to my madness as I pile the eclectic mix of cloth and colors onto the bed. Once the closest is empty, I tackle the dresser, packing the items into boxes on the floor. Something hard and decidedly not a sock catches my attention in the back of a drawer. I fish it out and find a small box wrapped in tattered paper.

Wait, I know this box.

It's the same one I planned to give James that first Christmas before everything got...complicated. I can't believe she still has it—unopened, too. I grab it and rejoin her in the kitchen.

"Look what I found," I tell her as I hold up the small package. Her eyes flare and her mouth gapes.

"Oh my God," she gasps, and her bottom lip starts to quaver. "I can't believe I forgot about that. I'm so sorry."

She grabs the package from my hands and tears into it. My now-empty fingers take a pass through my hair as a grimace forms on my lips.

"I doubt it's even worth it at this point," I tell her with a shrug.

"Why," she asks and pulls the lid off the top. Her gaze drops to its contents: two tickets to a pop-up art exhibit that has long since passed through. "Oh." She pulls them out and studies them for a moment before her face falls. "I'm so, so sorry."

"Why? We weren't even talking at that point. I figured you either threw them away or went with someone else. It's not a big deal."

"Not a big deal," she repeats, her voice rising with exasperation. "I know how much tickets to these things cost. Fuck, Morgan, you could have visited your parents with that."

Sure, I could have, but she and I both know that never would have happened. Money was never what was holding me back; fear was. I was never going to take that step without a firm push, and she gave me that. She showed me that the gap between me and my parents wasn't as big as I thought. I'll never be able to thank her enough for that.

"I wanted you to have them," I tell her with a shrug.

"But I wasted them," she protests, and her eyes shine with fresh tears. "I'm so sorry."

"That's enough of that," I tell her and wrap her in a gentle embrace. "I'm not upset, pretty girl. It was years ago. There's no point in dwelling on it. I wouldn't have even brought it up if I knew it would upset you."

She hugs me tighter, nuzzling her head into my chest.

"I love you, Morgan," she says with a sigh.

"I love you too, James."

We spend the rest of the day packing our things and breaking down the bulky furniture into maneuverable pieces. It's well into the night by the time we finish and drag ourselves to bed, far too tired to make good on the promises we made earlier in the day. Even with my love in my arms, sleep is elusive in a way it hasn't been in years.

My body grows more and more weary the later it gets, but I can't force myself to relax. Anxious thoughts swarm through my head like angry bees, and my gut roils with the same energy.

Tonight is the last night I'll fall asleep in this apartment.

Tonight is the last night I get to call this place home.

We fell in love between these walls. Every important milestone in our relationship has happened here, and leaving it feels like we are leaving part of us behind.

What if things aren't the same in the new place? What if we fall apart without these walls holding us together?

I know my fears are irrational, but they're the same fears that kept us from moving out sooner. James has been talking about finding a house to rent near her job since the last time our lease needed to be renewed. The fear that idea inspired turned my center to ice. It took almost a full year for me to get comfortable with the idea, and now that I have no reason to be this close to campus, there isn't an argument for us to stay. Not when the alternative is the logical choice.

Knowing that the choice is right doesn't make the anxiety go away.

"Hey, pretty girl," I whisper, testing to see if she's still awake.

"Hmm," she answers with a sleepy hum.

"Are you nervous for tomorrow?"

She rouses a bit more and turns to look at me in the darkness of our room. The moonlight that filters in through the blinds is enough to bathe her in an ethereal glow.

"Not in the slightest," she tells me.

"How? This place is our home."

"No, this is an apartment. You are my home. How could I be nervous when you are with me?"

Her words act as a balm, soothing all my worries easier than I thought possible. I kiss the top of her head, and she snuggles back into my chest. It only takes a few minutes for her to succumb to sleep, taking the last of my worries with her and leaving nothing but love in its place.

Afterword

Want more James and Morgan? How about the rest of the Cutter's Crew?

You're in luck. I'm not done with them yet. The gang will return in book two of the series, which will feature Gage's story.

Visit my website, www.valeriekain.com for bonus epilogues and other exclusive content.

Acknowledgements

I know I promised I wouldn't mention you, but you didn't believe that, did you?

This book would not have gotten finished without your unwavering support. Thank you for believing in me when I didn't believe in myself, thank you for the time you put in to offering feedback on an unreadable draft, and thank you for not being afraid to tell me when my shit sucked. I could go on for pages about how much it all means to me, but I won't because you would give me crap and say I was being "cringe".

I'll leave it at this: thank you for being my Kuo-toa.

About the author

Valerie Kain has a lifelong love for telling stories filled with drama and angst. Some of the earliest home videos from her childhood are of her blabbering her tales at whoever would listen. It was only a matter of time before she took that passion to the page. As a Georgia native and UGA alumna, the city of Athens holds a special place in her heart which is what inspired her debut series.

She is currently in her contemporary romance era but has projects in the pipeline that span multiple sub-genres, including dark romance, paranormal romance, and romantasy. Stay in the know by following her @valerie.kain.w rites on Instagram and Tiktok or by joining her newsletter at valeriekain.com.

Also by Valerie Kain

Classic City Romance

Dear Roomie

Sunflower Persona

Book 3 (TBA)

Book 4 (TBA)

9 798990 439214